Dan Sugralinov

CLASS-A

THREAT

*May every new day
in your life
become a Level Up day!*

Dan Sugralinov

DISGARDIUM Book One

Magic Dome Books

Class-A Threat
Disgardium, Book One
Copyright © Dan Sugralinov 2019
Cover Art © Ivan Khivrenko 2019
Art Editor © Vladimir Manyukhin 2019
English Translation Copyright © Andrew Schmitt 2019
Published by Magic Dome Books, 2019
All Rights Reserved
ISBN: 978-80-7619-031-3

Table of Contents:

Chapter One

Sandbox

FOR MY BIRTHDAY, my parents got me an *Infinitum 8*. Not a very expensive model of immersion pod, but one of the best in its class. It was the present I wanted most for my fourteenth birthday because that is the age you can finally start playing the coolest and most popular game on the planet – *Disgardium*.

As soon as the birthday party was over and the guests had left, dad smiled:

"Can't wait to test it out?"

I nodded. How could I!? An immersion pod is not some steam-powered VR-helmet with sensor gloves!

"Go on then, Alex," mom said and laughed, embracing dad.

"Don't go in too long your first time!" he shouted after me. "Alex?"

"Yes, dad!"

I answered, almost running to my room where the new pod awaited me. Just think, it was already installed, calibrated and ready to use! I hurriedly got undressed and went inside. It was vertical, but could change orientation to better reflect the virtual world. Gravity is a heartless little bitch and it's difficult to convince someone that they're standing when their real body is horizontal.

I grabbed the metal handles and waited. A few seconds passed, but nothing happened. Was this thing defective? I was about to run down and call the manufacturer when a stern voice rang out in the pod:

"Alex, your heartbeat is too rapid for your first immersion experience! Access denied."

"Oh come on!" I shouted.

"Apologies for the inconvenience, but characters can only be generated in baseline physical state..." the voice muttered, probably quoting the user's manual. Then it followed up with some helpful advice: "Alex, please do your best to calm down and try again. Thank you."

With a sigh, I climbed out of the pod and walked out onto the little balcony off my room. There were all kinds of silvery delivery drones flitting about on the backdrop of the starry sky, landing and taking off from the windows of our huge residential complex.

Higher up, a procession of public flying cars

darkened the sky. As of today, I was legally allowed to pilot them without computer control. I couldn't wait to try it out. Of course, I would have to pass the license test first, but I had no doubts about that.

A cloud of condensation burst out of my mouth. The cold damp wind made me shiver even though, earlier today, it was pretty clearly turning to spring.

A few minutes later, I was calm and back in the pod. This time I saw no warnings, and the immersion process was able to initiate.

Intragel flooded the pod, going over my head, but it was perfectly alright to breathe. Finally, I closed my eyes.

And when I opened them again, I was in outer space. The sensation of weightlessness took my breath away, and I could barely resist waving my arms and legs. Not that there was much reason to: the pod assumed control over my muscles, keeping them static while the intragel kept my body suspended and out of harm's way. That way, if something went wrong and it lost control of my body, the gel would protect me from injury.

Good evening, Alex!

Please select your preferred immersion environment.

The text was immediately read out by a breathy female voice. In terms of environments, there wasn't much choice. I had the moon-sized test world *Infinitum*, made to demonstrate the pod's capabilities, or the huge *Disgardium*, which came factory-preinstalled on all pods.

And that was what I chose. Some system logs ran before my eyes:

> **Biological age confirmed.**
> *Access to* Disgardium *permitted.*
> *Notifying Department of Education...*
> *Complete... Status confirmed.*

> **Initiating first immersion experience!**
> *Scanning body... Complete... Character appearance generated.*
> *Approved world type:* **Sandbox.**
> *Recommended location:* **Tristad.**

Unfortunately, I would be relegated to a sandbox until I reached sixteen. They were private locations where only underage players were allowed. Adults from the full version were not permitted, and all content was strictly age-appropriate...

All around me, I saw a flurry of majestic cities and abandoned villages; epic battles and ghastly monsters; the six not yet entirely explored continents; heavenly gardens and fiery wastelands; a billion active players and just as many non-player characters, which was to say nothing of noncitizen workers; seaside resorts and city blocks, teeming with forbidden pleasures...

Welcome to Disgardium, Alex!

Welcome to a world where dozens of nonhuman races live in harmony. A world where sword and magic reign! A world where anyone could one day become a king or hero! A world where you'll want to live! A world where fate...

I didn't even think of interrupting the intro, savoring the massive scale and brilliant colors of this world that was so recently off limits. I had been dreaming of this moment for far too long.

The primer on *Disgardium* came to an end. I was immersed in darkness for an instant and suddenly found myself in a room full of people.

It was a few boys and girls. We were all wearing identical canvas garb and looking around in surprise. I was just overcome and couldn't hide my glee. It was all so real! The wooden floor creaked underfoot, rafters peeked out from behind the high ceiling, and light from the windows jumped along the walls, playing off our shadows. I could smell a sappy tree, dust whirled in the rays of the sun. The canvas shirt fit loosely over my body and when I touched it I could feel my ribs through the fabric. Unbelievable!

"Woah!" shrieked a girl with long black hair. "Who pinched me?"

Everyone laughed. The girl sneezed, and that caused a new burst of laughter.

"Happy birthday, all!" I shouted.

"Happy birthday!" rang out discordantly through the laughter.

All of us had just reached our fourteenth year, that was obvious. Who in their right mind would put off their first taste of *Disgardium*?

"Hey, wait a minute! Shouldn't we be seeing our names?"

"We haven't even generated characters yet, dummy!"

In our feverish anticipation, we didn't notice at first but the door had opened.

"Welcome, new visitors of Tristad!" came a sonorous male voice.

We turned. In the doorway, hiding a smile in his whiskers, there stood a respectable man with graying locks. Over him hovered the words:

Peter Whiteacre, level 30
Chief Councilman of the city of Tristad.

"It is my pleasure to welcome you to the free

city of Tristad, where everyone has a place be they hero or warrior, bard or wise man, hunter or mage, druid or common quarry worker..." the councilman listed a few more series of classes and professions. Then he ran down the list of races inhabiting the Commonwealth: "And we are equally glad to see people, elves, and gnomes..."

For my part, I was quite engaged. Studying information online was one thing, but finally becoming part of all this was another. The councilman then gave us a brief overview of the state of the world: all races of the Commonwealth were at war with hordes of orcs and barbaric nonhuman tribes. They also repelled raids from the Nether and the senseless attacks of the Reavers, and resisted the dark brotherhoods, the Sleeping Gods, the Goblin League...

Lots of things happened in this world, and it was possible that some of us would remain in the Commonwealth after transitioning to the adult world. Others would certainly take the chance and change their character to a different faction, though.

"I can see that you're all tired from the long journey," Whiteacre said finally. "Now please complete your registration with Carlson the scribe, then I'll answer any questions you may have. If you have no questions, go out and see the city, meet its inhabitants and bring it good fortune..."

We started heading toward the registration desk. There was a plump rosy-cheeked scribe sitting there. I took up the back of the line.

"Complete these arrival forms," said Carlson, handing them out.

That paper, once in hand, unfolded into a character registration form.

In a sandbox, you could only play a person, so it wasn't clear why Whiteacre had listed all the races of the Commonwealth. And we could only choose a class at level ten, so now we could only fill in our name and allocate attribute points.

There was a name I was planning to use for a long time, ever since my dad read me tales from ancient history as bedtime stories.

Name: Scyth.
Confirmed.

I might have said it had no meaning, but that wasn't true. I hope I can live up to the name.

Scyth! You have 15 main attribute points.
In many ways, your attributes will determine your entire life in Disgardium *from your combat strategy to the way others perceive you!*
Take your time and think carefully! Your

attributes cannot be reset!

In school I heard that, no matter what class you choose, you need a ten at least in every attribute. Strength so I could carry lots of weight. Agility and perception so I wouldn't miss my targets and land critical hits. Intelligence defined mana regeneration, and mana was used to make special attacks, even for warriors. And with low charisma, I could forget about good quests and discounts from vendors. Luck, meanwhile, had a small impact on just about everything.

So then, after some brief thought, I put two into each one. I added the extra point to endurance without really thinking, just because it was there.

Scyth, level-1 human
Real name: Alex Sheppard.
Real age: 14.
Class: not selected.

Main attributes:
Strength: 2.
Perception: 2.
Endurance: 3.
Charisma: 2.
Intelligence: 2.
Agility: 2.
Luck: 2.

All finished, I handed my arrival form to the scribe. He scanned it, snorted, gave a strained smile and, with exaggerated enthusiasm, announced:

"Welcome to Tristad, Scyth!"

When I emerged I stopped on the stairs, looking down the central street dreamily and smiling.

Disgardium, say hello to your new hero!

Chapter Two

A Year and a Half Later

THERE WAS ONLY five minutes left in class, and the students were starting to get restless.

"The bell hasn't rung yet," Greg Kovacs, our history teacher, noted sternly. "Take your seats! Edward! Sit down this instant!"

Ed Rodriguez, leader of the Dementors clan, was scraping his desk along the floor. He quickly sat back down despite himself. Modern history was our last lesson for today, and he just couldn't wait to get back into *Disgardium*.

"I'm not finished," Greg frowned. "Alright kids, class is extended by two minutes! You know who to thank."

"But teacher!" Ed objected. "Mr. Kovacs..."

"No 'buts,' Rodriguez!"

Tissa, the blonde girl sitting behind Ed, hissed out something that sounded very much like "shit!" She was in Ed's clan and, seemingly, they had a raid scheduled today.

"Let's make that three minutes, Melissa Schafer," the teacher corrected himself nonchalantly. He continued the lecture: "After the collapse of the world banking system..."

Tissa rolled her eyes and gave a loud sigh, not unclenching her lips. Ed, turning around, blew her a kiss. Tissa shot him a middle finger back.

"... the UN," Greg said, writing the name on the whiteboard and underlining it. "That led to the creation of the Worldwide Bank and the global monetary union. Who can tell me what their new unit of currency was called?"

"The phoenix," the class answered in unison.

"Exactly," the teacher nodded. "And who knows what a phoenix looks like?"

Silence. Knowing Mr. Kovacs, it was better to answer. Otherwise we could end up sitting here for half an hour.

"The phoenix is a mythological bird that can burn itself up and rise from the ashes," I said. "The first written mention of the phoenix myth is found in Herodotus."

"I appreciate your knowledge of mythology, Alex, but I was asking about the currency. The

---

phoenix doesn't have a material form. It is a digital currency, independent of economic and political considerations. In the same year, another important change took place in society..."

He had moved on to the mandatory citizenship tests. Ours would be coming soon enough. And Greg touched on the pitiful existence noncitizens were shackled to, the fact that they outnumbered citizens, and that they were dying *en masse*, abandoned and forgotten by society... But by the end, no one was listening anymore. For the last seconds of our extra minutes, we were drumming on our desks and shouting out a countdown:

"Three! Two! One!"

The thunder of every chair scooting back at once drowned out our homework assignment and the date of an upcoming test.

The Dementors were the first out of class, driven on by Ed. They took *Disgardium* seriously, because they saw it as their future. Snowstorm Incorporated, the developer, was the first company to ever pay people to game.

And since then, it is the most widely played full-immersion game on earth, even receiving certification from the United Nations itself. And now, it was where noncitizens and underqualified citizens spent their days and earned their money. For many, it was the only way to improve their lot in life.

But definitely not for me.

It had been a year and a half since I first loaded up Dis. I remember thinking I was very clever investing equally in all attributes. How wrong I was! That gave me a character with piss-poor damage and dispiriting aim. I was hardly fit to live. Unfortunately, even though I had read a few guides before my first session, I never read the best way to make a new character. I knew that every level would give me five attribute points so I figured, if anything was wrong, I could just fix it in no time at all. Gaining just a few levels seemed trivial.

But it wasn't all puppies and rainbows. Bots were in no rush to give me quests, and farming mobs turned out to not only be tedious but difficult!

Level-one rats refused to be easy farming, and took me down in a couple of bites every time. I had to land ten or so blows, constantly swinging, just to take down one. And that was if I had someone holding the rat for me.

And when I joined a group with beginners like me, those drips of experience turned into mere dewdrops. When I realized that, my enthusiasm was extinguished. And this wasn't exactly an uncommon experience. Some just stopped playing, others opted for social quests.

But leveling like that was hopelessly boring and never-ending. Just to get one experience point, for example, you had to spend a few hours doing social labor like cleaning stables or pulling weeds. Half a year in the game to get a couple levels? Oh nether!

And one day I quit the game, but the next I was inspired by the success of a few classmates and entered again with new hopes and plans. But the longer I played, the more disenchanted I grew.

At the beginning, I couldn't get any equipment, armor or weapons. The lowliest knife in the weapons store cost a few silver, and I'd have had to complete fifty social quests to get just one silver coin. Fight rats with my bare hands? Ha! Those things were so big they'd have the upper hand on a rottweiler IRL! And even if I could kill one, the reward was just one experience point, maybe two if I got really lucky.

So in the end I just couldn't stand it. After a few weeks trying every which way to level, my experience bar was no more than five percent full. I didn't even hit level two.

For some reason known only to the developers, it was impossible to delete a character and create a new one from scratch in sandboxes. Maybe that was to make us take more responsibility for our decisions.

Meanwhile, I was disgusted by the idea of

spending real money on the game both then and now. I mean, I knew how hard up my parents were for cash. It wasn't like basic gear would cost some astronomical amount but, by the time I considered it, Dis had already lost its charm to me.

Sure, at first it was fun to explore a totally new world with its own laws, rules, geography, history and races. It even had different physics, given both magic and teleportation were possible.

But that was only truly enthralling for the first few days. Weeding or respawning time and again after the fatal bite of some overgrown spider? No thanks.

What was more, my heart yearned for outer space. The first settlements were being made on Mars, and it seemed to me that exploring a real new world was somewhat more interesting than a virtual one. I greedily devoured any materials I could find about space expeditions, studied the requirements for getting into university and prepared for exams. My parents supported my ambitions too, and had set some money aside for my studies.

But I still had to play Dis. And every day.

From the age of fourteen, everyone was required to spend at least one hour per day in the game. Snowstorm Inc.'s long tendrils reached deep into the UN Department of Education. Now it was thought to be an important part of a child's education, providing necessary social skills and preparing us for adult life whether in the real world or *Disgardium*.

Every day was exactly the same for me there. I usually spent the whole hour sitting on a bench opposite the Bubbling Flagon tavern. Just after I entered the game, the neighbor girl Eve O'Sullivan would come join me. She couldn't stand even a hint of pain, so she didn't find the game much fun either. And for that reason, she would sit around killing time with me.

The sooner we got to our citizenship tests the better. After that, I could be done with this onerous requirement.

With that thought in mind, I hurried to leave school. Our parking lot had a limited number of public flying cars, and if you didn't manage to get one on the first go around, you'd have to wait for one to come back.

And that's just what happened. Or more accurately, one of the last ones still had an empty seat, but I wanted one to myself so I could drive it manually.

The school lot was on the roof, next to a solar panel array. Eve was sitting there. She always waited for me so we could fly home together. Her father's business was really taking off, but they were still in our apartment complex.

"Alex!"

Eve's face lit up. I might have thought she liked me, but that didn't do anything for me. She was sweet, but not at all to my taste. Plus she didn't mind her figure, eating chocolate bars in quantities that far surpassed Department of Health guidelines.

"How was your day?"

"Like normal, Eve. Two periods of ethics of modern society, two of programming domestic robotics and two of modern history. Dullsville."

"Oh god! I never understood why we need history!" she shouted. Then she changed her voice, trying to parody Greg's distinctive manner of speaking. "The last president of the United States..."

"Mhm."

Eve got distracted and started thinking. I threw off the backpack and sat down next to her. All the flying cars were gone, so we would have to wait here at least ten minutes. Then a tarry column of acrid bitumen shot up into the air from the asphalt of the launch pad.

"That damned Dis again," she sighed. "When are you gonna play today? Right after you eat like normal?"

"Mhm. The sooner I start, the sooner I can finish. Then I can do whatever I want."

"So, what would you rather be doing?" Eve asked, emphasizing the word "rather." She even attempted a languid tone, drawing out the last word and cocking an eye.

Aw, nether! Flirting was definitely not her strong suit. Where had she seen that move? Nevertheless, I was caught off guard.

"Probably not what you had in mind," I answered with a smile. I didn't want to offend her, she was a great girl and I had known her since childhood. "I'll be studying materials on the Leman expedition to Mars."

"I see. I just thought... Maybe you'd want to..."

"What?" I didn't want to embarrass her, but it was better to break this off before it turned into an upwelling of unjustified hope.

"Maybe... Maybe we could watch it together?" she blurted out in one breath.

"Sorry, not today. My parents are working on a new project, I don't want us to distract them."

I tactically said "us," although I meant only her. My father and mother had finally gotten an easy order, but the client was fickle and it was best to keep risks to a minimum. Money had been tight for us recently.

Dad suspected mom was having an affair, which was driving him more and more to the bottle. And when he drank he got paranoid, suspicious and aggressive. Mom, of course, didn't like that. And so she left home on the sly and came back around morning. I definitely think she's seeing someone.

Their constant fighting ruined my mood so much I didn't even want to do my homework. And that was a problem. To get into university, I need high average points.

"We can watch it at my place," Eve wouldn't relent.

"We can talk about that later," I answered, hoping that by then her spark would have gone out.

Flying cars began returning to the parking lot. We got into one, and I gave a nod to Eve:

"So, are you flying, or the computer?"

"Me."

I changed steering to manual and took off into the air. Flying... what could be better? Only the stars.

Chapter Three

Bad News

AFTER EATING, I went on Dis. Eve and I sat on the bench across from the Bubbling Flagon tavern which was, by the way, the only one in all of Tristad. We just chatted and looked around.

The city had a rhythm all its own. Players ran around willy-nilly, coursing between the market square, bank and the auction. There was so much noise that, twenty minutes after loading, I truly wished I could know what it was like to be deaf. Everyone around was screaming, arguing, negotiating, inviting people to groups and just-formed clans.

The energetic whooping of criers and barkers for local merchants and craftsmen cut into the din. Maneuvering between them all was a challenge with my low attributes. Couriers and other low-level players were darting here and there, carrying out social quests for the city.

And they all ignored the red-faced town drunk Patrick, just pretending that he didn't exist. That's how much he bothered everyone. That unlovable bot was always begging for a copper. Yet there were rumors that if you cranked your reputation with him up to max, you could get some legendary quest. But few had tried because, at a rate of one rep per copper, it was too steep for most noobs.

A bit further down the street some restless gnomes were causing a ruckus with a group of dignified dwarves. Even from so far away, I could tell that they were negotiating to buy some new gnomish invention, and both were driving a hard bargain. A city guardsman was standing at the entrance to the tavern watching passersby like a hawk...

By the way, in the sandbox taverns players were only served cream beer. No alcohol! Explicit language was bleeped and penalized with experience points, too. What was more, it wasn't even possible to get fully undressed here. Instead of sex organs, we all had... nothing down there. Like a child's doll.

Too bad, of course. I had no problems with girls, but the very thought of something greater than a normal conversation made me twitch. I would not have said no to a bit of practice.

Class-A Threat

Just so you know, that does not apply to Eve O'Sullivan though. Not one bit. Though based on her chosen nick, Aphrodite, she may have had a different opinion. Still, I couldn't discount the possibility that she simply didn't know who that was.

When I did dream of taking it further than a chat, it was always with Tissa Schafer. And it just so happened that she was walking on the other side of the street with Ed and the other guys from the clan just then. They were talking loudly and laughing.

Based on how they were barely moving their legs, they were all encumbered and heading to auction on the market square, to the smith or to a merchant stall to get rid of all their loot before another raid. They probably didn't have anything of value, maybe just a hunk of rusty scrap from the mine of the hyena-like gnolls. That was not the most complicated instance, but it had to be done before raiding the dungeon of the man-eating ogres where they were going. And maybe they were planning to go run the new ins in the Olton Quarries, which everyone was talking about in school...

"Does she have to shake her thighs like that?" Eve asked in annoyance, looking at Tissa.

I led my gaze over Melissa's tall and well-proportioned figure, wrapped in the short white dress of a priestess of Nergal the Radiant, the main deity in this world. At the very least it was the god with the most adherents, and thus faith points. I couldn't look away. It was a captivating spectacle, and only Eve's look of admonishment in the corner of my eye made me stop leering at Tissa Schafer's backside.

Here all characters were an exact copy of the people who played them but, in the real world, Tissa never wore clothes like that. There she usually loafed around in oversized pants and baggy hoodies. So I could only admire her here. And that was the only thing I liked about this game.

Of all the players I knew in Tristad, only she and Ed "Crawler" Rodriguez had become mages. Magic was an inalienable part of the world. In theory anyone here could master it, but it cost unspeakable sums of cash to learn. A tome of basic magic of any school cost at least ten thousand gold! That was approximately the same number of phoenixes, about the same as a flying car.

But neither of them bought any tomes. Tissa randomly found a quest object that brought her on a long chain where the final reward was light magic training in the Temple of Nergal the Radiant.

And Ed got the fire magic class supposedly after finding a tome as loot in an instance. Either fate had been kind to him, or he was just entitled to the loot as the clan leader. I didn't know for sure.

"I'm bored," said Eve, looking at me demandingly.

"Do you want to take a walk around town?"

"Not really," she shook her head, and I understood that I had guessed wrong. But I wasn't going to play her naïve little flirting game.

"Then let's please just sit quietly."

Eve went silent.

I would gladly have read something, but there was no way to bring stuff in here. This was a medieval fantasy world, where the highest technology available were primitive powder guns made by the gnomes and dwarves. So I'd have to read, or more accurately, reread the in-game encyclopedia: "Gnomes provide the dwarves with various kinds of powder weapon: rifles, muskets and even cannons. And they do not disdain steam power either, among other sorts of technology..."

Boring. Why should I care about steam power in the modern age, when humanity had already begun colonizing the Solar System?

Damn, time was drawing on so long! Too bad I couldn't break up the required hour per day into several sessions. That was for health reasons. It was thought to be harmful to the psyche, constantly changing between realities. There were recorded cases when people didn't properly adapt after a virt session. In the game, they rakishly carry heavy two-handed words, but in the real world they were weaklings, which at times led people to overestimate their abilities and injure themselves.

Feeling bored, I once again opened the interface menu and looked at my profile:

Scyth, level-1 human
Real name: Alex Sheppard.
Real age: 15.
Class: not selected.

In sandboxes, you had to show your real name and age. It was thought to cultivate a sense of responsibility in schoolchildren for their behavior in the game. In the first few years, only your nick was shown in your profile and you could generate any appearance.

That was a truly blessed time for dorks and losers, who took revenge on their real-life bullies in the game. Then a wave of parent outrage swept the globe and, after brief discussion, real names were added to sandbox profiles and characters were required to look like their IRL counterparts. The next day, almost none of those gankers came to school...

Eve stood up. She probably wasn't mad. She

---

always forgave me for stupid jokes.

"Where are you going?"

"I'm sick of sitting here," she answered, turning. "Wanna go take a walk?"

I also stood up and we headed to the city gates. On the way I remembered that, five minutes earlier, I had suggested we take a walk and she had refused. Girls...

Mills, the gate guard, tossed us a passing gaze and gave a signal to his partner:

"Let them pass!"

For the next few seconds we waited patiently for the gates to open enough to get through, then we left the city limits. Eve said something about a gift her parents were getting for her birthday, but I was barely listening.

The edge of the forest was just twenty yards away when we were caught by a group of running players. I spit out a curse. The last thing we needed were the Dementors. I always thought their leader Ed "Crawler" looked at me funny. Plus he teased me whenever he got the chance.

"Where are you guys going?" he asked, giving a jocular smile. "A romantic date in the Gloomwood? Or are you off to raid some rabbits?"

"Come on, Rodriguez," I answered.

In the last few months, I had grown used to my classmates teasing me. It always followed the same scenario. Now Malik "Infect," a swarthy Thief would make some joke about my progress, and "Bomber" Hung would pile on. Then Tissa would frown and try to bring her clanmates to reason, and Crawler would balk, saying they had no more time to waste on pathetic noobs...

"Not likely," Infect said. "A rare mob just popped up by the rabbits. They won't be able to take it; their equipment is too low level."

"Do you think they'll attack the butterflies?" Bomber asked, keeping the serious expression on his face. His father was Chinese, and his mother Swedish, which at least partially explained how Hung turned out a six-foot-six wall of muscle. "They're gonna get wiped, one hundred percent."

Ed stopped the act early, though. Waving his rare wand, he left a stream of fiery sparks in the air. Then he took a few steps toward me and said in confidence:

"Listen, Scyth. I understand that Aphrodite's family has it made, and her parents will set their daughter up with something cozy. *Disgardium* doesn't mean squat to her. But what about you?"

"What about me, Ed?"

"Call me Crawler, Scyth. This is the game, not the real world!"

"Back off!" Eve screamed.

She stood in front of me and shot Tissa a mean look.

"Hey Aphrodite, we were having a little talk

here! For you all this," Ed led his hand over everything around, "means nothing. But for us it's very important. Much more important than what happens there, where the world is ruled by hypocritical bastards like your parents!"

"Don't you dare talk about my parents that way!" Eve flared up. "You have no idea what you're talking about!"

"Oh, is your father going to be elected prefect? That's what everyone's saying. How many butts did he have to lick? Or is Mr...." Ed made a face and spit, "O'Sullivan not going to share the wealth with his special little princess?"

"Up yours, dumbass!"

"Choose your words carefully, fatty," Tissa said lazily.

"And what if I don't? Are you going to kill me? Ha!" Eve was going nuts, and I anxiously placed a hand on her shoulder but she threw it off. "It's impossible to even really kill someone in your stupid game!"

She took a step forward and gave Rodriguez a slap. Ed easily dodged, then unwittingly threw a fireball. His flaming left hand came unclenched, launching a spurt of condensed plasma the size of a walnut. It reached Eve in one second, and fire covered her body like napalm.

Her clothes – a standard novice's dress – caught fire and burned up in an instant, while her health points fell sharply downward. Eve screamed. Sensations of pain were significantly dulled here, but they did exist. The girl fell to the ground, trying to beat out the fire, but the damage was too much for her level one. A few moments later, she died.

"Geeze Crawler, what was that for?" Tissa wrinkled her nose.

She could hardly have been talking about the fire. Tissa Schafer visually mocked Eva's plump body, which was now only in underwear and beginning to flicker. Five seconds later it was gone. She left the world.

"What, you won't even go to bat for your stupid girlfriend?" Crawler asked acridly, egging me on.

"If you're talking about her intelligence, she's not stupid," I objected calmly. "Definitely not dumber than you."

"No, she isn't dumb. You're right there. But still she's a big piece of crap like the rest of her family!" Crawler provoked me, cradling a new fireball. "Well! Come on!"

"Do you really need a moral justification to kill a much weaker player? At the end of the day..."

"Mouthing off again, Scyth?" he interrupted. "You'd rather use your tongue than your hands? Ha-ha!"

"Good one."

Class-A Threat

He was thinking of his reputation with the city. Eve attacked him first, so he was defending himself there. It was his right to kill her. Now he was expecting me to do the same.

"Coward," he said, hawking another loogie.

"This is pointless, Eddie. There are four of you, all level fifteen. I won't even get through your armor. I mean sure, I could get myself whipped up into a righteous anger and tell you to go to hell. I could even call you a jerk and run at you swinging if that helps your send me to respawn with a clean conscience."

"So, he is running his mouth. Right guys?"

"Yep, running his mouth is all he's good for, Crawler," answered Bomber. "You want me to swat him down without all this heckling? You know, I could..."

"Let him be," Tissa interrupted. "We're wasting time!"

She turned to leave, but Rodriguez got what he was after. Regardless of what I said, their words hurt me and I wanted to respond.

"Hey, Ed..." I called. "You know what?"

"What?" he shuddered.

"At the end of the day, this is just a game. Nothing more! No matter how cool you make yourself here. No matter what you're worth in the game, real life still means something..." They were all listening carefully, even Tissa, but they kept silent and I continued: "And you know what? No matter how hard you try, you're gonna have to live in a fake world. And that's if you can pass the citizenship test. Otherwise... The virtual mines? Working on plantations? Street sweeping? Is that life?"

Not one muscle twitched on the Dementors' faces. Just a light shadow ran by on Tissa's cheeks: she had lost her mother, and her father worked in Dis. She had no chance at university.

"Come on, to the nether with him guys. We're wasting time!" she said.

"Just a sec, guys. The ogres aren't going anywhere." Crawler walked up to me, coming forehead to forehead. "As long as I've known you, Scyth, you've always thought you were above everyone else. I might not be so smart but, at the very least, I have friends. Do you have any friends, Alex Sheppard?"

"Yes. I do."

"And who are these invisible friends?"

I had no response. Only lonely kids dreamt about space. Everyone else had someone to lose.

"Exactly," Ed nodded. "Think about that... smarty pants. Tissa, buff me!"

The priestess of the Radiant God renewed everyone's movement speed buffs and they ran to the west, not looking back.

I exited Dis.

Class-A Threat

Scyth, you have left Disgardium.
Please wait to adapt to the real world.
Remaining time: 00:59... 00:58... 00:57...

I was immersed in impenetrable darkness. I felt deaf, dumb and unconscious. Just the flavor of ash was left in my mouth – a trick of the mind as I involuntarily recalled Aphrodite's burned body.

Just then the pod went vertical, it's sensors relinquished control over my body and handed the reins back to my brain. Then the intragel, which provided balance, shock-absorption, and also maintained muscle tone, was sucked into the pod walls for antiseptic treatment and filtration.

My senses returned. I was standing in the middle of the pod. It's doors slid aside silently.

I crawled out and froze. My hearing was back, and I could immediately tell that my parents were fighting loudly in the other room. Their fights had become a daily occurrence, nothing out of the ordinary.

I put on my shorts and t-shirt and went into the kitchen to get a couple sandwiches and a bottle of mineral water, which I was planning to consume as I studied the materials on the Leman expedition to Mars. But I stopped and listened. My father was trying to get something through to my mom, and he was calm. Now that was weird.

"... you'll have to tell him, Helene. He's a smart kid, he'll figure it out."

"Mark, you're so heartless! This is his last year of school, citizenship tests, do you even understand what a blow this could be to him? He might not recover!"

"No, you don't understand!" My father raised his voice. "Sooner or later, he'll have to find out! And let it be sooner rather than later so he has time to think it all over and decide what to do!"

What were they talking about? What was I supposedly going to figure out? I just happened to come out when my mother's mouth was open to answer. Seeing me, she gave a noisy sigh:

"Alex..."

"Mom, dad? Is everything alright?"

"Everything's alright buddy, everything is fine..." father muttered. His hands rested on my shoulders and we sat on the couch. He tossed a gaze at my upset mom and, looking aside, quietly said:

"Alex, your mother and I are getting a divorce. No-no, not now. We're going to wait until after your citizenship test."

"You're getting a divorce?" I repeated stupidly. "What about me?"

"Yes, you..." my dad looked at my mom. "Helene?"

"No way, this was your idea, you say it. I

don't want him to hate me for the rest of his life!"

"Oh this was my idea now?" he asked, outraged. "You should have been thinking about our son when you..."

"Mark!" my mom whispered. "Not in front of Alex!"

My father nodded at her enraged gaze again, but held back. Their flares of tension were so intense I could almost hear them.

"Hey, so what's all this? Care to explain calmly?"

"Alex..." dad coughed out. "We can't afford to pay for your studies. I'm sorry."

"But why?" I figured I'd misheard. "Why?!"

"Divorce will automatically lower our civil status to G. There won't be enough money to pay for university, and we can only help you get set up. You're gonna have to start working, son."

Working? With no education? And what, pray tell, did they think I was going to do? Oh nether, but they were saving for my studies! Or...

"And what about my college fund?" I made up my mind to ask, already knowing the answer.

"There he goes!" mom answered with particular vengeance, looking at my father. "What do you think we've been living on all this time? We haven't had a decent project for a long time!"

I looked helplessly at dad and he, working his jaws, looked away. But mom just kept coming at me:

"Our income is going to be barely enough to live on. Congratulations, Alex. You'll be an adult soon and you're gonna have to learn to fend for yourself..."

But I couldn't hear her or my father, who was saying empty words. Just one idea was clanking around in my head? No outer space? Then I exploded.

"This isn't right!" I shouted. "Mom! Dad! What are you talking about? What divorce? Everything is fine! And sure, you fight sometimes, but so does everyone! Every couple fights, but they don't all get divorced!"

My face twisted and, trying not to burst into tears like a baby in front of my parents, I turned away.

"Sorry, son. Our minds are made up," came my father's voice from some unfathomable distance. "When you get older, you'll understand..."

Sensing my mood, our catdog AT rubbed up against my leg. He meowed and tapped me with his big forehead. I mechanically picked him up, brought him to my room, and only there let my silent tears out, my head buried in a pillow.

No work without higher education. No education without money. My basic income would only be enough for a cupboard in a building for poor L-class citizens, and all I'll have to eat is flavorless universal nutrient blend.

So, all I have left is *Disgardium?*

Chapter Four

Back into the Game

I WAS IN NO MOOD to watch materials on the Mars expedition now considering that my path there was blocked, perhaps forever. After all, I couldn't get a scholarship, for that I'd have to be a particularly bright student at least on my city level. But we had plenty of kids smarter than me. Maybe Ed Rodriguez thought me a "smarty-pants," but I was never so truly enthralled with learning to go beyond mandatory coursework.

I didn't know how long I sat there, staring aimlessly at the ceiling. I didn't pay any attention to my parents' fight flaring up again in the guest room, or to my communicator beeps. The only thing running through my head was how could two adults be so selfish that they could deprive their only son of his future. What happened?

My mind was searching fitfully for other options of how to solve the problem, refusing to accept my new reality and hoping it could all be solved. I even tried to talk to my mom and dad again, but that just got me in trouble and made everything worse. Seemingly, they hated one another so much that they didn't give a damn about me or my future. All they wanted was to forget one another and never see each other again.

That's when it dawned on me. Their relationship was like a shattered cup. It could never be glued back together. I'd have to look for other ways of getting money for my education. And the only way to do that was *Disgardium*.

And that actually comforted me. Now I knew what to do, though I didn't yet know what I'd do in the game.

But how to get back there? It may have seemed stupid, but I was worried how Ed, Tissa and the rest would react after all the stuff I'd just said. Why couldn't I have just held my tongue?

I was also sorry that I hadn't gone to bat for Eve. After all, today she was my only close friend, and I was leaving her message unread!

Feeling pangs of conscience, I picked up my comm and listened to her recorded message:

"Hi! How's it going?" Eve's hologram moved into the middle of the room. "Did those bastards finally leave you alone? Don't worry about them, Alex! They're just jealous..." she kept silent, not having made up her mind to continue. "Uh...

Basically, remember when you said you were gonna watch something? If you want, I could come to your place. I mean it isn't urgent or anything, I just thought..."

She finally got too embarrassed, squeezed out a "Bye!" and the message came to an end. I valued her tact. She didn't call, she sent a message, so I didn't have to answer. But I did answer, though I kept it brief: "I'm going back on Dis. I'll explain next time I see you."

After that I went into the kitchen for food so I could force down some cold sandwiches and mineral water. I was planning to spend a lot of time in the pod, and I didn't have one of the advanced versions that could keep you fed and healthy.

I just couldn't forget about my parents' divorce. What went wrong in their lives and when?

Aw, to the nether with all that. Why keep putting off the inevitable? It was time.

Undressed, I walked up to the pod and placed my palm on the sensor. It read my prints, lit up green and gave a welcoming beep. The pod doors opened.

Going inside, I grabbed the handles and launched start-up. The pod closed, the lighting went out and intragel quickly filled the tube. I winced reflexively.

Loading...

I opened my eyes. I took a breath, filling my

lungs with piney air and feeling rays of the sun baking my skin. I was surrounded by a bright and astonishing forest. A huge butterfly flew by, brushing my cheek with a wing. Trying to catch it, I took an awkward step and heard a branch crunch underfoot. My bare foot shot with pain, and I swore for a while then spent a bit of time sitting on a stone on the roadside, fishing out the splinter.

I finished and looked around in search of hostile mobs, then decided to think up a plan of action. I had to begin with a look at my character.

This time I wasn't just browsing my stats in boredom, though. I was looking carefully, absorbed.

Scyth, level-1 human
Real name: Alex Sheppard.
Real age: 15.
Class: not selected.

Main attributes:
Strength: 2.
Perception: 2.
Endurance: 3.
Charisma: 2.
Intelligence: 2.
Agility: 2.
Luck: 2.

Secondary attributes:
Health points: 23/23.
Mana points: 12/12.
Recovery speed: 9 health points per minute.
Movement speed bonus: 2%
Base damage: 1.2.
Carrying capacity: 108 lbs.
Accuracy: 20%
Spell power bonus: 2.4%
Dodge chance: +4%
Critical damage chance: +5%
Vendor discount: +2%
Chance of receiving a unique quest: +0.2%
Chance of receiving improved loot: +0.2%

Fame: 0.

As for clothing, I was wearing only standard novice stuff, no bonuses. Canvas pants and shirt, not even any footwear.

In the game's quality scale, my stuff was *grey*. The items were such low quality no vendor would even buy them. Normal *white* stuff was a bit better, somewhat more durable, but no bonuses.

Bonuses started with the unusual, *green*. At the first levels, getting an enchanted green object was akin to a miracle. There were also supposedly rare *blue*, epic *purple* and *orange* legendary, as well as some *set* and *scalable* items. But I hadn't crawled far enough into the thicket of the game encyclopedia to even know what the last two were.

And it was probably not going to be relevant for the foreseeable future. This was my gear:

Novice's canvas pants
Shoddy
Cloth armor.
Armor: 1.
Durability: 4/10.
Requires level: 1.
Sell price: 0.

Novice's canvas shirt
Shoddy
Cloth armor.
Armor: 1.
Durability: 7/10.
Requires level: 1.
Sell price: 0.

The pants had less durability than the shirt after a memorable battle with an aggressive level-two bunny. I could probably have repaired it, i.e. gotten a patch and sewn it on, but that required a separate skill. Or to pay a tailor... That was the most painful issue in *Disgardium*, especially when you realized that, after the sandbox, game money could be easily withdrawn as real phoenixes. And by the way, I personally didn't have a single bronze coin to my name.

Basically, this novice gear was given to everyone. If I died, I could find a new set in my personal chest in the tavern. Identical canvas pants and shirt down to the stitching.

Farming mobs unarmed with my stats was not only a drawn-out process, it smelled of masochism. So I would have to earn XP with long and routine social quests: fetching, delivering, cleaning, collecting... Experience and money. Money and experience. I needed to get together at least ten silver for more serious gear and maybe not a sword, but at least some shabby dagger.

"Outta the way!" Someone hit me with their shoulder as they ran past.

Unable to keep my balance, I fell off the road face-first into mud. A few more people ran past after him.

"Where are you going?" I threw out, not expecting an answer.

"A Class-Z Threat!" A strangely dressed level-six archer turned and shouted back at me. He had a helmet on his head that looked to be a cast-iron pot, and was forced to hold it with one hand to keep it from falling off as he ran. "Some necromancer raised a churchyard!"

Ah, that was it! The game gave generous rewards for eliminating "threats" to the world (if

Class-A Threat

you let a necromancer go wild, he might take over the globe!) ...

I got up, shook off the clods of damp soil and, walking cautiously on the edge of the path, headed to town. Players were rushing not to miss the threat and that was only to my advantage. Maybe we'd be able to take some kind of quest before evening while the city council was at work. A large amount of Tristad's quests were given by the Chief Councilman. Although that was only during the day while he was at work. Other NPC's lived their own lives and gave out quests only if they actually needed something.

Approaching the city walls, I saw a row of black-market merchants stretched out along them. These were players just like me who didn't want to pay commission to the auctioneer or waste money on a market license. Or maybe they just wanted to unload their goods on the cheap. Now, honestly, there weren't very many people. I guess most of them had run off to eliminate the threat.

The sun was already starting to sink behind the city wall, and shadows were falling on the market stalls. The monotone hum of commerce split into distinct cries of admonishment and the sound of people doing business.

"Woven battle jacket! Plus two strength! Just three gold!"

"Minor healing potions! Bulk discounts!"

"Endurance and agility scrolls! From levelling prof, selling at cost!"

"Just what do you think you're doing?! Those ingredients are worth a penny! And what are you selling those things at, you miser?"

"I don't have any anti-greed scrolls, keep walking!"

I decided to walk past and get some prices. I would have to get somewhat more appropriate gear and figure this all out eventually. For the most part, they were selling trash, second-hand goods, things grown out of. Nothing of particular value, often missing some durability. Still it was cheaper than buying new.

"Are you looking for something in particular?" someone's hoarse voice made me turn around. A short lean level-nine player with the apt nick of Underweight looked over what I had on, then shrugged and came to a conclusion: "Not likely."

"You a beginner?" asked a very tall girl by the name Overweight sitting next to him. In fact, she was half a head taller than me.

In front of her there were piles of weapons sorted by type. Underweight had primarily clothing and armor. Sure, I guess they'd found their niche – take stuff on consignment or buy for more than the NPC merchants then resell at a premium.

"I don't think so," Underweight answered. "He's fifteen, that means he's already spent a year here at least."

"Wait a minute... I think this is that weirdo who's always sitting next to the tavern! That's right!" She turned to me. "Is it you?"

"Yes it is. Scyth."

"How can we help you, Scyth?" the traders asked in unison.

"I'm getting an idea of what I can buy to easily farm mobs."

"Got it!" the boy exclaimed. "We'll show you everything! So... Level one... What's your strength?"

"Two."

"How much? Two? Uh... That, putting it lightly, was pretty dumb bro... I see. That means plate and mail are out. Give me a minute..."

Underweight snorted, digging through the cloth and leather armor, setting things that might work for me in a separate pile. I shifted from foot to foot, thinking and listening to what the other sellers were shouting. I could make it to the city council building, there was still time, but then...

"Don't listen to him," Overweight said. "Maybe you want to be a mage? Or a bard? Is there some reason you just hang around the tavern all the time?"

"I haven't really thought about it..."

"Well, there is still time. You can still make it. But you better figure it out now so you level the right stats from here on."

"Thanks."

"Think nothing of it. It's common knowledge."

"Still thank you, Overweight. And hey, why do you have that nick?"

"You can't tell by looking? What do you think?" she snorted. "He's a hat rack and me... I've got big bones, ha-ha!"

She couldn't be called fat, but she definitely wasn't delicate either, more like curvy. Plumpest of all were her thighs. Laughing it off, she took a skeptical look at her partner, his head buried in a pile of gear, then asked:

"Well handsome, got any money?"

"Not even one copper," I admitted. "I haven't done any work here."

"So then, what made you waste all that time?"

"I wasn't having fun," I shrugged, not knowing what else to say about my lack of activity in Dis.

"It happens. But it's a shame. And you know why?"

"I can guess."

"Because we don't sell on credit!" the merchant shouted. "Listen, Undy! False alarm!

Class-A Threat

This schmo doesn't have any money! Empty pockets!"

"What?" he whooped, throwing some shoulder pads in a fit and raising his head. "What are you doing wasting my time then, lazybones?"

Underweight finished up and was not planning to continue. He stood at the improvised counter and looked angrily, puffing his nostrils. He was a head shorter than her, even though he was human not a gnome, which was funny to look at.

"I'm not here to waste your time, uh, Mr. Underweight. I said up front I was just looking, not planning to buy. So you think you can tell me what you've got?"

He looked untrustingly, did the math and a smile spread out on his face:

"My apologies for the... flare-up. That was just a misunderstanding. Our small but proud enterprise is always happy to give some help to beginners!"

"And what does your small but proud enterprise have to offer a noob like me?"

"Well, take a look," Underweight turned serious. "I picked out some cloth armor for you and a few leather pieces. The main one is a normal cloth Condor set: a chest wrap, pants, braces and shoulder pads. All *white* with no bonuses, but all together it gives a good boost to strength. I recommend you take leather boots right away and high ones at that. The main mobs are shorter than you at the beginning, so the first thing they'll bite at is your feet. I've got a leather belt too, though it is a bit shabby. But it does have a one-point endurance bonus. That'll help you survive a bite or two extra. Also, it's best to take leather gloves, but I don't have any right now, sorry."

"Come on, Undy!" Overweight shot out.

"But will he ever get money?" he smiled.

"We don't sell on credit!"

"There's a first time for everything, Rita," not turning his gaze from me, the trader kept smirking. "I'm gonna do you a favor, brother. I'll give you this whole excellent set of beginner armor, which is worth more than two gold if you do two little things for me..."

"I pay you back twenty for the two?" I smiled skeptically.

"You pay me back exactly what I give you. Two gold and twenty silver. And that's with a wholesale discount!" Underweight raised his index finger. "But! When you grow out of the set, you give it back to me."

"So you'd lease it to me?"

"Yes. What kind of timeframe were you thinking for payment? How about a week?"

"No thanks."

"No? Are you serious? In that gear, you'll be mopping up the city jail all by yourself tomorrow!"

Class-A Threat

"Haha, very funny. Not likely. But thanks for the offer. As soon as I manage to earn some money, I'll come back and buy something. Sorry for wasting your time."

The girl elbowed her partner in the ribs. He cast a dismayed gaze and sighed:

"Okay, bro. But this is a special offer and only because you're such a weirdo!"

"Underweight, thank you, but I have to go," I still needed to reach the chief councilman, and I had no interest in continuing to discuss money lending. I didn't know why, but I wanted to live within my means.

"Hear me out! Fifty silver a week. Hm?"

"Alright, I'll consider it. Thanks."

"Alright," he nodded and patted me on the shoulder. "If you reconsider, you know where to find us. Good luck, brother!"

I had already taken a few steps away when one of them called out.

"Hey, Scyth!" Overweight beckoned, holding a stick of some kind. "Here. On the house! This'll be bit better than bare hands..."

Large bear bone
Shoddy
Bashing weapon.
Damage: 1-2.
Durability: 8/20.

Sell price: 0.

"Take it, take it!" She practically forced it on me. "There you go. No need to thank me, no one wants that crap anyway, it's just taking up space."

I imagined the best way to grip the bone and how much it might weigh. I'd guess ten or fifteen pounds. I'd have to hold this in both hands.

"Good, now beat it," Overweight finished rudely. "Aren't you in a hurry?"

"Thanks," I looked into her profile. "Thanks, Rita!"

She rolled her eyes.

"Beat it, Sheppard!"

Chapter Five

Officially Displeased

I THREW THE CLUB over my shoulder and walked up to the gates to the appeals of the merchants, but I was stopped by guardsman Mills:

"Put your weapon away, young man!"

"Is this really against the rules?"

"For you it is. The city doesn't trust you. I don't trust you. Put your weapon away!"

He placed his hand on the handle of his sheathed sword and stared at me with a look of anticipation. I see, I didn't have enough reputation with the city. Honestly, I had none whatsoever, and the locals treated me with distrust. So I nodded in agreement and put the club in my inventory. That was one of the old-school gaming conventions Snowstorm left in Dis to the detriment of reality. Inventory here was independent of space and volume. The only things it measured were number of slots and carrying capacity in weight.

I walked toward the city council building down the straight central street and could sense Mills' suspicious gaze boring into my back.

Crowds of people were walking around Tristad even despite the fact that many had run off to fight the class-Z threat. That hapless player had probably become a necromancer almost by mistake, and almost certainly got more than he bargained for. I didn't know so much about it, but I'd heard that threats in *Disgardium* were often triggered accidentally. That was to put some variety into the gameplay and stave off stagnation in player development, constantly generating more and more "threats" at all levels.

Another question was what the benefit was to the threats themselves. I didn't know. At some point, I got curious and tried to dig through the forums. I didn't find anything but rumors and riddles. I got the sense that the corporation simply forbid all players who had ever been one of these global scapegoats from saying anything, and had powerful levers they could use to cut-off any attempts to do so...

With my poor attributes it was no easy task for me to get through the crowd. Everyone around was stronger, heavier and more powerful than me.

Slipping between a warrior in plate armor and

some girl, I stepped on the hem of her dress. The fabric stretched and began to audibly tear. The girl's legs were left bare and she nearly tripped, but the plate-armored dude grabbed her. With another hand he managed to snatch me by the shirt collar.

"Hey, don't you move!" he barked out menacingly.

"I'm not moving," I sighed in disappointment.

After the news of my parents' divorce, it felt like everything was rolling into a bottomless chasm, and this was just another of life's mean jokes.

"Excuse me, you have damaged the lady's attire!"

The "lady" was a level-one fourteen-year-old girl named Vista. While the pedigree bull trying to pass himself off as a knight was a level-twelve warrior named Crag, aka fifteen-year-old Tobias Asser. Jesus, what a cheap pick-up attempt! But Vista was into it and looked at me demandingly.

"It was an accident. I beg your apologies..."

"Apologies aren't gonna get you out of this one! She must be compensated fairly!" Crag said, drawing out his words and looking to Vista in satisfaction. She gave a suggestive smile, not at all embarrassed to be half naked.

"Come on, compensated for what? This is a standard novice's dress. Have her die and go to her room in the tavern, then pull a new one out of the chest..."

"Well I'm in a hurry, my friend is waiting for me!" Vista threw out. "And now I have to go respawn all because of some butthead?"

"It was an accident!"

"Pay for the damage, otherwise I'll call the guards!" the warrior bellowed.

"I don't have any money to pay for the damages, so..."

"Guards!" Crag shouted out suddenly. "I have apprehended a criminal!"

Come on. What bullshit! Was he serious? I tried to get out of it, my shirt ripped then the warrior grabbed me by the arm. He really was gonna do this!

"Come on, Crag. Why bring the guards into this? I really don't have any money!"

"Yeah, sure buddy. You've been here more than a year and expect me to believe you haven't found even one little copper? You can explain yourself to the guards... Ah, there they are now!" Crag placed me before a trio of guards that ran up. "Guardsman Gale! This criminal has damaged the elegant lady Vista's dress and must be punished!"

"Let's let the judge decide if he's a criminal or not," Gale grumbled. "Take him away, boys!"

The guards lifted me by the armpits. Gale pointed them where to go and barked loudly:

"Make way for the guards!"

Class-A Threat

The people cleared a path. "You're so strong!" Vista's voice rang out behind me. I no longer heard Crag's answer, but I thought he was happy. Picking up girls in the game was nothing new. And neither was the fact that some of them were not opposed to being helped by a high-level player, drawn in by a passing glance of their pretty little eyes.

"You're all off your rockers!" turned over and over in my head until the guards put me down. People here were behaving as if this was real life, not simply playing a character in a role-playing game. That rubbed me the wrong way...

We made it a few blocks, then the guards brought me to an empty alley and pressed me against the wall. Senior guardsman Gale brought his face close to mine and, his boozy breath intermingled with meat and onions, loudly belched and whispered privately:

"What say we come to an agreement without the judge? Three copper, one a piece, and you're free to go. Shake on it?"

"I don't have any money, guardsman Gale."

"What if you think about it?"

"I could think all day, I have no money."

"Not even one copper for us guys to blow of some steam after our shift?"

"If I had a copper, I'd have given it to the girl, guardsman Gale."

"Nether!"

He angrily pounded his plate-armored glove on the wall and furrowed his brow, considering what he could squeeze out of me.

"Well Gale, we gonna drag him to court?" one of them asked in dismay. "Maybe, well he..."

"To the nether with him!" Gale gave his verdict. "Let's go, boys. And you, Scyth. Keep your head down in Tristad. We are now officially displeased with you!"

Your reputation with the city of Tristad has been lowered by 5.

Current reputation: mistrust.

The guardsmen left, forgetting about me instantly. In their minds, they were already at a table with their friends, carousing and playing cards.

I looked at my Tristad reputation progress bar. It was not yet hostile, but getting close. I couldn't allow myself to tumble that far, otherwise I'd never get back into the city.

Alright, no big deal. I could do some social quests to restore my rep and even increase it to *friendly*. That would up my vendor discount, and give me a greater variety of missions. Overall it would just make living in Tristad more comfortable.

With these thoughts in mind, I ran to the city council building before it closed. The entrance had a bulletin board hanging near it with current missions:

> **Street sweeping.** *One full work day. Reward: 1 copper coin, 1 experience point.*
> **Mail delivery.** *Requires agility over 5. Full work day. Reward: 2 copper coins, 2 experience points.*
> **Weeding.** *Full work day. Requires Herbology level 1. Reward: 2 copper coins, 2 experience points.*
> **Guarding the border with Gloomwood.** *Full work day. Requires level over 10. Reward: a share of the loot, 10 silver coins, 30 experience points.*

All told I read a few dozen of the so-called "dailies," quests for the public good that were renewed once per day. But every ad had a stamp reading: "Mission unavailable. Come back tomorrow!"

Alright then, made sense. Day was already turning to night, plus the number of vacancies was limited. You couldn't very well send a thousand people to weed a single garden. Weeds here were impossible to kill and grew back every day, but everything had reasonable limits.

I couldn't get a daily today, but I could try my luck with Chief Councilman Whiteacre.

I walked into the building. In a small cozy wood-floored hall with a huge chandelier, Whiteacre met me personally. He was pacing the hall with his hands folded behind his back but, when he saw me, he stopped and melted into a joyful smile:

"Scyth! How glad I am to see you! Have you been enjoying your stay in Tristad?"

His kindliness, no matter how false it seemed, pleased me for some reason. I understood he was an NPC controlled by artificial intelligence but, after seeing those guardsmen behave a bit too realistically, even that warmed me. Just some amicability.

"It's a great city with welcoming locals, Councilman Whiteacre. I like everything here!"

"Wonderful!" he said, his joy still overflowing. "How can I help?"

"I'd like to be of use to the city. Think you might have some missions for me?"

"Of course, esteemed Scyth! We're always glad when our visitors want to help. So... Let me think..." he raised a pointer finger. "I have an extremely important assignment for you!"

"I'll do everything I possibly can!" I stood at attention, because usually he didn't say the words "extremely important" and just got straight to business giving the quest. "What needs to be done, Councilman Whiteacre?"

He tossed a skeptical gaze over me.

"Hm... You see, this is a very delicate assignment. I don't even know if I can ask you..."

"Of course you can! I'll do it as fast as possible. And of course, this stays between us."

"Okay then..." he nodded, his mind made up. "Go to the pastry shop Piping Hot. You'll find it on Bakers' Street. Do you know where that is?"

"I do, councilman."

"Excellent!" he said, rubbing his hands together. "Go there and tell Mrs. Grossman that tonight is canceled due to... unforeseen complications on the right flank."

"And?" I didn't see a quest window, and I was surprised. Maybe this was the introductory part of some unique chain? "Will that be all?"

"Yes, esteemed Scyth. That is all. Will you do it? Do you remember what to do?"

"Mrs. Grossman, Piping Hot. Tonight is cancelled in view of unforeseen complications on the right flank. I'll run right there, Councilman Whiteacre!"

I flew like a bullet straight to Bakers Street. I knew exactly where the pastry shop was. I had taken a walk there with Eve a few times. I carefully doubled around passersby so I wouldn't land myself in more trouble, and I ran to the shop just as my energy bar hit zero. But my deadline was in five minutes.

The store was empty. The sweet-looking stately Mrs. Grossman heard me out with a stony expression on her face and nodded in silence. I shuffled my feet, expecting a response of some kind, but she just went back to placing today's unpurchased pastries into a large sack.

"I'm sorry... Mrs. Grossman?"

"Yes? Is that all?"

"Yes, I told you everything word for word."

"Then what do you need? Wanna buy some fresh pastries?"

"Uh... No, I just wanted to ask if maybe you have some requests for me? Maybe you'd like me to send a message back to the Chief Councilman?"

"No, nothing. Although..." a shadow ran over her forehead. "Tell him something must be done about the right flank. It can't go on like this. Alright, go. You're getting in the way."

There it was! I'd see how Whiteacre reacted! My energy was back, so I ran all the way back as well.

"Something must be done?" he clarified when I brought Mrs. Grossman's answer. "Alright. Thanks, Scyth!"

The councilman smiled coyly and, whistling, headed into his office. What? No experience? To the nether with this quest chain, it didn't even give

---

me one meagre copper. And that was fine, but not even one experience point?

"Councilman Whiteacre! Wait!"

"Yes?" he turned around, his feet tapping in impatience. "What do you want, Scyth?"

I took in some air and exhaled slowly. Okay, sure. Business as usual in an online game. I wasted ten minutes, no big deal. Now I needed a quest I could complete with this character.

"Maybe you have some more missions for me?"

"Oh, Scyth, what a pity!" he threw up his arms. "All missions for today have already been given out, come back tomorrow and I'll think up something for you."

"I'll definitely be back tomorrow, Councilman Whiteacre, thank you. But still... maybe you've got something more interesting than street sweeping or delivering mail?"

It was as if the smile was glued to his face, but his eyes had stopped smiling. He studied me with his gaze. An indistinct thought flickered in his eyes.

"Something more interesting?"

"Yes. Less boring."

"Less boring? I see. I'm afraid I have to explain that cleaning communal areas and timely postal delivery are very important to our city. There are many things in this life that are vital to society, but could never be called interesting. You see, work is not supposed to be fun. Fun, generally, is not something people get paid for. Visitors do a service to our city by taking on these, as you put it, boring tasks. And the city repays them with respect and welcoming. But if newcomers turn up their noses at fundamental tasks, the very things which make Tristad an attractive city with a comfortable lifestyle, that means... That means those visitors have no place in Tristad. The city cannot entrust important functions to visitors such as you, Scyth."

"Excuse me?"

"I'm afraid I have to turn you away. The city will no longer hire you for daily social tasks. No matter what. At least as long as I have any say here."

Your reputation with the city of Tristad has been lowered by 5.
Current reputation: mistrust.

He turned away, letting me know that I could go. My reputation took another step closer to hostile. But even worse, this was the only place in my whole sandbox where a player of my level could get a quest. I needed to turn this around!

"Councilman Whiteacre!"

"We're done here," he answered, not turning

around.

"Sorry, my bad! I misspoke! It's just that... I couldn't wait to start doing good for the city, and all the public works have been finished for today..."

"What?" seemingly I had piqued his interest, and although he wasn't smiling, he had stopped walking and turned toward me.

"Maybe I could still be of use to the city? I'd really like that!"

"Alright then..." he bared his teeth again, but the smile was much sincerer than before. "Alright! I understand that for a young person such as yourself, it can be hard sometimes to formulate your thoughts properly..." seemingly he was mocking me and had just called me an idiot.

"Sorry, you're right. I really do have a hard time with that," I played up to him. "Making the words out of letters, and the words into sentences..."

"Enough clowning around," the councilman cut me off midsentence. "The Temple of Nergal the Radiant. The crypt. Something is happening down there. Something bad. See what it is and take care of it!"

And with his last words, a mission window popped open.

Chief Councilman of Tristad Peter

Whiteacre would like you to figure out what is stirring up trouble in the crypt of the Temple of Nergal the Radiant and take care of it.

Reward: 1 silver coin, 100 experience points.

Recommended minimum level: 5.

Penalty for refusing mission: reputation with the city of Tristad lowered to hostile.

Now he really was having fun with me. I turned from the mission to the councilman, trying to gauge if the expression of confusion on my face looked authentic enough.

"You're still here? Go and prove your worth to the city, Scyth!"

Oh nether, he wasn't joking! I accepted the quest, and Whiteacre nodded.

"How much time do I have?" I asked, fitfully thinking the only option was to level up on mobs using the club I thankfully just got then go into the crypt, even if it was in a month or two.

"You've got plenty of time," he answered favorably. "More than enough! I expect results by tomorrow, end of the work day. Off you go!"

Off I go? I had been given the send-off so many times today that I didn't know how I would go on.

Chapter Six

A Curse and a Blessing

ON THE WAY from the city council to the temple, I ran into Eve. She had left the tavern in a new novice's dress and was looking around. As soon as I saw her, I noticed a flickering chat notification: "I'm on. Where are you?" And I remembered I'd left her a message.

"Hi, Alex! My mom wanted help picking out new furniture, we just left the VR store. I came straight here when I saw your message. What happened? Why are you back on Dis?"

I briefly told her about my parents and their upcoming divorce, but she couldn't comprehend the gravity of the situation. Not to waste time, I kept walking to the temple as we spoke.

"And you're just giving up on your dream so easily? After all, this isn't that bad. Their status will be lower after divorce, but that's all temporary.

They'll have it all back by their next attestation, then they can pay for your studies!"

"It isn't that easy, Eve…"

"And why not?"

"Well, they work best together. Their weak sides are covered by the other one's strong suit. Dad has awesome ideas, but he can't get them off the ground without mom's love of minutiae. And it's that way with a lot of things, which means they'll never get their status back on their own."

"So why don't they just keep working together?"

"Their work would be evaluated independently because they have stopped being a family. Those are corporate categories…"

"Then why are they getting a divorce?" Eve exclaimed.

"Who can say?" I swallowed a lump in my throat, feeling tears start to well up. "I guess they just reached a point where it was harder to live together than work apart."

"And now you think there's no way out except this stupid game?" she exclaimed. "God, tell me you're joking! This is a joke, right?"

"I don't have any other ideas. I don't know how else to pay for my studies. To be honest, I still have no idea how I'm gonna live without my parents' support… That is, I understand that when I get my citizenship, I'll have to make it on my own anyway because of the law... But I've got a long time before I'm twenty-one!"

"That law about mandatory independence for adult citizens? Greg just told us about that yesterday..."

"I beg sincerest apologies!" came a ringing voice, interrupting Eve.

Our path was blocked by the city beggar Patrick. The NPC or bot as nonplayer characters were called, was controlled by artificial intelligence. His age was hard to tell, but his level was relatively high at twenty-five. That was higher than the city guards, for example.

"I wish you the greatest of evenings, young man and woman!" he said, removing his tattered and holy hat.

"Good evening to you too, Patrick," we answered.

"Allow me to make an inquiry, if I may. You wouldn't happen to have an extra copper to lend some color to a drab evening, eh?"

We shook our heads, and Eve answered:

"Sorry Patrick, we don't have any money."

"Are you sure? What about you?" he asked his bulging eyes staring at me morosely. "Dig deep, little one! I know you can find a little copper for old uncle Patrick!"

While his eyes bored inhospitably into me, I remembered how hard Snowstorm had fought to keep physical cash in their world. Players demanded they simplify game currency, but the corporation balked and now we were forced to haul coins around everywhere. Good that they at least didn't limit the number of coins you could have in your inventory.

"We have no money, Patrick! All the best!" I bid him adieu fairly sharply, because he was a bothersome character and if he sensed a lack of confidence, he'd just keep pushing.

"Alright then, it's deplorable to know that visitors to this city couldn't even dig up one pitiful copper for an honorary citizen of Tristad!" He spat at our feet.

"More like honorary town drunk," tore itself out of me.

"What did you just say, fleabag?" he furrowed his brow and walked forward, looming over me. "Do you have any idea who you're talking to?"

"A pitiful boozer, a beggar?"

Patrick took in a full chest of air, pursed his lips to say something but then... just waved a hand. And only when Eve and I exchanged glances, surprised at his behavior, did I realize:

"Curse you, you wee bastard! May your soul never know peace, just like my poor dry throat!"

After his farewell, Patrick spat out a few curse words with some spittle and walked away.

Class-A Threat

What an unpleasant mob! I was just trying to have a chat, but Patrick was only polite and affable to those willing to part with a coin. And idiot that I am, I gave him my last one ages ago. My reputation didn't change, I didn't get a quest. Ten minutes later I met him again and he trotted out the same old "spare a copper" song and dance as if I hadn't just helped him out.

"Where are going?" Eve asked, leading a gaze over Patrick.

"The Chief Councilman gave me a mission to inspect the temple crypt. I need to finish before tomorrow evening."

"Can I come?"

"Of course, but it's dangerous. It's a quest for level-five and up, which means it's not exactly going to be a walk in the park. It might hurt!"

"Bad?" Eve winced.

"If we don't try, we'll never know."

Shortly after that, we were there. There were always many people at the temple. The Radiant God gave generous bonuses to his adepts, but he did require strict observance of the main principles of the faith. One of them was that his followers must visit the temple and pray to him each and every day. And by doing so the players increased their reputation with Nergal and got buffs to their attributes.

Getting through the crowd, I considered how

to approach the mission. Walk a circle around the temple to find a separate entrance to the crypt, or go straight to the high priest and say I was here on a mission from the Chief Councilman? Eve kept back. With her build, it was even harder to get through a big crowd.

"Scyth?" Tissa's voice rang out next to me. Now there's a surprise!

"Hey, Melissa!"

"Look at you in your torn-up rags. How'd that happen?" she asked.

I looked at myself and grew embarrassed. My ripped shirt revealed a heaving chest and protruding ribs. It was hard, but I got myself together: it was just a game.

"Torn-up? Ah, I happened across some 'defender of the meek and powerless.' He ripped my shirt. Some guy named Crag..."

"Crag? Ha-ha-ha!" Tissa laughed. "Did that loser raise a stink over some girl's skirt again?"

"Exactly."

"Don't pay it any mind. He's an asshole. There aren't many of them. That's why he's not in a clan. He always gets thrown out. He's such a crap-head..."

"To the nether with him!" I interrupted her, then it hit me. "Hey, it's actually cool I saw you. Think you could help me out? I have a quest in the temple. There's something in..."

"You? A quest?" Her eyes went wide in astonishment, but Tissa was even more surprised when she saw Eve. "And what is fatty doing here?"

"Come on, don't call her that. Her name is Eve," I corrected her, hoping she was far enough away not to hear.

"Ah, screw it. What did you want to ask?"

"Chief Councilman Whiteacre said something was going on in the temple crypt. I'm supposed to check it out."

"Pfft... I could have told you that. A pack of undead have taken root! Like, you know, skellies and zombos. The boss is a small but very mean lich. Me and my clan did that mission a long time ago. It isn't hard."

"How do you get in?"

"Go through the back door into the temple, you'll see a ladder going down. You go down it, through a short tunnel then you reach the entrance to the ins... And that's all! What made you wanna get quests all of a sudden? What about this whole 'I'm too cool to play childish games' act?"

"I got bored. There was nothing to do, I decided to check the game out a little more." I tried to keep on my mask of indifference, but I wasn't sure I succeeded.

"Hm... let's say I believe you. Did the cow take the quest too?"

"You're the..." Eve exploded, walking up, but realized she could never call Tissa a cow. "Beanpole!"

"Come on Eve, calm down. I'm not talking to you," Schafer answered. "Alright, I'm in a hurry. I've still got to bless some new adepts. You two, by the way, would you like to accept Nergal as your protector? It gives a bonus to dark magic resists, and damage against undead. Plus, the more faith points Nergal has, the higher your reputation. And that's just the beginning! Scyth, it will definitely help you in that ins, what do you say?"

"No thanks. I want to read up on all the gods before I make my choice..."

"You still haven't figured it out? Nether, guys, what have you been doing here all year? Polishing that bench?" she asked, rollicking with laughter.

"Very funny!" Eve snorted, but quietly so Tissa wouldn't hear and laugh even more.

"We've got to go," I said. "Thanks for the tip."

"Sure. Good luck with the ins! Actually, wait... Are you level one? How are you going to pass it?"

"I'm helping!" Eve threw out.

"Sure, just... Guys, you're funny! Do you even have a weapon? You'll be chopped into coleslaw before you even touch any mobs! They will do increased damage to you, and you will do the opposite! You won't even be able to hit them! You'd better get a group together, maybe you can find someone... Although it isn't likely. Loot will only drop for people who have the quest. And what kind of loot will it be? Scrap metal and bones? You'd be better off paying a power-leveler! For a few gold, you can find a high..."

"So you can't help?" I asked, finding some boldness, which I immediately regretted.

"Me? Definitely not. Sorry, Scyth. You're a nice guy..." Tissa drew out her last word, then interrupted herself: "... if a bit strange, but Crawler won't understand. Especially after everything you said today. See you in school!"

She left, heading to the main entrance but then turned around and winked. For a second, I was enshrouded in light. Tissa had cast a +5-strength buff on me. Unfortunately, me only.

I heard sniffling behind me. After enough time with Eve, I was used to that.

"A strange, but nice guy? What was that about?"

"I have no idea. Well, are you coming?" I turned and looked skeptically at my combat buddy. "Those aren't rabbits, it's gonna hurt!"

"I think I'll manage," she answered and looked away. "Too bad you can't just break a branch in this game and fight with that..."

Yes it was unrealistic, but if an item was not

classified by the game as a weapon, the damage it did was generally equal to zero. What a mechanic!

Chapter Seven

When You're not Prepared

WE PUSHED THROUGH a crowd of people listening to the senior priest giving one-day buffs along the way. Then we got out in the open and breathed more freely. The smell of one hundred and fifty unwashed bodies was faithfully recreated in the game.

We walked along the side of the temple down a cobblestone street. The building was in excellent condition: ideally clean, undamaged with no dirt or anything else a normal city building might have. Even the city council building was scratched up. It was as if the temple wasn't even made of stone but cast marble if such a thing were possible.

In the twilight it was especially easy to see the faint glow of the walls. And it was not an earthly light. When I raised a hand to it, my hand stayed dark. The divine glow gave no warmth, no illumination, it had just one function: to announce the presence of the god.

We finally found the back door near the far end of the temple wall. Following Tissa's instructions, we reached the entrance to the ins in just a few minutes. We would have made it faster, but Eve tripped on a big cobblestone and nearly died. What it was doing in this tunnel we had no idea. Then I turned to check a side passage, which led to a dead end, just wasting time. It was always that way in this game. Any hole, passage or abandoned cave, most likely was simply generated by a heartless artificial intelligence. There were usually no hidden objects or treasure chests, or even decaying bodies with intriguing notes to kick off a quest chain.

Back in the tunnel, we reached the flickering pall of the quest instance Crypt of the Temple of Nergal the Radiant, and tried to enter. Eve even went first.

"I can't!" she said. "It says: 'you have not been assigned a quest associated with this location, and are not in a group with someone who is.'"

I hurriedly added her to my group, took a deep breath and dove into the instance. I took a look at the first room. It was dimly lit by a couple smoldering torches on the walls. There were bits of a spiderweb in the corner, but I didn't see its eight-legged maker, nor any other aggressive creatures. Eve appeared at the entrance soon after.

"Don't be afraid, no one is going to attack now, it's empty," I said.

Eve squinted, looking deep into the crypt. I then took out my club and suggested a plan:

"Just wait here, I'll scope things out. If I die, you leave."

Eve nodded in agreement and stayed at the door. The first and most important rule of going through instances was not to die. If the whole group died, you had to do everything over from the beginning. But if Eve didn't die and left the crypt, I'd also have to start over again, I just... I just didn't want her to get hurt. What was more, she was wearing a light dress that didn't even reach her knee, and was totally unarmed.

I left her and looked into the corner. There was a narrow dark corridor, and I could see a vaguely moving silhouette at the other end. If I listened closely, I could hear a scraping sound. I stared a bit and saw what it was:

Raised skeleton warrior, level 5

The smell of rotting flesh struck my nostrils, and I could barely keep myself from vomiting. I held my breath, grabbed the club in both hands and spent a few seconds getting set up.

You can't postpone death with a deep breath – that old saying was extremely relevant now given the horrid smell of rot. I took a decisive step into the next room with my club at the ready and swung it, also moving towards it. The languor of the undead creature played into my hand. The skeleton didn't even have time to turn around and took a blow to the back of the head. The bear bone slammed into its human bone. I heard its skull crack. I saw some not-fully-decayed bits of flesh fly.

You have critically damaged Raised Skeleton Warrior: 4!
Health points: 35/39.

Even if he could wince, he wouldn't have. Turning unflappably, his short rusty sword shot up and landed a blow I just couldn't dodge. In the end, he wasn't as slow as he looked. This mob was an energetic runner.

Raised Skeleton Warrior has damaged you: 7.
Health points: 16/23.

The flash of sharp pain in my chest quickly

---

passed, but I was not exactly burning with desire to experience it again. The exchange of blows after that was clearly not going to end in my favor, and I instinctively took a step back. But when the skeleton took a step toward me, I caught him moving the opposite way and swung.

Miss!

And so, trading blanks, we walked all the way to the beginning of the ins. The battle was silent. My enemy didn't make any sounds, except the cracking of its bones. In silence and with the perseverance and unflappability of a robot vacuum cleaner, it landed a scripted chain of blows: straight at my chest, from left to right, from right to left, straight on...

I started to get scared. It was depressing to see it instantly change tactics to suit me and my attempts to dodge.

Raised Skeleton Warrior has damaged you: 8.
Health points: 8/23.

I had enough health left for one more hit. And if I landed it, this undead creature's life would go down by just three health points.

The skeleton thrust forward, Eve squealed

behind me and I got distracted, taking a fatal blow. The skeleton's sword cut through my neck, and this time a dull wave of icy cold burned through my whole body.

After dying, I didn't head straight for respawn at the graveyard, using the allowed ten seconds to sit in my dead body and see whether Eve pulled it off. At least I had some luck. My body was facing her.

"Just run!" I thought, but I couldn't even write her in the group chat. Dead people can't talk, and I was dead.

But she didn't run! Squeezing out a cry of rage, Eve closed her eyes and flew at the mob like a predatory chicken. Her little fists thrashed the evil skeleton, but even without logs it was obvious she wasn't hitting.

And the skeleton didn't miss once. He was so much higher level that every blow landed, and the damage was increased. Eve gave one last shout of terror and fell dead.

Just then, my respawn timer counted down its final second and the dialogue window disappeared. I was back to life. What the heck?! I didn't come back in the graveyard! I was right back in the instance!

The undead fighter, already on its way back to the patrol zone, sensed a new enemy and immediately turned around. What was happening?

Raised Skeleton Warrior has damaged you: 6.
Health points: 0/23.
You are dead.

Back in a corpse. The respawn timer started counting down again. I pressed the respawn button.

And again found myself in the same room. The skeleton had walked away again, and looked back at me a bit puzzled and didn't attack right away, just took an unconfident step.

I looked at my life bar: 1/23. Come on, what the crap?

"Where are you?" Eve wrote in the group chat. Hmm, where was I...? I had a fleeting thought of Shakespeare. "Wherefore art thou Scyth?" But I was never strong in poetry, especially with a living corpse coming after me.

The skeleton was already next to me, and I was infuriated. I took a step to the right, but then immediately shifted my weight left and jumped past so I could grab the club I dropped after my first death. The system did not agree with my estimate of my own agility, so I was only half able to execute my plan.

A short jab of the skeleton's sword caught

me midjump. Too slow!

Raised Skeleton Warrior has critically damaged you: 9!
Health points: 0/23.
You are dead.

This time I was in no rush to resurrect. I figured let the bastard get some distance, then I'd just grab my club and ditch this stupid ins. Eve was still bombarding the chat, and one of her messages drew my attention: "I can't enter the ins! It says you're in battle!" Well, that made sense. As long as at least one group member was in the instance, the others couldn't get out after respawn. Otherwise any boss could go down in flames by a group coming back to fight multiple times after dying.

The skeleton was in no rush to leave. It was standing next to my body and slowly turning its skull like a tank tower, looking suspiciously all around. And all that in dead silence.

The timer ran out and the show "One on One with a Stinking Corpse" picked back up with its guest Alex aka Scyth aka the most pathetic loser... Nether it hurt! The rusty sword with a chipped blade – I got a very good look! – went right between my eyes as I tried to get my club up off the floor.

Class-A Threat

Raised Skeleton Warrior has damaged you: 7.
Health points: 0/23.
You are dead.

Freaking a! Why had I reached for my weapon when I was planning to get out of there. Hell knows, but then why had my desire to leave been replaced with white hot rage? Something in me was stubbornly saying: that thing hurt me too many times. It must be punished!

Only then did I notice that the mob's health was stuck at 32/39. I guess this little skeleton couldn't last forever! I guess if I had respawned at the cemetery, the instance would have rolled back, but I was still here, though I was a ghost most of the time.

I respawned again and mentally I was swinging. As soon as I was in my body again standing next to the mob, I punched the bony bastard in the forehead.

Miss!

I managed to get in two more swings before dying again. And the last time I hits!

You have damaged Raised Skeleton Warrior: 1.

85

Health points: 31/39.

**Raised Skeleton Warrior has damaged
you: 8.**
Health points: 0/23.
You are dead.

And although I was lying on the ground, just
a corpse, and my enemy was grinning in self-
satisfaction and pulling the rusty sword from my
chest, inside I was smiling. Until level ten, dying
didn't take any experience. And I just had to land
thirty-one more accurate blows to crush this bony
shitheap into dust! Then I could get to the bottom
of whatever bug was making this happen to me...

After thirty deaths I finally lost count. By
then, I had the skeleton's life down to 19/39. After
one respawn I managed to grab the club. It
happened when an especially forceful attack sent
me back and I died a few steps away. It allowed me
to land just one blow with the club, but what a
blow it was!

**You have critically damaged Raised
Skeleton Warrior: 5!**
Health points: 14/39.

Eve had been writing for a while already, but
I hadn't been able to answer: the dead can't talk,

and these brief seconds of life were not enough to type an answer. In that regard, the corporation was also conservative. If you wanted to use your voice long distance, you could buy a *signal amulet* or a *mirror of far sight*. Obviously, Eve and I had neither...

They say people can get used to anything, but I just couldn't get used to being stuck through with a sword every ten to twelve seconds. I instinctively winced or covered my eyes with a hand every time I came back, hopped, crouched, and dodged. Basically I was doing everything in my power not to die right away and get off a hit.

And expecting a flare of pain every time, I could literally feel my heartbeat speeding up in my chest IRL. If you think pain reduced many times is bearable, try poking yourself with a needle. First in the eye, then the side, then the chest, try it on your stomach or neck, too. And keep doing it every ten seconds. How quickly would you give up? I was just about at my limit.

My occasional hits – approximately one per five or six deaths – were made with my bare hands, and they never did more than one point of damage. I hated this bony creature with every fiber of my being. It was seemingly scoffing at me as it killed me with a blow to the groin. My teeth just clenched!

At first my only consolation was the fact that

the skeleton's health was not infinite, but then I got a boost to my enthusiasm. After a successful attack, lying dead, I read the logs and felt a strange satisfaction.

I had discovered my first skill!

Unarmed Combat skill discovered!
Damage dealt without a weapon increased by 10%
Attack accuracy increased by 10%.
Current level: 1.
Improve this skill by fighting enemies of your level or higher for additional bonuses and new special attacks.

You have learned a new special attack: Hammerfist!
Cost to use: 2 mana points.
Deals 150% of normal damage.

You have received experience points for discovering a new skill: 10.
Experience points at present level (1): 36/400.

I got my first twenty-six experience points in my first weeks in the sandbox, before I finally lost all interest. And now, ten at once!

I could see a light at the end of the tunnel. I

hadn't looked further ahead or thought about what to do next yet. Leave the instance or try to go further down it the same way? That way, I might complete Whiteacre's quest at least. In the second option, I might simply go mad, but I decided to think it over later. But now... I activated *Hammerfist* and my hand turned blurry in the air. It felt like my hand was wrapped in a steel glove. That was about how loud the crack was when it went through the skeleton's ribcage! Fragments of bone flew around the room!

You have critically damaged Raised Skeleton Warrior: 5!
Raised Skeleton Warrior is dead.

Experience points received: 10.

By the end of my second hour in the crypt, the torment was over. The bone warrior fell to dust. With a vengeful kick at what remained of the skeleton, I could feel my anger gradually receding.

I was so tired I was in no rush to see the fallen loot, I just sat down next to it and took a ten-minute breather with my back up against the wall. Eve was no longer in Dis, but I still wrote in the group chat that I was stuck in the instance and couldn't get out.

While I caught my breath, my health went

back up to full. That made me even happier than the loot. And actually, it was worth checking what fell. I stood up, happy, and picked up the gear and one copper dropped by the skeleton.

> **Etched leather spaulders**
> *Common*
> *Leather armor.*
> *Armor: 5.*
> *Durability: 60/60.*
> *Requires level: 1.*
> *Sell price: 1 silver coin, 15 copper coins.*

Would you look at that! Earning that much money with low-level social quests like picking weeds would take a whole month! Now I see why the Dementors devote all their time to clearing ins's.

I thought for a minute about whether I should put on the spaulders, but decided "no." Enough fighting, dying and pain for today. Sure, maybe I'd fail the quest and be unable to clear the temple crypt after school, but the game wasn't going anywhere. If I failed tomorrow's modern history test in Greg's class, though, it would be a blow to my final grades. As my uncle Nick, my mom's brother, always said, "a fella needs to be able to keep his priorities straight."

I headed for the exit from the instance. But

a pall at the door gently pushed me back.

You cannot leave the Crypt of the Temple of Nergal the Radiant until you finish the quest or defeat the boss of the location.

Alright, makes sense. That was so a group wouldn't run outside to heal or stock up on food and gear. But I had no desire to keep dealing with this. I wanted to get back to my cozy room as quickly as possible, study for the test, then finally watch the materials on the Mars expedition...

I glanced at the word "Exit" in the game interface. A warning window jumped in:

All your progress will be lost!
Confirm?

And those sage words gave me pause.

So what, did I just spend two hours dying here for no reason? I closed the interface window and thought. I had gotten the Unarmed Combat skill and the *Hammerfist* attack, which gave me reason to hope it would get easier.

I opened my attributes window, reread the information about my new special and saw another line in my character's profile that wasn't there before: *Restless Soul.* I focused in on it and a very bad word burst out of me. So that was why I wasn't respawning at the cemetery!

Restless Soul

You have been cursed! You must have insulted someone or left them out in the cold when they needed you most. This curse was heard by the universe, acquired force and took form. From here on out, after dying, your restless soul and cursed body cannot enter a cemetery. You will always respawn in the same place you accepted death and with one health point.

"Damn that Patrick! May your throat always burn! May you drink and never get drunk! May ale and wine forever taste like piss to you!"

I kept shouting, hoping that my curses would also be heard, but I already knew this game was over for me. No matter how many levels I got after ten, a group of gankers would beat all the experience points money and gear out of me in no time.

"Patrick! You alcoholic bastard!" Tearing my throat and coughing, I kicked the wall, taking damage. And I could only hope that drunk was at least hiccupping.

Chapter Eight

Skeletons and Zombies

I T TOOK ME more than an hour to clear the wine cellar. In the corridor where I encountered the first skeleton, I discovered a door in the wall. It was locked, and no matter how I went at it, I just couldn't get it open. I started thinking it was simply a decoration like those smoking torches on the walls that couldn't be removed – just part of the way the world looked.

I was supposed to ignore it, but I was haunted by the idea that there might be something interesting behind it. Furthermore, I thought I could hear a rustling.

The next patrol down the corridor was not a warrior, but a Raised Skeleton Keymaster and killing him was much easier. It took just a quarter hour of respawning, and gave eleven experience and a keyring.

Locked door, dropped keys... You didn't have to be a genius to figure out what it wanted you to do.

I went back and started trying keys one by one until one of them worked. But as soon as I opened the door, I heard a high-pitched shriek that nearly burst my eardrums. First a few rats rushed at me, shedding bits of decaying flesh and shrieking the whole time. A bit later, waiting to respawn, I saw their exact number. There were five of them at various stages of decay. And that whole endless string of lives between deaths was accompanied by their constant squeal.

While their pack was full, it was hard to get even one hit in without dying. Plus I couldn't always hit the same zombie rat every time. I just wanted to damage at least one of them. Thankfully, using *Hammerfist,* I could take more than one sad point, giving two to four every time. They also had less health than the skeleton warrior. Still the battle was tough going.

The last remaining rat stopped attacking at ten percent life, trying to hide among the wine barrels. Then I had some time to restore my health, pick up the club and calmly land the final blow.

The wailing of the huge zombie rat came to an abrupt end when my club smashed its head into a wall. Silence descended. I could hear my heart beating, a vein pulsating in my temple, my breath wheezing. But other than that, total calm and grave-like silence reigned.

The time had come to pick up loot. I dug through their bodies in disgust but, other than *Zombie Rat Innards*, I didn't find a thing. No pelts which, to tell the truth, they never especially had, and no claws which they did have and just so happened to be frighteningly powerful. No coins or other items fell either.

The only uses for the innards were given in a few scant lines: "Alchemy ingredient. Cooking ingredient. Value: 2 copper coins." Cooking ingredient? I made a mental note to figure out which dishes contained this and never to try them. But as for the value... Well, fifty rats added up to one silver. That could be a pretty good business.

I finished that and looked at the time. It was getting near midnight, but I had already decided not to sleep tonight. My room was locked and my parents would think I was already asleep. Tomorrow morning I would take a shower, run through the materials for the test, get some breakfast and fly to school.

And for now, I would keep clearing this instance. At the back of my mind I knew that Patrick the drunkard's curse was the only way for me to finish the Chief Councilman's quest. I didn't know how long it would last, but the very ability to spend one night farming up a mountain of experience and money was worth something. And that was not considering that I was also leveling *Unarmed Combat*, which was growing much quicker because I was fighting enemies five times my level.

Right after I killed my fourth rat, the skill and special both levelled up. My damage and accuracy in *Unarmed Combat* were now increased by fifteen percent, while *Hammer* beefed up my normal damage another twenty percent. While fighting the rats, I got the hang of kicking when I realized I wasn't hitting with my fists, but I hadn't gotten an attack for that yet. Either I hadn't used my legs enough (kicking barefoot, you take more damage than the enemy) or new attacks were linked to skill progress.

Clearing the rats from that wine cellar gave me a strange satisfaction. A thought flickered by, seemingly from genetic memory, that I needed to make sure my rear was clear.

I did a bit more common-sense thought and even put on the leather spaulders to raise my defense before my first death in the next battle. And I had no doubt I would die a few times.

But suddenly, when I reached the end of the narrow corridor I heard a voice. "Boo-uh..." And a few seconds later: "Yghgh-uh..."

I heard some more rustling of feet on the

floor, accompanied by disconnected sounds as if someone was about to barf but couldn't. The next room was three times bigger than the last. The torches only provided good illumination in a small radius so, in order to see who was there, I had to come up as close as possible. And when I did, the name of the nearest mob flickered up.

Brainless zombie, level 6

The group of risen corpses was ambling in a circle in the middle of the room like convicts in a prison yard. They were bad at coordinating their movements unlike the skeletons I'd come across and constantly ran into one another, hobbled, wobbled and clearly because of that constantly bickered in zombie language. There was an arrow protruding from the head of one mob, and it was constantly catching on a rag hanging off the zombie in front of him.

I watched them, already thinking where best to die and whether I could retreat and kite them closer to the ins exit. I was nourishing a hope that, if I brought them out of this room, after I died they would leave and I could restore my health in peace. At the same time, the first flickers of a new plan were born. It was more cumbersome but, if it worked, I would die less.

Then I took a critical look at myself. I was

totally naked apart from the boxer shorts I couldn't remove. My first shirt had lost all durability points and was decaying into dust, then three to four deaths later my pants also met their end. It all happened back at the first skeleton, and that made the stretched-out spaulders look extremely funny on my body. To hell with it. It was better this way. Otherwise I might lose them too. I put them in my inventory and my gaze hit on the rat innards. What if...

I equipped one unit of zombie rat guts and, holding my breath so I wouldn't get nauseous, threw them into the crowd of walking dead. Sure zombies normally don't eat zombies, but what if?

The first zombo to be alerted was the one with the arrow in his head. Hearing the flesh slap onto the floor, he stopped, turned his head and his eyes latched onto the bait. The one behind him ran into his comrade, also stopped and asked:

"Oowuh-uh?"

"Hoo-wuh," the arrowhead replied and took a step toward the chitterlings.

His buddy hissed and kept walking, but arrowhead took a few cautious steps toward the guts. I took a step toward him and he saw me. Forgetting the guts, he gave an elated gasp and sped up! Sure he was still hobbling and wobbling, but his step had a lot more pep.

I started walking back into the hallway,

---

hoping I could kite him away from his compatriots, but it was all in vain. Arrowhead made a few especially loud exhalations of "Boo-wuh!" and a moment later all the corpses were walking in my direction.

"Fresh brains! Fresh meat!" I was sure that was exactly what these monsters had in mind.

The zombo with the arrow was out in front in this race but, no matter how he moved his decayed legs, I was faster.

I reached the wine cellar and slammed the not totally flimsy oak door and locked it tight.

"Eeugh-woo!" came a walking corpse from the other side, somehow particularly disappointed.

While they held a meeting, exchanging ideas for how to break the door down, I suddenly got the impression I could discern nearly intelligent speech. That is, without lips or a tongue, which had long since rotted away. Not many sounds could be produced, but I could make out a certain logic in their moaning.

Thinking that over, I rolled the wine-filled barrels along the ground one after the next and barricaded the door. I managed to brace it with a few rows of heavy barrels and I was greatly hoping that would be enough to pull off my plan.

"Boom! Boom! Hrrss!" the zombies were still knocking and scratching at the door.

I unlocked it with the key and took a step back. The narrow gap was immediately filled with several hands and feet. And we're off!

Full force I swung down along the gap and hit the hands of two of the living dead, taking two or three health points each. They were getting in one another's way, trying to climb inside. As for the one with the arrow in his skull, he was stuck, which blocked the way for everyone else once and for all.

I looked at the club and considered whether I should start hitting with my bare hands to level the skill, but common sense took the day. They could grab me and pull me toward them, and with my stats I would not be able to escape. No, I'd stick with the club.

You have critically damaged Brainless Zombie: 5!
Health points: 43/50.

The zombies lost it, and in the groans of headwound seemed to now contain notes of offense:

"Boo-wuh?"

"Hoo-wuh!" I squeezed out with my next blow.

The process was ongoing...

With its last health points, arrowhead tried

to get out of the gap, but his own comrades were blocking him.

> **You have damaged Brainless Zombie: 3.**
> *Brainless Zombie is dead.*

The body of the now doubly dead creature collapsed with a smashed skull. In his place another came to test out my club. He was already dented up – he got hurt when I was swinging at random. The zombie extended a hand and nearly got me with his petrified nails, which oozed with a thick black substance. I needed to be more careful. The last thing I needed was to take a debuff from some kind of corpse poison.

With that thought, I landed an especially good blow. A powerful smack to his nose pushed the flesh inside his skull.

> **Bashing Weapon skill discovered!**
> *Damage dealt with a bashing weapon increased by 10%*
> *Attack accuracy increased by 10%.*
> *Current level: 1.*
> *Improve this skill by fighting enemies of your level or higher for additional bonuses and new special attacks.*

> **You have learned a new special attack:**

Battering Ram!
Cost to use: 2 mana points.
Deals 150% of normal damage.

You have received experience points for discovering a new skill: 10.
Experience points at present level (1): 126/400.

I grinned, got a better hold on the club then activated *Battering Ram*. That made things a bit less bleak. I was still missing frequently and doing little damage, but it *was* better. Mana practically didn't regenerate in battle, and I had to intermix my attack with normal blows. But knowing that every successful attack gave a couple points to skill progress put me on a real hot streak...

The whole pack of six zombies took me no more than half an hour. Feeling safe once they were gone, I leaned over to pick up the loot. Just then something grabbed me by the hair and tenderly said:

"Oh-wah-ya? Ah-ah-ah!"

I tried to escape, but it was holding me tight. I turned my eyes and saw a zombo I'd missed before. He bared his teeth in glee and repeated:

"Oh-wah-ya! Oh-wah-ya!"

Why did I seem to hear the word "gotcha?"

"Gotcha?"

The zombie nodded with enthusiasm: "Oh-wah-ya!"

It was almost friendly, if he hadn't bit into my shoulder at the same time.

Brainless Zombie has damaged you: 8.
Health points: 15/23.

The pain drove me on. I braced my legs on the wall and gave a sharp push, yelping in pain. This zombie was stuck in the passage but had part of my hair and a piece of my flesh. I then rolled back into the middle of the wine cellar, dropping my weapon. The zombo, chewing what he'd bit off, looked after me disappointed, not trying to slip through the narrow gap. What a weird mob.

I picked up the club and cautiously came near. A miss... The zombie walked back, disappearing behind the door. Was he really brainless?

I changed the viewing angle and saw he was standing beyond where I could reach, looming in the hall. Seemingly, this one wouldn't be so easy to kill. Well, I guess I'd have to die.

Chapter Nine

Cursed Lich

THE "SMART" ZOMBIE sent me to respawn twenty times. After realizing that I respawned right where I died, he was always on guard, never going anywhere and waiting next to my body. In the space of a second, I wasn't always able to get off even one accurate blow, so I had to play on the element of surprise. Sometimes I went right to respawn, other times I waited the whole ten seconds.

He really had me whipped up, too. It was like he was mocking me, letting out belittling comments, laughing and even making indecent gestures. One time he didn't even kill me right away, walking a few yards back prudently. He made a whole speech, of which I didn't understand a thing except that it was a question.

"Ah-eegh uh-woh yeh-ah-yeh? Eegh oh

---

eegh-wuh? Oh-wah ooh-wuh!" After that he shrugged and attacked.

I did kill him in the end. It seemed like he was letting himself be killed, and was even relieved. He was just so sick of it. And that was finally enough experience to push me over the equator: 210/400. The thought that levelling up would give me five more attribute points gave me strength. The only thing that really upset me was a growing thirst. I wanted to drink so badly I had to fight the desire to do make an emergency exit, crawl out of my pod and drink to my heart's content.

The loot from the zombie pack was a final reason to keep bearing it. For someone like Tissa, it was like *gray* shoddy stuff, not worthy even of a place in her inventory. But for me anything was a big help: the cloth *Robber's Vest* (+2 to armor), *Worn-out Arm Braces* (+1 to armor) and, best of all, *Worn-out Shoes*! Sure they gave just one point of armor, but now I wouldn't be barefoot! All in all it was worth a bit more than two silver, but I was not going to sell it. As soon as I got out of this idiotic ins I would finally get some clothes on.

After the room of walking dead, I went down the next corridor which had a couple skeletons on patrol. I had to mess with them for a bit, because one was carrying a round wooden shield, which he used deftly to protect himself from my blows.

Those two took me a bit more than an hour, but in the end I got a rusty *Flimsy Sword* that did 3-4 damage, and immediately equipped it, putting the club in my inventory. The shield unfortunately did not drop. A few extra copper did though.

And I also got my first achievement. My body lit up for a second, illuminating the corridor. My mana and life were completely restored and, accompanied by a brief horn fanfare, in came a notification:

> **Achievement unlocked: I'm on Fire!**
> *Defeat 15 enemies who are more than five times higher level than you.*
> *Once is a coincidence. Ten times can happen. But fifteen? That's an achievement!*
> *Reward: +10 health points.*

Of course, I immediately forgot about my desperate thirst. This was starting to be fun.

In the hallway, I discovered another locked door but, after opening it, I found nothing but a room full of bones. I scratched it all up with my hands and feet, but there was nothing of value. Just trash – bones and chips of bone.

And then, the serious problems started. The next room had a platoon of skeleton archers. Sure, there weren't twenty or thirty, just four, but that was plenty for me. As soon as they saw me, they ran away a certain distance, shooting from afar.

Luckily, they didn't just stay in one place and kept wandering aimlessly, sometimes ending up right where my harried corpse fell. When that happened, I respawned and managed to land one or two *Hammer* blows. They had less health than the skeleton warriors so, as a rock can be sharpened by droplets, I eventually did the pack in. As a reward for my torments, I got *Torn Leather Gloves* giving +4 armor and worth twenty-six copper and four silver.

The next door was to the left and led to a room full of zombies. They were all of the brainless variety, and both packs of six I lured by throwing rat guts. They ran at me, and from there it went the same as the first pack of zombies, even though they didn't have a smart and talkative one. That just made it take less time. What was more, I started using the sword! Sure it only did two or three damage more than my club, but it was also just easier to use.

Achievement unlocked: I'm on Fire – 2!
Defeat 30 enemies who are more than five times higher level than you.
We are starting to suspect you're a cheater! Haha! Relax, it was a joke. But still... Thirty? Something just ain't right!
Reward: *+20 health points.*

After that, I started to understand achievement chasers. No, seriously. They were nice enough all on their own, but also gave significant bonuses! My health points were already two and a half times higher than before, and that was all down to the achievements.

As for the loot, unfortunately just one thing fell, a low-quality *Decayed Leather Helm* (+3 to armor) and around fifteen copper. But now I was just about up to level two: 358/400. I also discovered a new skill:

One-Handed Swords skill discovered!
Damage dealt with a sword increased by 10%
Attack accuracy increased by 10%.
Current level: 1.
Improve this skill by fighting enemies of your level or higher for additional bonuses and new special attacks.

You have learned a new special attack: Sneak Attack!
Cost to use: 2 mana points.
Deals 150% of normal damage.

You have received experience points for discovering a new skill: 10.
Experience points at present level (1):

Class-A Threat

It was just about four o'clock in the morning. Now I was so thirsty not only was my throat parched, my eyes were starting to stick together. And in the game I experienced the same thing as my real body. But I wasn't going to abandon all my progress when I was half way home. Thinking it over, I had completed more than half the crypt. There was actually not much left.

After clearing the room, I started a new corridor, also on the left-hand side. There was a mixed patrol: a skeleton warrior, a skeleton archer and two brainless zombies. All four I kited back to the wine cellar, where I handled them the same way, except for the archer. He was being tricky and not coming close to the gap, just looking at me and shooting from the corridor. I had to take a risk: I put on my new gear and started to fight.

To my delight, he couldn't shoot as fast as I could hit. I didn't even die. The archer collapsed into a pile of bones.

You are now level 2!
5 free attribute points available!

I no longer even had the emotional capacity for a torrent of joy. Instead I just sat there frozen for a while, studying the attributes list. Given my current reality, I figured the best possible strategy was increasing perception. I weighed it all again and put all five points there, raising my accuracy to forty-five percent.

Then I went back into the corridor I lured the last patrol from. There were two locked doors. And I shouldn't have opened the first...

Foul Quease, level 7

The mob's bulbous ten-foot-high body was seemingly sewn together from the corpses of several people: three legs, one sticking out of the stomach, four arms, eyes on shoulders and a huge lipless mouth packed with teeth. When the monster saw me it just ran, extending all its arms and the one leg out to greet me. And it charged with unexpected verve. I turned tail, hoping the monster would get stuck in the doorway but it must have ducked or something, because it got out.

I had to run with all my might, hearing it's disgusting breathing and sniffling behind me. I soon realized these sounds were actually coming from the oozing wounds on its body. I reached the trusty old wine cellar, closed the door and barely managed to lock it shut. The quease started slamming the door and nearly broke it down while I, slightly panicking, put the barrels that got moved back in place.

Then, following the repeatedly proven plan, I unlocked the door and immediately took a flat blow to the forehead, losing a quarter of my life. That was thanks to the helm (and I hadn't yet figured out if all my armor was cumulative), otherwise the damage might have been fatal.

But at that point the quease's health bar fell below white and, a few minutes later, its joyless life was also at an end. My sword stuck into its rotting body like a knife through butter, not only knocking out health points, but bits of flesh as well. I got coated head to toe in viscera, and the nauseating smell of rot was just stuck dead on me.

It dropped no loot, and the just twenty experience points hardly compensated my horror and disgust.

I went back to the room it came from and, behind the second locked door, which I opened cautiously, ready for anything, I found an empty room with a small chest. It was not locked, and inside I found a few small vials of healing and mana potion. I put that all in my inventory along with two silver coins. In comparison with the old poor Scyth, I was a rich man now! I could finally afford to drink cream beer in the tavern! And of course I'd treat Eve, too...

"Just what you like to see," as my uncle Nick said. It was already almost six AM. In an hour my parents would be up and calling me to eat breakfast. But I was still in the game. My stomach had gone on strike, demanding food. My guts were churning, my throat was like an emery board, and I still had the final boss ahead of me.

I could now see him at the far end of a huge room lined with some kind of temple vessels. The boss cut a fairly undaunting figure. He was short, plump and didn't look like much of a problem. Especially with my curse from Patrick the drunkard. I imagined it would be quite easy: land a blow or two, die, respawn and keep going until the boss was dead. Sure he was a custom creature, but what difference did that make.

Dargo the Cursed Lich, level 10
Crypt Boss

My gaze slipped over him. I was totally equipped. Ready. I gathered my courage and took a step out to meet him.

"Who dares disturb my slumber?" his hissing whisper filled the whole crypt.

What a tired phrase. But not counting that clever zombie, I hadn't spoken with anyone in so long that the answer burst out of me as I held my sword horizontal and walked toward the boss.

"My name is Alex Sheppard, aka Scyth, and I am here to kill you."

"You are a mere weak mortal," the lich's said, emotionless. "I have been summoned by the Destroying Plague. It is not for you to tussle with me..."

I made a blow, trying to hit his unprotected neck, but Dargo easily dodged and threw a magical pinkish black ball, which looked like a clump of dirt and worms. The ball slammed into my stomach with a swish and went inside. The cold of eternal rest entered my blood and ran over my whole body.

Dargo the Cursed Lich has damaged you: 49.
Health points: 4/53.

With a wail of pain while falling, I made a *Sneak Attack* with my blade into the lich's thigh and died after a tick of DoT.

You have critically damaged Dargo the Cursed Lich: 8!
Health points: 272/280.

Not wanting to waste more than an hour on this bastard and be late to school, I didn't wait and immediately respawned in the same place, naked and unarmed. My gear was just lying on the floor and I didn't have time to put it back on. I ran at the lich as he walked away to hit, but I didn't get a hit off.

I got back up, ran... Died. Got back up...

On my eighth respawn I immediately drank a health potion, and I was able to cut Dargo the lich in his noseless face.

You have damaged Dargo the Cursed Lich: 2.
Health points: 278/280.

Lying dead at his feet, I looked at the battle logs in disbelief, then over to the boss's health bar. This bastard was regenerating much faster than I was doing damage!

This had to be the end.

Remaining time to respawn 9... 8... 7...

Chapter Ten

You Scratch my Back and I Scratch Yours

A FEW SECONDS to die, another few to respawn. No less than four deaths per minute. More than one hundred in the first half hour of battle with the Cursed Lich.

I had only seen grit like this in the movies. Our intrepid hero was defeated, his efforts fruitless, yet he continued stubbornly. Not did it look pointless, it looked stupid. But he just kept going, "making moves" as my Uncle Nick liked to say. Apathetic and totally drained of confidence, faith, spirit and energy, he pressed ever onward.

That was about what I felt like. Like a rat with an electrode in the pleasure center of his brain, I pressed the respawn button time and again and went balls to the wall hoping for a miracle. Sometimes I managed to hit him, but usually not.

He was also starting to get burned out, but probably more mentally. Seriously, he even stopped ominously whispering: "You pitiful weak mortal!" every time I came back.

After killing me fifty times, he changed tactics and started alternating between deadly balls of grave worms, covering half the room in bubbling smoking slime, and just resorting to physical damage by knocking me on the head with his staff, which was crowned with a heavy black stone. The logs told me the names of his spells, one more foreboding than the next: *Scourge, Plague, Blight...*

I managed to think that all over during my next few attempts, having made peace with failing the quest and being expelled from Tristad. I just... decided to try one more time. I had half an hour left.

Dargo the Cursed Lich has damaged you: 37.
Health points: 0/53.
You are dead.

Oh, Patrick, Patrick, you old boozehound! Couldn't you have given me a curse that would make me respawn with full health? That way I'd have a chance, but now... Wait!

After respawning, I mentally tensed up expecting a flicker of pain, but still I ran at the lich. A blow! *Hammer!* Another blow! None of them landed, the boss easily dodged, laughing. Not understanding what was happening, I stopped, breathing heavily. Dargo was looking at me with... pity?

"You pitiful weak mortal! I have been summoned by the indomitable, merciless Destroying Plague. And together we shall conquer all *Disgardium*. It is not for you to tussle with me..."

As he said these words, the lich beckoned me with a finger, then pointed at the earthen floor. After making sure I saw him, he wrote with the handle of his staff: "You don't give up, do you?"

In amazement, I couldn't squeeze out a single word. I just nodded. He erased that and wrote more: "I see. Well, I'm sick of this." He was writing one thing, but saying another:

"You worm! Do you really not understand how pointless this is?"

"But I have no other way out, Dargo," I explained. "Failing the mission will destroy my reputation with the city, and *Disgardium* is my only chance to earn money for school."

"School?" the lich wrote and said bombastically:

"Feeble human, your self-assurance will be your ruin!"

"Yes. I want to go to university to be a space guide," I of course was confused but was now sure the boss was being controlled by a real person. "As long as I can remember, I've always dreamed of working in space."

"You'll be devoured from the inside!" he started conjuring a ball of grave worms, but threw the curse away from me.

"Cali Bottom, 270-36. Ask for Clayton. Bring donuts. UNB just makes me sick anymore!" the lich wrote with his staff, then looked closely and attentively at me.

UNB, by the way, is universal nutrient blend. It contains everything a human needs, and is cheaper than drinking water. A synthetic cocktail, it comes artificially flavored with hundreds of variations but they all taste like paper.

"Cali Bottom, 270-36. Got it. That's a two-hour flight from me..." I said, already thinking what I'd tell my parents. "I'll come right after school. I'll be there near evening."

Dargo nodded. Then he stashed his staff, spread his arms and looked up at the ceiling.

I looked under his legs and saw only two words: "Hit me."

Not looking away from the bizarre lich, I

---

walked over to where my stuff was piled in a heap that fell after my first death, got dressed and picked up my sword.

"It'll be faster this way," I explained to the boss, raising the sword.

He blinked. He understood but kept showering me with stuffy phrases:

"Shut your mouth, worm! It is not for you to tussle..."

A *Sneak Attack* cut him off midsentence.

You have critically damaged Dargo the Cursed Lich: 9!
Health points: 271/280.

Missing every other time, I mixed my only special with normal blows, squeezing my two strength points for all they were worth. I tried not to raise the sword so I wouldn't hit him in the head because it seemed wrong, although maybe I was just making it harder on myself. To the nether with all this.

Yet another *Sneak Attack* landed a crit for twelve damage. Dargo didn't even wince, maybe because he didn't feel pain.

By the end of the second minute, I was done with the crypt boss. A moment before the last blow, he threw up his hands and, his thumb and pointer finger touching, formed a ring.

"Donuts?" I asked with an exhale.

He didn't have time to answer.

You have critically damaged Dargo the Cursed Lich: 5!
Dargo the Cursed Lich is dead.

Experience points received: 90.
Experience points at present level (2): 117/900.

You have completed the Crypt of the Temple of Nergal the Radiant!

The damp and crumbly soil floor, which smelled of rot and decay started changing from the place the boss died. Murky and barely lit by the smoldering torches, the room lit up with faces of the Radiant God on the wall. The damp went away, the earth instantly went dry, then just disappeared, leaving a fine wooden floor.

A series of flashes followed, then a victorious fanfare, and my vision was obstructed by interface messages. I gathered my things, then returned to the lich's body and sat next to it, my hands crossed on my knees to catch my breath. I looked over my rewards.

Tristad   Chief   Councilman   Peter

Whiteacre's mission completed.

You discovered that an unknown evil stole into the crypt of the Temple of Nergal the Radiant – an emissary of the Destroying Plague, Dargo the Lich. The lich managed to raise quite an army of the undead, defiling the very foundations of the Temple, feeding off emanations of faith from adepts of the Radiant God like a parasite and threatening the blessings of all city dwellers.

By your efforts, the Temple has been cleansed of profanation!

Tell Tristad Chief Councilman Peter Whiteacre to receive your reward.

Experience points received for completing the Crypt of the Temple of Nergal Radiant: 100.

Experience points at present level (2): 217/900.

So there were plusses to soloing through instances. All that experience would mean precious little if I had to share it with a whole party. Eve was still in my group, but she probably wouldn't get experience because she was outside the crypt. Although maybe it would count as her passing it?

Somewhere behind me, a door screeched

open. I turned around and saw a flickering pall in the doorway. The exhaustion and ambivalence that had overtaken me a half hour earlier were swept away by glee. Smiling like an idiot, I swallowed trying to somehow wet my throat. I raised my cottony arms in a sign of victory.

There was just one message left unread. I purposely left it for last, already knowing what came next, and wanting to savor it.

> **Unique achievement unlocked: The Lich is Dead! Long Live the New Lich...**
> *You defeated the main crypt boss all on your own (!), and it was five times (!) higher level than you. Better yet, you didn't even take any damage!*
> *Dargo the Cursed Lich is dead, never to return. But before he shuffled off this mortal coil, he inadvertently transferred you a modicum of his power.*
> **Reward:** *Mark of the Destroying Plague.*

I opened my profile and read the description of the ability, trying to hack through but my brain was categorically opposed to working at full steam.

At first glance, the ability seemed to be of dubious utility. It came with bone-chilling side effects, and the name didn't seem to promise anything good.

Mark of the Destroying Plague.
Passive skill.
Current level: 1.
When taking a killing blow, you have a 1% chance to receive Curse of the Undead. If it triggers you will not die, and all damage you take will be reduced by 100%. However, your living body will begin to visibly decay!
This curse will remain active until you completely restore your health.

Another curse? Was the one from Patrick not enough? I thought about it and decided to figure out how to live with this later. I grabbed the loot off the floor. It was illuminated by the interface. It contained some strange and unpleasant feeling scaled belt. I threw it in my inventory and ran to the exit.

The workday in Tristad hadn't begun yet, and that meant I would have to first fly home after school to pass the quest, then go see Dargo/Clayton after that.

The sun was already peeking up over the horizon, coloring the roofs and temple spire a beautiful shade of gold. After the murky and musty crypt, Tristad shone with new colors. The air was transparent, and the smells of fresh morning inspired joy. And I was happy, in no rush to leave this world.

Somewhere in the city, a bell rang three times, making my temples shoot with pain. I slipped my gaze over a global notification about a new threat. I had seen plenty of them when I first started, but I thought I turned off threat notifications. Strange that this one it through the filter... Ah, there was the issue – the potential threat level was higher than normal:

> **We have detected a disturbance in the strings of creation! A new evil has awoken in Disgardium!**
> *Estimated potential threat class: L.*
> *Current threat class: Z.*
> *Most likely location: foothills of the Nameless Mountains.*
> *Now that this evil has awoken, we mustn't let it grow more powerful. Be the first to find and eliminate it, and the powers that be will reward you generously!*
> *And if you succeed, oh bravehearts and heroes, the gods will be favorable to you as well!*

Nameless mountains? That might be somewhere nearby, but it might also be on another side of the world. It was a mountain ridge that went on for three hundred miles. To the nether with that, I was late for school. And oh how I want

to drink...
    I focused on the "Exit" button.
    Oh nether, let me be free.

Chapter Eleven

Cali Bottom

I TOOK A SHOWER and got ready for school, then went to the dining table to have breakfast, followed by AT the catdog. Father sluggishly traded curses with mom, while AT laid next to them, occasionally wagging her tail. The robot cleaner hurriedly wiped a red spot on the couch. By the looks of things, mom was drinking wine last night.

This was not a usual morning. There was none of the usual animation, with father acting nasty toward mom and her quipping back. My parents, fully immersed in their own problems, didn't even notice that I hadn't slept. The cold and damp of our unheated apartment was making us all shiver.

I finished a bowl of wheat flake cereal, then hurriedly left. Eve O'Sullivan was waiting for me outside as usual. Like always she was wearing an ironed uniform, a crisp white shirt and a long gray dress. In her hand she held a compact airstream umbrella. I was in such a rush that I forgot mine at home, but she gladly let me stand next to her.

On the way to the parking lot, without getting into the details, I told her how I spent all night in the crypt. She didn't express particular interest, just surprise like "how could you voluntarily lose sleep over some stupid game?" The new Alex Sheppard didn't quite fit into her regular and easily understood world.

The school lot looked like a batted beehive. One after the next, glassy droplet-shaped vehicles silently whirred up, either following an automatically generated route or on manual control. Most people preferred not to bother with manual, entering their destination and dozing off for the whole flight. Still, no matter how badly I wanted to sleep, I opted to fly.

Not listening to Eve's chirping, I was mentally in the game. I had already begun to understand Ed and Tissa's behavior in school. Hours spent in the real world for them were the same thing as my required Dis time before. Everything there was brighter, more significant, more dynamic. In one night I had experienced most likely more emotions than in one month in our world. Take those balls of grave worms for example. I still shuddered just to think about them.

I wasn't the only one in class who hadn't slept. "Bomber" Hung was yawning so much his jaw almost came unhinged, and Malik "Infect" just laid his head on his folded arms. With makeup on, Tissa could hide most of the evidence of a sleepless night, but there was nothing to be done about the burst blood vessels in her reddened eyes. Ed wasn't even there for the whole first period. But eventually the chief Dementor did come to school. And he was in a good mood, which immediately spread to the rest of his clan.

I only understood why that was later when talk spread throughout the class that he had successfully prevented a Class-Z Threat with the potential to go Y. The clueless necromancer deemed a threat to the world was accidentally outed.

Realizing there was nowhere to hide in our sandbox, the kid decided to sell his identity. A deal was struck just hours before sunrise, when there were almost no players remaining in the region.

But Ed had stayed back to sell his loot, a couple high-level alchemy ingredients, through an illegal auction.

"Why doesn't everyone do it like that?" Tim, captain of our soccer team, asked during a break.

"Everyone who becomes a threat?" Ed

clarified.

"I mean, yeah. Like that guy. He made some money, got rid of the problem, and now he gets to re-spec with a new toon."

"Because the closer you get to meeting your potential, the higher the rewards from the corporation." Ed shrugged his shoulders as if he didn't understand how someone could not know such rudimentary things. "And they go up by orders of magnitude! He never made it past the minimum Z-Class, and all he'll get from the corporation now is a thousand gold or two."

Tim gave a whistle, then squinted skeptically:

"And how do you know what he got? No one talks, you know that. Don't you know what kind of problems that can cause?"

Ed turned away, hiding his smile, and Bomber answered for him, whispering forebodingly:

"Believe me, Cap. Ed knows."

"Oooh," Tim wailed, imitating a ghost. "Boys, that game is making you nuts! Why should you eliminate a threat when it's a little caterpillar if you can let it level up and destroy it as a butterfly?"

"Because, Tim," Tissa answered readily. "The preventer's reward, i.e. for the one who eliminated the threat, depends only on potential class, not present one."

"Ah, I see. Then better to suppress threats while they're weak," the captain nodded.

"And you don't want..." Tissa started, but the bell rang.

"Class, attention!" Mr. Kovacs announced. "Your first semester examination..."

The modern history exam consisted of two parts: a regular test and an essay question. I wasn't even remotely worried. I was first to turn it in and, with Greg's permission, I left school without waiting for Eve. I told her not to wait for me, then flew home to pass the chief councilman's quest.

The black clouds had dissipated, and it was much easier to drive the flying car than this cloudy morning.

It was completely quiet at home. My parents were working on a project, immersed in their joint virtual workspace.

AT was in energy-saving mode as a cat on the windowsill, lounging in the rays of sun and recharging her batteries while the robot cleaner did the same, nestled in a wall nook.

I hopped into my pod, taking my clothes off as I went, loaded up Dis and ran to the city council building. The game beeped out new messages and notifications, but I decided not to get distracted and look that over tonight. Cali Bottom was not the kind of neighborhood where a young person should be after dark and, in order to make it before nightfall, I'd have to hurry.

Chief Councilman Whiteacre looked at me ambivalently and listened to my report on the temple crypt.

"I've already been made aware of your success, Scyth. Here is your reward," he extended me a silver coin.

Some logs came up saying I finished the quest and received one hundred experience points. And another five points of reputation with the city brought me that much further from hostile.

"Thank you, Advisor! Is there any other way I could be of use to the magnificent city of Tristad and its residents?"

"Without a doubt, Scyth!" Whiteacre nodded eagerly. "You can familiarize yourself with the whole list of available city council missions on the bulletin board. It is to the right of the exit, which is right behind you. Have a nice day, Scyth!"

My hopes of receiving another unusual quest were dashed. I was not going to weed gardens or sweep streets most of all because the rewards for that weren't even close to worth the time they took.

So then, leaving the building, I left my character at the bulletin board and exited the game.

Dargo was waiting, and I still needed to buy donuts.

* * *

My parents were fairly beneficial to society, so they were assigned the status "F." And we lived in an apartment block of the same category. It wasn't as luxurious as, for example, E- or D-category blocks, but still better than those where citizens with low social significance lived. My parents had a separate bedroom, for example. And I had my own room. Plus we had two bathrooms and a guest room adjoining the kitchen. There was nothing to really complain about. There was even space for catdog AT and a robot cleaner.

Cali Bottom, which took me more than two hours to reach, was a different world. My flying car came down on the roof of one of the huge drab residential buildings – one-hundred-floor dormitory number two-seventy. This neighborhood was so tightly packed that I couldn't find anywhere else to land.

This wasn't the safest area, but I didn't think anyone would touch me. Noncitizens were subject to immediate sentencing for crimes with little to no judicial process. Punishment came right after any infraction. At the very least that's what Greg told us.

And this artificial city of uncategorized residences was built for noncitizens. Apartments here were called cubbies. That was how cramped they were inside. Toilets and showers were in the same room and shared for all residents of one block. There were a few blocks per floor, and many of the cubbies didn't have windows.

This was not the kind of information I would have sought out on my own, but it was part of my education. Greg even brought us on a field trip to show us the various classes of residence, seemingly to motivate us to study harder.

I got out of the flying car and tried to get my bearings. I was looking for block thirty-six, so I read the numbers on the signs. But my arrival did not go unnoticed. Groups of people in various states of poor dress started closing in around the flying car. Mostly they were teens, but I also saw an old man in a wheelchair and a few old women on a bench staring at me.

I walked up to them, shivering at their dark and sullen gazes. One of the boys, a lean swarthy pipsqueak in a t-shirt, was blocking my path.

"Where'd you come from, goody two-shoes? And in a flying car, come on! So jerkoff, you from out here?"

I turned around and realized I was surrounded. One of the people standing behind me spat at my feet, another was thoughtfully clapping a short piece of rebar in his hand.

"I'm looking for block thirty-six," I said. "I'm here to see Clayton."

"What you got there?" the skinny kid pointed at a paper bag in my hands.

"This is for Clayton."

"What are you even talking about! Clayton this, Clayton that! Do you think we know who that is? I do not give a shit who the hell Clayton is! Give me the bag!"

"Boys, I'm just..."

"Who you callin' 'boys,' jerkoff?" the skinny one asked angrily. "You sound a little mixed up."

Someone ripped the bag of donuts out of my hands and gave a celebratory squeal:

"Aw, nether! Just look what he's got here! Mmm..." the last word bore witness to the fact that one of the donuts was already in his mouth.

Well then, where was his punishment? Where was the orbital crime detection system? Where were was law enforcement?

They tore the bag to pieces, a few donuts fell out, and a hunchbacked boy picked them up, gracefully crawling out of the free for all. The hunchback brought the donuts to the old man in the wheelchair.

Two ideas were fighting in my head: run while I still had the chance, or go try and find Clayton? I turned my head, bewildered and saw the old man in the wheelchair beckoning to me.

And so I went.

"Hey, jerkoff, I'm not done with you yet!" the

skinny one shouted behind me.

I quickened my pace, hearing running behind me, but I turned around and saw the skinny one standing in place and staring at the old man. He made a hand gesture I didn't understand. The boy nodded and lost interest in me.

I walked up to the old man. He studied me for some time. The donuts were lying untouched on his legs, which were covered in a blanket. Only then did I realize the hunchback was no kid, just a very small adult. He came up to my shoulder, if not lower. His face was too aged. There were deep wrinkles in his forehead, and his skin looked unhealthy and gray.

"Hello. I was invited here by someone named Clayton. Sorry to say I don't know his last name. He lives in block thirty-six."

"No Clayton livin' here," the old man mumbled.

"Mhm," the hunchback nodded. "No Clayton."

"I talked with him this morning! Well, not here..." I stumbled, not knowing if I should talk about the game. "He asked me to come here..."

"Clayton is gone now!" the hunchback looked at the sky.

"Where did he go?"

"This morning he kicked up daisies. He died," the old man said, taking a nibble of a donut.

His shoulders heaved and I couldn't tell if he was laughing or crying. "He bought the farm."

"What happened?"

The old man choked and coughed for a long time before he could answer. The hunchback knocked heartily on his back but that didn't help. Finally the piece of pastry dislodged from his windpipe. The disabled man wiped away sweat and tears.

"Why did you want to see him, sonny?"

"I... owe him," I muttered. "What happened?"

"Too much Dis," the boy answered.

"What do you mean?!"

The old man sighed and said:

"He and I... were neighbors. He used to be one of those – one of those citizens. He piloted freighters, said he'd even been to Mars. Then one day he crashed and got crippled like me. In the end they took his citizenship and he ended up here. He worked in Dis, taught common sense to Trixie here," he said, nodding at the hunchback. "He was a good man."

"Good man!" Trixie confirmed, nodding rapidly. "What a shame!"

"So, what happened?"

"Uh..." the old man mumbled, choosing his words. "This morning his pod alarm went off. A medical module flew in and took his body. He was already dead. As for what happened or why, they don't tell us. The dickheads!" the old man clapped a hand on the wheelchair lever. "I hate them so much!"

Dying in a pod was business as usual, considering that many people spent most of their lives in one. And that went double for Clayton, considering his disability and the conditions he lived in.

I had nothing more to do here. Apparently, Dargo/Clayton had no relatives or close friends, and his body was immediately taken away for recycling. I'd never get the chance to thank him. That thought made me feel bad even though, just a few days ago, I had no idea he even existed.

"Very sorry for your loss," the proper words just bubbled up in my memory. "May he rest in peace."

"You're a good kid," the old man rasped back. "Clayton can hear you from the heavens."

"Clayton can hear you!" the hunchback's face melted into a smile and that smile was kind, open and sincere even though his mouth was missing many teeth.

With a nod farewell, I silently walked to the flying car. No one got in my way: the young people were up to their own business, having lost interest in me, and only the old people on the bench, actively gesticulating and arguing, wouldn't take an eye off me.

Once in the flying car, I saw them run over to the wheelchair to ask what happened. The hunchback was not next to the old man. In fact, I saw him next to my flying car. I lowered the window. He moaned and groaned, pretending to be a zombie.

"Oh-wah-yah, Scyth! Oh-wah-yah!" he started grinning into the window and gave a rollicking laugh.

I took off sharply, not realizing right away what he was saying. As soon as I left Cali Bottom, a sticky sweat came over me. It was not hard to connect Trixie with the unusually smart zombie from the instance, plus the hunchback recognized me and called me by my nick. That connection led me to a logical conclusion. What if Dargo giving up and Clayton's death were connected?

And what if someone from the corporation decided to try and line up my passing the temple crypt with my trip to Cali Bottom...

My leg slammed unwittingly into the floor, sharply speeding up the flying car. Considering the vast amounts of interest and money in *Disgardium*, cheating in the virtual world could lead to a very real prison sentence.

Interlude One

Clayton

"HE'S GONE NOW," said Trixie.

"How is he?" Clayton asked.

"He's a good kid, Clay. He didn't chicken out! He just flew away!"

Clayton nodded. Trixie's uncle had already called and told him that the boy was driving the flying car manually. To him that said a lot. From his window on the thirty-sixth floor he watched a flying car pass by. That must have been Scyth.

A sad smile crawled onto his wrinkled face. With his one good hand, he raised a donut to his nose and drew in the long-forgotten smell – an aroma of childhood. His Russian grandmother called them "pyshky" and when her grandson came to visit she made so many that, for the next few days, Clayton himself would look like a donut.

Pyshki fried in oil... Clayton laughed and

took a little bite, taking in the flavor. The last time he ate something like this was many years ago when he was a successful spaceship pilot. And he had more than five thousand days in space! If only he hadn't gotten in that accident! The rescue shuttle didn't work right when entering the atmosphere, the harsh landing... Almost his entire body was paralyzed, his status was changed, he lost his citizenship. The months in a coma ate through his savings and the compensation payed out by the company before he even woke up. And he could only dream of an operation and implants.

"Sorry, Clay," said the man from the union, his eyes downcast. "The guys are sympathetic, but... We already spent so much on keeping you alive."

The only thing he had left, other than the easy way out of suicide, was Cali Bottom and dis. Only that, nothing else. Just dis, an inferior product. A mere substitute for real life.

And now he was locked in the body of the Cursed Lich, boss of the local crypts, but that wasn't so bad. At the very least he could walk in that world.

In *Disgardium*, the developers didn't bother making multiples of the same instance for different groups of players. It was thought this would make it more realistic. An instance was a separate, persistent part of the game and, if there was someone inside, no one else could enter.

As a rule, they were populated by scripted hostile characters, but this year the corporation cautiously started implementing the "human factor" in some locations.

A number of non-key characters in less densely populated locations started coming under control of hired noncitizen players, selected by some criteria known only to Snowstorm. It was all top secret and disclosing it could be punished with a lifetime ban. And for a noncitizen, a lifetime ban in dis was basically like being sentenced to death by starvation. No one in their right mind would share that they were playing a "mob" or "bot," as the players contemptuously called them, instead of some miner, cleaner or lumberjack.

But Trixie was not in his right mind. To be honest, he was mentally a child. And to Clayton and his uncle, he was just a boy even at his nearly forty years. He was significantly behind in his mental development, stuck at the level of a kid. So he quickly shared his new role in the game world – he was a zombie in the temple crypt. No one took the hunchback seriously, or believed him. Other than Clayton who was friends with his uncle, so he immediately realized what was what.

He then became an Emissary of Destroying Plague, which would the next global cataclysm dreamt up by the corporation. Dargo the Cursed

Lich! Ha!

For the first few weeks, he reveled in his role as crypt boss. As soon as he was alerted that players had come into the ins, if he wasn't in the game, he dropped everything and loaded up dis. Sometimes, he stayed in the game to sleep during the odd gap between incursions.

The first few skeletons and zombies obediently got in line, carrying out his commands. As he grew in level, he learned new things, and his crypt army gained new slots.

He managed to infect a rat with the Curse of the Undead, and it spread the infection. That was how a new type of mob appeared in the instance – zombie rats. It was a shame, but they did not obey him. That said, they didn't take up any slots in his army, so he left them locked in the wine cellar to stop them from gnawing at his human zombies.

After that, he experimented with the cursed magic he had available and managed to create the Foul Quease – a disgusting creature sewn together from bits and pieces of human bodies. This particularly strong mob might be crypt boss one day, if it leveled up enough. A little work on his abilities, combining attributes and skills, was fun although also stomach-turning. Still Clayton had long stopped turning up his nose and now looked on his mobs as pets – his personal guard. And really, that was basically what they were.

Class-A Threat

One day, as the alarm rang out to say a new group of players had entered, he cleverly changed tactics, placing limited contingents throughout his dungeon. Obviously, sooner or later the group would pass his crypt, killing everything right down to the lich himself. But Dargo studied his enemies and changed tactics every time, not letting them just have it and tricking groups of players that came into his – his! – dungeon for easy gain.

Dargo and his underlings all earned experience and slowly but surely grew in level. Too bad only one of them was being controlled by a person and didn't obey the primitive behavior scripts. And it was doubly bad that this underling was Trixie. He was, to put it lightly, not the brightest bulb. Still, say what you will, it was company. And when there was nobody in the instance, they found things to discuss.

As for earning experience, it was slow going because every time he died some of it was lost. But they had an eternity ahead of them. A game eternity at the very least, or so said the introductory briefing Snowstorm sent him when he started this assignment. At least until the threat of the Destroying Plague was eliminated by the forces of all *Disgardium*.

And there would be new assignments after that, not necessarily playing evil. Although to Clayton's eye, they were the evil ones. Fat and happy, having replaced real life with three-dimensional renderings.

Damn these game conventions! If only it were possible, he would gather up all his mobs and have them greet the players together at the front door...

In two or three years, Dargo might take over the whole temple of the Radiant God and grow beyond a local instance into a global one like, for example, the infected ruins of Tristad.

But yesterday that weird kid came by. He wouldn't die or disappear from the crypt, time and again respawning right where he died. At first Clayton figured it was some bug and sent a ticket to tech support. But he was told it was all part of the game.

A crypt boss complaining about a cheap player, haha. Clayton smiled. Trixie interpreted that chuckle his own way and handed him another donut. The last one.

"Here you go."

"You're still here? Go on, Trixie. Your uncle's waiting."

"Okay," the hunchback nodded.

He didn't need to say anything twice. Said and done. For Trixie, that was the easiest way to live.

"Trixie, wait."

"Yeah, Clay?"

"If you come across that kid… Alex…"

"Scyth?"

"I always said you're smart, Trix! Yeah, Scyth. If you meet him – here or in dis – help him out. Alright?"

"I'll help. I'll help Scyth. Clay says, Trixie does."

"Thanks. And another thing. Tell your uncle he's a good guy."

"Uncle, good," the scamp smiled, revealing his sparse decaying teeth.

When the hunchback walked away, Clayton, slowly savored the donut, finished his UNB and spent a long time sitting and staring out the window. Yeah! He had a window. And from it he could see the sky. Sure it was tantalizingly just out of reach but, in a way, it kept him anchored to earth.

Seeing that kid, who kept trying to kill him even when it was obviously hopeless, had stirred something in him. He wasn't like the others. They always gave up after a few failed attempts. The lich could sense their frustration. No, his kid reminded him of himself at that age, when the sickly asthma-stricken Clay used to smile, running around the building until he coughed his lungs out so he could finally earn a commission and one day join the flight academy.

All his rage at the injustice of the world, at

life, at how fate had turned its back on him, found embodiment in this series of killings, which he quickly grew bored of. Clayton killed the boy every way he could, mocked him and sneered, using all the phrases in his control panel – the corporation didn't let him talk on his own.

But the boy wouldn't break. At a certain point he thought this Scyth must have been a bug, not a player. Just a system error.

But it was no error. Tired, Clayton decided to figure out what was happening, and didn't kill him. Apparently, this was a real teenage boy. A real person, and he was reaching for the stars.

And then Clayton broke. He activated hardcore mode, which made character death final, then the instance disappeared and he allowed himself to be killed. That option was put in for spice, giving those like Dargo the Lich ten times more experience and letting them play on their nerves. He stood to lose months of progress, after which he would be starting over in the body of, perhaps, some brainless zombie. Not much of an alternative. And that wasn't exactly the risk Clayton was taking.

This morning he decided to quit this job and get back to what he was doing before – working in a quarry. He still had old friends there and, even if the pay was less, at least he had more people to talk to than Trixie the zombie.

Class-A Threat

Scyth killed him, the temple crypts were cleansed of evil, and Clayton himself was completely satisfied with his decision, left dis and wheeled down to the only shower for the whole floor to get cleaned up. When he came back, he discovered a notification from Snowstorm. He had been accused of unfair conduct and breaking his contract. And at the end of the sparse message, they slapped a lifetime ban on the noncitizen Andrew Clayton. And that applied to all game worlds.

There was no longer anything to live on. Or for. Clayton figured the boy didn't need to know, so he asked Trixie's uncle to keep an eye out for him. If Scyth came, he asked him to say that Clayton was dead.

But still, something made him wait until evening. Either he wanted to make sure he wasn't wrong and the boy was worth his salt and would keep his promise or he was simply dreaming of having one last donut. Maybe it was a bit of both.

But now his final goal in life had been achieved. And there was no more reason to stick around. But in the afterlife... there might still be some fun to be had.

Clayton rolled over to the narrow, wide-open window, pulled himself up onto the sill and, for the last time in his life, he flew.

Chapter Twelve

Threats and Rewards

*T*HE SUN WAS almost down when I got home, tired and harried by the traffic on the airways.

Mom immediately flung herself at me.

"Alex, where have you been?" she asked insinuatingly.

The question seemed strange considering she could always track my location and see exactly where I was and when.

AT poked my arm with his wet nose and licked my hand. I pet the catdog, he wagged his little tail and, not raising my gaze I answered:

"I went to see a friend, mom."

"How could you have any friends in Cali Bottom?"

"From Dis. He's gone now."

"What does that mean?"

"He died."

"What?!"

I walked coolly into the bathroom, giving curt answers to all my mom's questions. Based on her reddened face and somewhat raspy voice, she and father had just come off a ghastly squabble. And now father was nowhere to be found, probably off drinking in some bar to wait out mom's rage. When she got mad, it seemed to me, her eyes flared, her voice turned pebbly and some black wings sprouted from her back. I mean, you know, like in movies about the devil possessing people.

Finally, she said her fill and left me in peace, mumbling that my lunch had turned into dinner, and I could heat it up myself if I cared to. And I did not. Not tasting anything, I shoveled down the cold synthetic-meat cutlets and dove into my pod.

When reality flickered and disappeared, replaced in an instant, I noticed in passing surprise how rushed I was to get into Dis.

I had a ton of stuff to do: see the loot from Dargo (just then, I started feeling bad that I never got to know Clayton); read all the notifications and messages I didn't delve into earlier; take a look my gear and, if anything didn't belong, try and sell it to Underweight; and take a peek at the city council bulletin board – maybe there would be some missions. I also needed to find Patrick and figure out how to get rid of his curse. I just wanted to walk around town and talk to random locals too. Maybe they'd give me a decent mission.

As for my curse, by the way, I had an interesting idea. And if it worked, well… I could live with it for now.

I also needed to figure out how to level from here. Overall, to borrow a phrase from my Uncle Nick, I had a metric crapton to do.

In Tristad, night was also beginning to fall. Sandboxes were tied to one's physical location on the planet. All the teens I shared mine with lived somewhere nearby. Time was synchronized too, of course.

I showed up right where I left the game earlier, and a player immediately came at me – some puny level-one beginner.

"Watch where you're going!" he declared in a deep bass, totally removed from the logic of what was happening.

I watched him walk away in astonishment. To look at him he was thirteen but what a voice! Just to be safe I walked away and looked at my inventory. What dropped from Dargo the Cursed Lich?

First I saw an amulet and gasped for joy. My first *green* – unusual – object that gave a bonus to attributes!

Heavy Bronze Amulet

Unusual
+5 Endurance.
Requires level: 5.
Sell price: 98 silver coins, 50 copper coins.

The amulet was strung onto a pleated leather cord meant to be worn around the neck. Too bad the level requirement was too high for me to wear it yet. Still I imagined that at auction something like this could fetch at least three or four gold. Actually though, I'd better hold onto it for now.

I put the amulet back in my inventory and moved onto a scaly-textured belt. At first I couldn't believe my eyes, but after I made sure my vision wasn't deceiving me, I couldn't hold back a victorious yelp, jumping and shaking my fist. The leather belt was *blue*! Rare!

Corrupted Scale Belt
Rare
Leather armor.
Armor: 4.
+9 Strength.
+12 Endurance.
+3% critical damage chance.
Durability: 90/90.
Requires level: 10.
Sell price: 7 gold coins, 52 silver coins.

Chance of losing after death reduced by 50%.

"Dang! Where'd you get that, little noob?" turning my head, I saw a warrior I had the displeasure of knowing quite well, level-twelve Crag, aka fifteen-year-old Tobias Asser. The one who turned me in to the city guard for ripping a dress.

He bared his teeth happily through an open visor, but his gaze was glued to my belt. And his hand, in no hurry, was reaching for my loot.

"You won't be able to find this where I got it now."

I quickly stashed the belt in my inventory, watching the warrior. He pretended he just wanted to scratch the back of his head, just with a very roundabout trajectory. Could he get a lot of scratching done through a plate armor helm I wonder? I heard metal scraping on metal. The warrior wrinkled his face in annoyance.

"Sell it to me!" Crag told me. "That thing is for strength and endurance, you have no need for those! And it's too early. You'll have to level up for half a year to even put it on. I'll give you ten silver right now!"

"Not for sale, sorry."

I turned to walk away, but the warrior's heavy hand landed on my shoulder. I turned around and saw him squinting.

"Twenty," Crag said affectionately.

"I can palm this off on a vendor for seven and a half gold."

"Are you an idiot? At auc you could get three or four times that..." he stumbled.

"Exactly. Exactly, my dear Crag."

"Well here's my advice to you, uh... Scyth! Just sell it, otherwise you'll never be able to use it!"

It reached me that he wouldn't let up if I kept talking. So I stopped responding and he just kept trying to convince me he'd give me everything he had – all two gold. And the rest he'd add in the real world, just not right away. Gradually, over a year... I was just calmly reading old messages though.

"Alex, I have plans tonight, so today I'm alone in Dis for the first time. And just so you know, without you here, it's a million times more boring!" Eve wrote earlier in the day.

"Woah! Look at all those achievements!" Oh nether, I forgot that logs about important events were added to group logs. No matter, Eve is a friend. She won't tell. "What does Mark of the Destroying Plague mean? Did they give you a new skill?"

Another couple messages of congratulation followed – in her boredom she had studied all the loot I picked up. Near the end, she announced she'd had enough, then she left the game.

I didn't know why, but I didn't want Eve to keep getting information about what was happening to me. I exited the group. And by the way, she got no experience for passing the crypt. Well, at least that made sense. Otherwise everyone would level that way.

"Knock-knock! Hey, little noob! Anyone home? Knock-knock!" I closed the chat and saw that Crag was clapping his metal-gloved hands before my nose in an effort to get my attention. "Three gold right now!"

"You're getting in the way of my gaming. That's one. You don't understand the word 'no,' and that's your problem. That's two. And three, I'm calling the guards. Any questions?"

"Well little noob, I'll remember you!" Crag threatened and walked away.

"Took you long enough to learn my face..." I answered, distracted by private messages.

Or more accurately, one message. There was just one, but it wasn't mere spam. This came straight from the developers.

Greetings, fair Scyth, from the gods of Disgardium!
Whether random or not, your recent actions have earned you a place among our most special and unique players. You have become a threat to the world!

Class-A Threat

The system of classifying players as threats to the world is an important and inalienable part of our game. It is the key factor that makes Disgardium inimitable and beloved by our many devotees the world over (the boring world you come from at any rate).

Potential class of your threat to the world: L.
Present class of your threat to the world: Z.
Threat traits: under the radar, part of a global cataclysm, Destroying Plague, pandemic, non-linear character development, hidden advantage against higher-level enemies.

Achieve your full potential and reach maximum threat level!
As your threat class goes up, more interesting events will start to generate around you and more players will come join the hunt!
But what do you stand to gain, beyond unbelievable and captivating adventure?
After the threat is eliminated you will receive:
— A new character with a unique skill!
— An in-game reward starting at level one. The higher your final threat class, the more

valuable the prize!

— A monetary bonus paid to an individual account of the Global Bank of Snowstorm, which will also be determined by your final threat class.

What next? Play! Grow as a threat and always keep your special status a secret. Always, even after elimination!

That will help you hold out as a threat to the world as long as possible and allow you to develop your potential to the max. What's more, if you reveal your status at any time, even if it happens outside the game world, the Snowstorm corporation shall retain the right...

I read up to that point and spent a long time trying to recover, turning this morning's events over in my head again and again. What brought me to this point? Patrick's curse? Killing Dargo and the achievement? The *Mark of the Destroying Plague*? Based on the threat traits, I was not far from the truth.

So then, that global notification was about me? The foothills of the Nameless Mountains... Exactly! Nether, what a hunt the preventer clans would put on for me now!

Although... First they'd have to find me and second, they had no access to our sandbox. And how could they ever know? It wasn't exactly stamped on my forehead! Or was it? I opened my profile, studied it closely: there was nothing there about me being a threat to the world.

Okay, sure. I got back to the message.

What followed was a list of possible punishments, going all the way to extrajudicial deprivation of citizenship (for citizens) and huge fines. The full text of the agreement was sent in a separate message as soon as I accepted the conditions. And why not, really? I had nothing to lose. I was not especially attached to my character, especially now that he was cursed.

The agreement was written in boring legal language, but I didn't find anything new other than that my threat status had no time limit, but I was required to spend no less than eight hours of real time in the game every day. It separately laid out that if I achieved my maximum potential, the corporation would compensate me with a pod that provided all the essentials, and if I got sick or was forced out of the game for any reason I would have to make up the time I missed.

I was not okay with the path that necromancer took. I had a fire in my belly, and I was not going to just be satisfied with class Z.

At the end of the first message, it explicitly defined "eliminating the threat." I could die as many times as I liked, but only up until I was outed as a threat. I could be identified by a brand on my wrist, visible only in the light of a *True Flame*, a very expensive artifact which required extremely rare ingredients to craft.

Whoever revealed the threat could eliminate it by killing the character and performing a full excarnation ritual. It was a very primitive ritual. All you had to do was stick any sharp object into the heart and solemnly declare: "I expel you from *Disgardium* forever!"

After exposed and positively identified, the game assigned a *knowledge* tag to those who have seen evidence of your status. Only after getting that tag could a player actually eliminate a threat once and for all. Then on elimination, the threat would drop a colored crystal and the higher the potential threat class, the larger it would be. And that crystal, once activated, would open a temporary portal into a treasure room that contained the preventer's rewards.

I thoughtfully bared my wrist and saw a black brand shimmering with toxic green light. Some text popped up:

Brand of a Class-Z Threat, with Class-L potential.

"How's it going, Scyth?" came a deep velvety voice. "What you got on your wrist there, hm?"

Chapter Thirteen

The Bubbling Flagon

I SHUDDERED. Overweight, and that was who it was, started laughing. In a couple of heartbeats, I opened my inventory and put the amulet from Dargo back into my hand.

"Oh, Rita! I was just coming to see you! Look what I found..." I extended the loot to show her. "What do you think, should I keep it?"

"I mean..." she said, intrigued. "*Green?* Well... not bad. Five endurance at level five couldn't hurt. For two and a half gold, buyers would rip off your arms to get it. But, if you're not in a rush, you could probably get three or four."

"That's what I thought," I said with a nod of satisfaction, stashing it in my bag. "I'll keep it then."

"Good choice. Just put it in your chest first, otherwise you might get ganked and lose it." she tossed a gaze over me. "You get some gear? A successful farm?"

"Sure. Thanks for the club, you really helped me out!"

"Yeah, it's nothing really. I just wanted to get rid of it," she shrugged.

"By the way, Rita. I wanted to drop by and see some of what Underweight had to offer, then keep leveling from there. Could you tell me where best to go at my level?"

"Definitely not Gloomwood," the girl laughed. "Not a lot of people go there, and if they do, it's with a strong coordinated group. Have you ever heard of Crusher?"

"Uh... No."

"He's a rare mob who got announced not very long ago, a kind of local boss," Overweight explained eagerly. "A big old wolf as tall as you, a level-fifteen elite. He hunts local mobs all alone. To put it briefly, no one has been able to take him down yet. He can cast a *Fear* spell by howling and at half life he summons a pack. And that's when it's all over."

"I see. I won't go there alone or with a group. But what about the rest?"

"Listen, I don't remember where I even leveled. Undy and I used to comb through everything around here. We got our first few levels quick. To the west the murlocks will eat you up, so all you have left is the Mire if you don't want to do socials. Walk around – there's a hunting camp over that way. They might give you a mission to genocide local animals. Most important though, don't get near the needlers! Those are these huge flies. They lay eggs inside you, and the maggots crawl around under your skin and start burrowing... Yeesh..." she shuddered.

Rita's hand dived into the pocket of her leather jacket. She pulled out a bag of sweets and extended it to me.

"Treat yourself."

"Thanks, I don't like candy."

"What? These randomly give one to an attribute or plus ten percent to movement speed!"

"Are you serious?" I pulled a candy in a rainbow wrapper from the bag, unwrapped it and tossed it back. In a matter of seconds it dissolved on my tongue, leaving an aftertaste of strawberries and cream.

You have eaten Sweet Joy.
Positive effect received: +10% movement speed.

"And what if..."

"Doesn't stack," she interrupted. "It lasts one hour. If you eat another one, the bonus just changes."

"Thanks!"

"Bon appetite! Undy is the one of us who handles the *Cooking* by the way. If you get any ingredients, feel free to bring them to him. He'll buy whatever you got. You'll get less than at auction, but all at once and fast."

"Ah, you know I just so happen to have some..." I dug in my inventory and pulled out the rat innards.

"Ick, that stuff is nasty," Overweight wrinkled her nose. "I've never seen anything like it. Where'd you even find a zombie rat?" Her eyes went the size of a gold coin. "Were you in Gloomwood or something?"

"Me? Do I look like an idiot?"

"Honestly... yes. At the very least you did all that time you spent wearing through the seat of your pants outside the tavern. It's just that a zombie rat... I have no idea where else you could happen on one of those other than Gloomwood. I never saw any rats there, but there are wraiths."

"First room in the temple crypt. There's a wine cellar with these rats."

"Ah, I see," she nodded. "Check auction prices, because I have no idea how much that might cost or what it might be used in. Well, or ask Undy. He should know."

"Gotcha, I'll do that. Thanks!"

"Look me up sometime, Scyth. Alright, we've

been talking too much. I've gotta go to the auction, then the real world. I've got stuff to do. If you require our services, you know where to find us," Overweight shoved my shoulder and left.

She really was pretty. You know how that happens? Like a person doesn't really make an impression at first, but the longer you talk the more you find them attractive. Well with Rita Overweight, that was about the size of it. I discovered that she had an infectious smile, pretty eyes and an attractive face. And I wouldn't call her fat. She still had a long way to go before Eve's level. She had a guitar-shaped body, and if... Nether, where has my mind gone?

I tore my eyes away from Rita's buttocks, wrapped tight in her leather pants. She was rushing and her thighs were shaking side to side, hypnotizing me like a pendulum...

Was Undy her brother? Or boyfriend? I never thought to compare last names.

On the announcement board, I didn't find a thing worth doing. What was more, almost all the jobs were already taken because it was evening. I wasn't high enough level to patrol the edge of Gloomwood, and now after the fast leveling in the ins, you'd never drag me down to weed gardens for a couple copper and a droplet of experience.

Now last night's torments and suffering no longer seemed so horrible. I mean sure, I got wiped a couple hundred times but I passed the ins, got some gear, leveled up, earned achievements, discovered new skills and improved my character!

That reminded me, Patrick! I'd have to find him and thank him with a couple coins. But first to the tavern to toss this rare belt and unusual amulet into personal storage.

The Bubbling Flagon tavern, which I had spent so much time outside of, was always full of people. Bots after work; noncitizen laborers, in the sandbox on a job, relaxing after a long day in the quarries; a group of bards, kicking out retro-rock jams on some archaic musical instruments; the usuals too, like Patrick when he had the money; the backup dancers, who earned money and experience at the tavern... All kinds.

There were also duels for money in the back yard and, from time to time, the bot owner Tashot put on tournaments. It, of course, was no Arena but there were no formalities, and it was closer to town.

Considering the limited number of seats, the principle of, "If you don't order anything, don't sit down!" was loudly espoused by the owner. So for a moneyless noob like me, getting inside was unthinkable.

Fortunately, I could reach the individual rooms via another entrance. And I did just that.

I went up to the second floor, walked down

---

the hall which had just twelve rooms, to my door. Eleven of the rooms were just like normal: for tavern visitors who wanted to have some private time. There was no sex, sure, but you could make out as much as you liked. And many did just that.

But door twelve was special. Individual rooms were generated like instances – an independent space, different for each player. And you could get into your room from any tavern in *Disgardium*. You could upgrade your room all the way up to Royal, which would make it both larger and more luxurious. And yes, you could decorate it however you wanted, as long as you had the money.

And in that I had never had any money here, my room spoke to that. It was a little room that fit only the basic eight-slot chest, a bed the game designers had made creak and a small wooden nightstand, which had somehow been broken.

I didn't spend any time in my room, just tossed the loot from Dargo in. But when I came down to the first floor, I heard a lively dispute coming from the kitchen. I got interested and walked up closer. From behind the closed door, I could hear voices:

"That's what I'm saying, I just splatted it out on the floor! With this very boot!"

"You really splatted it, Mr. Arno!" a girl's voice egged him on.

"That's what I'm saying, I swatted the thing dead. But then it jumped up like nothing happened and ran!"

I cracked open the door and glanced into the kitchen. A well-fed chef of around five-hundred pounds, waving a broad knife, was arguing with a young female cook. He cast a dismayed gaze at me, opened his mouth to say something, but was interrupted by the lady shouting in fear. She jumped up onto a chair and yelled:

"There it is!"

Me and the big guy turned to where she pointed. There we saw a small gray rat walking aimlessly in a circle with its head turned one hundred and eighty degrees. It's fur was all matted, in places it had open wounds. One of them had a bone jutting out.

A level-eight zombie rat! How'd this hostile mob get into town? It must have come up from the temple crypt. But that was impossible! An instance is an instance, mobs have no way out...

"Mother of my wife!" the chef yelped in a falsetto, awkwardly flinging his knife at the rat.

It hit the floor handle first and flew away. The rat bared its teeth, gave a ghastly squeal and ran at the knife, biting at the blade and trying to grab it. Realizing the target was not alive, the rat stayed in place and turned its head to point its eyes at the chefs. The zombie rats chose a new target and started off. Their squealing went ultrasound.

The fat one darted off for a pan filled with boiling oil.

"Lord, lord, lord Nergal the Radiant..." the lady muttered. "Reveal your light and destroy this stinking creature..."

Arno poured the bubbling and hissing oil on the zombie, then quickly jumped back. Just like a dog, the rat shook it off, then ran on the attack. One solid jump was enough to get next to the chef. Then the rat jumped high and bit at the chef's thigh, going through his pants and his whooping joined the rat's screeches and girl's screaming.

The cook threw the rat away, yelling all the time. The creature twisted its body and landed on its feet. Its head turned forty-five degrees threateningly. Its tail was twitching nervously, tapping on the floor.

But I bucked up, gathering courage. Just one rat? I killed a whole pack last night!

My blade found its own way into my hand and I threw myself into the fray.

"Die!" tore itself from me when I cut into the zombie.

You have critically damaged Zombie Rat: 2!
Health points: 55/60.

My rusty sword cut the rat in two with a dull thud and sunk into the well-oiled wooden floor. "Yes sir," came a whisper echoing in my head.

Zombie Rat is dead.

Wait, what? I looked at the dead mob in astonishment. Based on the logs, it had enough life left to send all the kitchen staff running for the hills, then eat me to death. And it gave no experience.

On autopilot, I crouched and picked up the loot. It was more innards. I threw them in my inventory and turned my head in incomprehension when the chef's soft hand touched my shoulder. I only then realized that it was completely silent, even the crackling of logs in the stove had stopped.

"How are you, little one?" Arno asked.

"Fine."

I got up, reaching for the outstretched hand.

"You came just in the nick of time!" the chef laughed. He started speaking quickly like a person who had just survived a test of their nerves: "At first I thought: what does he want down here? All kinds tread these floors! The fact that you're a visitor to Tristad is obvious! But are you a guest of the inn or not? We have a strict rule here, outsiders are not allowed. And we don't hesitate to

---

call the guards. But just look how it all turned out! You do good work with that hunk of metal, well-heeled warrior!"

"I am no warrior, I just got lucky... Mr. Arno."

"Fortune favors the bold," the chef said, raising his pointer finger to share that tidbit of wisdom. "Thank you, Scyth!"

Rada the chef girl came down from the chair and pulled a big tray of pies out of the oven. The smell of yeasty pastry wafted into my nose. She deftly cut a slice, walked over and extended it to me.

"Take this as a sign of gratitude, warrior!" she said, her eyes downcast. "It's filled with porridge, herbs and meat. Only Mr. Arno knows how to cook like this."

I took it and couldn't hold back. I bit right into the burning slice, savoring the flavor.

"One won't be enough," Arno announced. "I've heard that visitors to Tristad are generally amenable to learning the ins and outs of a new craft. So Scyth, would you like me to teach you to cook?"

The Chef of the Bubbling Flagon, Arno, would like to teach you the basics of the Cooking trade.

Do you accept?

Limitation: no more than one trade for every

ten levels.

While the chef patiently awaited an answer, I thought, studying the mobs as I did. Something in his status seemed strange. A debuff icon?

Arno, level 22
Chef of the Bubbling Flagon tavern.
Infected.

I focused on the icon and a moment later an explanation popped up:

Hidden debuff, visible only to emissaries of the Destroying Plague.
Effect triggered. Will turn into a zombie after death.

Chapter Fourteen

Nonmilitary Trade

"**A**ND NOW, we take the meat off the flame and serve, wrapping it in a tender lettuce leaf. And that's all, Scyth! You wanna try cooking something?" Arno asked, shaking off his apron. "Ah, okay. I guess the hearth is occupied. Don't forget to bring flint and steel, a pot and some wood."

We had just finished studying the basics of *Cooking*. It took ten minutes. While the *infected* chef told me about cooking methods, some system messages jumped in.

> ### Cooking trade discovered!
> *You now have the ability to cook food. Prepared dishes can give various temporary effects when eaten. These effects may improve attributes or, in rarer cases, give you*

an unusual ability. To prepare food, as a rule, you must first light a fire.
Current level: Pupil (0/100).
Chance of cooking a dish with known recipe: 100%
Chance of inventing a new dish: 1%

Cooking recipes added: *spiced bread, fried rabbit, boiled chicken egg, spider-egg omelet, rat soup, roast lamb intestines, herb-encrusted venison filet, needler kebab...*
To improve your skill in this trade, prepare dishes with known recipes, come up with your own recipes and experiment with ingredients.

You have received experience points for learning a new trade: 50.
Experience points at present level (2): 267/900.

"I have nothing more to teach you, Scyth. If you bring your craft up to level one hundred, come back. I'll teach you new methods and increase your professional rank to journeyman." The chef gave me an approving pat on the shoulder. "Sorry, I've gotta get back to work."

While he was teaching me, several times panicking waitresses had run back demanding

---

some dish be produced at once, and Rada just got mad and looked at the chef.

"Thank you, Mr. Arno," I said, squeezing his hand.

Outside, I stopped to think. The city was still vibrant at night and lit by street lamps. A cart came up to the tavern, and some grubby miners poured out, then holed up in the tavern all together. I turned my head and crossed the street, nearly landing under the hooves of a guard horse. There I sat on the bench that felt almost like home and thought.

The main question was not about the *infected* chef, but my plans. I was so exhausted that the flow of the game was just carrying me at this point. How would this help me in the future? What was the point of leveling this character? Could I earn any money here? Would it cover even part of what it would cost to go to university? I had no idea. On the other hand, what else could I do? Half the planet couldn't come up with anything more lucrative than working in *Disgardium*.

Well, I'd play actively for a month at least then I could make some conclusions. But for now I'd get back to Arno's strange status.

Maybe I was a newbie in Dis, but I wasn't stupid. If the chef's debuff was only visible to emissaries of the Destroying Plague, I must have been one. The message from the developers led me to that conclusion when it listed the traits of my threat, but now I had that confirmed.

Another question: how had it happened? Dargo? But he gave me the entirely concrete achievement and skill *Mark of the Destroying...* Son of a...! Of course! The name contained the answer to my question!

Then there was a different question. What should I do with that? Would some messenger be coming tomorrow from the Destroying Plague with a special sabotage mission? And what was this Destroying Plague? A global raid boss? A spirit? A deity? An anomaly? I'd have to browse the forums.

Also, where should I go from here? The plague ability was geared toward the idea that I would die, or reach the edge of death. Then something would trigger and a system somewhere in the bowels of the servers would roll dice to see whether I would be made invulnerable or not.

So I'd rather die in a place where the chance of encountering others was minimal. Otherwise they'd take me guts and all and that would mean goodbye to increasing my threat class. I set about studying the interactive map. Almost its entire surface was concealed by a murky fog of war and I could only see the outskirts of Tristad, the same as I'd scouted out in the first few weeks.

To the south down the river was Gloomwood, which teemed with high-level mobs. Many dozens of miles to the east of that was the unending impassable Mire. To the west it was calmer, and that was where the Dementors usually trained, but if they took a risk and went too far they could end up captured by a patrol of snake-like nagas or ambushed by murlock fish people. Beyond their chaotic settlements was a shore lapped by the treacherous waters of the Bottomless Ocean. To the north, the Nameless Mountains towered over Tristad...

"What are you frowning for, Alex?" Tissa asked, coming over to me and waving her hand in greeting. For a second, light enveloped me. Another friendly push from the priestess of Nergal, +5 to strength.

"Hi! Thanks for the buff!"

"It's nothing," Tissa sat next to me and rubbed her forehead. "Ugh, I messed up healing on Crusher! We got a bunch of scrubs in a group, then they just went past Bomber toward the boss! Wipe on wipe! Dang! So, you gonna wear through your pants outside the tavern again? And where's your girlfriend, Aphro-fatty?"

"She already worked off her punishment. And I'm thinking where to go next in my uber gear. Do you know where a guy could rack up bunnies around here?"

"Bunnies, you say... I could power level you in the Jail.." Tissa looked me from head to toe.

"But I'm afraid we'll get wiped. We'd need a decent tank, but that'd want gold. I've had enough of scrub tanks for today."

"And where are your badass friends?"

"Uh..." Tissa waved a hand. "I told them to screw themselves! They need to think about their behavior and about how they'll get along without a heal."

Up until we were in fourth grade, me and her used to talk all the time. Then she changed. Her mom got in an accident: some psycho slammed into her at full speed with his flying car. That was hard on her dad, and Tissa had to grow up early in all senses. She blossomed as a lady, started thinking more seriously about the future, her interests changed. And two years ago, she started hanging out with Ed, Malik and Hung and stopped talking to me once and for all. My attempts to interact came across as naive and childish and, due to my successes in school, she started looking on me as a geek.

Strange that she started talking to me again recently. It was... unusual to say the least.

"Thanks, Tissa," I couldn't find the words, and squeezed out something I never would have said in a normal situation: "You wanna go somewhere together?"

"What? With you?" her pretty eyes went wide.

"Crap, sorry. That isn't what I meant..." feeling my cheeks go red, I started to spin a yarn. "You just said you could power-level me and that would mean we'd go somewhere together... Right? Or did I misunderstand you?"

"Ah!" her face lit up. "I thought you were asking me out on a date, and..."

Was it just me or was she embarrassed too?

"Come on, what're you talking about?!" I protested. "I would never ask you on a... date, not at all..."

"And why might that be?" Her eyes narrowed and she raised up. "Do you think you can't ask me out?"

"Come on Tiss, you're misunderstanding me..."

"I'm understanding you just fine! Go on a walk with your tub of lard friend, idiot!"

She threw her head back, adjusting her hair, straightened her spine and walked proudly into the tavern. I was such a dumbass...

I spent five minutes getting my thoughts in order, trying to stop thinking about Schafer. It wasn't easy, but I managed, remembering what I stood to lose if I tanked in Dis.

To nether with girls! What was I thinking about before the priestess of Nergal showed up?

Ah yeah, how to level the *Mark of the Destroying Plague*. I needed to die somewhere no one would see. That could be arranged. In theory, there were two options: an instance or a badass mob that cannot be killed so no one comes near. Like that Crusher thing.

The second option was perfect for testing another of my ideas, too...

First I dropped by Underweight and sold him all the shitty gear I gathered in the Temple crypt. There was no sense in dying that many times just for this sad equipment. But still, at least it was a few copper. I kept only the rusty sword and zombie rat guts (I had four, but Undy wouldn't buy, saying he had no idea what they could be used to cook). He payed me four whole silver for everything – more than an NPC vendor would have given.

Then I put my basic novice clothing back on. From there my path went to a merchant's stall. Not a weaponsmith or an armorer, just a normal trader of anything and everything. That part of the plan was not supposed to take much time, but only Nergal knew when I'd get back to the city.

There was a line in front of the vendor. Friday evening: many were buying up stock of ingredients, food and other small items so they could leave the city for a while. No one here had their own mount, and a week was not enough to cross the whole sandbox on foot. And that was without grappling with any mobs, which grew both more numerous and ferocious the further you got from town.

While I waited, I decided what to buy. First a pot, some wood and firestarter. Thank all the gods that it was only a formality, but basically, if you had all that in your inventory, starting a fire was something like activating an ability. Second, ingredients: herbs, spices, flour and spring water. I'd have liked to have gotten some fishing stuff too. After all, that would make a good combo with leveling *Cooking*, but I didn't have enough money.

After making my purchases, I left town and walked into the forest. In a clearing, I started a fire and began baking bread. It was the simplest recipe made of the cheapest ingredients: flour, water and spices, then wait ten seconds by the fire and it was ready to be pulled out of the pot.

You have prepared Spiced Bread.
Spiced Bread (1) added to your inventory.

Cooking trade: +1.
Current level: Pupil (1/100)
You have received experience points for progressing in a trade: +1.

I glanced into my bag. It now contained a bread icon. The description said that eating bread would restore ten health points. Not bad.

The ball was rolling. Sitting by the fire, I kept

cooking, appreciating the scent of fresh baked goods. The experience points came as a pleasant surprise. It was easier to get like this than spending half a day hunched over in the quarry.

Ten minutes later, my bag was twice as heavy, half-filled with spiced bread – fifty little fist-sized rolls.

Cooking trade: +1.
Current level: Pupil (43/100).
You have received experience points for progressing in a trade: +1.

The last points in the trade were an ordeal. The recipe was too simple, and in order to keep levelling, I needed to make more complex dishes.

I stood up to get to the next part of the plan, but then it dawned on me. Aw, what the nether?! I pulled the *Zombie Rat Innards* out and threw them in the pot.

They were still "fresh" so they hissed and spattered, and a smoldering black smoke rose up out of the pot. The guts sparked and caught fire. A few seconds later, all that remained was char. And a second after that, it was gone too. Only the black smoke curling upward was left to remind me.

Attempt to create a new dish!
Failure!

That bad? But I was on the right track, right?

I snorted and threw another set of chitterlings into the pot.

Failure! Another failure!

I pulled out my last one. I'd forgotten to check the value of this "ingredient" at auction, and now I was tormenting myself imagining that I was destroying something that might be worth an unbelievable amount of money. *Very rare alchemy ingredient. Required to create invincibility potion. Value: 1000 gold*, I imagined.

At first I hesitated, then I decided not to get too crazy over this. I mean, when had a rare ingredient ever come from a noob ins?

Without a doubt, I threw the last rat zombie innards into the pot...

"Chh!" a plate armor boot, scattering the coals, kicked the pot so hard it flew seventy feet.

Iron clanged and a wide blade pierced just under my ribs.

Player Crag (Tobias Asser) has damaged you: 31.

Health points: 22/53.

I turned my head and saw the lamentably familiar warrior. He was smiling. Vista was standing next to him, now level three, and another player I didn't know named Rashidos was with them at level nine.

"You're pretty hard to kill, scum," Crag said in dismay, and twisted the sword.

Player Crag (Tobias Asser) has damaged you: 7.
Health points: 15/53.

"You shouldn't be sticking your nose out of town," he said. "We'll find you every time, got it? Although... I'm in a good mood today. I trust you brought the belt?"

"Nuts to you, no..." I coughed and, twisting like a rotisserie chicken, collapsed to the earth.

What would happen when I respawned right here, how would I explain that? You can't leave the game in battle, nor can you exit while dead. Damn, damn, damn...

"Finish him off, Crag. What are you drawing this out for?" Vista said. "If he has the belt, won't it drop?"

"Not for sure," the warrior frowned. "He could have hidden it in his chest, plus the drop chance for *blues* is not one hundred. So Scyth, I'm going to ask you again. Do you have the belt?"

"Go f..." I started coughing again.

Crag stuck the sword between my eyes.

A sharp pain pierced my head. I screamed.

Player Crag (Tobias Asser) has critically damaged you: 52!
Health points: 0/53.
You are dead.

Remaining time to respawn 9... 8... 7...

"Aw, nether, no belt! Just potions, some bread and a rusty sword!" Crag kicked my things in disappointment, and Vista ran to pick them up. "Come on, drop that trash! Let's hurry to the cemetery! We'll head him off there before he buggers off to his room!"

"Yeah," Vista agreed. "He'll be more talkative with the memory of your sword in his stupid face!"

"He should be glad you didn't go for the ass!" Rashidos jeered right in my face.

They laughed and ran off toward the city gates. Even when Ed mocked me, it didn't hurt much. But now I felt a true rage.

Remaining time to respawn 4... 3... 2...

Still, it came together in my favor. They left and I was in the glade – alone. Also...

I couldn't smile as a corpse, but still I was laughing inside. No, not because those bastards didn't stick around to dance on my corpse. I was delighted by the logs I saw before I died:

Attempt to create a new dish!
Success! You have created a new cooking recipe: Roast Undead Rat Chitterlings!
Experience points received for new cooking recipe: +100.

You have prepared Roast Undead Rat Chitterlings.
Roast undead rat chitterlings (1) added to your inventory.

Cooking trade: +10.
Current level: Pupil (53/100)
You have received experience points for progressing in a trade: +10.

In one second, I'd stand up and see just what these *Roast Undead Rat Chitterlings* really were!

Chapter Fifteen

The Road to Gloomwood

THE BLACK AND WHITE purgatory was replaced with the world of the living once again. Not moving from place, I took a look around: there was no one in the clearing. A few steps from me a level-one grass snake slithered past but didn't see me. I never saw a status bar over it. A fuzzy bumble-bee flew past as well.

The fire was out, and around the huge spread of ash there were white chunks of bread. My sword, and the health and mana potions I found in the underground chest had been taken by Vista, and the bread constituted no more than one stack. No biggie, I'd write them off as a loss.

I added Crag, Vista and Rashidos to my enemy list so I wouldn't miss them coming near again. The bread, wood and fire-starter took back their slots, and I went to find my pot.

I had to search in the overgrown bushes for a long time and, when I found it, I couldn't hold back an explicit outburst. The cast-iron pot had a hole in it! Either Dis had realism problems, or Crag's strength was so high he could rip through cast iron like paper.

Not feeling sorry for myself – I'd buy another one – I opened my inventory. Now I could see what kind of new dish I'd managed to invent. I wondered whether it was my success chance, or just that Crag had quickly taken it off the fire.

Roast Undead Rat Chitterlings

Ingredients: Zombie Rat Innards.
This truly shameful dish can boldly take its place among the worst plates of food ever made! Its inventor Scyth is probably not too proud of his creation. After all, these disgusting rotten undead rat innards spent only a few seconds over scorching heat. Still, that was just enough to tame their unique tang and give them a razor thin golden crust.
Special effects when eaten: +1000% to skill levelling rate for 1 hour.
Effect is removed after death.
Value: 1 gold coin.

I turned the unappetizing seared glob over in my hand, then it flew into my inventory.

Class-A Threat

No idea better than selling it at auction came to mind. Seriously, to me it was useless, because I died more often than a hummingbird's heartbeat. I suppose I could hold onto it for better times to level skills. Although... Nether, I'm stupid! Evidence of the sleepless night, no two ways about it. I was yawning now as well, risking dislodging my jaw. But I decided to bear it.

I needed to figure out the optimal route – not the longest, but the one that would keep me from encountering any Tristad guards. I really didn't want there to be talk about a weird level-two noob.

The map was showing my path first through the forest to the East, then over the Tremitelle river into Gloomwood. And that path would be full of pain and death.

My death.

The first problems began just one hundred yards from the glade where I was cooking. And even that distance was not made easily.The dark forest with its high trees had a canopy that didn't let one single bit of light through from the moon of this world, which was called Geala the thorny bush...

But I overcame it because I knew that my body was safe in my pod at home, and the scratches and injuries I was taking would heal in a matter of seconds. What was more, I now had a new skill:

Night Vision skill discovered!
Vision radius in the dark increased by 10%.
Current level: 1.
Improve this skill by staring into the darkness, but take care. It might start staring back at you!

You have received experience points for discovering a new skill: 10.
Experience points at present level (2): 330/900.

The new skill helped, or I simply had gotten used to the dark, but I saw the spider before it attacked.

Night Spinner, level 6

The long-legged blood-drinker gracefully descended from a higher branch. I got scared and not only because of the spider's anomalous dimensions. I was also just scared of the deep darkness this was all taking place in. I didn't manage to dodge, the attack was lighting fast and hit me on first try.

The damage from the bite halved my life, but the DoT of nasty poison was quickly taking down the rest. Still it was not fast enough to kill me right away, so I managed to jump on the spider. My teeth clenched in pain, now particularly acute due to the little spines that covered its back, I pressed down with my feet and rained down a hurricane of blows. In real life, it would have been hard to miss. I mean, my whole field of vision was occupied its body. But here misfires happened often.

Still, my fists made a dent in its chitin, doing one damage here, zero there and missing, slipping off, my knuckles were cracking and bleeding and... I died.

You are dead.

Remaining time to respawn ... 9...

I didn't wait. I respawned that very second, and the spinner's squeal of celebration was cut off when my fist clabbered its mandible.

Bite! Death. Get up! *Hammer*!

The enraged insect ran a leg through me like a spear and I died again. Then I made another attack.

When killing, the mob chirred victoriously time and again. I started to seethe with hatred for that specific spider. Driven on by adrenaline, I tried to tear a piece of flesh off it whether with my teeth or fingernails.

Between deaths, I had time to read about a new skill and accompanying ability.

Resilience skill discovered!

Resistance to all types of damage increased by 1%.

Pain reduced by 1%.

Current level: 1.

Improve this skill by fighting enemies of your level or higher for additional bonuses and new special attacks.

You have received the Stoneskin ability!

Cost to use: 3 mana points.

Increases resistance to all types of damage by 10%.

Duration: 1 second.

You have received experience points for discovering a new skill: 10.

Experience points at present level (2): 340/900.

Only a masochist like me could level this skill! I chuckled, reinvigorated, but the laughter gave way to a cough when the spider spit poison and it landed in my mouth. He got me!

His dim bulbous little eyes stared senselessly until I started pulling them out one after the next. Each eye I removed took a few deaths, but soon all twelve were gone. How do you like that, blind freak?

Class-A Threat

Unarmed Combat skill improved: +1.
Damage dealt without a weapon increased by 30%
Attack accuracy increased by 30%.
Current level: 3.
Improve this skill by fighting enemies of your level or higher for additional bonuses and new special attacks.

Hammerfist improved: +1.
Cost to use: 2 mana points.
Deals 250% of normal damage.
Ignores 2% of armor.

Pay a visit to a master of Unarmed Combat to learn more special attacks!

Now there was an idea. I guessed that the higher my enemies' level, the faster my combat skills would improve, but I hadn't found a confirmation in the forums. In a world where any victory was the result of gallons of spilled blood and years of time, and where your success defined your future in the real world, no one shared any real guides or secrets.

With a third of its life remaining, the Night Spinner tried to run, but I caught it in a jump and grabbed it by the leg. Its leg joint couldn't take the strain and just popped out. Ichor spilled from the wound, I licked it carnivorously, took a DoT of poison and died. After getting back up, I looked around for my victim, but its trail had gone cold. Probably hidden up above, the vile bug!

I was not in combat, so I took my fallen bits of bread and devoured three, restoring my health. I needed it to climb up the tree in one piece and find this thing.

My breathless body fell off the tree fifteen or so times. Nothing remained of the spiced bread, but I balked. I climbed up the tree again and again, flaying my whole body, found a huge cavern that served as the spider's den, and tried to take down the mob as it recuperated. It met me on the threshold. Poisons, punctured organs, falling from a tree, bits of web gluing me in place – the variety and amount of damage I was taking leveled *Resilience.*

That in turn improved *Stoneskin,* which turned out to be a very useful ability. It was the very reason I eventually was able to take down the spider. I had just a few bits of health left, and landed two *Hammer* blows. One of them was a crit. The chirring stopped and the arachnid splayed out at the cavern entrance.

I got twelve experience and a quick look around netted me the same number of spider eggs. These were *Cooking* ingredients for an omelet. But unfortunately I'd just lost my pot.

Class-A Threat

I came down from the tree feeling tired. My adrenaline had boiled off. I considered the fact that this was only the first mob in my long road to Gloomwood and felt despair. Fainthearted, I thought it would be nice to get some sleep so I could continue my journey tomorrow with renewed strength. But while I thought and found more and more new reasons to leave Dis, my legs started moving all by themselves.

I continued arguing with myself, but didn't stop. I encountered no mobs, and eventually reached a dock in the Tremitelle river. The swift waters of the river just flew into the Bottomless Ocean, and the question of how to get out without drowning occupied me for ten minutes.

I made up my mind and jumped in the water. The current immediately pulled me down and dragged me along the stony bottom. I tried to keep my head above the surface as I paddled toward the opposite bank. And it should be said it didn't really work.

Many damage messages poured in, first about scratches and blows on rocks. Then I was brought down to the bottom, and damage was added form the bites of some small but very sharp-toothed little fish called Stone Grabbers.

The water was too cloudy to see what they looked like, but they really ripped my flesh. Whoo-ee! I used the timer between deaths to the maximum, so my body would be carried as far as possible from the predatory fish.

But a few seconds later, they were next to me again. I got the impression that the river was teeming with them, but that was to my advantage. *Resilience* leveled up to three, reducing pain and incoming damage by three percent.

I resurrected, activated *Stoneskin* and took a few paddles to the opposite bank. Eventually I did get close enough to it to latch onto the root of some huge oak. The hardest part of the swim was not forgetting to pick up the baked chitterlings that dropped after I died. Good that the river carried them at the same speed as my body. I had plans for them. But I lost the spider eggs and didn't even realize.

The sky began to glow when my foot stepped into Gloomwood. My eyes closed, I was falling off my feet in exhaustion and lack of sleep but I was satisfied.

Suddenly in the complete silence, I heard a barely audible rustling from the bushes. I raised my eyes... and my gaze started rushing around in search of the exit button, having seen a huge dark silhouette approaching me with the description:

Crusher, level 15
Wolf
Local boss

Class-A Threat

Softly stepping on the damp loose soil and noisily pulling in air, the wolf headed in my direction.

But to heck with him! Exit!

Chapter Sixteen

Curse of the Undead

I SLEPT THROUGH school. My smart alarm clock detected sleep deprivation, did the nice thing and deactivated harsh wake-up mode.

Based on the recordings I saw when I woke up, father returned home in the morning and he couldn't stay on his feet. His clothing was all dirty as if he had crawled from his flying car to the apartment. Probably that was why mom hadn't slept all night either. That said, when she disappeared all night, dad's worrying meant nothing to her.

But all that made them forget about me completely. They must have figured their son flew off to school unnoticed even though all that time I was out like a dead man. And as a matter of fact I had died. Five hundred times in fact.

I woke up after midday feeling absolutely

broken and dispirited. AT was kneading her feet on my chest and issuing a measured satisfied purr. He could sense feelings and transform into either a cat or a dog. Though to be fair he was a bit glitched. At some point a firmware update installed wrong and, remaining a cat, he ran around the house and barked in a deep bass like a German shepherd. What a sight that was!

I mechanically stroked my pet, feeling a calming measured vibration under my hand. I laid like that a few minutes then, pushing the cat off, got up.

There was no sense in flying to school but, to clear my conscience, I listened to the condensed version of the lectures I missed while I went about my morning routine. I washed up, did a couple exercises and had breakfast. Again those repellent cereal flakes with synthetic milk. My parents were on the warpath again, so they didn't have the energy to refill the nutrient cartridges in the kitchen. I ate, shoveling down two portions so I could spend more time immersed.

My parents were already fast asleep by then, recovering from their wild night. Mom was in the parents' bedroom and dad was in his clothes and half on the couch. He didn't have the energy to get up any better, and his feet were just sitting on the floor.

After that, I spent a long time warming up

under a hot shower not wanting to crawl out into either the clammy real world of my unheated apartment or the twilight of Gloomwood in Dis. In fact, I didn't want anything at all. Both life and the future felt like impenetrable darkness, and only force of will could get me into my pod to launch the game.

I appeared in the world mentally prepared for instant death in Crusher's teeth. But nothing happened, the local boss had left and it was all clear.

The washed-out clay riverbank where I'd left my character was slippery under my bare feet, and I had to get on all fours to reach dry land. Water was burbling behind me, teeming with an overabundance of Stone Grabbers. The little fish started jumping onto the land, trying to get a bite of a foot, then nervously flipped back down and rolled into the water. And finally I was able to catch a glimpse of the things: the ugly little fish were the size of a hand and had a snake's neck with a huge set of jaws and protruding fangs. I stomped a few vengefully, smearing their guts over the black sticky clay. No experience, no loot. Just useless animals.

But then I had to cut and run. From a nearby eddy, a group of level-eight Magnetic Toads jumped over to see what all the commotion was about. The plump amphibians emanated a weak aura of submission. The Stone Grabbers calmed down in an instant, shoaled up and swam over to the shore so they could jump out of the water all at once.

The magnetism of the toads almost worked on me too. I got a minute-long debuff that significantly lowered movement speed but, much to my delight, the little fish were closer to the toads. While they slurped down the Grabbers, I hauled ass.

It took me a minute to get sixty-five feet away and out of the aggro radius of the overgrown toads. Flaying my elbows, I crawled on the desolate earth through a dried-out bush. A bit further away I found a small but fairly deep flood gully and tried to hide. But I ended up stirring up the blood-red cockroaches that lived there. Thankfully they didn't attack me, instead ducking into their burrows.

Last night I had a clear plan of action but today... A wave of hopeless despair rolled over me. I felt it was all in vain. My parents would divorce, I would fail my citizenship test, move to Cali Bottom and never find success in Dis. It was too hard to level without using real money, and it would only get harder. I mean, I was just level two!

Thoughts were turning over and over in my head. The forest was imposing with its mere presence.

To my side, a level-eleven Acrid Wraith hovered past. Every crack in his joints seethed with green and black smoke. I pushed myself down into the tree trunk, not exactly thrilled at the idea of jumping right into another series of deaths. Most likely it would be a big waste of time. I probably couldn't even do one point of damage.

So I sat like that for more than an hour while the Wraith periodically popped up in my zone of visibility. By then I managed to gather my thoughts and stop feeling sorry for myself. I had already nearly decided to start fighting to level skills when I suddenly got a new one:

Stealth skill discovered!
Chance of remaining unnoticed by enemies increased by 1%.
Current level: 1.
Improve this skill by hiding near enemies of your level or higher!

You have received experience points for discovering a new skill: 10.
Experience points at present level (2): 350/900.

Well, well. That was new! One more bar appeared over every mob, showing my *Stealth* level. The Wraith groaned and stopped short. The

---

bar started filling in red. I fell to the earth. My visibility level froze in shaky balance. The Wraith spent some time boring its black eye sockets into the spot where I was hidden, then silently hovered in my direction.

The not-fully-decayed corpse was wearing scraps of browned cloth. It floated over the earth, enshrouded in wisps of dissipating black smoke. A hood covered its face if it even had one. Its feet were nowhere to be seen, as if dissolved in air, just absent in this reality.

Then my *Stealth* bar disappeared and I suddenly saw a notification:

Stealth check failed! You have been detected by Acrid Wraith!

There was nowhere to run. I was in Gloomwood. And why the hell try? This was why I came in here! Standing sharply, I interlocked my fingers and stretched upward, shaking the indecision from my muscles. The wraith came closer.

A *Hammerfist* swung through the air, making contact with the otherworldly abomination...

I missed, as I did the next few times. Its level was just too much higher than mine.

Then I died. With yet another swing of its

extended bony fingers, the wraith pierced my chest. It looked like the mob clenched my heart in its fist, dealing me a huge amount of critical damage.

The never-ending series of deaths, respawns, attempts to land blows and new deaths was drawing on and on. *Unarmed Combat* and *Resilience* went up by one level, while *Stoneskin* now lasted three seconds. But none of that was really changing anything. I was still dying just as quickly.

This was probably what it felt like to lose your mind from torture. The only difference was that I could stop this at any moment by just leaving Dis. And that was enough to get me through it. But when it was all over, my pent-up frustration found a way out. I started laughing softly and kept snickering like a madman, lying on the ground as the Acrid Wraith attacked me impotently.

You carry the mark of the Destroying Plague and have evaded fatal damage!
You have been given Curse of the Undead: all damage taken reduced by 100%!
This curse will remain active until you completely restore your health.

Mark of the Destroying Plague improved:

202

+1.
Chance to receive Curse of the Undead: 2%
Current level: 2.

While I lost my mind, unable to calm down, green and black spots covered my skin. My skin even receded in places, revealing bare flesh. The pain went completely numb, and the mob's attacks started to feel like light brushes. Seemingly, I had lost my sense of touch.

All the wraith's strikes lost power as soon as they touched my body. Recognizing that, I again just about lost it laughing, but got myself back together. Time was ticking. I picked up the culinary masterpiece that fell after my first death and one it, trying not to think about what it was made of.

You have eaten Roast Undead Rat Chitterlings.
Positive effect received: +1000% to skill levelling rate for 1 hour!

I calmly stood up and laid down a series of blows so fierce that, by minute two, I was withered and had lost tempo. None of them had done even one point of damage, but the games had begun. I now had a high-level training dummy to level my combat skills on. And the only drawback was that

I didn't have a weapon. I had given the bear bone club back to Undy and Vista took my sword. It would be nice to level more than just *Unarmed Combat*. Still, I had a truckload of Dis time ahead of me.

> **Unarmed Combat skill improved: +1.**
> **Unarmed Combat skill improved: +1.**
> **Unarmed Combat skill improved: +1.**
> **Unarmed Combat skill improved: +1.**

After skill level ten, the life of the acrid wraith began to slowly crawl down. First every tenth blow landed, taking one health, then I started hitting more and more often, slamming into its bony body. At that point crits started mixing in with the normal damage too.

When the Wraith's health was half emptied, I realized I was digging myself into a hole. If this mob died, I would no longer be in combat, so my health would start to regenerate. That would put me back to full health fairly quickly. The curse would go away and I'd have to die another hundred painful deaths in hopes of triggering the Mark. And that realization led me to a decision. I started hitting the wraith less often, and began moving deeper into Gloomwood to gather more hostile mobs.

And when I was done, I didn't even have to

aim. Every swing hit something.

Unarmed Combat skill improved: +1.
Damage dealt without a weapon increased by 110%
Attack accuracy increased by 110%.
Current level: 21.
Improve this skill by fighting enemies of your level or higher for additional bonuses and new special attacks.

Hammerfist improved: +1.
Cost to use: 2 mana points.
Deals 1150% of normal damage.
Ignores 20% of armor.

Pay a visit to a master of Unarmed Combat to learn more special attacks!

By evening I had nearly half the mobs in this part of the forest after me. There were huge spiders and black rats, reeking corpses and more wraiths. There was even one *rare* cursed bear with ribs outside its skin. And all these bumbling mobs were constantly getting in one another's way as they piled on me: biting, chomping, scratching, trying to tear me to pieces, puffing in acid clouds, wrapping me in spider webs and spitting poison. Right after Curse of the Undead activated I stopped feeling pain but, as the damage I took grew, it started to slowly come back. There was no time to think about why, but I quickly came to the conclusion it was some hidden downside to the curse.

Still, soon I grew so accustomed to the never-ending pain that I stopped feeling anything.

But then exhaustion started taking over. A few times I just sat down on the ground, piled on by the small herd of monsters and caught my breath. I waited for the exhaustion bar to zero out, then stood up and started methodically mowing down their ranks. My Unarmed Combat had reached level thirty, bringing my accuracy up so high that every attack hit my higher-level targets.

My mana was back up to two points, so I threw another *Hammer*, shattering an enemy skull with a satisfying crunch.

> **You have critically damaged Reeking Corpse: 84!**
> **Reeking Corpse is dead.**
>
> **Experience points received: 64.**
> *Experience points at present level (2): 817/900.*

The level-thirteen body collapsed into a pile and I had to take a few steps aside. The bodies of the dead mobs were not disappearing, just piling up to wait for me to take their loot. Experience was gushing like a river, the only thing holding me back was a lack of mana. In battle it regenerated very slowly, and I couldn't use *Hammer* as often as I might have liked. Normal blows meanwhile, took just two or three health.

I fought that crowd of mobs until almost midnight. In the fury of battle I felt no hunger, no thirst, but I did start missing more. My exhaustion bar never left the red zone and I had to take frequent breaks. Strange of course that my cursed body was getting tired, but I didn't wrack my brains over it and simply took it as a given.

You are now level 3!
5 free attribute points available!

I hit level three casually, sandwiched between yet another reeking corpse and the *rare* cursed bear. I was worried that my health would come back and the Curse of the Undead would leave me. But for some reason that didn't happen. My mana came all the way back though. I threw five points into intelligence, nearly doubling my mana reserves, and I started using *Hammer* more often.

When only five mobs remained, I got an achievement:

> ***Achievement unlocked: I'm on Fire – 3!***
> *Defeat 60 enemies who are more than five times higher level than you.*
> *This is why people like you get labeled a threat to the world! We're afraid to even imagine what will come next! A bit of friendly advice: you can keep your character info secret with the privacy settings in your profile.*
> ***Reward:*** *+100 health points.*

I didn't put that off either, hiding all the information. Now everyone else could only see my name, current level, and health and mana bars were shown to others only as a percentage scale.

By the time I had only one mob left, I stopped fighting and went to gather loot. The black rat, its snout shattered and paw broken, started hobbling over to me, trying to bite. I didn't kill it so the curse would stay with me.

The loot was rich. Enchanted *Corpse Ash* at five silver a piece took up a whole slot. Another was occupied by *Black Spider Webs* to sell to tailors, almost one gold per stack. And a third went to the web glands, which were used as an alchemy ingredient. They were worth no less.

Due to limitations on carrying weight and bag slots, I had to throw out my normal *gray* and *white* gear. Unfortunately, I couldn't wear any of it. It required level five at least. Another three slots went to *green* items: pants, boots and a jacket with bonuses to strength, agility and endurance. The last two were taken up by rare *blue* items.

As soon as I saw them, my heart skipped a beat and a hamster crawled out of somewhere deep in my subconscious. With a voice not its own, it screamed, "move your butt into town and get this loot stashed as deep in your chest as possible." And I was in complete agreement! Both the weapon and boots were incredible:

Skeleton Club
Rare
One-handed bashing weapon.
Damage: 24-36.
Durability: 80/80.
Possible effect on hit: corpse poison, dealing 7-9 damage.
Requires level: 15.
Sell price: 29 gold coins.
Chance of losing after death reduced by 50%.

Lynx Paws
Rare
Leather armor.
Armor: 5.
+7 Agility.
+7 Intelligence.

+7 Endurance.
Durability: 100/100.
Requires level: 10.
Sell price: 8 gold coins, 94 silver coins.
Chance of losing after death reduced by 50%.

I looked around and noticed that the bodies of the dead mobs had disappeared because I had taken their loot. All that was left nearby was the huge black rat. It was latched into my calf muscle and jerking its head, trying to rip off even one bit of flesh. I bopped it on the nose. For a few seconds it shook its head, coming back to its senses after my crit *Hammer*.

In the distance, I suddenly heard walking and breaking branches. I looked and saw a group of people tearing through the forest glade. The last thing I needed!

Sh-sh-shu-ugh! The space nearby lit up, and a fireball slammed into the rat's side. The fire covered its pelt and the rat squealed in pain. I smelled burning fur.

"Run, Scyth! Run, you idiot!" Tissa screamed.

The Dementors had come to pay me and the black rat a visit. Infect and Bomber unsheathed their blades as they ran, and Crawler came behind them, casting another fireball. Tissa took up the rear, enshrouded in the aura of a priestess of

Class-A Threat

Nergal the Radiant.

I could smell a noxious sweet scent coming off me. Then I remembered the ulcers and festering wounds all over my body...

And ran away from my classmates.

Chapter Seventeen

Crusher

I RAN THROUGH the darkness into the forest, covered in cold sweat. It was supposed to take me seventeen minutes to completely regenerate, and I could not let the Dementors see me before then. Otherwise it would all be for nothing. They'd smash me, identify me as the threat and take me down. And with such glee!

A potential L-class threat is no little Z-class necromancer with Y potential. For eliminating someone like me, Ed and company would be showered with bonuses they couldn't even dream of. And it would be easy for them to catch me with a buff to movement speed from the priestess. I hoped something was holding them back.

The trunks of dead trees flew past, and their dry branches poked holes in my skin. Finally, I reached the familiar ravine of red cockroaches and laid down. Much to my delight, I didn't get a single mob aggro'd the whole way, and my health was gradually regenerating: 72%... 81%... 97%...

My heart, which seemed about to burst out of my chest, calmed down. I even risked sticking my head out and immediately dove back in – the Dementors! But they saw me. My blood was boiling, quarts of adrenaline flooded into my real body. 100%!

Curse of the Undead removed.

In just a few beats of my mettlesome heart, my body started looking normal again. The ulcers and seething wounds disappeared, my muscles filled with blood and my flesh was covered with clean healthy skin.

"Scyth?" Ed appeared at the edge of the gully. "Are you hiding?"

The others appeared behind him. Tissa shook her head. Infect snorted. Bomber lowered his heavy shield to the ground, leaned on it and asked:

"Sheppard, are you an idiot? What made you wanna come to Gloomwood?"

"Hey yeah, good question," said Tissa. "When you asked where to level, I thought you'd come up with something better than out here!"

I got to my feet and climbed up. Ed extended

a hand, firmly grasped mine and helped me up.

"Thanks."

Crawler nodded, not turning an eye. He was expecting an answer.

I shook off the sticky clay and looked at myself from a third-person perspective: wearing only underwear, unarmed, level three... They were right, I looked like a mental midget.

"I was leveling on that side of the Tremitelle," I started explaining calmly. "Then some gankers came at me and I ran. I fell into the river and it carried me to this side. I figured I had nothing to lose from taking a look around and went into the woods."

"How did you get past the Grabbers?" Bomber asked in surprise.

"Uh, what are Grabbers?" I asked.

"They didn't get you? You got real lucky, Sheppard. They're these little fish like piranhas, they can eat up a character in seconds!"

"I guess I did get lucky. And then I got lucky again. I saw a boss in the distance. A huge wolf..."

" Crusher," Ed nodded. "Where'd you see him?"

"Right from this gully. He walked away, and I hid down here. Then I walked through the forest, got the stealth skill and figured this was a great place to level it. I crawled around a bit, too. Well, until the rat came after me."

"I see. And what are you gonna do next?"

"I want to get back to the city. Is that where you're going?"

"No, Scyth. We're looking for Crusher."

I looked at Tissa, she gave a slight nod. Aha, that meant they had made up and were going to try again, this time without hangers-on.

"You obsessed or something?"

"He's a new boss," Ed explained grudgingly. "We want to get *First Kill.*"

"An achievement? I see. Alright, thanks for the help. I'm gonna head. See you in school."

I headed for the river, but didn't even reach the bank before Crawler shouted:

"Hey, Scyth! You're taking the hard way! Just die and you'll be back in the cemetery where you belong. You've got nothing to lose, right?"

"Oh yeah..." I agreed. "I just want to get there on my own."

Oh, nether! But the Stone Grabbers! Damn! I mean, they'd eat me right up in full view of the Dementors, then they'd see me respawn right where I fell! And I had so much in my bag! Nether!

"You sure?" Ed snorted.

His hand lit up. A flame flickered in his fist, growing and filling with plasma.

"I mean, I could help! It won't hurt... probably."

He laughed and raised his hand, closing it.

I saw a vision of the future before my eyes: my *blue* loot would drop, I would respawn, Tissa's eyes would go wide in amazement and delight, then Ed would put two and two together and realize something was up...

"Wait! Don't kill me! I don't want you to."

"Alex, what's the point?" Tissa asked. "You won't survive. The river is teeming with Grabbers, just look."

I took a glance despite myself and saw the surface of the water frothing. Those big-toothed little fish were really whipping a fit. They could see us and were jumping excitedly out of the water, rolling out the red carpet.

I shuddered, remembering what it felt like to have hundreds of toothy maws ripping my flesh at the same time. It was like being run up and down a cheese grater. A shiver went up my spine. But I couldn't let them kill me – I'd be giving myself away.

"I said 'no!'"

"No?"

"No. What's so hard to understand about that, Rodriguez?"

Unlike normal, Ed didn't tell me this was Dis and here he was Crawler. Instead he fell silent, thinking it over, then walked up closer. There was no fireball in his hand, he had canceled the cast.

"Something isn't adding up here, Scyth. I

know you're a smarty pants and always look out for yourself. Me killing you is for your own good. You'll save a bunch of time and lose nothing. Your experience will stay the same. You don't have any gear on. Plus, you don't want to see what the Grabbers bite like. I'm the one who would lose one rep with the city, so I'd be taking the hit. I mean, this is just a friendly favor, and you're refusing? It's weird."

"Are you a sadist? A pyromaniac? Have you ever tried burning yourself?"

"A pyro... what?" Ed frowned. "Burning? What about burning? You'll die right away, you're all squishy and my fireball will take you down in one second. But the Grabbers will take a long time... And yet you don't want me to help! That just isn't right..."

"Come on, just leave him alone, Crawler." Tissa said, walking up. "What if he's just afraid of fire? Right Alex? You got pyrophobia? Want me to kill you? It'll be light magic. I could slap you with a *Hand of Nergal*... One and done!"

Seeing the frantic chatter, Malik and Hung walked up. Now they were also suggesting ways of killing me one worse than the next:

"What if I just cut your head off? Scyth, you won't even feel it!"

"Listen to him, yeah! What about me? I could just slit your throat," came Infect. "Or first break your back. That'll take the pain away!"

"A *Light Arrow* to the eye!"

"Better a *Wall of Fire*! So he can't change his mind and run!"

The Dementors were having fun discussing and snickering at every suggestion. Bomber was laughing so much he fell into the gully, taking Infect with him. That caused a new outburst. What simpletons! Sure, boys will be boys, but Tissa found it so funny her eyes were tearing up!

To hell with these idiots! I couldn't have thought up a better opportunity to leave the game if I tried. I opened the command menu and looked at the exit button.

> **You cannot exit Disgardium while in combat mode.**
>
> *To exit, leave combat mode or activate emergency exit by using the command on your immersion pod or in your interface. The battle will be considered lost, and your character will be considered dead!*

While I read the message in confusion, the laughter went silent all at once. Ed shouted:

"Crusher is here! Bomb, get up! Tissa, buff! Then all heal on tank! Inf, dust!"

But the well-organized group already knew what to do without his commands. Bomber was too slow getting out of the gully though. And that threw a wrench into Crawler's plan.

The monstrous black wolf lunged at the closest one to him. That was Tissa. She froze in his jaws like an inanimate doll. Crusher turned his head, shaking out ten percent of the priestess' health.

Infect saved her. The swarthy thief used a class ability, throwing a handful of enchanted dust into the boss's eyes. Blood gushed out. Crusher unclenched his jaws and, whimpering like a dog, started to scratch his snout with his paws.

Tissa ran behind her friends', healed herself and buffed the group. The Dementors' bodies were enshrouded in flashes of light and icons appeared by their names for regeneration, light shield and a movement-speed bonus.

Bomber was already standing at the boss's snout by then and, hiding behind his shield, started generating aggro with his sword. Infect was nestled up tight against Crusher playing hole-punch at the speed of a sewing machine. His daggers flickered in the air, dripping poison. Crawler was launching various types of fireball, starting with fast and frequent bolts and ending with incendiary nuclei with decaying DoT.

It all happened so fast I kept looking without moving and totally forgot what I wanted. What I wanted was to run and now was the best possible time. But for some reason I didn't.

The skill and exactingness of my classmates' work captivated me, so I kept watching. I was especially impressed by Melissa Schafer. She was casting concentrated spells, healing Bomber or healing up Infect if he landed under a *Swipe* – the boss's ability to hit all melee fighters. And all the while she was dealing damage with *Hand of Nergal*...

The Dementors had taken no less than half its health. The wolf howled, summoning his pack. Next to him, five elite level-thirteen wolves materialized out of thin air.

"Got 'em!" Hung shouted.

Generating aggro, the warrior stuck his sword into the ground, and a vibration emanated out, reducing even my health points. All the mobs threw themselves on him. Tissa bit her lip and concentrated only on the tank. A healing flash of green extended from her outstretched hand toward Hung.

"Focus on fire!" Ed commanded.

It was the first time I had seen him like this. Calm, confident, and sure of what to do next. He stuck a flaming bolt into the fur of one of the summoned wolves. It burned up. Infect and Bomber turned to him and got him away in a few seconds.

"Next!" Ed announced, throwing a fireball.

Class-A Threat

Like that, they cleared all the adds and turned back to the alpha. Crusher's health points were crawling steadily downward.

Just then, Tissa noticed me, swallowing a mana potion. She threw away the empty flagon and shouted:

"Alex! You idiot! Run the heck away! Run..."

And so I ran. We all ran, because Crusher gave a fearsome howl. And that gave us all the Fear effect, another of the boss's abilities. Though our minds could recognize what was happening, our bodies ran in panic. I totally lost control: I couldn't say anything and my body was acting all on its own. My mouth gaped in a heart-rending cry, my hair was standing on end... Nearby, Infect and Tissa started wailing in fear, and Ed was way out in left field, fallen into the gully.

Over the ten long seconds the boss's ability lasted, I managed to run up to my knee in the water. The *Grabbers* were all around and had already taken down a third of my health. And that was fifty hitpoints no matter how I looked at it. Quickly pumping my legs, I ran out of the river. But there I was awaited by a shameful scene.

Without Tissa's healing, Crusher had chewed Bomber to death. The body of the tank was lying in the same place and not disappearing. Clearly Hung was hoping the priestess would respawn him.

The wolf jumped into the gully. From there I quickly heard Crawler yelping as well. A mage's rags are not exactly a warrior's plate armor. No protection.

And next came Tissa. The wolf ripped her chest open with its massive claws and landed a *Swipe*. Tissa was cut in half.

Infect tried to escape by disappearing, encircling himself with a smoke screen but didn't consider the wolf's sense of smell. Crusher tore him from invisibility and, holding him down with his paws, ripped off his head with his mouth. Then he turned toward me.

With no hope whatever, I activated *Stoneskin* and got ready to use a *Hammer*. There was no reason to run, but this way I might be able to get one hit in on his ghastly fanged snout.

A moment later the boss jumped and he was next to me, slamming me into the ground. His nightmarish fangs grabbed me by the head and his jaws clamped shut. My health bar was instantly empty. I respawned right away, but died again at once.

This time, four deaths was all it took...

You carry the mark of the Destroying Plague and have evaded fatal damage!
You have been given Curse of the Undead: all damage taken reduced by 100%!

This curse will remain active until you completely restore your health.

Mark of the Destroying Plague improved: +1.
Chance to receive Curse of the Undead: 3%
Current level: 3.

I snorted as I knocked out one of Crusher's fangs with a *Hammer*. It occurred to me that, in the Tristad cemetery right now, Crawler was probably turning his head in surprise trying to figure out where his loser classmate, cursed geek Alex Sheppard, was.

Chapter Eighteen

Emissary's License

A NEW MESSAGE notification beeped. In the corner of my field of vision, Tissa's icon flashed.

*Player **Tissa (Melissa Schafer)** would like to add you as a friend. Accept?*
You may set privacy settings to determine friends' information access level about your character.

First I set them to maximum, so it wouldn't even show my online status and location on the map. Only after that did I accept her friendship. All that time I was trying to kick the big wolf away, but it was in vain. He weighed around one ton, and my strength was just two. His stinking saliva covered my face when he, roaring savagely, gnawed me like a bone. Everything around smelled like a dog and, enraged, I bit him right back.

The wolf pressed me to the ground with his paw, clenched my head in his teeth and turned his head, trying to tear it off. My neck would not give. The damage wasn't registering, but I also couldn't move. So I was flailing my fists at random, not forgetting to throw a *Hammer* when I had the mana. The special ability took much less health than it did from normal mobs, even when it was a crit. And normal blows, meanwhile, barely got through the boss's thick hide.

You have damaged Crusher: 19.

Tissa wrote a PM asking where I'd gone. I answered that I was running from Crusher in the woods. Then she warned me that they would be changing into their backup outfits and coming back in forty minutes. Some gear had dropped, and Crawler was huffing and puffing at losing his epic cloak. There was just a ten percent chance, but it dropped!

I told them it was no rush. I said I had climbed up a tree, and the wolf was trying to get me, but their valuable stuff was right where they left it, including Crawler's epic. Tissa answered with a big greeting from Ed containing more threats than anything sensible. But I understood.

Or to be more accurate I understood now. Epic is epic. If Crag was willing to act shitty for some *blue*, and of quite a low level, what could I say about *purple* gear? The chance of getting it in the sandbox must have been just a hair below zero.

> **You have damaged Crusher: 1.**
> **Miss!**
> **Miss!**
> **You have damaged Crusher: 14.**
> **Miss!**
> **Miss!**
> **Miss!**
> **You have damaged Crusher: 2.**
> **Miss!**

That was how my fight with the boss was going. He wasn't using *Fear* or calling his pack, just methodically gnawing, growling and trying to bite off chunks. I thought it was good that he wasn't controlled by a person like Dargo. Otherwise, he would know something was off and... give up? Write to tech support? Haha.

With a laugh, I kept going with my fists, and the wolf's life bar crawled inexorably downward. Ten minutes later, he was all out of health.

With a tenth of his last percent of life remaining, he gave a whimper and ran off, losing interest. My eyes were covered with wolf spit, the moonlight cast shadows off the trees and I didn't realize right away that I was alone in the glade. But as soon as I did, I shot to my feet. No, no my dear. You won't be getting away!

Crusher was crawling through a bush, dragging his feet. There was a tree in front of him, and he was poking his big snout into the trunk as if struck blind. For a moment I was reminded of AT in German Shepherd mode with low batteries, and I felt bad. The omnipotent and previously undefeated king of the forest was now being made to run from a level-three noob.

But I had to hurry. Battle mode was still active, and I needed to lose the curse or hide far away before the Dementors got back. I still hadn't decided.

I walked around the wolf and grabbed him by his fearsome furry snout. He made a vain attempt to break free, his huge teary eyes squinted and his tongue lolled freely out of his mouth. He raised a paw and placed it on my chest. His colossal claw left a scratch, taking some scraps of skin and flesh with it, but it wasn't damage, just a visual effect. The claw got caught on a rib and stuck. The bone didn't break, but my legs shuddered under the weight. Then he licked my face. What?

I nodded, stroked the wolf's ear... and slammed his wet black plate-sized nose with a

Hammer. My vision was fully occupied by system messages. But before reading them, I looked into my bag, pulled a couple of the cheapest *greens* out and threw them to the ground, making room for the loot from the boss.

You have critically damaged Crusher: 47!
Crusher is dead.

Experience points received: 500.
Experience points at present level (4): 310/2100.

You are now level 4!
5 free attribute points available!

Achievement unlocked: First Kill: Crusher!
Of all the players in your sandbox, you were the first to kill this local boss. Crusher, a titanic level-15 wolf, was once alpha of the Gloomwood wolf pack. While a pup, he was touched by the fell breath of a Sleeping God. With time his judgment grew cloudy and one day he killed his entire pack, including his own cubs. That gave him new powers: the ability to summon his former pack and Ghastly Howl, which strikes fear into the

hearts of his enemies.

Now you have laid Crusher to rest forever but, before he shuffled off this mortal coil, he inadvertently transferred you a modicum of his power.

Reward: *active skill Ghastly Howl.*

Ghastly Howl
Active skill.
Current level: 1.
When you howl, your enemies are filled with fear. The blood turns to ice in their veins, their soul sinks into their boots, their hair stands on end and they run away in panic.

This ability works on all enemies, however, the higher their level, the higher their chance of ignoring it.
Duration: 10 seconds.
Active radius: 30 feet.

All hail the hero!
Would you like to make your name public? Doing so will give +100 reputation with the city of Tristad and +5 fame.

No! No matter how much I wanted easy rep with the city, the unwanted attention was less desirable.

Nope, nooope. I refused the privilege.

Attention all sandbox players!
An anonymous player has successfully made the First Kill of the Gloomwood boss **Crusher**! Residents and visitors of Tristad, hats off to **an anonymous player**! All hail the hero! All hail **an anonymous player**!

Less than a second passed and I was inundated with friendship requests from Crawler, Bomber and Infect. Messages poured in from Tissa:

"What the heck?"

"How?"

"Tell me that wasn't you!"

"Actually no, tell me it was you!"

"We'll be right there!"

I accepted friendship with the guys and Tissa's contradictory messages were joined by direct ones from them:

"What dropped?" Crawler wrote. "Scyth, damn, what the crap?"

"The loot belongs to us!" Bomber claimed presumptively, adding some friendly threats. "Sheppard, I'll strangle you! I'll knock your head off! I'll drown you in a urinal in school! I'll smear you!"

"Wait!" Crawler again. "Scyth, god damn, how?"

"Don't do a thing! Wait for us! Guard the

cloak! Pick up the loot and hide! Run away! Don't go anywhere! Better just die! An epic? An epic! Come on, answer! I'll break your neck!"

Reading these erratic messages, I imagined what was happening among the Dementors. They had a common goal and they didn't even consider that I might have my own opinion. They imagined that their higher level gave them the right to order me around. It looked very much like what happened in the real world with citizenship statuses.

Oh well, they'd see they were wrong. It wasn't that I wanted to keep all this stuff necessarily, but talking to me with that tone? They should have had some respect. I mean, I was a hero! First Kill! I smiled sarcastically, but then rushed off because I couldn't stay where I was. A pair of green eyes were glimmering from behind the trees and, to be honest, I wasn't sure what to expect.

The attribute points from level-up were placed into endurance and strength. And I did it as I ran up the river, ignoring everything Ed and company wrote. I answered only Tissa: "I didn't touch your stuff or the loot from the boss. It's *green*. It isn't safe, so I had to leave."

The curse would pass in three minutes so I jumped into the river and took broad paddles to the other bank, not even noticing the frothing

Stone Grabbers. I discovered the swimming skill and, clearly, that helped me reach the other side faster.

From there I had to be very careful. Curse of the Undead was gone, and the stuff in my bag made me want to avoid any fights. So I crawled cautiously, staring into the darkness until my eyes hurt and avoiding any mobs, which leveled *Stealth* and *Night Vision* by three points each.

Coming out of the forest, I could see the glow of Tristad. The city wall was patrolled by guardsmen with torches. My goal was close at hand. I figured I could enter the city, catch my breath, then throw this stuff in my chest. And I had plenty: beyond the *blue* and three chopped-up monsters in my bag, I had loot from Crusher.

Locket with a Girl's Portrait
Unique quest item.
This dull, dingy bronze locket seems to have been chewed by a very powerful set of jaws. It contains a portrait of a smiling young girl who lived in Tristad several years ago. Nevertheless, the one who once loved her can barely recall her face.
Someone remembers this locket. Find them.

It was a quest item, but had no information about rewards. And I didn't get an actual quest.

But all my theoretical experience said a unique quest item taken from a boss wasn't going to lead to recovering five stolen chandeliers from some kobolds for one copper or one experience. Basically, I was not going to give this locket to anyone if I could help it.

And any player in the sandbox would sell their soul for the thing in my bag's last slot.

> **Whistle of Summoning**
> *Legendary*
> *Unique item.*
> *Single use.*
> *When activated, permanently summons mount: **Legendary Spectral Wolf.***
> *Requires level: 40.*

The road to the city was deserted. As much as the players loved this game, everyone in the sandbox was at school. And the night before a weekday was not the best time to be in Dis. Every kid got no more than three passes per semester, with demerit points on the citizenship tests given for any beyond that. While in school, it wasn't a hard choice. Dis wasn't going anywhere, and the chance to get good grades came only once in a lifetime.

I made sure the road was clear and quickly walked up to the city gates. Just fifty yards remained when an alarm rang out – enemy near! I glanced at the mini-map. Red dots for Crag, Vista and Rashidos were approaching me from three different directions, cutting off my path to the city.

Aw nether! I began to fret, but quickly got myself together. My gear? It was all digital items, just ones and twos. At level twenty I wouldn't give a damn about this old crap. Sure it was a shame to lose the mount, but maybe I'd be able to do better than a *blue*. Better to lose it than reveal myself as a threat.

Crag walked up and raised his hand in a gesture of peace. His hangers-on were standing to my side with their weapons drawn.

"Scyth old buddy! I've missed you! We've been waiting so long! We combed the whole town! Yesterday, today... We even had to get in touch with your parents to make sure you were actually in Dis!" The warrior chortled. "Don't be surprised if your mom mentions your new friend Tobias, by the way. You never know, your mommy just might ask about me..."

"End him, Toby!" Vista exclaimed. Why was she acting so bloodthirsty? Was this all over that torn dress? Or had she gotten a taste for easy money?

"Calm down, babe," Crag looked at her unhappily. "Why would we want to kill him right away? So we have to chase him around the whole sandbox later? He'll give us what we're after, isn't that right, lil' Scythy?"

"Of course, Crag," I nodded. "You win. I admit it. Dying really hurts. I spent two days in the woods to stay away from you but, as you can see, it was no use. So why should I get jumpy? I suggest we all go to the tavern together. I'll take the *blue* belt out of my chest and give it to you."

"Good boy," said the warrior. His lips stretched back into a smile, but his eyes didn't look friendly. He was pointing the sword at me and slashed it in the air a few times in front of me, making a whishing sound. "Not trying to be rude, this is just payback. For making us wait. We'll see you at the tavern..."

And he swung his sword.

Chapter Nineteen

Gankers and Dementors

A SKY FULL of stars lit up the wasteland beyond the city wall. The illegal traders were gone and I didn't see anyone who could might to my aid.

If Crag thought my agreement to give up the rare *Corrupted Scale Belt* automatically meant I would let him just kill me, he was mistaken. What was more, it no longer made any sense to give him anything.

He could have taken the easy way. We were on our way to settle it! But now, I guess it'd have to be the hard way. All these thoughts flashed by in an instant while I looked around for the button to activate *Ghastly Howl*. At the same time, I ran toward Vista, dodging Crag's sword as it cleaved the air. The lupine howl echoed off the city walls and rolled to the edge of the forest but, to put it lightly, it was not an impressive sight.

Crag shuddered, Rashidos's jaw hung down in incomprehension. It only worked properly on Vista. She screamed and ran away in panic, which gave me an opening. So I beat it...

... but didn't consider that my opponent was a warrior. He made a *charge* in front of me. His powerful armored body slammed into me, throwing me a few yards and taking a quarter of my health. I somersaulted aside and jumped to my feet. But Rashidos was already flying at me, waving his club. But an instant before he hit I put my *Stoneskin* on and held out a hand in defense. And I used my other hand to land a *Hammerfist*.

You have damaged player Rashidos (Oleg Dmytryk): 61.

The skill ignored some of his armor stat and left a dent in his chainmail. He stumbled back. Unfortunately, that took less than ten percent of his health. I had to start ramping up my strength as soon as possible. I took the opportunity and ran a wide curve toward the city gates.

A half-second's squeal of cloven air presaged another *charge*. Another quarter of my health down, I was lying on the ground. Vista's wailing grew more distant, but the other two gankers were next to me as soon as I got to my feet. One was behind, and the other right in front.

"You've really stepped in it now! Stand up straight!" the warrior ordered, preparing for an attack. "I'm gonna teach you a lesson..."

"You aren't gonna touch him," Crawler came up to us. His epic red cloak was fluttering gently despite the lack of wind. "He's with us."

All three of us, me Crag and Rashidos turned our heads toward Ed in surprise. The other Dementors were standing behind him: Hung bared his teeth, Malik walked out of stealth for show, Tissa frowned, warming a ball of light in her hand, a *Hand of Nergal*.

"What the heck, Crawler? Since when do the Dementors let in noobs?"

"Ever since we kicked out all the dumbasses, dumbass," Tissa said.

"You know, he doesn't exactly look like a Dementor," Crag snorted distrustfully. "What, you couldn't even get him equipped? And no clan emblem..."

"He doesn't have a clan emblem because he hid it, douche!" Hung said, baring his teeth. "So he thinks he's big and strong now? How about a duel? Warrior versus warrior, even-steven!"

Tissa hushed my gaze of incomprehension. I gave a very slight nod. We'd handle it later. Vista froze ten steps away. She knew the drill and was keeping her distance. "Get lost!" the priestess of

---

Nergal threw out with just her lips and her trail went cold. She just exited Dis.

"Found the idiot," Crag grumbled. "You're three levels higher. You already have *Destruction*, one hundred percent. And better equip!"

"Aw nether, what idiot?" Tissa exclaimed. "So the fact that Alex is level four and totally naked didn't throw you off?"

"What about it?" the ganker didn't understand. "He's a noob and a victim, you gotta milk that. Or I should have..." he corrected himself. "But no matter what he owes me a *blue*! We agreed on that before you took him!"

"What *blue*?" Infect asked, on guard, his voice ringing out from behind Rashidos' shoulder although he was cloaked. "What could possibly have made him want to give you a *blue*, if he doesn't even have any gear, and walks around Dis in his underwear?"

"Scyth?" Crawler raised a brow.

"I had two options: never stick my nose out of the city again, die or give up the *blue*. I got it in the temple crypt from the Cursed Lich. I can't wear it yet, I wanted to hold onto it but then this guy," I said, nodding at Crag, "noticed and forced me to sell it to him. I refused, then they took me down in the forest while I leveled *Cooking*. And now they found me again, so I had to let them have it."

"So this is who you were running from?

When you fell in the river?" Ed asked, just about catching me in an inconsistency.

"No, that was someone else."

"I see. Well, all items of quality higher than unusual are property of the whole clan," Crawler declared to the gankers. "We can decide what to do with that *blue*. You're free to go, you degenerates!"

"Got it?" Crag took a step forward, but Bomber took a step to meet him. He was a head taller and a good deal beefier.

"Questions?" Hung spit at Tobias's feet, knocked his plate-armored hand on his head then gave him a light head-butt. A dull metallic clang rang out. Crag walked back and Bomber shrugged: "No questions."

"This isn't what we agreed on, guys," Rashidos said. "This isn't fair! You're gonna have big..."

The sound of daggers cutting through chain mail interrupted him. He began to twitch. The thief's curved blade stuck out of the ganker's mouth. Meanwhile a hand with another dagger appeared from the shadows and ran under his chin. Crag's partner collapsed and headed to respawn. Malik hid his weapon, looked at Crawler, nodded and took all the loot.

"Come on, what the heck?" Crag whined, looking around nervously. "At least give back the gear! I'll let it go, I have no problems with you! Not

Scyth, or you, or the *blue*."

"Good," Ed agreed easily. "If you so much as look at him wrong again, you or your loser friends, we'll put you all on our KoS list. And you just know half the clans in the sandbox will join us. Jackals like you need to be bled out. Is that what you want?"

"No," Crag whispered barely audibly.

"Alright, get out of my sight. Tissa, slap him with a *Palm* if he's still in range in five seconds..."

Stomping noisily, the warrior ran into town. The guard at the gate blocked his path and said something. Crag stashed his sword. Clearly, he also had an unsavory reputation in Tristad.

"Okay, Scyth. Now tell us what actually happened with Crusher," Ed said, leading his gaze over Crag.

I was ready for this. And with my mouth already open to recite my answer, he raised a hand in warning:

"Just so you know, we've studied the mechanics of Dis very well. Infect died last and saw that the boss had more life than you would have been able to take down. Even considering the DoTs still on him – burning and poisons – you couldn't have taken him down even if you had all epics on. The difference in level is just too high."

"Yeah Alex, tell the truth," Tissa supported her leader. "You know how important Crusher was to us. It was our chance to take First Kill. But you not only got it, somehow you made the boss transition into its next phase. And don't say you didn't take the achievement! There was no one else around!"

"I took the achievement, but that stays between us," I admitted. "But as for the next phase... What do you mean?"

"Just what I said," Crawler answered. "When we went back, the boss's body was gone. We took that *green* you left there to trick us, but then we had to run. And you know why? You do and should have warned us!"

"Sorry, what?" I shouted, pretending not to understand.

"Crusher was back. But now he isn't a boss, just a normal elite mob. Punisher. The same level, looks almost the same. But now he's like... not exactly alive," Ed started chuckling hysterically, but quickly got himself together.

"What does that mean? There's a new boss called Punisher, but it isn't a boss, just an elite? And someone already killed him? I mean... you said he's not alive..."

"He's not alive because he became a zombie, Sheppard!" Hung boomed out in his deep bass. "A huge zombie wolf for Christ's sake!"

"Pf-f..." I replied, trying to affect disbelief.

Before the lethal blow I dealt to Crusher, a

hidden effect of the *Mark of the Destroying Plague* kicked in. The system gave me the option to infect my victim. The mad alpha of the pack died, but was *infected*. Did that mean he was back? I didn't get any notifications, and nothing new appeared in my interface. But I figured it was worth popping back into Gloomwood to see how the new mob would treat me.

"Boys, Tissa, I'm out of here! How should I know about these phases and other problems? I've only been really playing for three days now! I have no idea how any of this stuff works!"

"Alright, we'll go with that," Crawler accepted my explanation. "Snowstorm must be up to something again. Last year's escape from the nether wasn't enough for them!"

"What about the League of Goblins? How did those little green vermin have the brains to take over the entire criminal world?" Malik exclaimed. "My brother plays a gnome in big Dis. He works in a bank. Some goblin crime ring has scared off all their clients! Those little pipsqueaks aren't afraid of anything! And now they're shaking hands with the mayor of the capital!"

"So people don't control everything there?" Hung asked in surprise. "Why..."

"Alright, enough rattling!" Crawler barked. "So then Scyth. We aren't going to hurt you, but we will be very disappointed if you don't tell us the truth. Something happened after we got wiped. Something that killed the boss. And we would really like you to show us the real loot, not this trash. Hung!"

The tank nodded and shook the two *green* items out of the air.

"Hm? Go get them, they're yours. And give us what belongs to us."

"What the heck makes it yours exactly?" I freaked out. My nerves were shot to hell with all the stresses of the last few days and nights. "You said it yourself: you got wiped. That's all! And I could have taken down Crusher myself without your help!"

"What?" Crawler choked with indignation.

"What is this heresy, Scyth?!" Bomber asked, picking his jaw up off the floor. "Did Crag hit your head too hard or something?"

Tissa gasped for air in silence, but her eyes were laughing. I realized that the best approach to hide the most important facts was to reveal things of secondary concern. To the nether with that, blind luck would take me.

"Well Dementors, let's do this!" I called them closer. "I'll show you that I can take down a rare on my own, explain how it happened, and you leave me alone. And you don't claim the loot from the boss. Shake on it?"

Crawler looked at my outstretched hand

mockingly. Hung jabbed him in the shoulder:

"Yes!"

"Alright, Scyth," Crawler squeezed my hand and the other Dementors put their hands in on top. "And you'll also explain how you got three levels in less than three days."

"Ok. Then stay here, I'll be right back."

They didn't have time to answer, just Infect grumbled in dismay when I grabbed the *green* and ran into town. I quickly reached the tavern, threw everything of value in my trunk, filling it completely and putting what didn't fit in my inventory. And meanwhile I put on my novice's canvas clothes. A quarter hour later, bombarded by messages from my classmates, I was back.

"Well?" Ed asked impatiently.

"So..." I looked at all of them one after the next. Still trying to find the path of least resistance, I pointed at Tissa: "Melissa, kill me."

"I don't understand..." she drew out her words. "Kill as in to death?"

"Exactly. But make it quick, I want to get at least three hours of sleep before school."

"Come on, *Palm* this freak already!" Infect pleaded. "Tissa!"

A clump of condensed light lit up her hand. Tissa waved and I was held down tight. I just about went up to my knee in the dirt, but I was still alive. An indifferent white beam drifted in my direction, a bolt stuck in my chest and I died. Nether! I guess light magic wasn't that kind after all!

The phantom pain of death slowly faded away while I lay there lifeless, staring at the Dementors.

"Crawler, I think he tricked us," Hung exclaimed.

"I don't understand," Crawler shook his head. "Where's the trick? He could have just left Dis. Why make us kill him?"

"To make us look like bigger idiots than Crag!" Malik shouted, enraged.

Tissa kneeled next to me and, looking into my dead eyes, asked:

"Alex, what's going on? Are you making fun of us?"

Alright, it was time. I got up to the shouts of amazement and splayed my shoulders, stretching my stiff muscles after respawn. Tissa frowned as usual when she didn't understand something. I answered:

"I wouldn't make fun of you. You're serious people, you don't like jokes. But if you want, kill me again. The same thing will happen."

"What the crap? How?" Crawler asked. "And how the hell aren't you dead? Why do you respawn without full health?"

"I'll reveal my debuff info for a minute. Look carefully..." Burbling their lips, the boys slowly read the description of Patrick's curse. "Basically, I got back up and hit him again. Hundreds of deaths, guys, hun-dreds..."

Tissa, who was the fastest reader, looked dreamily into the starry sky. And when the others had figured it out, Ed "Crawler" Rodriguez gave me a slap on the back. And with all his dumb might, he hugged me and lifted me up, tearing my feet off the ground and shouting right into my ear:

"Sheppard, you son of a bitch! We can use your buff to clear raids in hard mode!"

"What?" Just in case, I walked away, a bit closer to the city. "What the crap makes you say we? I didn't agree on any 'we!'"

Crawler exchanged glances with his clanmates and announced ceremoniously:

"We officially invite you to join our clan..."

Chapter Twenty

Friendly Strangers

DREAMS REFLECT reality. Or so said one ancient psychologist. The three hours I managed to sleep before school, though, didn't reflect any reality. In my dream I accepted Crawler's invitation and joined the Dementors.

Ed's idea was basically like this: raid dungeons would not reload as long as at least one group member was still inside. And the only survivor after a wipe would always be me. But I could use the *Stone of Resurrection* to bring Tissa back. They told me it was an extremely expensive crafted item that could raise any dead group member as long as they were still in their body. And a player could lie as a corpse as long as at least one member of their group remained in the raid.

The Dementors had emptied out a large part

of their clan stores to get the money for this artifact. They were planning to take advantage of Infect's invisibility. He could leave combat mode, raise Tissa, then the priestess of the Radiant God could use her ability to bring back all the rest. A great idea. This way the whole clan wouldn't have to run back after a wipe to redo a whole ins from the beginning, just hoping no one else got in there in the meantime. But as it happened, the high-level mobs would drag Infect out of stealth and tear him to bits. The artifact was no use, but they hadn't sold it at auction. They kept it.

In our whole sandbox, there was only one raid dungeon that hadn't been passed yet. It appeared long ago in the Olton Quarries and was called Evil from the Depths. The minimum recommended level for it was eighteen. And no one in the sandbox was that strong. It took Crawler nearly two years to hit sixteen. And after two years in the sandbox were up, players got forcibly transferred to big *Disgardium*, even if they wanted to stay.

Basically, all that time Evil from the Depths was sitting there ripening, expanding, conquering new territory. Now, the reward for passing it was the stuff of fairy tales. The city council increased the prize for passing Evil just about once a month. The bosses and mobs inside were growing in level, and along with that the drops improved qualitatively. And most importantly, it was a guaranteed achievement: first pass and First Kill of a final boss, who few had even seen yet.

So basically, I dreamed I joined the clan and we passed the Olton Quarries. And I didn't die there, instead getting taken by the Curse of the Undead. And the very same day a hunt was declared for me not only by my own clan, but the whole sandbox, including Patrick the drunkard. In my dream they were chasing me around Tristad with torches and pitchforks then caught me. And before once and for all expelling me from Dis, Chief Councilman Whiteacre ceremoniously announced:

"Undead must lie in a grave!"

And Patrick nodded, saying: "Cursed undead! Could have found a little copper for old uncle Patrick!"

My dream was so overwhelming I almost chickened out, and played sick to skip school. I would have had to fake an illness for that and send it to the system. I didn't actually know how to do that, but I had heard it was possible and I was about to look into it. I heard, for example, of classmates who had raised their body temperature by drinking a ton of coffee or by taking a few drops of iodine.

While I thought about it, not getting out of bed, my mom walked in and unceremoniously forced me awake so she could get my bedsheets off to be cleaned. I meanwhile decided it was easier to sit through my lessons than figure out how to get to a pharmacy for some iodine to raise my temperature.

I got to school as usual with Eve. She was talking the whole time, but the color of her room in her new house seemed like such a trivial problem that I just about slapped her. Good thing I held back. I mean, was she even remotely at fault for having an easier life?

The city was blanketed by a featureless sheet of clouds. The skies were only cleared over neighborhoods for citizens of category D or above and our neighborhood was not one of those.

Eve, sensing that I was getting farther from her and not listening, jabbed me in the shoulder!

"Alex!"

"Sorry, I wasn't listening. What were you talking about?"

"A gift for my birthday! I asked my parents to get me the 'Total Babe...' It's a package including plastic surgery, face correction and..." Eve went a deep shade of red.

"What?"

"Alex! Don't make me say it!"

"A sex machine?"

"No dummy!"

Eve got mad and didn't say another word to me until we arrived.

I knew that her gift included a robot lover though. And it would teach her... everything. My parents had an old-fashioned mindset when it came to that stuff. They thought all that was overkill. Most kids tended to agree. It wasn't a cool thing to own. Admitting that you used a doll, even one identical to a person was basically social suicide. And that was why no one talked about them in school, but I knew for sure that Aaron Quan got one from his parents that looked like Denise Le Bon. Sure, he denied it, but he slept with her at least once. Haha, of course we believe you, Aaron "Robolover" Quan!

Just as an aside, Denise Le Bon got paid one hundred million phoenixes for the right to use her image in erotic VR worlds and as a model for pleasure robots. As my father loved to joke, humanity opted not to mend their flaws, just make them less harmful.

In school after first period, Ed and the guys dragged me out into the schoolyard and started giving me another go around. At night I refused them and left the game as Bomber cursed ornately. In the morning they were standing watch at the front door of the school, but I arrived with the bell and Tissa just stared at me all class. From behind, Hung kicked me in the back and Malik whispered my name forebodingly: "A-aa-le-ee-ex!" When I turned around, he had his hands folded at his chest, pretending to pray. I shook my head and didn't look back again.

"You little bitch, Sheppard, don't make me push hard!" Hung pressed me to the wall with his hand, holding me in place.

"Alex, hun, why do you break so easy? You're like a little girl!" Tissa joined in on the fun. "Oh well, if you don't want to be in the clan, that's your right. But join a group and come with us. We'll get the achi and you can go. How about that?"

"Aw nether, Alex!" Ed shook a fist at the wall next to my head. "What the heck?"

"God! Boys, Tissa, do you realize you're making this much harder than it has to be? Who taught you to negotiate like this? I could get through that dungeon on my own once I level up. That's one. And two, you can't intimidate me with violence! Okay, let's say I join the group, we go to the ins and you die. I could just not use the *Stone of Resurrection*! Weren't you told that people only work together if everyone benefits? Sure, you get what you want. But what about me? Why should I share experience and loot with you?"

"Like I said, he won't do it!" Malik cried. "Tissa, I always told you he was a freak! So he's playing Dis now, who cares? Inside, he's still the same Alex Sheppard we've known since first grade!"

Ed cleared his throat, then said gloomily:

"Hung, let him go. Let him waste his time."

"We shouldn't have helped him yesterday!" Malik kept up his malice. "He wasn't worth it!"

"Not at all," Ed disagreed. "We never let outsiders take one of our own... no matter how big of assholes they are."

Tissa wanted to say something, but kept silent. Ed understood that I was not going to answer, and waved a hand:

"Beat it, Sheppard! Use your cheaters' ability, level up... If you change your mind, you know where to find us. Let's go, guys!"

Hung took his hand away. They left. But I just stayed there for a while, sensing a strange frustration burbling up in my chest.

When I got back to class, my cheeks were burning. I was trying not to meet eyes with the Dementors. Ed made me feel really bad, and I was thinking about it the whole next class before I made up my mind.

It wasn't easy but I seemingly had begun to understand what Rodriguez meant when he burned Eve and said I didn't have any friends. Yesterday when they went to bat for me it was... Not just nice but somehow... special or something. It gave me a rich mixture of emotions. Joy, pride, satisfaction at a just conclusion. And all that from a positive ending to the Crag situation. So I decided to take a risk.

Class-A Threat

After class, when I wanted to talk with them, Greg held me back. The history teacher dug around in his tablet and brought up my success profile.

"Look, Alex. This is your report for the week. Your activity level in class has fallen by eighty-four percent. Is everything alright? Is something wrong?"

Actually, a lot was wrong: my parents' divorce, the fear of not passing my citizenship test, keeping my threat status and my relationship with the Dementors. But admitting to any of that would mean coming under observation of the academic council. Of course, their purpose would be to help me, but I couldn't see a single way that might be to my advantage. Most likely, they would just pile on with questions, do my parents' heads in and assign me a mentor. And a supervisor was the last thing I needed. So I smiled and shrugged:

"I'm doing just fine, Mr. Kovacs. Just wonderful!"

"Oh yeah?" he angled his head in mistrust so he would seem the same height as me – another of the psychological tricks Greg was famous for. "Alex, you can be honest with me. I remember you on your first day of school when you were just six. I've watched you grow up!"

"Everyone grows up, Mr. Kovacs..." I shrugged again, looking around nervously. I

---

wanted to talk with Ed, Tissa and the others but not in Dis.

"You can call me Greg, Alex."

"Greg, everything is A-okay! Can I go now? My friends are waiting."

"Alright, go. But if you want to talk, you know where to find me..."

Hey, what was that? This was the third time I had heard the words "you know where to find" today! This morning, after breakfast when dad forgot he was going to divorce mom, and asked her where his socks were, she answered:

"You know where to find them, Mark! And if you don't, better learn to leave your things where they belong!"

To be honest, she was not right. My father and I always remembered where we put our things. The robot cleaner didn't touch them, but mom had a habit of "putting things away." That was when she moved our stuff to where, in her opinion, it belonged. And those places were always changing, so finding a t-shirt you threw on the couch in the morning could be a truly legendary quest by evening.

There was a bothersome fine mist coming down outside. The launchpad was already empty. Not even one flying car, and almost no school kids. Only two people stood out under the roof: Eve wrapped in a beige overcoat and under her airstream umbrella, and just next to her was Tissa, shivering. Schafer's face was under a hood, and her hands were in the pockets of her baggy hoodie. When she saw me, she waved. Eve took an indecisive step toward me and glanced at Tissa.

I walked toward them.

"Wanna stand under my umbrella?" Eve offered.

"We need to talk," Tissa said.

"Eve, thanks. I'll be just fine," I said, turning to Shafer: "I also need to talk to you."

O'Sullivan puffed up her face. I felt awkward, as if I had traded my old friend for new ones.

"Can all three of us fit?" I asked.

"I don't know... I can try turning up the airstream," Eve led a finger down the handle. "Okay. Stand next to me!"

I got under the umbrella. Tissa squeezed in between Eve and me despite herself. So close... My heart sped up.

"Okay," we all said at the same time and Tissa faded into the background.

"Alex, are you going to play Dis today?" Eve asked unconfidently. "Shall we sit outside the tavern like before? If you want, we could level together. I decided to buy game currency so I can get some gear. Want me to get you some too?"

Tissa wrinkled her nose mockingly.

"It stinks here," she said. "Like grease. And

overcooked food."

"Cut it out," I said. "Eve, Tissa is joking. I'm going to be in Dis, but you'll have to level on your own for now. I'm level four already. I have my own quests. Catch up!" I encouraged Eve and tried to pat her on the shoulder.

"Alright, Alex," Eve said quietly, her eyes welling with tears. "I'll catch up. Then I can help you."

I didn't feel this lousy even when my parents told me about their divorce. And that made it all the harder to answer Tissa when she then said:

"Listen, Alex, I decided to bail on Dis today. I wanted to fly out to the southern district to a water park. Wanna come? It'll be fun! And later we can go to Caramba! A friend of mine is a bouncer there, he'll let us in. We'll be able to drink... What do you say?"

"Of course," I nodded, keeping an eye on Eve. "Let's go, sounds like a good time."

The umbrella shuddered and I barely managed to catch it when it left Eve's hands.

Chapter Twenty-One

Tits and Dragons

WE LET EVE take the first flying car, then flew off in the next one. And everything would have been great, if my childhood friend hadn't suddenly gone gloomy when she got into her vehicle with her head drooping and shoulders slouched. She couldn't even hide her glistening tears.

And it was only made worse by the fact that nothing came of it. Tissa had to go before we even got to the water park. As soon as we reached the southern district, she got a ton of calls and messages from her clan.

If there's a gap, something will come to fill it. Crusher was gone from Gloomwood, but now his place had been taken by Punisher. And now, with him also gone somehow, out of the woodwork came Bloodsucker, a spider with attributes comparable to the alpha of the wolf pack.

Infect accidentally found the new boss while trying to stealthily find and track the zombie wolf Punisher – a sort of non-boss boss, but still elite, so the Dementors had a certain interest. After a few hours of pointless wandering, he still couldn't find Punisher, but he did witness the birth of Bloodsucker. The earth yawned and nauseating waves of crawling arachnids scurried out of a deep crack. And at the very end, the new boss crawled out of the hole with a creak and a squeal.

To hear Malik tell it, that part of Gloomwood was unrecognizable now, quiet as the grave! Nothing was left alive, everything was covered in spiderwebs. Basically, gloom.

When she heard that, Tissa abruptly rerouted the flying car toward home. And when she saw my downcast face, she explained despite herself:

"Alex, I'm sorry! I just can't miss another First Kill! You can come with us if you want."

I shook my head. I had my own stuff to do in Dis without overgrown spiders, and I didn't hear particular insistence in Tissa's voice.

So I shook my head in silence and headed home.

There my parents were in the kitchen eating. They were sitting opposite one another, discussing a project peaceably and seeing them this... calm was unbelievably nice. Especially after the scene with Eve and my ill-fated date with Tissa. What was more, the girl of my dreams had given me a plain demonstration of my position in her priorities. I think if Eve were in her place, she would have gladly traded an alien invasion and winning the lottery to spend a day with me. But her love was little solace. To me she remained a nice if somewhat plump girl. A friend.

"You have a big appetite, Alex," mom said, stroking my head. "More?"

"Uh... Yeah, another half portion, mom. Thanks!"

Mom must have been in a good mood, because she didn't print our dinner tonight, she made it herself. She had roasted a chicken, all coated in spices and garlic, with potatoes underneath and swimming in her special sauce. It was unbelievably tasty! And I took advantage of that to eat my fill of tasty grub before a long Dis session. Then I spent a long time sitting with my parents, enjoying their placid company.

Father, meanwhile, asked how I was doing in the game. And he had a real interest. After all, he and mom were virtual reality architects. At one point they even managed to have a hand in a few locations in greater *Disgardium*. I had already begun amply and vaguely answering, but then I followed a wild hare and interrupted them:

"Hey dad, when you design a location, do you consider all the mobs that will live there?"

"Of course," he nodded, setting aside the news on his tablet. "Developers closely track the balance of each location's ecosystem. They even consider potential migrations of individual mobs. The food chain must function like clockwork. Every unintelligent mob has a stat for exhaustion, thirst, hunger and satisfaction of base instincts. And if we don't provide, say, enough Jerway oak, the acorns of which make up the bulk of the diet of red-eared boar, those boar will either die out or be forced to migrate. And then, in their turn they serve as prey..."

"Dad, I got it," I cut him off impatiently. "But I wanted to ask about hidden treasures. Like, let's say I pass an instance and find a chest in a room..."

"Oh, wow! You get an epic?" my father's eyes lit up.

But mom sharply brought him down a peg:

"Mark! Don't start, please! Remember what tripped us up with the Space Harem project!"

Dad cringed. He really had mucked up that episode. He was so entertained by Dis that he had even founded a clan and led raids. I was eight or nine then, and I used to count the days until I could go be a part of that world. Father hadn't found great successes there, but they did lose the

Harem project at roughly the same time. Dad just didn't have enough time or inspiration. He was up to his ears in the game.

"Nothing good, no," I shook my head, "but here's my question, dad. Who places these treasures?"

"It isn't a person," He snorted. "The world of Dis is alive, it's constantly changing. Dungeons form and disappear of their own accord. All of them will be passed sooner or later and eventually they will all see their final run and will go away. But really, speaking of mysteries, Alex..." father stroked the back of his head. "The artificial intelligence of a boss picks up loot from dead players and hides it wherever it can. And that's all because nothing in Dis ever disappears or is created from nothing. Weaponry is forged by smiths from ore mined by miners. Buildings are made of lumber from the lumber mills and stones from the quarries. Food..." he shrugged, "well, you get the idea."

"And what about legendaries?" I couldn't quiet down. "Those come only from smiths and armorers of a certain level..."

"Well legendary items, as a rule, are unique and were woven into the fabric of the world when the game was first launched. They have their own place in *Disgardium* lore. By the way, where did you find a chest?" father asked.

"In a locked empty room," I shrugged my shoulders as if saying something insignificant. "But the keys fell from the second skeleton I saw."

"That means," father nodded in satisfaction, "the main boss never managed to complete its plan. It was probably going to get up to the mob slot limit and make some kind of guard. Maybe even a boss."

"Aha! And the items themselves have a durability score and sooner or later they are destroyed and disappear from the world?"

"Exactly..." father suddenly laughed and extended a hand, expecting me to shake. He had taught me when I was one and a half, and ever since we had a secret handshake. "Exactly right, boy..."

As I struck hands with my father, a wave of sorrow rolled over me. I suddenly realized he and my mom were getting divorced.

He clearly remembered too and looked away. I stood up silently, gave a hug to him then mom and went into my room.

* * *

In half an hour I was in Dis and found Eve almost instantly. In a lather, she was darting about the city on a social quest as mail carrier. As Chief Councilman Whiteacre once said, "timely postal delivery is very important to our city."

And that was probably why she just gave a tiny nod to acknowledge me, not stopping to talk. I meanwhile managed to see that she was wearing a fine suit of leather armor, which meant she had in fact put some money into the game.

My main goal for the day was to reach level five. That way, I would no longer be relegated to the crap gear Underweight sold, and could finally wear some *greens* with bonuses. But I still couldn't use anything I got from Gloomwood, so I decided to sell all my unusual stuff at auction or paw it off on a reseller. It would depend on what was more profitable.

Holding onto it all was no use. The *blue* scale belt from Dargo the Lich would only be available at level ten. And the only thing I had any chance of using any time soon was the bronze amulet giving +5 endurance. It was easier to sell than wait.

So then, before getting into yet another series of deaths, I decided to take care of some business in town: run to auction, level *Cooking* to journeyman, learn new recipes and do some quests. I didn't have any missions now, but I did have the quest item from Crusher. And based on the description, I needed to immediately find someone who knew the girl from the locket.

And there was no better place to start my

search than the Bubbling Flagon. So that's where I headed.

Meanwhile, I took a peek at the city council bulletin board, but there was nothing interesting. It had all the same missions for weeding, sweeping and doing dishes in the tavern probably under *infected* chef Arno, and patrolling the border with Gloomwood...

Walking past the auctions, I figured now was a good a time as any to go check out prices. Trading here was global. The market was shared with the world of greater Dis. Krauss the auctioneer handed me a catalog, the system brought up a window and I started studying.

What I found was no consolation. *Green* stuff like I had was worth between two and five gold from official sellers. And whether or not they would buy an item was impossible to say. Yet you needed to pay fifteen percent commission on each item's declared value to put it up for sale. I snorted skeptically and shook my head. This was definitely not my best option.

At the same time, I took a gander at the price for a *Whistle of Summoning*. The cheapest possible one, which summoned a horse, was worth one hundred gold. And more advanced mounts cost more depending on breed and attributes. Still, I wouldn't say no to a creature like that – even a slow old nag gave +200% to movement speed. The riding skill was not required but very desirable and, in its turn, gave additional bonuses to speed and animal stamina.

Overall, the variety of mobs impressed me so much it made my eyes spin. There were water mounts like sea turtles, and air mounts like gryphons and hippogryphs. Among the terrestrial mounts I found elephants, hippopotamuses, deer and boar... Basically something for all tastes. However, prices started at a few thousand gold, and that was for normal ones, not even rare. It was too early to think about any of that before level forty.

I had heard somewhere that Horvac, leader of a top clan The Wanderers, bought the egg of a ghost dragon for a few million. But to me that was something beyond the realm of mere mortals, something as far away and removed from my real life as Denise Le Bon's space yacht.

So I leafed lazily through the catalog a bit longer, didn't find anything I could even remotely afford and returned it to the auctioneer in disappointment. Then I walked to the resellers to unload my *green* junk.

After one glance at my goods, Undy warned me honestly that they would have to pay me thirty percent below established value, but I would pay no commission and they would pay in advance. With a sigh, I asked them to pick me out a level five set with a slant toward strength and endurance.

"Are you getting anywhere, Alex?" Rita asked while Undy looked over my stuff and, muttering to himself, calculated the value. "Level four already, come on! It hasn't even been a week!"

"I'm really giving it my all. I wasted so much time before..."

"That's for sure!" she treated me to a Sweet Joy and changed topic. "Someone took down Crusher, did you hear? You know that boss I told you about. All alone! Without a clan!"

"Yeah, he must have gotten lucky," Undy sighed. "The loot must be unreal. And that achievement probably gave big-time bonuses..." He wanted to add something but unexpectedly an archer named Justasec cut in, digging through jewelry at the neighboring trader's stall.

"I just so happen know who it was!" he exclaimed joyfully. "I saw him, a level-eleven boy with a pimply face. And I know what the loot was too..."

He made a theatrical pause, and Undy jabbed him with the wooden end of his spear. He really wanted to know!

"Well, don't sit on it! What did Crusher drop?"

"A legendary mount!" he declared in celebration. I froze, overcome with sticky sweat. "A

---

phoenix! A flying firebird," he continued, his eyes bulging. "And it has a thirty percent movement-speed bonus! I'd give my teeth to say he's waiting for offers from all the big clans right now..."

"Sure, of course, what a crock!" Overweight squinted in disbelief. "From a low-level boss in the sandbox? You're such a liar, king of the jackoffs!"

"Wanna bet?" Justasec lit up. "I bet five gold against your whole stall that it's true!"

Overweight and Underweight exchanged glances, and a competitive glimmer flickered up in the latter's eye.

"Okay," the girl turned decisively to the archer. "Let's see the five."

The archer bared his teeth:

"No worries," he drew out in self-satisfaction, "I have the money. So, here is how it went down..."

Underweight glanced at the boy as he sang like a nightingale and gave a loud chuckle:

"Alright, take a bath, you lost already!" he exclaimed, clasping his hands together with a clap. "You can read it right there in *Disgardium Daily*," the trader said as he weightily shook a folded newspaper in the air as evidence. "It says that an anonymous player has put a flaming phoenix up for auction, a unique legendary mount. He's already been offered seven million gold. But the lot was opened three days ago, and Crusher was taken down only yesterday."

The archer's face broke out in further spots and pimples, and a brown shade came over him. Meanwhile I realized that selling my legendary spectral wolf might solve my money problems.

"Well then?" he exclaimed in hot temper. But everyone already knew he lost. "Maybe it was a different phoenix?"

"Are you an idiot?" Overweight snorted. "Does the word 'unique' mean anything to you? There's only one," he said, repeating the last word for emphasis. "So that's it. Give me the five gold!"

"What?" the archer went sour. "We never shook on it!"

"Wasn't the bet your idea?" Undy chuckled in satisfaction. "It was. Overweight accepted. We have witnesses. Scyth?"

"Hand over the coins, Justasec," I said, sincerely joyful. "You lost."

For a second the archer looked around in confusion, blinking his whitish eyelashes. Then he gave a loud exhale... and took off! Like a cowardly rabbit, lifting his bony knees up high, he ran into town.

And on his way, he managed to grab a handful of jewelry from the trader's table. That tricky little...

Still, it wasn't exactly a smart move. Cursing, the jewelry seller dashed off after him, and Undy after him. I watched them run, deciding

---

whether to join in the race, but Overweight stopped me.

"One witness is enough," Rita said. "The bot guards will take him to court, and they'll deal with him. They'll bring in a *truth seeker*, who will confirm the testimony. That Justasec is a moron. Idiotic nick for an idiotic guy. What was he hoping for?" she shrugged.

I remembered the way the guardsmen treated those they brought to court and snorted. I didn't have to worry about that now. I looked at Rita in her revealing shirt. Its top buttons were undone. My eyes were drawn to the alluring gap like a magnet, and I just couldn't look away.

"Hey, Alex!" Overweight shouted. "At least pretend you're looking me in the eye!"

I shot up and exerted some effort. It was hard, but I managed.

We spent a bit more time chewing the fat, then Undy came back shimmering like a gold coin and counted my money for the gear. The archer, pushed against the wall by the guards, scraped everything out of his pockets, and the weapons buyer came out ahead. Still Justasec categorically denied the theft and left the game.

The jewelry vendor came back next looking glum. As he ran away, Justasec threw some cheap jewelry, but nothing was found on his person. The trader picked up a few rings on the way back, but he couldn't say whether he'd found everything. He had no system of bookkeeping, so he had a hard time saying what he had in the first place.

I also looked over his goods just out of curiosity and a few of the rings really caught my eye. But with a wallet as thin as mine, there was nothing to buy. I said goodbye and ran to the Bubbling Flagon.

I saw Patrick when I came near the tavern. Figuring it was long since time to have a chat, I got a copper ready to make him more talkative. But the drunkard called out to me first. Revealing his rotting teeth, he asked me with a smirk:

"Well, how's life with a curse, boy?"

"That's exactly what I wanted to talk to you about, Mr. Patrick. Here," and extended him a copper.

"Stick this small change up your ass!" the old alcoholic wheezed, chuckling. "For once the heavens listened to me! I swear on the stinking hole I crawled out of to reach this world that this is only the beginning! Praise be to Behemoth!"

The madman's laughter drew the attention of some passersby. They were used to seeing Patrick belting out songs, cursing, indulging in self-pity and clinking coppers together, but they had never seen him jubilant. I needed to do something before his strange drunkard's behavior drew even more attention.

Class-A Threat

"You want me to treat you to a drink, Patrick? I've got money now. Here..." I scraped a few silver coins from my inventory, showing the drunk.

His laugh cut off as sharply as it began. Patrick froze in place and stared at the handful of silver, intrigued.

"You want to smooth over your sins, eh?" he asked, serious and no longer slouching. "Why didn't you say so? Alright, let's go boy. We can sit and have a drink. Just one thing... I will not protect you and I cannot remove the curse! I don't know how it happened, or what triggered it. It's never happened before."

"Come on, old Patrick. You know," I smiled. "I'm getting by just fine. I wanted to talk about something else..."

Interlude Two

Patrick

H E WAS a middle-aged man, tall, stiff and entirely confident in himself and his boys. He looked around and couldn't hold back a smile. The girl behind him smiled back.

"Jane, my wife," Patrick O'Grady turned the thought over a few times, savoring it. He felt like he could stare at her pretty face until the end of time and still couldn't believe they'd be getting married in just two days.

How long he had courted Jane! He first noticed her as a long-legged, gangly girl with knobby knees running around the streets of Tristad. He always thought that one day she would blossom into a beautiful woman.

And she had grown up now. Patrick found out her name and what family she was from and tried to get to know her father to have an excuse to talk to Jane more often. But she didn't even want to look at him. Her father, a trader of expensive fabrics, had an entirely different future planned for his girl. He wanted her to study at the University of Magic, then getting a career as an enchanter in the big city. You see, Jane had the gift of magical perception, and her doting father ordered her a pair of voluminous folios from the first caravan that came through town after her abilities revealed themselves. One was for elemental magic and the other for nature.

And the coming of a new mage did not go unnoticed by the city council. Chief Councilman Whiteacre had convinced Jane's father to let his daughter join the city guard and help the patrols. And they didn't have to ask her. What could be a greater honor than helping one's city?

And that was where things began to take a turn. Jane started to consider Patrick as a partner. Not a handsome man, but recklessly brave, he was reliable in battle and very kind outside work as well. The boys in the squadron loved him with all their hearts. And at first their unreserved loyalty to their leader rubbed off on Jane, then her feelings grew into something larger...

That very day, City Guard Captain Patrick O'Grady was patrolling the border with Gloomwood. His shift was coming to an end – very soon Mills' group would arrive to take over. Then he, Jane and the boys would go to the Bubbling Flagon to celebrate their last joint patrol. And it really would be their last. Patrick had decided to quit and take Jane to the capital of the Darant Commonwealth to hone her magical abilities.

And he... He was strong, disciplined and had great recommendations from Tristad city council. What was more, at his mere twenty-five years of age, Patrick had been made an honorary citizen for his heroism during an outbreak of the nether. In the struggle to hold it back, he had distinguished himself, a fact that made him well known in Tristad. So he would have no trouble finding work in the capital guard.

"Captain! We've got action on the right" cried Frank, a younger guardsman.

Patrick held back. Frank had high Night Vision, but drew attention with his shout. Now even the captain could see the thing coming in from the forest. It was a few wraiths: six level-fifteen offspring of the nether and one level-twenty elite.

"Lukas, you take the little ones!" Patrick commanded. "Boys, focus on your targets! I'll hold off the elite for now. Jane, heal on Lukas! As soon as you're done with them, come join me!"

The squadron started carrying out their captain's orders without a second thought. Patrick's experience and clear command in battle was the main reason he hadn't suffered a single loss in more than a year. And that was something of a record among the patrol squadrons of the Tristad guard.

The captain himself made a jump at the elite wraith and dealt a series of special attacks, generating aggro. With his trusty motions and very high *Dodge* and armor... This elite didn't stand a chance.

The guys quickly chopped their targets into coleslaw, then turned to the elite. Patrick walked back, giving Lukas some space, then allowed himself a quick breather. Looking toward the city, he saw torch lights – that must have been Mills' boys.

The high-level undead was just a few blows from death when it retreated. And that was strange because the beasts that inhabited Gloomwood always fought to the last breath, if such a thing can be said about that which does not breathe. But this one was behaving unusually. The wraith lit up with an otherworldly fire, blinding Patricks' soldiers for a few seconds and ran off.

He could not be left alive. His vision returned, Patrick saw where the thing was going, shouted an order and dashed off, first on the chase. The wraith was covering ground quickly. That thing could not be allowed to leave combat mode and restore its health! Somewhere behind, tripping on something, Jane shouted. The captain let the boys go ahead, himself returning to help the girl. The two of them quickly caught the squadron. It picked up the pace and dashed out ahead.

But the picture that revealed itself made him pump the breaks then stop altogether. The wraith had gone upward and was hovering in midair. And right behind him began a wall of foreboding fog, which flickered with green light.

"Wait, Patrick!" Jane exclaimed.

He didn't listen. The elite wasn't running and, expecting some kind of trick, the captain was careful in his approach. The squadron stayed where they stood, not having any orders.

But his sword just split the air, not touching its target. The wraith dissolved in the fog.

"Got away..." Patrick spat out. "Let's head back, boys!"

He turned away from the fog, took a step and, much to his surprise, found himself covered in stinging wet goo. There was such a dead silence in the air that he thought he had gone deaf. In the fog he saw some silhouettes, and Patrick took an unconfident step toward them.

"Jane? Lukas? Frank? Slava? Phil? Claudio? Carius?"

The figures disappeared. Then Lukas appeared right in front of him. He was grinning with superiority and shaking his head.

"You're such an idiot, captain," he said.

"What happened, Lukas? What are you talking about, old friend?"

"Jane... You still expect it to happen, don't you...? Your wedding? Didn't anyone tell you that girls need *it*?"

"What exactly?"

"They've got an itch," Lukas said with a whinny. "An itch, you understand? And it needs scratching, it's human nature! And she dropped you plenty of hints, but you're too much of a dumbass! And so O'Grady, what choice did I have when she came to me?"

"Lukas, let's discuss this in the city. It isn't safe to stay here. Let's go, old friend!" Patrick tried to embrace his squadron's secondary tank, but Lukas dodged and threw his hand away.

"Go to hell, Captain! You aren't even worthy of her pinky finger!"

Patrick went crimson. He wasn't a dazzling intellect and often didn't understand things, but this reached even him.

"Is there something going on between you?" he asked.

"You son of a bitch, how can you be so stupid?" Lukas started cackling. "Open your eyes, O'Grady. We're sleeping together! Us! Me and her! Getting it on! Doing it, you son of a bitch!"

Patrick then felt like he was dying. His heart stopped, his breathing seized. All the blood ran into his head, he stumbled and dropped his sword. Then he keeled over, unable to carry the weight of this betrayal.

When he woke up and opened his eyes, the fog was gone. His squadron was all around.

And they were clearly up to something! Jane's false wailing tore his soul to bits. That dog!

Lukas leaned in over him and snorted:

"You doin' alright, cap?"

On the other side, the new kid Frank patted him on the shoulder. Patrick saw in his eyes that he also harbored a sense of superiority. He knew! Or maybe he was also playing him like a fool? Patrick extended a hand and felt for his fallen sword. Without giving away his intentions, the captain grabbed the handle and, with a sharp exhale, stuck the sword right into Lukas' dastardly mug. A moment later he jumped and cut Frank's throat in a lightning-fast motion. Clutching at his neck, he collapsed. The blood gushed out of his young body. His youthful eyes went glassy.

"What the nether? Captain?" They threw themselves at him to take his weapon.

He broke out of it with his superior strength and level and cut Slava and Claudio down in just a few slashes. Traitors! Somewhere to the side, Jane was squealing and trying to heal – not him! –

the others that were still alive. How many were left?

Carius threw his weapon and ran. He had always been a coward, and this squadron was no place for the weak! Patrick threw an axe into his fleeing back. Gotcha. The deserter fell dead as a doornail.

Groaning with madness, he dashed at the next one. With a vengeful grin, Patrick slammed his shield into Phil's nose. He was the one Jane was trying to heal. So, him too? Fuck other peoples' wives in hell, scum! Patrick jabbed the sword into his heart.

Now only Jane was left. She was weeping and drying her tears.

"Why Patrick? Just why?" the slut wailed. "What did they do to you? Lukas, Phil, Frank, Slava, Carius... Why?"

He felt like the part of that governed emotion had been yanked out. Lukas wasn't lying. She said his name first, which must have meant she was crying for him. Patrick shoved her against a tree and sharply drew his dagger across her throat. Choking on blood, she slumped back. A look was frozen in her once beautiful eyes... shock?

To make sure the enchantress wouldn't heal herself, he cut off her head. The headless body stayed on its feet for a few moments and fell. A locket flew off her neck. It was a gift from Patrick

– a portrait. And inside it was his own face – young, with a dashing moustache and a boyish smile. But it looked was a stranger's face now, not his. He didn't feel like that person anymore.

He picked up the locket and opened it. He saw Lukas's smirking mug.

Patrick issued the enraged yelp of a wounded animal, tore a bronze chain from his own neck with an identical pendant gifted by Jane and threw it as far as he could. Somewhere in the distance, a wolf howled, but it barely registered.

He was very tired. A twelve-hour shift, a few battles and the last – with traitors – had him completely bugged out. Patrick laid down, feeling like he just couldn't move a muscle. His eyes closed, and his mind went quiet, enjoying the silence.

He woke up to a bitter cold. Snow had fallen. The dismantled bodies of Jane and his boys were still lying on the ground around him as if to prove this was no nightmare. There would be no wedding now.

With that thought in mind, Patrick stood up. He took a step and slipped on the locket that had fallen off Jane. He picked it up and, not thinking, opened it. And the portrait was a gallant image of himself smiling – young and with dashing moustache.

It was then that Patrick realized exactly what

had happened. His knees started to buckle, but he found the strength inside to find his fiancée's head in the bushes.

And after that he spent a long time trying to get it back on her body…

For the next few days, Captain Patrick O'Grady wandered the forest aimlessly. Back in town he was considered missing without a trace. The knowledge of what he'd done slammed into him like a ton of bricks. He saw no sense in continuing to live and was attacking any living thing he encountered, hoping to die in battle. But he won every time no matter how he wanted the opposite. And he was not going to give up or kill himself – that went against the teachings of Nergal the Radiant.

A week of wandering later, he reached the Mire. The creatures there didn't touch him for some reason. A huge Snakehead he encountered on one of the little islands refused to fight and soundlessly dove underwater.

And that was approximately the same day he started hearing the voice. It whispered that there was a way to fix all this. It told him what to do. When he was hungry, the voice told him where to find food and it always knew where to look. The first time Patrick found the body of a hippo that had recently died and filled his stomach with raw swampy-flavored meat. Another day, he hit upon a pack of magnetic toads around nightfall. They seemed to have hypnotized one another, so he easily tore them to bits and ate them.

Led on by the voice, Patrick wandered the Mire always knowing precisely where to place his feet to stay alive.

He spent many long days in motion, obeying the voice. It was the only thing keeping him alive and sane. Or so he thought. The voice told him about what used to be. In the distant past, long before the first human foot stepped upon the earth, it was ruled by entities we now called the Sleeping Gods.

Patrick tried to ask what happened and where the Sleeping Gods had gone, but the voice gave no answer. The whispered reply could hardly be considered that.

Patrick reached a patch of dry land any normal person would call a muck heap rather than an island and there he collapsed, totally drained. And the voice said he'd reached his destination. This was his place. Where he was supposed to be.

Patrick himself could feel it, too. There was a slight vibration and monotone hum coming from somewhere deep beneath him.

"What next?" the former guard captain

asked aloud.

"We make a deal, mortal," the voice whispered. "We have been forgotten, no one believes in us. That is the cause of our weakness. We can handle that later, but now..."

The voice gave him some curt but concise commands: return to the city, cover up his involvement in the slaughter, say the fog killed his team and reoccupy his place in the city. Once back in the city guard, by the spring equinox, find a suckling babe and bring it to the Mire to sacrifice in the name of Behemoth – the one true god.

"And how will that help get Jane back?" Patrick asked. "And what will become of me?"

"You shall be our first apostle," came the rustling voice of Behemoth. "We can protect you. We will bring in more adepts, our power will grow. My power will grow! I will bring Jane back to you..."

By the end of the short winter, Patrick was back in Tristad. No one recognized him: gaunt, bearded and gray, O'Grady had been cause for discussion for quite some time. The mysterious story of the disappearance of the top patrol squadron was talked about all winter. But all the crazy hypotheses were overturned by the return of the captain himself, who explained everything.

The hardest part turned out to be looking Jane's father in the eye when he told him. After losing his only daughter, the widower closed his stall. And after talking to Patrick, he gave all his property to the city, becoming a servant of the temple.

Patrick resumed his service with the Guard, but refused to patrol, preferring to serve as a common gatekeeper, just opening and closing the city gates. And they understood.

The day appointed by Behemoth was fast approaching. The voice abandoned Patrick when he left the Mire, and he would have forgotten about it if not for the daily reminders of Jane. They used to love walking down this street, and under that tree is where they had their first kiss.

Then one of his partners had a baby girl, and Patrick made up his mind. He dropped by to pay the man a visit, picked up the baby and entertained it as much as any childless middle-aged man could entertain someone else's baby. He threw it in the air, did baby-talk, made faces... And the baby got used to him, relaxed in his arms. That was all he needed.

A week before the spring equinox, Patrick was ready. He had a stock of food, his weapon was ready, he had a bag packed full of milk bottles. He told his partner he wanted to visit the place where Jane and his boys died, then headed to his house.

He went through the window into the bedroom and made sure the baby was in its crib.

Class-A Threat

The young mother, exhausted by her routine and sleepless nights, was sleeping nearby in the marital bed.

Patrick stood for a long time staring at the baby girl's tranquil face. Then he stroked her forehead, feeling the warmth of the child's body with the tips of his fingers. Suddenly, he heard a rustling behind him and turned. The child's disquieted mother was turning over in her sleep. Her forehead was soaked in sweat, her bare thigh was lying shamelessly over the comforter. She herself was basically still a girl. Not much different than his Jane...

He adjusted the baby's blanket and, not turning, climbed back outside. Then he went back to the city gates, waved at his partner and headed into the forest. He didn't have a clear plan, but did have the glimmer of an idea. After a day of searching, he found what he was looking for.

Patrick pulled a wolf pup out of a wide burrow. The mother was clearly gone either to hunt or drink some water.

The pup was blind, mewing and poking into his arm trying to find something to suckle. Patrick tossed it in his bag and ran toward the Mire.

He spent two days underway with breaks to feed the pup and a wolf howling behind him. The voice came back to help him get the wolf pack off his trail.

After he reached the Mire, Patrick did exactly as Behemoth instructed. He dug a deep hexagonal pit, carved strange figures into the soil and let the voice guide him.

Then he produced many strange guttural hissing sounds and began putting the soil back. The vibration and hum grew stronger. A sharp pain pierced Patrick's head. He lost consciousness.

Somewhere in the forest, the wolf mother howled in sorrow.

Then the momentary flood of memories came to an end. He could barely make out what the cursed boy was holding in his hands.

"Mr. Patrick?" he asked. "Are you doing okay?"

O'Grady reached for the glass of gnomish swill and drained it in one gulp. Then he wiped his moustache and drew air into his nose. The day he buried that wolf pup, everything ended for him. The Sleeping God was enraged that he used a pup instead of a human baby. Everything went wrong and leaving Patrick alive was not an act of mercy, but one of impotence. The Sleeping God had clearly been awoken, but he was so weak he couldn't even move.

Still the deity's rage was strong enough that everything after that happened in a fog. Patrick ran, fell in the water, got out somehow and kept running. Onward! Onward!

Back in town, he quit the guard. But the connection with Behemoth remained. The voice continued to whisper and demanded he fix everything, put it right. The nightmares the Sleeping God sent him even in waking life only left when he drank. So the only time Patrick felt alright was drunk as a skunk...

And now he was trying to achieve that – to drink himself into a hole with the money from that foolish kid, taking him for as much as he could get.

"I've been doing bad for a long time, boy," he answered. "What would you like to know?"

"I asked if you knew who this locket might belong to."

Patrick raised his head. The idea glimmering in his head formed into a fully-fledged plan. After all, this really might work! And why not?

"I do," he called back, revealing his blackened teeth in a crooked smirk. "But if you want to hear the answer, boy, you'll have to do something for me."

"Of course, Mr. Patrick. How can I help?"

"You're nobody's fool, Scyth! Haha! What have you heard about the Mire?"

Chapter Twenty-Two

Immaculate Impulses

"WHAT HAVE YOU heard about the Mire?" Patrick asked, tapping the table two times loudly. "Another!"

Lulu the level-seven waitress, played by Luciana from my school, rolled her eyes. A minute later, a huge mug appeared before Patrick filled with fresh fiery Black Mountain ale. He drank the first practically in one gulp right after I showed him the locket. He turned it over in his hands, then opened it and stared at the portrait for some time.

"The Mire? I heard its full of these terrible monsters called needlers. They stick a larva under your skin and it is usually deadly, especially if you give them time to dig deeper in your body."

"Needlers?" Patrick took a swallow and wrinkled his nose. "Believe me, boy. That isn't the worst thing out there. Those swamps harbor true horrors..."

He muttered something indistinguishable and nasal, then went completely silent, staring into the distance. Rocking in place, Patrick seemed to be looking past me. I followed his gaze, but there was nothing there. Or...

In the far corner of the tavern there was a brigade from the Olton Quarries. They were all level two or three except the foreman. He had hit five.

The workmen were concentrating on moving their jaws, savoring the tasty food they couldn't get in the real world as noncitizens: roast boar ribs with mountains of pearl barley, enriched with ground chitterlings, pepper and oil. My *Cooking* was a great help in recognizing the dishes served in this tavern. I remembered my plan to level that before I headed off to farm. I'd have to pay Chef Arno a visit. Maybe he'd toss me some new recipes...

"Watch where you're going, birdbrain!" The thunder of breaking dishes and stream of curses that followed reached the whole tavern.

I recognized that voice. It was Crag. I turned my head and saw him shaking some workman, lifting him two feet off the floor. "Manny, level 5. Quarry Foreman," said the words over his head.

"Aw jeeze... I'm sorry, it was an accident. My

bad..." the foreman murmured.

"My ass it was an accident," Crag squeezed out between his teeth. "Well, let's go. I'm turning you in to the city guard!"

"Please, not the guard!" Mannie rasped. "For god's sake, they'll make me pay or go to prison! How will I work? I have a family, a child..."

"What god do you follow?" the warrior asked, looking interested as he set the workman down. "Tell me a name!"

"What god?" he asked, batting his lashes in bewilderment. "You know, God. What else is there? The father, the son..."

"Excuse me, half-wit! What is this nonsense? One day you will come to know that Nergal the Radiant is the one true god! And for that blasphemy, you'll be beaten to a pulp! Come now, let's go, step to!"

The man looked to be forty years old. His brigade looked on gloomily, but there were no attempts to help. With their levels and reputation, messing with the city just meant attracting problems. Only the very youngest one, around twenty, tried to jump up but the man next to him held him back.

That threw me for a loop. That cream beer glass he broke was worth just a quarter silver, but Crag clearly wanted to frighten Manny and take him for all he had as "compensation." In my experience, Crag was a big fan of demanding "compensation."

I glanced at Patrick, he was still in a trance. His vision was glazed over, his lips twitching soundlessly. His gnomish swill stood untouched.

Meanwhile Manny, spurred on by Crag, passed by me.

Oh, nether! Alright. I never got the chance to thank a noncitizen by the name of Clayton. I'd try to pay back my karmic debt this way. I got up sharply and stood between the ganker and workman.

"Hey there, Crag! How are things?" I only then noticed the warrior's gear had taken a step down. "Rough I take it?"

"Ah, Scyth..." his eyes squinted. "This doesn't concern you, stay out of it! This is between me and this *inwinova*!"

Inwinova? An individual with no value to society, a slang word for all noncitizens. I again remembered Clayton/Dargo, mentally putting him in Manny's place...

"Now it's my business. What is your problem with him? A mug of cream beer? I'll order you another one. We good?"

"Not on your life! Let me repeat, this doesn't concern you, stay out of it. Your clan will not help you, I am within my rights! You know it, he knows it, and everyone else knows it!"

He almost shouted his last words, attracting attention from the whole tavern. The room fell silent, and even the group of bards on stage stopped playing.

"People!" Crag exclaimed. "Here's basically what happened. This *inwinova* knocked a glass of beer out of my hands on purpose. The glass broke, I got soaked in beer, and now I'm feeling like crap! I want to turn this scamp in," he said pointing at Manny, "to the city guard! Am I right to do so?"

"You are! People like that must be punished! You're doing the right thing!" I could clearly hear a few players saying that in the disordered hullabaloo. The noncitizens kept silent, trying not to look at Manny.

Crag gave a satisfied nod and poked my shoulder. I flew to the side.

"Get outta my way! And I better not see you again, ever!" said the warrior.

I got up, thinking feverishly. I couldn't stop him by force, should I call the Dementors? I guess not. I'd have to have no conscience to do that, especially after all my refusals to join them, and after I was not able to agree to help them with Tissa. Pay Manny's fine to the guards? It would still hurt his reputation with the city. He might lose his job...

"I challenge you to a duel!" I shouted after him. "I'll put my *blue* belt up against five gold with the condition that you forgive this workman."

"What?" Crag froze in the doorway. He stopped the foreman and then came back to me and asked, intrigued: "One on one? Without your friends? You and me?"

"Yes. You and me. Tomorrow evening. At nine beyond the wall next to the market row."

"This guy's lost his marbles! Level four against twelve?" someone shouted. "Hey, this is that idiot who spent a whole year sitting outside the tavern!" came another person. "And that is Crag, PK'er extraordinaire and PvP specialist! I bet a gold Scyth won't last ten seconds!"

But there were other surprised voices as well. They were quieter, but the table of quarry workers was closer so I heard: "Who is that? Why does he want to help?" "Is he one of us?"

"Let's shake on it!" Crag bared his teeth. "So, do you all hear? Tomorrow at nine PM at the city wall I'm gonna punish this cretin for biting off more than he can chew! When I win, he will have to give me a rare belt!"

"If you win, not when. The rest is all true!" I said loudly.

"So you don't get cold feet, let me be clear about one thing!" the ganker strained his throat. "No limitations in terms of equipment, weapons, elixirs and buffs!"

"Accepted!" I nodded in agreement and

extended a hand. "Agreed?"

Crag held a pause, bared his teeth, looked around the room to make sure everyone was watching and clapped hands with me. With a crack, he squeezed, pulled me closer and whispered:

"I guess you weren't exactly 'in the clan,' huh? Maybe you never were even close. Have that belt ready, worm!"

Guffawing and unbelievably self-satisfied, he left the tavern, not forgetting to give poor Manny a shove so hard he slid under a nearby table.

I helped him up. The foreman opened his eyes and shuddered when he realized it was me, not one of his guys. He tried to tell me something, couldn't and just nodded. I closed my eyes for a moment, let go of his hand then got back to Patrick.

He was already back from the astral plane and watching with intrigue. I took a sip of cream beer.

"Your little hands are shaking!" the drunkard noted. "What'd you get yourself into, boy? Who did you piss off? Look at yourself, you're just common riffraff, but you jumped at a glorious warrior! Whatever for? Hoping for cheap glory?"

"Justice. Not glory."

"You're a fool," Patrick said evilly. "There's no such thing as justice!"

"I cannot change the world, but I can change myself," I answered in annoyance. "So let's stop talking about this. It's my problem, not yours. You said I need to do something so tell me about the locket. What exactly?"

The drunkard was still holding the item. He opened it again and looked at the portrait, then returned it to me decisively.

"You see, son... First I had a different idea for what you should do. Something I once could not do myself. But now, seeing and hearing you... I don't think you can help me. This seems more like a job for the guy you'll be fighting tomorrow."

"What makes you say that? You think because I'm lower level than him I can't do it? You don't know me!"

"Oh, believe me, boy. I know you very well!" Patrick laughed. "It isn't a level issue. This issue is... Ah, nether. Nergal smite you! Basically, listen. I'm not sure you'll be able to do it, at the very least because you won't be able to reach the Mire. And then you'll have to cross it. But that, as you say, is your problem."

He shouted to the waitress, ordering another ale and asking for a pencil. A few minutes later, Lu brought both. Patrick started making a rough sketch of the edge of the Mire right on the table, made a line for the main road from Tristad, marked the bits of dry land and drew the contours of the route to the destination.

"This is the dwelling place of Behemoth," he said.

"Behemoth?" I clarified. "Is that some big animal?"

"No, this is a different sort of entity. If it so desires, it will reveal itself to you. In any case, you must tell it that I sent you. And you must do as it wishes. And when it comes time for your reward, be sure to say you want what Behemoth promised me. Tell it these words exactly: the thing you promised Patrick. If it does not agree, well..." he went gloomy. "Then we'll call it even and I'll tell you about the locket."

> *Patrick O'Grady, former guard patrol squadron captain and honorary citizen of Tristad, would like you to go to the point he showed you in the Mire and offer your help to a spirit which calls itself Behemoth and, as a reward, ask for what it promised to Patrick.*
> *Rewards:*
> *— 1200 experience points;*
> *— reputation with Patrick O'Grady increased by 150;*
> *— Patrick O'Grady will tell you the story of the locket;*
> *— next mission in the quest chain.*

Penalty for not completing mission:
— *reputation with Patrick O'Grady lowered by 150;*
— *reputation with the city of Tristad lowered by 10.*
Recommended level: *at least 15.*

"Well boy, what do you say? Will you take it?" he snorted. "Just know this: I have no reward to give you. I'll tell you about the locket, but I don't think the story is quite what you want to hear. And by the way, there's no rush. I understand that you need to get stronger before trying to go there."

I thought hard. With my curse I was sure I could make it. What was more, the *Mark of the Destroying Plague* would show itself sooner or later, and I'd get there unharmed. I wouldn't have to kill anyone there, just talk, and that meant my level didn't matter. And the fact that there was no time limit was only to my benefit. I should level up a bit before sticking my nose in there though. Otherwise it would just take too long, killing aggro'd mobs for hours every day.

Accept Patrick O'Grady's mission?

Yes, undoubtedly. I added the quest and O'Grady nodded.

"By the way. As for your curse, you should

ask Behemoth. It was his doing."

"I see. Thank you"

"Well, will you treat old uncle Patrick to one more?" he asked happily. And he changed somehow imperceptibly. His shoulders weren't so tight or something, as if a heavy weight had been lifted. "The sun will be going down soon, but I'm not the least bit tired! Are you gonna treat me, or was tonight a bust?"

I nodded, took out a silver coin and placed it on the table.

"You blow off some steam, Mr. O'Grady," In the end, he wasn't lying about being an "honorary citizen," and that merited good treatment. "I've gotta go. Now I've got that duel tomorrow and I have to get ready!"

He patted me on the shoulder understandingly and barked, calling Lulu:

"Another ale for an honorary citizen of Tristad!"

Uh... But he just got one! I didn't even see him drink it. Alright, Nergal be with him. Levelling *Cooking* would be canceled for today.

I was planning to level while Crag slept. I had quite the night ahead of me.

Chapter Twenty-Three

City Jail

THERE WAS NO TOBACCO in the sandbox, but Dis didn't stop you from rolling up some herbs and smoking that. In fact, that had grown up into a whole industry and every day herbologists put new recipes on the market that gave various positive effects. And although they didn't last long, they were a relatively healthy consolation for people who couldn't rid themselves of the psychological habit of lighting and dragging on a burning stick.

After saying goodbye to Patrick, I caught the quarry foreman looking at me. He nodded and raised a hand, the rest at the table did the same. I waved back to them and, tacking between the players dancing in the smoke, walked across the room. I just about ran into a waitress as she left the kitchen with a full tray, then went up the stairs to the second floor.

In my private room, I filled a chest with money I got from Undy and completely cleared out my inventory. Ideally, I should have invested in something a bit more spacious than my basic starter bag, but even basic sixteen-slot storage started at five gold, and that was with no bonuses to reduce weight. The better ones were enchanted to make the contents have a lower drop chance if you died, too. Overall, I'd classify that stuff as "very important, but still out of reach."

My levelling strategy for the evening and upcoming night was formed before I even spoke with Patrick. Gloomwood and the land of the murlocks to the west were right out. Too much action there. Going to the mountains was no option either, nor was the Mire. I probably wouldn't be able to effectively fight the mobs there, because their level would be too high. Even *Hammerfist* couldn't help me against them and it gave me a 155% accuracy bonus on same-level enemies and dealt an additional 1600% damage.

If I understood the accuracy and damage calculations correctly, they were both reduced by about 10% per level higher than my own. So let's say I simply could not hit a mob sixteen levels above me. And if I missed, the attack wouldn't level.

So for those reasons, I decided to spend the

night in a dungeon. No one would see me transform when *Mark of the Destroying Plague* kicked in, the loot was better there and, at the end of the day, it was close at hand.

First I thought of the Evil from the Depths instance no one could finish in the Olton Quarries. But I weighed the plusses and minuses and decided against it. Sure, it could potentially give me a heap of achievements. And the years' worth of loot there were more enticing than Overweight's velvety hemispheres, but...

But the mobs were high level. That's one. It might take me a whole month to pass that ins, considering what I said before about damage and accuracy. And two, I had decided to go there with the Dementors even if they didn't know that yet. Well and three, it seemed like a big shame! With an eight-slot bag I'd have to leave most of the loot inside! The hamster on my chest would tear through my shirt! Well, to hell with that...

So I picked a different dungeon. The Tristad City Jail was just six blocks away. After the Crypt of the Temple of Nergal the Radiant disappeared, this was the only instance in the city.

As far as I could tell from the in-game encyclopedias, there were three bosses: a mad gnome scientist, a cunning goblin from the League and a draconid – a scaly four-legged creature with two arms.

The outbreak of the nether from a few years back had started in the right wing of the jail. And that was where they held prisoners convicted of the very worst crimes. The former prisoners were no goody two-shoes before, but after their minds got clouded and bodies mutated, they became a major threat to the city. The town was only saved by a Senior Mage from the capital who was passing through Tristad on business.

Still, the mage was in too great a hurry to properly clear out the jail and seal the portal, so he just cast a spell on the whole right wing, placing it in a separate pocket of space. That left the city's top minds scratching their heads, but they decided to just leave well enough alone and not build a new jail.

Whether that was the truth or a simple legend explaining why such an ins existed in the sandbox was immaterial. It wasn't the hardest dungeon. It was for players of level nine or ten. It had been passed successfully by many generations of players. And a new crop of players came through every two years, considering that the "graduates" of the sandbox passed into the greater world just as they reached sixteen.

There was practically no risk, and the only thing that might stop me was if someone was already in the dungeon.

But I jinxed myself. As soon as I walked up

to the jail, I got what I was afraid of. There was a group of players waiting for their group outside the instance portal, a fine layer of ether that glimmered shades of green. It was three characters in cheap mismatched gear, two boys and a girl, all level eight. They were sitting on the grass and talking about something. The text over their heads told me they were from the clan Schrodinger's Cats.

"Hi!" I said. "Are you guys gonna run this ins?"

"We're actually on our way out. We're just waiting for our tank and healer," a tall gaunt boy named Teller told me. "They were just about to finish off Pherax, he had less than ten percent HP!"

"Maybe we should give it another try?" the girl forwarded.

"No, Plancka. It's late, I've gotta go. Let's wait for our team and log off. What about you, Yukawa?"

"I gotta go too before father hits the emergency exit," said the third, a heavyset East Asian boy wearing chainmail and holding a bow. "I've got an algebra test tomorrow."

"Oh god! Who needs algebra? What good will it do us?" Plancka sniveled.

"Everyone needs it, quit your belly-aching," Teller grumbled. Based on their shared last name, he and Plancka were brother and sister. He looked at me and squinted. "And what's it to you, Scyth? There are no quests for your level here. And there's nothing else for you to do in this ins."

"Quests? They give out quests for instances?"

"It's like you just fell here from the moon! Cooper is the warden and he still hopes they can get the right wing of the jail back under control." He pointed me to the far door, leading to the administrative wing. "Cooper will give a mission to anyone: for boss's heads, clearing out the wing, closing the portal to the nether... But it's too early for you to think about that. See, the five of us are at level eight and we couldn't do it."

"I'm just asking," I said, spreading my arms. "I haven't been playing for long and, basically, I'm getting to know the city. I just wanna know what's what."

"I see. Well, best of luck.. Ope!" he looked up. "Our tank Mosely is down. That's gotta be it! And there goes Born! Wuss... Alright, let's go to the graveyard. We can meet up with them and do a quick post-game..."

Clamoring in disappointment, they stood up and went to the respawn point. I led my gaze over them, then walked past the instance portal.

The bulletin board at the main entrance looked like a scene from a Western. There were poorly drawn portraits of criminals with labels like

"Especially dangerous," "Wanted!" "Dead or alive!" And they overlapped, covering the whole thing. Among them was every kind of beast from the ocean to the Mire. They would give one hundred gold for the chief of the nagas, snake-people from around the coast. But the poster of Crusher was crossed out in red and stamped the same color with the word "Dead." Strange that this was the warden's job and not, for example, the leader of the city guard's.

These quests were given out automatically, and I took them all just in case, filling my list of missions. But first of all, I wanted to find out about the ones Teller was talking about.

I opened the door confidently and walked inside. I immediately found a guard. He was completely encased in plate armor with his helmet visor down. He put a hand on his sword handle and asked:

"Where to?"

"The warden."

"Against the rules," he answered, sizing me up with a gaze.

"I'm here about the right wing. I wanted to ask if the warden has any assignments."

"Assignments? For you?" the guard asked in amazement, guffawing. "Geezer, Miser! Boys, just come look at this little ragamuffin! He thinks he's going into the right wing! Hahaha!"

"Wait, Mario!" a hoar-headed guardsman with no helmet said quietly but significantly. The laughter immediately came to an end. "Who knows what kind of power might be lurking in this unprepossessing boy? What is your name soldier?" he asked, turning to me.

It was a strange question, because nonplayer characters always knew everyone's name. It was a mechanic of the world. They perceived all these levels, experience points, reputation, skills, attributes, interface hints and damage numbers as a given, just the fabric of their world. That was one of the most crucial issues of the first virtual worlds. In fact, when basic NPC scripts were first replaced with artificial intelligence, the Movement for Nonplayer Character Rights achieved their goal. Mobs were made equal with people in terms of access to information. They didn't get to respawn, though. That might break the reality of it. Aggressive mobs respawned, but key bots did not.

"My name is Scyth. I already know I'm not yet ready for an encounter with the beasts that inhabit the right wing, but I'd only be risking my own neck."

"You're right, son," said Geezer. He slapped me on the shoulder and turned his gaze to Mario: "Let him through."

He didn't argue with his superior and

---

pointed me to the hall:

"Last door on the right. When speaking with Mr. Cooper, always be clear and to the point."

"Thanks."

I had passed them when I was called out to from behind. The gray-haired guardsman came up, winked and barely audibly whispered:

"Thanks for Manny."

At first it didn't really register, then I put two and two together. Geezer was played by a noncitizen? Just like Dargo/Clayton? Well, well! I guess the corporation didn't stop at hostile mobs and was now injecting real people into NPC's like the Tristad guards.

I remembered Gale the guardsman who wanted to let me go for a copper, i.e. a bribe. His behavior was just too humanlike when he was supposed to be bringing me to court for ripping Vista's dress!

The thought buried itself in my subconscious while I walked toward the jail warden's office. Not seeing any identifying markings on the door, I simply knocked.

"Come in," came a peevish voice inside.

Digging through mountains of paper in the cramped office was a severe bald man, Warden Cooper. He raised his head, instantly saw my level and equipment and winced.

"Speak!" he barked.

"Good day, Mr. Cooper! You wouldn't happen to have any assignments for me, would you? I'm thinking of going to the right wing..."

"No," he replied and immediately forgot about me, immersed in the papers on the table.

"But maybe..."

"Geezer!" the boss shouted, not raising his head. "Why are there strangers in my office?"

I was baffled! Teller told me he'd give quests to anyone, but look at this. He wouldn't even talk to me!

Geezer came in, showered his boss with apologies and, grabbing me by the hand, led me out of the office.

"Low reputation with the city," he explained. "And I, idiot that I am, didn't think to check. Have you done any social quests at all, Scyth?"

"Social quests?" I stopped. "No. And you, apologies... are you human?"

"Human as they come!" Geezer replied, winking and shaking his head. "What do I look like a gnome?"

"I thought..." I nodded, realizing he may not want or be able to speak about his true nature. This may have been more or less exactly like my threat status. I remembered how that admission had turned out for Clayton. "In any case, thank you for trying to help, Mr. Geezer!"

I left the administrative wing, sensing a

stubborn gaze from the gray-haired guardsman. I wondered how it was to play that. If he wanted to quit and go do something else, would they let him? To what degree could he exercise control over this seemingly nonplayer character? I had lots of questions but practically no answers. And the only person who could help me with this was that midget from Cali Bottom.

However, that was just basic curiosity. I forgot all about the odd guardsman called Geezer as soon as I entered the dungeon.

* * *

The gloomy and practically unlit dungeon was once the right wing of the city jail, but now it looked more like the insides of some huge insect. All surfaces were covered in acrid slime and constantly buzzing like a living organism. This once spacious corridor was now an uneven tunnel with pulsating outgrowths all over the walls.

Ghastly Howl, which I used right after respawn, made passing the dungeon easier, especially after Curse of the Undead triggered. The ability's cool-down zeroed out after dying, and some of the pushy former prisoners scattered in fear every time. That let me land a blow or two more before I got torn to shreds again.

Kobolds, ogres, dark dwarves and gnolls – all

the prisoners had been *altered* by the entity that flooded out of the nether. These *altered* creatures grew mandibles, powerful fangs and chitin plates all over their bodies. They craved only one thing – flesh and blood. Unfortunately for them though, they did not eat one another, and they had no way out of the sealed wing. So their only food was people like me.

Almost all my attacks were hitting something, adding points to my progress in the Unarmed Combat skill and the only special I used, *Hammerfist*. I hadn't yet made it to a trainer for this school of combat. I didn't even know where to look. Nevertheless, that had one huge plus: sure I was leveling only one attack, but my patently unfair invincibility allowed me to level it on stronger mobs for a practically unlimited amount of time.

Mark of the Destroying Plague only kicked in on the second pack. The first one, made of six spiteful and ugly *altered* criminals, took me more than one hour. I lasted almost twenty seconds before my first death, then I managed to raise *Unarmed Combat* high enough and lay low my first mob. Each subsequent one took me two to three dozen deaths. I respawned with just the one life and each subsequent death spurned on my desire to speak with Behemoth, hoping it could do something about this curse.

Class-A Threat

By the time I'd reached the first boss, I had done everything I could. *Ghastly Howl* was up to level. Curse of the Undead had activated, which raised the *Mark of the Destroying Plague*. I had increased *Night Vision* and *Resilience* to level five. The last one made me especially glad, because it increased my resistance to damage by 5%, and brought up *Stoneskin* the same amount, which I could now have on for an impressive five seconds. Reducing the pain was also quite significant, considering how much I had to bear.

But that wasn't why I came into the ins. That was mostly for my main special attack.

And it had grown as well.

Quite a lot in fact:

Unarmed Combat skill improved: +1.
Damage dealt without a weapon increased by 185%
Attack accuracy increased by 185%.
Current level: 36.
Improve this skill by fighting enemies of your level or higher for additional bonuses and new special attacks.

Hammerfist improved: +1.
Cost to use: 2 mana points.
Deals 1900% of normal damage.
Ignores 35% of armor.

Pay a visit to a master of Unarmed Combat to learn more special attacks!

A bit more and I'd hit level five. Feeling inspired, I picked up the loot from the last pack. I got a few silver and copper coins, as well as an unusual *green* knife, which looked more like a sharpener but gave interesting bonuses: plusses to *Thief* and *Break-in*. The little knife took a place in my bag together with a rare *blue* grubby armband, which increased agility and *Stealth*. That brightened my mood and gave me cause to hope it would get better from there.

I got up off the slimy floor and took a step toward the boss section when suddenly I saw a silhouette split off a black unlit section of wall. If this hadn't happened in the virtual world, I'd have shit a couple dozen bricks. All hostile mobs were dead, everything behind me was clear, and before me was the boss room!

"Nether!" I shouted. "And who the hell might you be?"

In the light of some water-sac torches jutting out of the wall, I saw a fearsome figure three feet taller than me. It had a massive body, tail, hooves, a bull's head and a huge ring in its nose. I breathed a sigh of relief. Level eleven, elite. But I had already lain low three packs of that, even if none of them were human-bull hybrids. Seemingly this was a patrol mob. It came just as I finished taking down the previous pack. And just in the nick of time. Let it bash at me to keep the curse active. My health took a while to regenerate, but it was always better to have insurance.

"Here little bull," I lured it with my left hand while the other squeezed into a fist. "I'm gonna break off your horns!"

"No, I'm gonna break you...!" the tauren bellowed out in the deep bass of a five-story building.

Hammer launched at him like a cannonball, but didn't hit. The mob deftly stepped back, then poked his good hand into his chest and said:

"Don't fight, Alex. Trixie is here to help. Clayton said: Scyth is good. Trixie will help Scyth!"

Trixie from Cali Bottom? The same one who used to be a nameless zombie under the temple? I started suspecting there were no nonplayer characters in this game whatsoever.

"Trixie?"

"Mhm," the tauren grinned. He pointed over my head, clearly at my health points bar. "You are so weird! Why don't you die?"

Chapter Twenty-Four

Stopped in the Act

"**A**LRIGHT,**"** Trixie easily agreed with my suggestion to kill him. "Will you bring donuts? I like them! But they made my stomach hurt..."

The tauren was still giving short broken phrases in a booming bass, talking about food, his grandfather, his hate for universal nutrient blends and other commonplace things he found important. Before that he expressed an eagerness to help me get through the jail and, in confirmation, he banged on the tunnel wall. That made a clump of seemingly living tissue fall off, splattering into a black slime. Then he showed his bull's biceps. I imagined what a joy it must have been for a little person like him to be so big...

I refused his help though. First, it might cause him problems with the corporation, and

---

second I was trying to keep witnesses to a minimum.

I explained the fact that I had torn a pack to bits before his eyes with my bare hands and easily survived with one percent life by saying I had a special combat elixir. He just shrugged, which was a bit hard to see with his hefty torso and beefy neck. But I figured I should warn him one more time:

"Trixie, don't tell anyone what you saw here, okay? It's a secret! Do you understand?"

"Okay," he said and blurted out the longest thing I had ever heard him say: "I love keeping secrets! I collect them! If you tell someone a secret, then you have one less secret. That's a bad deal."

"Good. Ready?" I was looking anxiously at my health bar. While we were talking, it had gone up three quarters. "Attack!"

"Will you fly to my place?" He didn't hit right away, pausing his footlong claws at my neck.

"Yes, I'll come. You and I need to have a talk. I'm not sure it'll be tomorrow, but on the weekend for sure. Do you know anyone else like you here?"

He shook his head and slashed without warning. His claws went in under my clavicle. I howled in rage and slashed back.

Altered Tauren Criminal has critically damaged you: 247!

Damage completely absorbed by Curse of the Undead.
Health points: 178/220.

You have critically damaged Altered Tauren Criminal: 106!
Health points: 634/740.

As we agreed, the tauren kept swinging at me full force, but his blows weren't doing any damage. And meanwhile I just couldn't stop thinking about Clayton, who had died so strangely right after he simply let himself be killed in Dis. And so I decided to imitate a fully-fledged battle with Trixie.

Before dying, he rasped out something about donuts. The loot he was *Altered Ash,* just like most of the mobs down here. It functioned as an alchemy ingredient. In the system's reckoning, it was worth a quarter silver, but I could get more at auction. The system only showed the guaranteed purchase price from nonplayer vendors.

I needed twenty experience points more to reach level five – less than I'd get for a mob in this ins. So not wanting to waste any more time, I ran into the first boss room without preparation.

At one time this was a cell for ten or twenty prisoners, but now it was the dwelling place of the *altered* gnome Wimpy, a level-twelve mad scientist and inventor. He was alone but, based on his appearance, he didn't need any help.

Suddenly, the gnome raised his head and gave a sniff.

"Hm..." he muttered. "Change in atmospheric oxygen content detected! Hm-hm..."

Small, only up to my chest, the gnome was wearing a powerful exoskeleton of mysterious origin. Digging around in a pile of scrap metal, he suddenly got up, hit a button and... disappeared.

I heard a clap in the other end of the room, revealing where he'd gone: to a strange looking machine powered by a clearly living semi-transparent intestine coming from the surface of the floor. And there were black clods of something wriggling around inside.

What it actually was I didn't see. I was already flying across the inventor's lab. Pah! The attack went nowhere, the mana points burned for no reason. Meanwhile, a red beam hissed into my quickly frying skin. It was such serious pain that I stopped breathing. Tears filled my eyes. All that remained was to fall on the floor and squirm, trying to escape.

Wimpy has damaged you: 142.
Damage completely absorbed by Curse of the Undead.
Health points: 178/220.

Wimpy has damaged you: 134.
Damage completely absorbed by Curse of the Undead.
Health points: 178/220.

Wimpy has damaged you: 158.
Damage completely absorbed by Curse of the Undead.
Health points: 178/220.

New combat logs flickered up the whole time the laser was trained on me. Hiding behind some mysterious piece of machinery, I wiped the sweat off my face. What a relief...

Pah! Sh-sh-shu-u-uugh-gh-gh! Son of a bitch! Nether! I couldn't hold back and screamed. I'd definitely have to dig into the settings of my capsule! This was an order of magnitude more painful than before!

"Good news, old buddies!" the gnome cackled. "Tonight's dinner will be served hot!"

I rolled forward and aside and the beam burned into the slimy floor, heading for me. Screw it. It wasn't real, just visual effects. I ran over to the boss, but I only managed to hit once and not with *Hammer* because its cooldown time hadn't passed yet.

You have damaged Wimpy: 4!

Class-A Threat

Health points: 1196/1200.

Pah! The boss teleported once again and turned on the hyperboloid in his exoskeleton. Zh-zh-zh-zhoo-oogh-gh-gh-gh-gh! I clenched my teeth and, despite myself, covered my eyes with a hand and dashed toward the boss.

Resilience skill improved: +1.
Resistance to all types of damage increased by 6%.
Pain reduced by 6%.
Current level: 6.
Improve this skill by fighting enemies of your level or higher for additional bonuses and new special attacks.

Stoneskin ability improved: +1.
Cost to use: 3 mana points.
Increases resistance to all types of damage by 11%.
Duration: 5 seconds.

Level six *Resilience* gave six-percent resistance to all types of damage and lowered perceived pain by the same amount. From there it logically followed that, at level one hundred, resistance would be maximum. But that had to be impossible! That would give complete immunity!

Most likely the skill had a cap, some upper limit. Either that or here, as with damage and accuracy in *Unarmed Combat*, the numbers only applied to enemies of equal level.

The *Stoneskin* level-up caught me by surprise. The ability's active time stopped growing at five seconds, but the resistance percentage was still going up.

Basically, complete invulnerability made me feel relaxed. In a normal battle, players were always on edge, timing out their every move for maximum DpS while their tank and healer were alive, all while trying not to aggro the boss.

But here I was calmly thinking and trying to distract myself; reading logs, mechanically trying to get a hit in on the boss after cooldown and trying to ignore the burning beam putting holes in the scraps of my rotting flesh and frying the nerve endings of my dying body.

The battle just kept going. Wimpy kept gushing out stupid quotes like "I love the smell of fried meat in the morning!" and wouldn't let me land a series of blows longer than two. Every time he would disappear and come back with a "pah!" at the other end of the large room.

When I dashed over to him once again, I gained another level in *Resilience*. Then it dawned on me. The laser beam dealt constant damage, basically a DoT that ticked with every second spent in the active zone. I curled up in the fetal position on the floor, trying to mentally distance myself from the pulsating burning in my back and get as far from here as possible.

The laser burned constantly. And my *Resilience* progress bar slowly but surely went up. Meanwhile, the mad inventor began a scientific discussion with himself about the proper cooking level for human meat as I, gritting my teeth, wandered... or tried to wander in the clouds.

Why was I doing all this? The answer was plain to see: I had dreams of working in space, and for that I had to finish university. Online classes in virtual space wouldn't be enough. Despite profession's casual sounding name, beyond encyclopedic knowledge, a space guide needed a whole array of skills. And that included piloting a space shuttle and the required physical training.

A space guide had to be able to pilot an interplanetary yacht and be a master aerospace engineer so that, if anything went wrong, they could fix it. They also had to feel comfortable in zero gravity and be able to do space walks... Yes it was a lot to know, that was why studying to be, in essence, captain of a space yacht took six years in university then the same amount of time as a cabin boy and junior pilot on an active vessel.

And only the top ten percent of university graduates had their way paid by the taxpayers.

Another one percent each were taken on by corporations and private sponsors. But for middling students like me, the only option was to pay.

"Smells like... Mmm... Barbecue!" Wimpy shouted, knocking me off track.

I clenched my jaw when the laser passed over my unprotected neck. This wasn't the kind of pain I felt a few days ago, this was much stronger! And that was strange, considering that my *Resilience* skill had gone up.

So... No pain, I was just pretending. None of that existed, my body was safe and sound in a capsule back at home...

So then, my studies. That would take money. Lots of money. And here was why.

Twenty billion people lived on this planet and, in just a few decades, they had completely changed their conception of the value of human life. No one strove to "give everyone chance" or "support the working poor," as certain activist movements once called for. Every year there was a new crop of them from among the high-status citizenry. But all it took was lowering their citizenship class a level or two and they learned to keep their mouths shut. In fact, they all eventually came to sincerely repent for their ignorance.

The planet was not capable of feeding this many people, and even our early colonization of

Class-A Threat

Mars couldn't help. There were just two thousand people living there now and that would only double in a few years. They were less than a droplet in the ocean.

But after concepts like "social value to society" were introduced, fierce competition took root. People strived to increase their class however they could, and the only way to do that was by raising social value. And that meant becoming useful to society.

And that was possible only by having a high-demand profession which was only possible with higher education. No one wanted more competition for the small number of spots, and that was why the education had become so expensive. The needs of civilization were completely met by the ten percent of the population hardwired to be straight-A students so, collectively, we paid for their studies. The rest would either fall into the nether or have to pay out of pocket for further schooling.

Even if I did pass the citizenship test, and got assigned the lowest citizenship status of L, all I could hope for was a wretched existence in a shoe box scarcely more spacious than the cubbies they kept noncitizens in, a miserable basic income and a strictly regulated ration of universal nutrient blend. Medical care, luxury items, which now included even underwear, entertainment and subscription to the public flying car service... All that had to be purchased with money, and money had to be earned.

And without education, the only way to get any capital was in *Disgardium*. In the other worlds, wages for online work were lower and, due to lower popularity, their in-game items and currency were worthless. After all who would want some legendary set if there was nobody to show it off to?

My parents' upcoming divorce would lower their status. It was a strange rule at first glance but, like everything the UN did, it was aimed at lowering the birth rate. No one said you couldn't get married again, or even have more offspring. Technically the "one child per family" rule wouldn't be broken. But you would certainly lose citizenship level. And along with that your income would fall sharply, as would your guaranteed basic income.

I couldn't believe my mother and father decided to do that! I mean no one would have said a word if they just stayed married, and got new partners on the side! But no, and it was all because of father, I was certain. He was too proud and proper to go against the system and his conscience. Clearly, he had fallen out of love with mom...

My attention was drawn by the fact that my *Resilience* progress bar was stuck at 0% and had stopped going up, even though the mad gnome was still attacking. What was more, he had added stink bombs to the laser beam, which enshrouded me with impenetrable wisps of red smoke full of flecks of soot that curled around in the air.

I looked at the most recent logs.

Resilience skill improved: +1.
Resistance to all types of damage increased by 36%.
Pain reduced by 36%.
Current level: 36.

Stoneskin ability improved: +1.
Cost to use: 3 mana points.
Increases resistance to all types of damage by 26%.
Duration: 20 seconds.

My last skill-up happened more than a minute ago. Weird, what happened? Why wasn't it growing anymore? I focused on the bars but nothing changed. No hints, no warnings.

Okay, sure. I'd have to wade into the encyclopedia. Skills... Combat skills... Defensive skills...

Aha, here: "A skill will level in battle with enemies of your level and up, but only until that skill reaches three times the enemy's level."

Everything was coming together: Wimpy was at level twelve, and my *Resilience* was at thirty-six. I couldn't squeeze any more out of this mad inventor. It was time to keep going.

I stood up off the floor with a groan like an old man, hissed when the laser hit me in the eyes, then went blind for an instant and dashed at the boss. Stay where you are, pipsqueak! I'm gonna give you a real bop on the noggin for all that torture! This is an act of retaliation!

Emergency exit has been activated by: external command from immersion pod!
All progress in this dungeon will be lost!
Remaining time: 3... 2... 1...

"Son of a bitch!" I almost exclaimed as the intragel suddenly rushed out into the chamber walls. And good thing, because as soon as the capsule doors flew open, I saw my mom.

"Alex! Sorry for the interruption, but we're late!"

"To what exactly?" I bulged my eyes out, barely holding back.

They had robbed me of my dreams, they were getting divorced. They were the reason I had to spend all this time in Dis levelling masochism instead of studying. And now what was this? Now they were having troubles and I'd have to run this ins all over again!

"We're going to the O'Sullivans'. Did you forget? It's Eve's birthday!"

Chapter Twenty-Five

Eve's Birthday

"WHAT THE HECK, mom? Can you even do that?"

"What do you mean?" she asked, dumbstruck. "What are you saying I did?"

"I mean, you pulled me out of Dis while I was fighting a dungeon boss!" I kept objecting, but more out of inertia, still steeped in the fury of battle. "What's the hurry? The O'Sullivans live in our building, it takes two minutes to get there!"

"Since when do you talk to your mom like that, Alex? And why are you shouting?" father said in surprise, entering the room. "Wasn't it you who said no virtual game was worth wasting time in real life? Especially if we're talking about your best friend!"

Oh... Father was right. How could I forget? I flew back from school with her and talked with her after class. We spent so much time together, but she just left my mind like the wind. How could I not have wished her happy birthday? And plus that less than flattering scene with Tissa... Damn, damn, damn!

I turned completely red, remembering all the embarrassing things I had done in the last day. My problems in *Disgardium* had pulled me in head first! Even in the real world I was thinking about stuff in the game... and about Tissa.

"Sorry, mom..."

She looked at father. I noticed mom was wearing a nice evening dress with her hair coiffed and high heeled shoes... I hadn't seen her looking this pretty in a very long time. She looked younger. If you told someone now that she was twenty-five, they'd believe you. Dad was also dressed to the nines: cleanshaven, his hair was combed, and he had a suit on. Now he was leaning on the door with his hands in his pockets, spreading the tangy woody aroma of his expensive cologne.

"I'm gonna pop into the shower and get ready quick," I said hurriedly, jumping out of the pod. "What gift did we get?"

"The question is what gift did *you* get?" asked dad. "A few weeks back you, as usual, asked us to put fifteen phoenixes in your account. And you said it was for a gift for Eve... Did you forget?"

I really wanted to say I did forget and that I

forgot because of their stupid divorce! But I got myself together. They had just about stopped fighting and I didn't want to remind them of that incendiary decision.

"No dad, I didn't forget. Alright, give me a few minutes."

They exchanged glances and left. Mom looked at father accusingly, and he gave me a nod of pity. What was happening to me was very familiar to him.

Getting ready didn't take much time. My feverish search for a gift took longer than I was expecting. Last year I gave Eve a ticket to a virtual concert of her favorite group. That is, both the group and concert were completely real, but it all happened in U-City, a huge virtual entertainment city. It was a great gift... for a little girl.

But today she was turning fifteen! What could I possibly give to a growing young woman? I glanced at her online wish list, but everything she wanted had already been bought. Her parents probably just got everything on it.

So in desperation, I found a page called "The most popular gifts for teen girls" from an online gift store and ordered the first braided silver bracelet I came upon. I had just enough money, and the delivery time was just one hour. I could go out on their balcony and get my gift, feeding my location data to the delivery drone.

Buttoning up my shirt as I went, I flew out of my bedroom. We left home and, three minutes later, were standing at the O'Sullivans' door. The face recognition software worked its magic, something clicked and the door obediently climbed up. The smell of food and sound of fun came pouring out. There was loud music playing and the party was buzzing.

"Eve!" Mrs. O'Sullivan shouted when she saw us. "Go say hi to your guests!"

She hugged mom and kissed dad and me on the cheek. She smelled of wine and chocolate.

"Come in, everyone else is already here," she said. "Helene, can you help me?"

Mom nodded and together they ducked into the kitchen. I heard women's voices and laughter there. Help, as usual meant nothing more than chewing over the fresh gossip.

"Alright, Alex. I'm gonna go talk with the guys. Don't get too bored!" dad patted me on the shoulder and walked into the office.

"Mark!" Eve's father's voice rang out. "How long has it been?!"

The door slammed and I was left alone with the light cloud of tobacco smoke.

I had come over here so many times and it was always the same. The women drink wine in one room, the men lock themselves in Mr. O'Sullivan's office, smoke cigars, drink whisky and play poker, discussing recent news, women, sports and politics. And as always we were left to our own devices: Eve's room, a table full of food and children's games. Last year we played *Monopoly* almost all evening. We had so much fun we almost died! I'm lying, that's sarcasm.

"I'll be right back," came Eve's voice from the far room.

She went into the entryway and stopped, not having made up her mind to come closer. I also didn't know what to do. Eve was dressed up today, but not the same as normal. This time it was not a child's pink dress and a cardboard crown. I might have even said she looked adult. She had on a light lady's make-up, fashionably coiffed hair, an evening dress, high-heel shoes and a barely detectable air of perfume.

"Happy birthday, Eve!" I said. "Your gift is on its way."

"Thanks Alex," she nodded and bit her lip. "Let's go, I'll introduce you to the guys. You don't know any of them. They're dad's new friends' kids."

"Wait..." I hesitated, rushing to say my fill while we were still alone. "Sorry I didn't say anything this morning. And that I flew off with Tissa..."

That was a mistake. I shouldn't have reminded her. A shadow ran across her face.

Class-A Threat

"You see... I just haven't been myself lately... My parents are getting divorced, I'm spending whole nights in *Disgardium*... It's my fault that..." the more I said the more she bit her lip and looked struck. I could read in her eyes "stop!"

"Do you like her?" Eve looked me in the eyes. "Be honest!"

"I do. But..." I hesitated, thinking of how best to explain to her that she was much closer to me, just not romantically. "Uh..."

"Sure," she answered simply. "Let's go."

Lots of changes had happened to her room. The many video panels in the walls were no longer showing sweet cartoon cats and famous actors from preteen series. Every wall now depicted a landscape from adult *Disgardium*. A pink glow emanated from the ceiling. That was also new but, without it, it would all have looked somewhat gloomy. What was more, the cozy white rug that used to be on her floor was gone.

There were three people sitting around the small birthday table. The two eighteen-year old boys were somehow similar looking even though one was a bleach-blond Asian and the other was a strong white brunette with the neck of a bull. An instant later I realized what made them look alike: they both looked well-groomed, polished and arrogant. They didn't pay me any mind.

The only girl's head was half shaved. She

was also older than Eve and I, and was plainly bored, digging around in her communicator.

"Guys, meet Alex," Eve began with exaggerated cheer. "We've known each other since we were kids. Alex, this is Maria, Bill and Xan."

"Hi, Alex!" they said, their apathetic gazes sliding over me.

The boys returned to their conversation. As far as I could tell, they were talking about Dis. Only the girl even seemed to know we existed:

"So, you've known each other since you were kids?" she raised an eyebrow ironically. "You're still kids! Talk to me after you've passed your citizenship tests."

Eve didn't answer. Instead she sat at the table and started eating cake with a neutral expression. I took the only free seat and went after the hot food. Eve's mom was a great cook, but I wasn't sure she was still doing the baking. By the looks of things, they now had a chef.

"You shouldn't eat so much," Maria snorted and slapped her thigh expressively. "It's all gonna end up here."

"Ah, who cares," the birthday girl waved it off. "Dad's taking me to the clinic tomorrow."

"Plastic surgery? I see. Then yeah, this is a great opportunity. Use it to the fullest! After today you won't be able to indulge like this..." Maria buried her nose back in her comm.

Class-A Threat

She didn't try to talk anymore after that. I was not exactly burning with desire to chat either, though I did want to know what the boys were discussing.

"... and that cretin challenged me to a duel!" Bill guffawed. "He bet his flying car he could take me!"

"That clumsy idiot?" Xan asked in surprise. "And you agreed?"

"Of course! He figured as he's five levels above me so he can win easily. Aha, sure. Fat chance! One of my shields is worth more than his flying car! A legendary from the Svyatogor set!"

"So you've got the shield?" Xan's eyes crawled into his forehead.

"Between us two, yes. But it's transmogrified. For these exact circumstances, I made it look like regular epic."

"You got anything else from that set?" the boy's eyes began glowing greedily.

Bill waved his shovel-like hand with false carelessness:

"I may have something..."

"What?" he started pushing.

"Sorry Xan, you understand..." Bill said with a grin. "I can't say."

"So..." Xan wrinkled his brow. "One of the Russian clans has the helm, that's for sure. And I've seen the sword. Some sheikh has it..."

"Alright, no more guesses," Bill said pitifully. "It isn't exactly a secret. I have the horse. It's a combat mount. But it's almost no good, because I prefer to fly." I looked at him with respect and understanding, but he quickly disappointed me. "Those stupid poors never look into the sky! Easy kills!"

"That's right," Xan agreed and held up his hand for a high five.

I would have kept listening, but then my comm buzzed, notifying me the drone with Eve's gift had arrived. I apologized, ran out onto the balcony, accepted the fancily packaged box wrapped in ribbon and went back. I handed the gift to the birthday girl, and everyone spent a few minutes watching curiously.

"That's a fun little trinket," Maria observed.

"I like it," said Eve. She clasped the bracelet on her wrist and admired it, tilting her arm. "Thanks, Alex."

She kissed me on the cheek and blushed. The boys then, their brief curiosity satisfied, got right back to what they were talking about.

"You aren't gonna try to get the whole set?" asked Xan.

"Of course I am!" Bill slammed his hand on the table so hard the dishes gave a jump. "Do you know what it gives?"

"Uh... like a jillion billion strength?" Xan

asked with a lazy chuckle.

"That's all on its own," he said, waving it off. "It also has a bunch of plusses to every stat, and most importantly it gives a unique ability! It makes you ten times bigger for one minute! You can just crush everyone around you! Isn't that awesome?"

"Wait really?" Xan couldn't believe it. His eyes turned into dinner plates. "And how is damage calculated for that?"

"No one knows, buddy. And that's because the set has never been assembled before. The last element is the Svyatogor chainmail, which is worn under plate armor, and it hasn't been found."

"All the previous parts of the set came from reward chests for eliminating threats with potential M or higher. That means the chainmail will be for the same," Xan declared authoritatively, raising a finger.

"That's right," Bill nodded and tore into his roast chicken thigh. He chewed it, came up close to his friend and whispered barely audibly: "Did you hear about the new threat around the Nameless Mountains?"

"The potential L?" Xan asked, finishing a rainbow-colored drink. "Yeah, we're trying to find it."

"So are we," Bill whispered feverishly, and I perked my ears. "And you know what?"

"The sandbox," the Korean answered with

his lips alone.

"Exactly. We've got guys standing watch and checking all the noobs that come out with *True Flame*."

"We don't have that many people, but it's a good idea. I'll tell our guys..."

"Hey, that's our spot!" Bill objected. "And that was supposed to stay between us!"

"Oh come on! All the preventers already know! There's nowhere else for the threat to come from, unless they just quit the game for good. We checked everything in the mountains and nearby!" Xan looked at me sidelong. "Hey, what's your name... you wouldn't happen to live in Tristad, would you?"

I just about gagged. I was spellbound, chewing mechanically but no longer distinguishing flavors or able to even tell schnitzel from cake. But when they turned their attention to me, I shuddered in surprise and froze.

"His name is Alex, Xan! And yes, he's with me," Eve confirmed. "But I don't really understand what you're talking about. I just started playing, and now I'm getting power-levelled in Gloomwood. I'm level three already!"

"Woah, three! Not bad!" they admired, exchanging smiles. "And who you got power levelling you?"

"Some guys from Axiom, the number one

clan in my sandbox! By the way, they're champions of the Arena this year!"

"The noob arena, with players from sandboxes only," Xan said mockingly. "A bit more and you can start fighting! By the way, I recommend it. Everyone there is poor. If you've got good gear, you can easily become champion. And it's actually worth doing. In my day I won and got an elixir giving plus ten to all attributes."

"You got lucky," Bill noted. "I got plus ten to one stat, though I did get a choice." He turned to me. "And you, Alex, what level you at?"

"Almost five."

"I see. A bit weak... Anyway, about Tristad, listen. Have you noticed anything strange, like some player levelling way too fast?"

"Nah, I haven't seen anything. No one will even let me in a group. I'm levelling slowly and I don't want to go into dungeons."

"Alex, why so modest?" Eve exclaimed. "He soloed a level-five dungeon at level one. I was in a group with him, but I got killed right away."

"What are you talking about!" Bill admired, not looking away. "And how'd you do that, champion?"

"Solo at level one?" I laughed, but it came across nervous. "It wasn't exactly 'solo!' Eve left the game, I joined a group with some classmates and they dragged me through the dungeon."

"I see," Bill was disappointed and lost interest.

"By the way, Alex. Wanna level with me?" Eve offered. "I paid Axiom to get me up to level ten! And I get all the loot! Want me to negotiate to get you in too? That way we can sit and chat while they clear mobs. The experience just pours in!"

"Sure, why not? Let's talk tomorrow," I suggested. Was I really going to refuse her yet again on her birthday and upset her? No thanks. "After school?"

Eve lit up, but was immediately disappointed:

"I'm going to the clinic tomorrow, then I'll have to spend a few days in recovery..."

"Not an issue. Then after that?"

"Alright!" she said, blossoming.

And I nodded, already back to listening to the boys talking about something else. Now they were on to the Destroying Plague.

Chapter Twenty-Six

New Figure

W E WERE BACK home by midnight. My parents were pretty tipsy and even opened a bottle of wine in the kitchen so they could trade impressions of the O'Sullivans and their upcoming promotion. I said goodnight, but actually locked myself in my room and climbed into my capsule so I would miss it if or when they fought. I didn't go right into the game, having decided to wade through the forums and compare what I found there with what those rich kids were saying.

Fortunately, when Bill and Xan were talking about the Destroying Plague, Eve did not remember me getting its *Mark* in the temple crypt. When I got it, that jumped by in the group chat, and she even asked what it was. But hopefully she forgot.

I closed the forums in two minds. I didn't find out much news about that global cataclysm. Throughout *Disgardium*, including in cities, there were now small dungeons and locations filled with skeletons, zombies and other kinds of undead. In that world, such mobs were nothing new. But the main bosses of those dungeons all shouted that they had been sent by the Destroying Plague, and that made me think.

In places I had found reanimated animal corpses. Just like the zombie rats I had come across or the strange unkillable cockroaches. But that also leaked onto the forums only as mentions of quirks or new features added by the corporation. One player complained that he had been attacked in a peaceful location by a usually unaggressive deer and, only after dying, saw in the logs that this was no common deer, but an *infected* one. The only answer under his post was predictable: "You got killed by a zombie deer? Lol! You're such a dumbass!"

Nevertheless, the words Destroying Plague were trending in various contexts and the overall opinion was that it was none other than the next bane of all *Disgardium*. Whether it was a deity, some especially strong mob or a natural disaster like an epidemic remained unclear. But there was no question that it would be coming for everyone. And both the Commonwealth and the dark races were afflicted.

Meanwhile, I tried looking up information on threats, but I already knew everything that was publicly available. Sometimes, players did something extraordinary that made them more than a common player, and after that they were recognized as a threat to the world.

Some even drew an analogy to the real world, and assumed this all came from there. With varying frequency, there were babies born who presented a threat to humanity in a way that no one could have predicted: Genghis Khan, Osama Bin Laden, Adolf Hitler...

Or what about Jefferey Gacy? He was from an F-class family, successful, popular with the ladies. He had a loving wife, a child, a career in the space fleet. He was living the dream! How could he possibly have been a threat? But something snapped in his mind and he rammed a tourist space shuttle into an orbital shopping center. A few tens of thousands of people died, and most of them were high-status citizens of high social value.

I didn't find anything about the preventer clans other than scant information that they existed, tracked down all threats, found them and eliminated them. Every such clan had something like a hotline, which could be used to share suspicions, whispers and rumors. And they paid well for information, if it led to a real threat: one hundred thousand phoenixes and up for information about any threat with a potential higher than G.

And that just so happened to be exactly how much I needed for my first two years of university.

That made me think. What if I fed them my own identity?

To be honest, I would get approximately half that for my current potential, but nevertheless that was guaranteed entry into my first year! Or I could talk with the Dementors and share the reward...

But no, that was not an option. Snowstorm would find out. The pods scanned you every time you loaded up Dis. And they didn't merely register body health, they could read brain activity. The corporation claimed it was all done for good reasons like to make the world of Dis safe from maniacs and psychopaths, and track the mental health of its users. But obviously, if they could read one thing, what was to stop them from reading everything?

So instead I decided to stick to my initial strategy and build on my threat potential. The fact that preventers were checking people as they left our sandbox didn't have me worried yet. How long could they possibly keep watch there? I had almost another six months before my sixteenth birthday, and I seriously doubted they would waste the expensive ingredients for *True Flame* and clan time for so long...

In Tristad it was a warm and hectic night. A starry sky, city streets filled with pleasure-seekers. In the evening, *Disgardium* always felt like a party. Street musicians, bards, dancers both male and female could be found on every corner. Even next to the jail where I appeared there was an illusionist performing.

The streetlights burned bright. A huge moth, drawn to one near me, hit me with a wing. I batted it away and, squinting, tried to figure out what I'd lost in the emergency exit. I opened my profile and saw that I still had my improved *Resilience* and the experience from the three packs of mobs in the dungeon.

I was running out of time, so I didn't waste any. I couldn't miss school tomorrow, and it would be good to not only pass this instance in three or four hours, but also level *Unarmed Combat* as much as possible. But my only hope for tomorrow's duel with Crag was to at least get a bit of sleep. And right after class I'd have to find a location with higher-level mobs – no matter what I wouldn't be able to get around the maximum skill-levelling limit.

I walked up to the instance portal, but found only disappointment.

The Tristad City Jail dungeon is being completed by another group of players.
Current group progress: battle with **Wimpy** *– 91%. Alive: 5/5 group members.*

Nether! All that was left was to hope that the mad gnomish inventor would wreck them. I posted up next to the portal and attempted to enter from time to time so I could see their progress. After they killed the boss, I realized that there was no reason to sit and wait here. Better to do something else. I remembered my other plans, stood up and headed to the tavern.

I scraped some cash out of the chest in my personal room and ran to a vendor to get some *Cooking* ingredients. Unfortunately, he had nothing for my recipes other than spices and seasonings. I couldn't level bread baking any further. I'd have to buy some stuff at auction because I had no time to hunt rabbits or deer.

There I placed the *Altered Ash* up for sale, of which I had nineteen in the bag. The market rate was three times higher than what I'd get from a vendor, and I could easily spare the money for commission. I put up my items ten percent cheaper than others, and went to check prices for *Cooking* ingredients. I got a couple beeps to tell me a sale had gone through.

I checked my inbox and was pleasantly

surprised: everything had been bought, and my wallet was approximately eleven gold heavier! That was an astronomical sum considering that, one week ago, I couldn't even find one copper to pay for a ripped dress.

Gladdened, I decided to unload the *green* knife and *blue* armband I picked up in the jail. They were for level ten, and their bonuses were useless to me. But I had a change of mind. Tomorrow I'd drop by Underweight. That would be faster and maybe even more profitable.

For almost a whole gold, I bought a few dozen spider eggs, some venison and some rabbit meat. The meat went for ten silver a stack, because the auction was packed with such low-level loot. Everything I bought was instantly in my inbox, and it went from there into my inventory. My bag was completely full.

All that remained was to decide where to practice *Cooking*. It was against the rules to start a fire within city limits, but I didn't want to go out of town either. Crag wasn't the only ganker in Tristad after all. So I went back to the Bubbling Flagon, left all my money in my chest and went down to the kitchen.

Chef Arno recognized me, greeted me kindly and didn't refuse my request to use their extra fireplace and dishes to cook. The kitchen wasn't too busy. After midnight, people preferred to drink.

You have cooked Spider-Egg Omelet.
Spider-Egg Omelet (1) added to your inventory.

Cooking trade: +1.
Current level: Pupil (54/100)
You have received experience points for progressing in a trade: +1.

The ball was rolling. The individual experience points brought me a new level after my twelfth omelet. I couldn't hold back a smile. I could finally put on the +5-endurance amulet I picked up from Dargo!

You are now level 5!
5 free attribute points available!

I pushed the plus button five times and my strength went up to ten. My damage dealing abilities doubled, which was something to celebrate. Maybe adding six points to base damage wouldn't be a huge help in tomorrow's duel with Crag, but the power of my *Hammerfist* would also be doubling! And that, as my Uncle Nick often said, was a horse of a different color.

Meanwhile, another set of spider eggs spattered in the pan along with some venison and rabbit meat. At first the trade grew with every dish

I made, but after level ninety my progress slowed down significantly.

It took me twenty eggs just to go up one point. I tipped over one hundred with some *Fried Rabbit* and *Herb-encrusted Venison Filet.* They were considered harder, so I sometimes didn't succeed making them.

"You're getting somewhere, Scyth!" the chef congratulated me, observing my creations with curiosity. "I think you're ready to move onto the next level in this trade! If you like, I could raise your rank to journeyman."

"With pleasure, Mr. Arno!" I agreed, looking at the interface clock. "Just one thing. I don't have any money on me but if need be I can run and get it..."

"No money, Scyth!" the large man shook his head. "Fifty silver won't make me any richer, but it will make me feel like an ungrateful bastard. You saved my life, I am indebted to you!"

I started thinking that the developers had some hidden reputation stat for various nonplayer characters. How else could I explain Arno's selflessness?

It took me more than an hour to grasp the ins and outs of journeyman-rank *Cooking*! Arno couldn't just assign me the rank or tell me about new recipes. He had to show and explain, it was the only way. In fact, for all game professions it was thought that Dis should not only entertain, but teach. It was at least good that the devs had found a golden mean and sped up the "training" process.

By the end of the master class, I noticed anxiously that it was coming to two AM, and I still had a dungeon to get through.

"Sorry, Scyth," Arno yawned. "I have nothing more to teach you. Everything else I know how to cook requires at least expert level. Come back when you've leveled up some more…"

Your rank in the Cooking trade has been increased to Journeyman!
Current level: Journeyman (100/250).
Chance of cooking a dish with known recipe: 100%
Chance of inventing a new dish: 10%.

Cooking recipes added*: smoked bear, crab claws in spicy sauce, crocodile steak, peppered blood sausage, grabber fry-up, farmer's winter snack, bat appetizer, juicy pork ribs…*

To improve your skill in this trade, prepare dishes with known recipes, come up with your own recipes and experiment with ingredients.

Class-A Threat

Before exiting, I checked the chef's status. He was still labeled *infected*. What to do with that information I did not know, so I simply bid him a fond farewell. What did the disease even do? Was it possible to cure? Maybe it was like a curse, and a priest of Nergal the Radiant could remove it? I'd have to ask, but cautiously.

With those thoughts in mind, I went outside and headed for the city jail. This time the dungeon was free...

* * *

Trixie was still playing the same Tauren, but this time gave no indications of human intelligence. Along with his pack, he attacked fiercely. I still hadn't gotten Curse of the Undead to trigger before I reached Wimpy, and *Stoneskin* made no sense with my one health...

I spent almost two uninterrupted hours dying while the RNG laughed in my face. The curse wouldn't trip no matter how I tried and, at this point, I basically felt like someone cursed to die for all eternity. Haha. In fact I didn't find it funny because, at this rate, I wouldn't be able to pass this dungeon before school started, which was to say nothing about getting some sleep.

> **Altered Kobold Criminal has damaged you: 186.**
> *Health points: 0/255.*
> **You are dead.**
>
> **Remaining time to respawn 9... 8... 7...**

More and more often, I was using the ten-second after death breaks in their full measure. I let the enemy mobs go on their way, just savoring the lack of annoyance. The mantra that my real body was safe and sound was less and less comfort. The pain on the other hand was growing stronger and every time I shuddered in anticipation of the inevitable suffering, seeing that I was again being torn apart and devoured by *altered* monsters.

I was particularly upset that this series of deaths had been no use. *Resilience* wasn't growing, frozen at thirty-six, and when I tossed a gaze over the other skills, I mentally poured out a stream of curses so vile it seemed to reach even the mobs. At the very least, they walked somewhat farther from my dead body.

And I cursed myself with my last words for

wasting all that time. Clearly, my brain was finally slipping into madness when I decided to go back to this instance to level *Unarmed Combat*. I already had it at thirty-six! It hadn't grown a single percent in all this time!

In my rage, I decided to activate emergency exit and leave the game, but then I changed my mind. Instead I took out that white-hot anger on the pack I was facing now and all the *altered* monsters living in this jail. Not this time, maneaters!

The timer counted out the last second, and I respawned. It was the same kobold that killed me before. He grinned and ran at me.

You carry the mark of the Destroying Plague and have evaded fatal damage!
You have been given Curse of the Undead: all damage taken reduced by 100%!
This curse will remain active until you completely restore your health.

Mark of the Destroying Plague improved: +1.
Chance to receive Curse of the Undead: 5%.
Current level: 5.

Curse of the Undead enhanced!
New resource discovered: Plague Energy.

Plague Energy pool capacity: 10000 points.
5% of damage taken while Curse of the Undead is active will be converted into plague energy and stored.
You can use plague energy to increase the power of an attack at a rate of one energy point per HP of damage.

Trying not to mind the pain, I read carefully. And as soon as I was done I realized what happened and got a message:

Current threat class increased: W!

Leaning on the pulsating tunnel wall, I slowly got up off the floor. The *altered* creatures hit, bit and tried to tear off pieces of flesh. They slashed, jabbed and scratched. I meanwhile couldn't take my eyes off a new bar that had come up next to my life and mana ones. It was slowly filling with a toxic green color. The logs now showed not only damage I took, but also the energy I had saved.

Altered Kobold Criminal has damaged you: 163.
Damage completely absorbed by Curse of the Undead.
Health points: 1/255.

Class-A Threat

Plague energy points: 968/10000.

I intuitively wanted to use it all right away. I put it into *Hammer* and slammed into a vile little kobold, dislodging his jaw and stuffing his fangs down his own throat.

You have critically damaged Altered Kobold Criminal: 1307!
Health points: 0/710.
Altered Kobold Criminal is dead.

The mob's body fell dead. I raised my head and gave a carnivorous snort.
Now it was time to do some fighting![1]

---

[1] And yes, that was a reference to Phil from *Final Trial*. :-)

Chapter Twenty-Seven

Friendly Advice

THE REST of the ins melted in my memory into one uninterrupted battle. I was hurrying to finish this and get at least some three hours sleep before school.

The gnomish inventor Wimpy didn't even manage to get to the "good news" and fell in one blow backed up by nearly three thousand points of plague energy. And thank all the gods, it was not reflected in any way – not visually or in the logs. However, the amount of damage would make anyone who saw the numbers think. Already I was thinking that I would have to sluff off extra damage in smaller amounts in my duel with Crag, not letting it reach four-figure sums.

After Wimpy died, a door opened leading to a tunnel. I ran to the second boss without stopping. When I reached Zander, an *altered*

---

goblin from the League, I was accompanied by a large and noisy delegation.

The four packs of mobs and tricky assassin boss generated massive amounts of damage, causing my plague energy reserves to grow very quickly. It was going so fast that every *Hammer* I used did more than a thousand damage and was guaranteed to send whatever unfortunate mob found itself under my hot hand to its forefathers.

I didn't even notice when Zander died. He was equipped with poisoned daggers and shouting not only about the superiority of the goblin trade league, but also his plans to take it over. Very strange plans for an *altered* criminal confined to a small pocket of space.

I took a strategic place in the corner of the boss room, where the monsters piled on me in one huge mass such that I had to fight lying down. Not feeling like moving, I kicked, slammed my fists and used my special as often as the cooldown allowed. *Hammer* was now guaranteed to make contact with someone every time.

And suddenly it was all over. No one was hitting me, the pain was gone and, listening closely, I realized I was alone in this part of the dungeon. I got up from under the pile of bodies and mechanically searched them, picking up all the loot without looking and walked further, eating the rest of the food I cooked in the tavern as I went.

It gave insignificant bonuses to my attributes and, in theory, it wasn't worth it but I wasn't feeling decisive enough to just throw out the fruits of my labor.

I didn't want to repeat the experiment and collect multiple packs again. It was a bit easier to handle them one at a time. What was more, they were stronger now. Some ugly ogre enchanters had been added to the new packs, and they used a bizarre twisted magic.

The two-headed ogres could stretch out time, and suddenly a target I had just hit would be 10 feet away. They also could condense time abruptly and, in an instant, all the claws and fangs of every mob in the room would be tearing into me at once. One of these *altered* enchanters attacked by swinging a sharp blade from afar and, with every imitated blow, a real cut appeared on my body.

The first of these packs took me a quarter hour, and I wasted a fair amount of plague energy on misses. But eventually I found the rhythm of the mages' cooldowns and, dashing at their two-headed bodies, broke through their rib cages. After the mages were gone, taking down the remaining lesser enemies was a minute or two's work.

And that pack was where I levelled up.

You are now level 6!

Class-A Threat

5 free attribute points available!

In the heat of battle, I threw it all into strength, but didn't confirm, having realized that making normal blows do more damage was pointless now that I had plague energy. That made actually landing the blows more important. I placed all five points into perception, which increased my accuracy to seventeen percent.

And that decision proved itself almost immediately. The next groups of mobs before the boss didn't take me much time at all. I would build up plague energy, expend some mana, then calmly take down the rest one at a time.

By the time I reached the final boss, Pherax the draconid, my bag was full of *Altered Ash,* a few *blues* and four *greens.* I managed to get two rare items from the bosses: a bashing *Two-Handed Mechanic's Wrench* from Wimpy and *Silent Boots of the Assassin* from Zander. I didn't have any room left though so, estimating the prices in my head, I tossed out all the *green* and filled up the remaining slots with alchemy ingredients. I figured they would be easier to sell. I'd get more money per inventory slot, too.

I emerged from the last tunnel, which was so low that I had to stoop, hitting my shoulders on the walls before I reached a deep and spacious cave.

Its ceiling was adorned with undulating waves that oozed with black slime. The floor underfoot was also rocking, and it was no easy task to keep my balance.

Then, in the very depths of the cave, a hypnotic hole beckoned. There were concentric spellbinding circles going all the way from its edges to the center. Looking away from this portal to the nether was actually so hard I had to strain.

I looked for the boss and at first couldn't see its bluish black scaly body. The draconid was standing next to the portal and staring at me attentively. But it was silent, doing nothing to come closer.

I had to take a few steps forward myself, but even then he didn't start attacking. Instead, Pherax wrapped himself in darkness, stepped into the portal and disappeared. The exit from the cave contracted and closed up, pulling me inside. There were lots of small openings covering the surface, and a strange smoking substance seeped out of them like sweat from skin. A popup notification showed ticking damage. If not for my curse, the DoT would have killed me very quickly.

Inevitability of the Nether
−3% health points every 3 seconds.

The battle began suddenly, but not at all like

Class-A Threat

I was expecting. I was pulled into the portal and found myself in a replica of the cave, but in the Nether. DoT was still bringing my life down, but then another effect joined the party:

Desperation of the Nether
−3% to all main attributes every 15 seconds.

That was very unpleasant. The portal disappeared, and I had no idea how to get out without killing the draconid.

I threw myself at him and landed a couple hits, but some of them sailed past into thin air. And the boss disappeared and popped back up right behind me.

Pherax wasn't attacking at all, just keeping silent. I was full of regret that I hadn't read any guides on this instance. DoT damage was not converted into plague energy and in a few minutes my damage, already quite low for this boss, was approaching zero. I mean, I basically couldn't even hit him!

My eyes raced around the room, trying to find anything that might have significance in terms of battle tactics, but there were no hints. The world had turned black and white, there were no sounds other than monotonous white noise, and the draconid was keeping his vow of silence.

By minute five, I was clearly at an impasse.

There was no way to kill me, but my blows were doing such a tiny amount of damage it would all regenerate before I landed another blow. And by the way, his health regenerated!

Then I got an idea. Sure no one in their right mind would have thought of it, but I clearly was not in mine. I balled up my fist and slammed it full-force into my own skull. *Hammer.*

Even the game went a bit bonkers, but still did its job:

> **Player Scyth (Alex Sheppard) has critically damaged you: 354!**
> *Damage completely absorbed by Curse of the Undead.*
> *Health points: 42/280.*
>
> **Plague energy points: 18/10000.**
>
> **You have critically damaged player Scyth (Alex Sheppard): 354!**
> *Health points: 42/280.*

I imagine Pherax had never seen anything like this before. Trying to beat myself up as much as possible before my attributes fell to zero, I landed one blow after the next. Clenching my teeth, I grunted and gasped after especially powerful *Hammer* cracks. The boss was so surprised that he froze at the opposite wall like a stone sculpture. Was it just me or was he shaking his head?

By the time all my stats had fallen by two-thirds, I was doing zero damage with normal blows. Accounting for a possible miss, I built up enough plague energy to kill this boss two or even three times.

I landed the final blows while carefully moving toward him, but he was on guard. And just as I came at him, he disappeared. I ran at him and hit with my special once again, but I didn't waste any energy. And thank God for that. I missed. In a few seconds, the boss disappeared again. I meanwhile ran on the chase, counting out heartbeats.

Approximately ten seconds. That was the cooldown time on his disappearing and teleporting ability. With my last attack, I had four seconds. *Hammer*! One thousand plague energy additional damage!

You have damaged Pherax: 1049.
Health points: 722/1800.

Another blow, a miss. He disappeared.
But he didn't survive my next *Hammer*.

✳ ✳ ✳

"Why did you make that stupid bet, Alex?" Tissa flew at me at our very first break. "Are you crazy or something?"

Ten pairs of classmate eyes were staring at me. I yawned wide, covering my mouth and stretched. Something cracked in my body and Tissa rolled her eyes.

"Not here," Ed hissed, looking toward the door out of class.

I nodded. I would have to discuss the joint venture to the Olton Quarries with them sometime. I might as well get this out of the way and hear what they thought about my bet with Crag too. Bomber pushed people aside and jumped out in front. Ed, Tissa and I were close behind.

Rodriguez patted Malik on the shoulder and he stayed in class. He was probably waiting to see what everyone else talked about after we left.

We walked a bit away and got set up next to the windows: Tissa sat down, and the boys stood next to her. The sun outside was shining bright, but heavy leaden clouds were already making inroads. Rain was coming.

"Why?" Ed asked simply, looming over me.

"Why what?"

"Why the hell did you go to bat for that

inwinova? And against Crag? Were you trying to make us look bad? Or are you just suicidal?"

"What do you mean?" He caught me off guard. Was I missing something? "Explain."

"Alex, Alex..." Tissa sighed. "You and your little girlfriend Aphrodite know the score. You must have some idea of the status quo in Dis after that whole year of bumming around."

"Basically," Rodriguez said harshly, "we said you were in the Dementors, a fact which did not go unnoticed. We even went to bat against Crag and Rashidos for you. And now those two are screaming on every corner that we basically ganked them, broke our understandings and took their loot. Then with a ton of people around, you go to bat for some workman and challenge Crag to a duel? And you're level four..."

"Six now."

"I don't give a shit. Everyone is talking about level-four Scyth and Crag at twelve. And when a noob challenges a well-known ganker to a duel with expensive gear on the line, people start to think."

"What do you mean?"

"Well, maybe something with that noob is a bit... sketchy. I mean, you had no good reason to go against him, and you're very confident. And there's been all this talk around about how you're a Dementor now and the conflict with Crag. Back in the day, we threw him out of the clan dishonorably... Axiom is starting to ask questions..." said Ed, working his jaws. "It is none of your business, but most people think we want to teach Crag a lesson. The idea is that we're using you as a lure to get revenge on that idiot. No one understands why though, and that is causing questions and suspicion."

The bell rang but none of them even tried to go back to class. The conversation had just begun and the Dementors were clearly in the mood to finish no matter what.

"Ed, game politics and your reputation are not my problem." I jumped off the window sill and Ed had to take a step back. "Crag is an asshole if I ever saw one. He went after this workman out in the open and, if not for me, his family would be going hungry right now. I don't care about the gear, but I'm not planning to lose! And now we'd better get back to class. I've got enough demerit points this semester as is. We can talk later. What's more, we need to get back to Evil from the Depths. I've decided to help you."

"We can talk later," Ed frowned. "But you think about whether that duel really is worth it. Because no matter how it ends now, the preventers are going to take notice. And they're gonna start asking questions."

Chapter Twenty-Eight

Valor and the Feeble Mind

NO MATTER HOW I tried to keep it together during the conversation with the Dementors, Ed's words made me think. He must have been dropping a hint when he mentioned the preventers. Maybe he was letting me know he already suspected me? We didn't have any time to talk during the other breaks. I slept through the next one after dozing through a tedious lecture by Greg about changes to the map of Europe over the last two hundred years and no one woke me up. After that, the Dementors were gone.

But that was normal. On Fridays, last period was optional. Some visited movie club, others played football, and others still went to the school's studio for a lecture on art. I headed into shop to finish working on an artificial companion, but my eyes were drooping and I couldn't get anything done. I had to leave it without getting anywhere though, because I came close to really messing it up.

I came home alone because Eve was at the clinic. I tried to call but Mr. O'Sullivan answered and said she couldn't talk yet. And that she would likely be unable to until the end of next week. Seemingly, she had gotten some serious plastic surgery because that was a long time for recovery. No, I saw another reason why she couldn't or more likely wouldn't want to speak. No girl wanted to be seen like that.

My house was empty. My parents had gone somewhere. Mom left a message, which played as soon as I walked into the house:

"Alex, dad and I flew off to meet a client. We're going to spend the night there. We'll be back by tomorrow evening. Make sure you behave yourself..."

"Don't listen to her Alex, take your chance!" Dad cackled in the background. Mom hissed, unhappy with his encouragement, then the message was over.

The oven turned on in the kitchen to warm up the food they'd left for me. I changed into shorts and a t-shirt, ate a big dinner then overpowered my desire to sleep a few hours and climbed into my pod. My duel with Crag would be in less than four hours.

A short moment of darkness and the pod walls were replaced with the walls of my personal room in the tavern where I left the game this morning. I opened my inventory: almost four full stacks of *Altered Ash,* one unusual item – plate armbands – and three rare items from the jail bosses. I looked at the loot from Pherax and sighed in disappointment: all this stuff was for level ten at least. Better to sell it and free up the space.

Robe of the Sinister Ritual
Rare
Cloth armor.
Armor: 4.
+5 Intelligence.
+7 Endurance.
Durability: 110/110.
Requires level: 10.
Sell price: 7 gold coins, 19 silver coins.
Chance of losing after death reduced by 50%.

The bashing weapon and boots from the first two bosses found a place in the chest, and all that remained in my bag was ash, *green* stuff and the *blue* belt. Most likely Crag would want to see it before the duel.

With that thought, I ran to the auction, my mind made up to spend all my money on a bag that brought down drop chance. Ten minutes later, some alchemist had bought all the *Ash* and I became the owner of an excellent *blue* backpack. It was literally blue as well.

> ### Medium Blue Leather Backpack
> *Rare*
> *Container*
> *Capacity: 32 slots.*
> *Chance of losing contents after death reduced by 100%.*

The rare bag cost me almost everything I had earned on the *Ash*, sixty gold. But it was pretty sweet, hard to argue with that. But I had stopped thinking in terms of money. Now it was just three hours' worth of time. And that was basically one run-through of the Tristad City Jail. And that was not counting the *green* and *blue* gear that dropped. I had left a lot of *green* stuff behind because I didn't have space, and that would have been around twenty gold. That meant I could earn a stable one hundred gold or more in that instance if I counted the *blue* and *green* loot.

And when I realized that I froze mid-step. I was already half way to Underweight, and it struck me like lightning. If I went through such a low-level ins two or three times in one day, I'd be earning as much as father. It was hard to even imagine how much money I could earn in the future if... If my threat status was maintained. When a threat was eliminated, the character died once and for all. I'd have to start over from the beginning but without the OP curses from Behemoth and the Destroying Plague.

And I myself would go to the merchant kid, who I didn't really know to sell him the *blue* stuff from the final boss at level ten. And that was at the fact that, when I went to see him five days earlier, I was at level one. Back then I couldn't even find one copper, and got overjoyed at the gift of just a *gray* club.

"Hey, Undy, you wouldn't have happened to notice anything weird in your sandbox, huh?" some preventer might ask. And the geographic location of our sandbox was no secret. "Maybe someone is levelling too fast?"

"You're telling me, Xan," Undy responds, scratching his head. "We've got one guy, he's a real freak. In five days he went from one to six and keeps selling me *blues* from level-ten ins's!"

"Unbelievable! And what did you say this weirdo's name was?"

"Scyth aka Alex... let me think... Sheppard! That's right! Him!"

"Bingo!" a switch flips in the head of this

hypothetical Xan or Bill. "There's our L-Class threat!"

Sure they couldn't get to me, but nothing was stopping them from hiring Axiom, enticing them with promises of support in greater Dis. And if they didn't want to share, I wouldn't be getting out of this sandbox alive. They'd figure out my birthday and at midnight they would put extra guards at the exit.

In a flurry I went back to the auction, placed the *Robe of the Sinister Ritual* up for twenty-two gold, spending my last coins on the inflated auction commission for anonymous selling. Then I walked over the tavern and sat on my favorite bench.

I lowered my head, studying some scurrying ants as I thought. If I won the duel, which was easily possible with enough plague energy, it would look very strange. If I lost and came back in the same place, it would lead to more questions. But I could explain it as a curse from the town drunk. Everyone knew him, and that worked to my advantage. Still that was best avoided. And if I didn't die because the *Mark of the Destroying Plague* triggered, that would be *alles, kaput*. Pictures and videos would hit the internet within seconds. And that would mean "hello" to the preventers, and "goodbye" to my plans for a better life!

Then I considered the situation from an outside perspective. A wimpy boy throws a fit and insults a strong player, setting a place and time for them to fight for who's right. Who would be surprised if the weakling chickened out? Nobody. That was to be expected. So maybe I should just play up to that? And to make sure Crag wouldn't get mad, I could send him the *Corrupted Scale Belt* he so yearned for. Let him choke on it, I say. At the very least, it would sate his ego and play in my favor, telling everyone about the cowardly Scyth. I made up my mind and breathed a sigh of relief.

Yes, the idea of losing to that asshole made me angry, especially considering I could win – I really could! – and cut him down to size. But everyone would soon forget this. And what was a temporary embarrassment in comparison with my lifetime dream? Not a thing. Nada. Come to grips with this, Alex...

"Of course this is where you are!" Tissa's cheerful voice rang out next to me. "You aren't answering messages, your comm says you're in Dis... The guys are looking for you in Gloomwood, but I decided to check your favorite place just in case. Are you getting ready for the duel?"

"Yep. I'm levelling the sitting on my ass skill, as you can see."

"Alright, be serious. We figured out what you should do with Crag!"

I had already made up my own mind.

I scooted over and Tissa sat close to me. Too close. My voice cracked either because of her proximity or because I had just been pondering my own weakness and cowardice.

"I'm not gonna do it. I just won't show up, and nether with the whole thing!"

"Yes, we also considered that." Tissa frowned. "It was actually my suggestion. But Ed said that would be a blow to our reputation. And you have to fight him no matter what!"

"Why? I don't owe anyone anything in Dis. Tissa, I'm sorry but I don't give a crap about your clan's reputation. Sure, you helped me out with Crag that time, and I'm grateful for that. But that doesn't mean I'm your... basically I don't have to do what you say, no matter what Rodriguez thinks. I play alone. Plus, I decided to help you with Evil from the Depths, so we're even."

I turned away, not feeling strong enough to keep drowning in her eyes. She took that as a lack of desire to keep talking. With my peripheral vision I saw her bite her lip.

"Alex, just listen. Please. Ed has an idea where you stand to lose nothing, and you might even win. It won't lead to any questions, either. Got your attention?"

"Tell me!"

I shuddered, looked at her and felt myself

drowning in her smiling eyes once again.

"The Arena," she said simply. "Alex, insist on a duel in the Arena. Battles begin at eight PM there every day. You won't be high enough level to really be competitive for a while, so it's no wonder you haven't heard of it. Any player can register their own tournament with its own rules. So you just make a two-person tournament, and turn on No Deaths and Player Scaling. Voila!"

"Scaling?"

"Yes. The system will automatically bring Crag down to your level. It will also proportionally lower his attributes and equipment level, but leave all skills. That way," Tissa raised her pointer finger and sent me a downward gaze, imitating our algebra teacher Ms. Uptegrove, "you can keep your secret, and significantly increase your chances of winning."

"And No Deaths means..."

"You won't die. When you have one percent life left, the duel will stop and you'll be sent out of the Arena with full health. Well, what do you think?"

So everything came together. I was overflowing with joy that there was a way out of this dead-end, that I was important to Tissa and that she was now sitting next to me touching her bare knee to mine. I brought my face close and kissed her tenderly on the lips. Her eyes shot open in surprise, she blushed but didn't back away. And for a few seconds that meant more to me than anything else.

The three hours before our meeting at the city walls flew by like five minutes. After that kiss, Tissa got embarrassed, sharply stood up and said that she needed to tell her clan I decided to run that dungeon with them. I sprinted to the jail and, much to my delight, it was going to free up very soon. I didn't go all the way through, just built up some plague energy. Honestly, even that took a lot of time. Almost two hours I had to wait to gain then lose Curse of the Undead.

I finally handled the first pack and picked up the loot. Nothing of interest, just ash and a few coins. So I left the right wing of the city jail and once again ran to the auction to get rid of *Altered Ash*, then used that money to buy some equipment. It would be stupid and suspicious to go to the duel in my canvas novice gear and it was good I remembered that. It was too bad that that all the gear I'd earned through pain and rotting flesh was too high level for me.

As it turned out, I wasn't the only one who remembered. Tissa tossed me a couple messages I had missed while, teeth clenched, I cursed at the jail mobs on my ass. But her messages contained gifts! There was a full set of armor for my level, and an explanation: "Here, a present! Tissa."

There was nothing out of the ordinary in the packages: mismatched *greens* for level five, leather and chainmail, a few rings, a couple bracelets and two brass knuckles. But the fact that it was selfless and from Melissa Schafer automatically made them priceless in my eyes. Without delay, I dragged the icons of all that equipment into various slots and admired myself in it. For the first time in *Disgardium*, I was fully equipped. I felt like a real person, and that feeling surprised me even more...

There, at the city walls, Crag gladly accepted the new conditions for our fight. He was very self-confident, and with an audience there to watch the duel, he was clearly not planning to fall face-first in the mud. But he did walk up close and whisper:

"So in the end you were too scared to fight fair, eh Scythy? As we agreed? No problem, I can take you in the Arena just as easy!"

I looked at what I had on with contempt and snorted. My *green* against his almost totally *blue* plate armor did not exactly match, and even I could see that. But I didn't think gear would be defining this battle.

In the audience I saw a few groups of workmen and among them was Manny. When he saw me look, he nodded.

"Fans and onlookers!" Crag declared nonchalantly. "We all understand that my superiority in level makes dueling Scyth unfair! So I suggested that we hold our little standoff in the arena with scaled characters! The battle will take place in less than an hour!"

"Place your bets, ladies and gentlemen!" From somewhere behind the warrior, Rashidos came and made a circle, announcing coefficients: "Three to one for Crag!"

Then we all grouped up with the audience and walked over to the Arena. It was a small, hardly noticeable building. As it turned out it was many times larger on the inside. Its two large and four small arenas were surrounded by stands.

I spent the time before battle studying tactics used by the other fighters. Duels were fast paced, because in the small arenas they were all one on one.

Ed and the others sat next to me, telling me tactics to use against Crag. They explained that, in three versus three and five versus five battles, the time limit might be as long as half an hour, but that was the longest possible in the arena. Eventually, a sudden death debuff would kick in and the fighter's health points would start falling...

"Third small arena, meet your new fighters!" boomed the commentator's voice when it came to be our turn. "The unrated tournament Sad Mossy Crag is officially underway! Organizer: Scyth. Registered fighters: two. So then, let's get straight to the final battle! Would the only participants in the tournament please enter the arena. Audience, say hello to Scyth, at level six with no class, and Craig the level-twelve warrior!"

To the screams of the many viewers, we appeared at different ends of the oval shaped arena. Crag and I were separated by around one hundred feet. He pointed at me and led his thumb across his throat, then closed his helmet visor.

"Conditions of the duel!" the commentator proclaimed. "No deaths! Fighters scaled! Enhancing and defensive buffs, potions, elixirs and scrolls are allowed! The battle will begin in ten seconds!"

"Nine! Eight!.." the crowd shouted.

There was a surprising number of people there. As it turned out, both workmen and players often spent their evenings in the Arena. It was both entertaining and stirred the blood. Many of them were placing bets with the honest goblins scurrying around the stands.

"Exclusive bets!" I heard from the stands behind me. "Ten to one that Scyth lands three blows first!"

I looked around and saw that my rival Crag was still working the crowd. I wondered how the goblins would react? And... Wait! What if that idiot just figured he could make some easy money? He saw that I had brass knuckles but figured I had no way to get through plate armor so he would give me a three-hit head start? I laughed and, when I heard the gruff cry, "let's start the fight," I walked confidently toward my rival.

Crag, shuffling his boots in the sand, came out to meet me and spread his arms, a shield in one and a short blade in the other.

"Let's go, little noob! Old Crag is gonna give you a head start!"

Four hundred fifty health points versus my three hundred twenty – this guy was buffed up to his ears. Positive effect icons were bunched up in the space over his portrait like ornaments on a Christmas tree. However, I wasn't far behind. I had speed and regeneration buffs from Tissa, a fire shield from Ed, a few scrolls increasing attributes, and a scroll that made cooldown tick faster for specials... The Dementors, in service of their own reputation, had invested quite heavily in me. There were whispers that I was in a trial period with them, and that was why I was progressing so quickly.

When I reached Crag, everything was already calculated. All his plate armor would bring down my damage by a bit more than one hundred. My plan, to stay on the safe side, was to hit him with four blows dealing two hundred fifty damage each. For a well-leveled skill those numbers wouldn't shock anyone. And I'd be able to use *Hammer* with a two-second cooldown thanks to the elixir.

"And now we turn our attention to small arena number three! The warrior looks very confident!" a voice began commenting for the whole arena. "Can everyone see him just begging his opponent to land the first blow?"

Crag was bowing like a jester. I was now only ten yards away.

"And now look at Scyth! I've got his stats in front of me here and, wow, he has never once defeated another player!"

The audience started to laugh, as the commentator drew everyone's attention to our fight.

"The Arena has never seen such a loser before! He has been killed by other players twenty-seven times! And zero victories! Oh god!" the announcer guffawed. "I cannot tell you this, but the total number of times Scyth has died would rouse anyone's imagination! Only today this fighter has died... Uh-hm-hm," the commentator cleared his throat. "Sorry, it's confidential!"

I seriously hoped the commentator was artificial intelligence. Nevertheless, his note got me to change battle tactics. Killing Crag in four hits would be too much. I'd split the damage into six. First one hit!

"The loser is starting out strong! Well, well, well! A *Hammerfist*! The basic move of the *Unarmed Combat* school! I haven't seen it in action for quite a long time! What? Did you see that? Did you see? Crag the warrior stumbled! A warrior! In full plate armor! He almost fell over... Woah! Unbelievable!" the commentator choked, not capable of explaining what was going on. "Seemingly, the warrior wanted to give his enemy a big leg up! Scyth has attacked three times, and all three hit! The warrior isn't even defending himself!"

By then, Crag could tell something was off, trying to deflect my third blow with his shield, but he wasn't fast enough. A *Hammerfist* swung through the air, slid off the brim of his chestplate and slammed into it like a sledgehammer. Too bad his face was covered by the visor and I couldn't see his reaction. I didn't manage to land a fourth blow.

"That's gotta be it folks! The noble Crag gave his weak opponent a head start but now he has started taking this fight seriously!"

The stands howled in glee. Somewhere in the background I heard my name, got distracted and got what I had coming. The warrior slammed into me with a *Charge*, and my body flew fifteen feet. The damage wasn't very serious. I lost around ten percent. But that gave a short stun, so I lost control for a few seconds.

That gave Crag enough time to get close and cut open my right arm, which I threw upward in defense. The leather armor, though it reduced the damage, wasn't much help. The wound slightly lowered the effectiveness of my attacks with that arm, too.

I rolled away from the next attack then, jumping from crouch, slammed the brass knuckles into his leg. The plate armor caved, the ganker's knee cracked and that gave me the chance to land a series of blows, adding a little bit of plague damage to each one.

Crag's health was down in the red zone, he jumped and feverishly reached for a health potion. That took a whole second, but it was enough. I made a series of attacks: *Hammer,* four normals and another special.

His life bar hit bottom, and we froze. In the air, to the sounds of a fanfare, a huge set of words appeared above the stadium:

Scyth has defeated Crag!

And a moment later, I was back in the stands next to Crawler, Tissa, Infect and Bomber. They shouted gleefully, patted me on the back and an especially strong pat from Bomber made my breathing seize.

"Oh well..." the commentator grumbled. "Self-confidence and underestimating your opponent can spell ruin for even the strongest competitors! The champion of the tournament Sad Mossy Crag is officially level-six player Scyth! This is his first victory, so let us congratulate him! Unfortunately for him, it will not be counted in his official rating. And meanwhile, over in large arena number one, a new sensation is being born before our very eyes..."

"So," Ed said when everyone had calmed down. "Alex, Tissa, go to the tavern. The boys and I are gonna settle up for some bets and come join you to celebrate the victory and think about what to do with Evil from the Depths."

"I mean, they were right," Hung guffawed. "We really did teach Crag a lesson! Thanks to Scyth!"

With a laugh, they sharply hurried off not to miss, insofar as I understood, Crag and his partners.

"So, let's go?" Tissa asked. "It won't be long if you hurry. We'll tell you the flora and fauna in the dungeon, write out tactics, say how..."

"I'm in no hurry," I interrupted her. I was overflowing with glee and wanted this night to last as long as possible. "Tomorrow is a weekend, my parents are out of town, so..."

"What?" A bold little fire flickered up in her eyes and tiny devils ran in. "Are you inviting me over?"

"Well, if you want..." my tongue could barely even get those words out, but then it went like a knife through butter. "Father has a case of beer in the fridge too, for what it's worth."

"Easy," she nodded. "I'll fly right over. Toss me your address in a PM. But go to the tavern first for the ins plan! Otherwise the guys will get mad!"

"But..."

"Alex..." she frowned. "It's better if they don't know. Okay? Especially Ed. Shall we?"

I felt a very strong itch under my shoulder blades. Seemingly, I had sprouted wings.

Chapter Twenty-Nine

True Test of Character

"**Y**OUR PLACE IS really cute," said Tissa. She pulled a small backpack off her shoulders and ran a gaze over the room, searching for where to throw it. "How's it going?"

"Good. While I was waiting for you, I thought over the strategy for the ins. Here..." I took her backpack and hung it on a hook on the wall. "Come in."

Tissa walked into the guest room and sat with her legs up on the couch. She was wearing wide khaki pants, a baggy hoody with the hood down and high boots. Her straight hair was up in a long ponytail, but a lock of her fringe had fallen out, covering one eye. From time to time, she blew on it to get it out of the way.

I pulled a couple droplet-covered cans of

beer out of the refrigerator, opened them with a hiss, handed one to her and sat down on the armchair near her.

"Thanks," she said, taking a big sip with an exhale of satisfaction. "M-m-m..."

"You like beer?"

"I have weird tastes, you know," she smiled in embarrassment. "I can't stand all these sweet cocktails! I don't like wine, and I really hate liquor. But I love the taste of beer! What about you?"

"I... like apple juice. I tried some whisky once, didn't like it..."

"What are you talking about!?" Tissa shook her head mockingly. "Whisky...!"

We chatted about some more pointless stuff and, to be honest, I didn't remember a single word. I was just staring at her reddish face, long lashes, blue eyes, the pink little tongue she used to lick foam off her top lip... and I wanted to kiss her. I got closer, but she laughed and moved away sharply, placing a hand between us:

"Alex, just so there aren't any misunderstandings... We're just friends! Alright? That kiss earlier... You caught me off guard! Don't do that again!"

"I'll try, but no promises," I admitted with a shrug. "I like you."

"I know. I like you too, but... don't complicate things. I'm serious! If you try again, I might get mad. We're just drinking beer, having a nice chat then you can walk me to a flying car and that's it. Okay?"

"Alright," I answered, going in for a fist-bump with a smile. "Agreed, friend!"

She went in eagerly, our knuckles touched.

And to be perfectly frank, I wasn't expecting anything more today. In fact, I was a bit afraid, panicking at the very thought that something I wasn't prepared for might happen! What would I do? How did that all work? From a technical standpoint I knew, sure. But I remembered my first ride on a bicycle all too well. It all seemed obvious, but I still tipped over a bunch of times. Just imagine embarrassing myself that much with Tissa. What a nightmare!

So her plan was perfectly fine with me. I was more than fine with the very fact that her and I were alone at night and drinking beer – nether! And she said she liked me! Just a week ago I could only dream of this!

"And another thing. No more than three or four cans each," she said. "If we drink more than that, our capsules won't let us into Dis, and they'll tell our school. I don't need any demerit points."

"Me neither. We'll stick to three or four. Actually, I've never had more than one. So..."

"Don't be afraid!" Tissa interrupted me and said with a laugh: "If you get drunk and start getting pushy, I can handle you!"

"Experience?"

"Something like that. What, do you think none of those three boys ever tried? They've got T^2 dripping out their ears!"

"I thought you and Ed..."

"No! But he has feelings, and he's very jealous..." Tissa thought. "He won't say it, you see. But I can see how it hurts him."

"And why do you care?" The beer was going straight to my head and questions like that no longer embarrassed me.

"I love him," she answered simply and explained, "as a brother. Him, Malik and Hung. They know that, accept it and treat me the same. You gonna open another?" Tissa extended me an empty can.

I brought more beer. This time it was the whole case at once so I wouldn't have to get up again. I reached for the tab, covered with water droplets, opened it with a hiss and handed it to Tissa.

"Thanks. Come sit closer if you want," she patted the couch next to her. Her tongue was stumbling a bit, as were my legs when I walked to the fridge.

"Okay," I landed on the sofa, my foot touched

---

^{2} T: (slang.) testosterone.

her sock and my heartbeat sped up. "What are your plans for Dis?"

"I have big plans, Alex. I have a few options, but it's all gonna depend on what we leave the sandbox with. All the good places in open Dis are already taken by clans. If you want to pass an instance, you have to apply to the owner, the clan that controls the location. Even applying costs money, and they might not approve."

"Then how do you level? How do you get equipment?"

"Well... Dis is a big place. Quests, social, farming mobs in open lands. As a priestess of Nergal, I'll definitely have something to do. There are a ton of class quests. The boys can find the same so I guess we'll end up doing that. But that's gonna take time..."

"Anything faster?"

"The frontier. Go to unknown lands." Tissa frowned. "That's Ed's idea. He wants to stay independent and grow our clan. But you can't really survive on the frontier until level sixty! And it'll be years before we're ready for that."

"What are your other ideas?"

"Come on, Alex," Tissa giggled and threw a pillow at me. "You're not a Dementor! I'm not going to tell clan secrets! Better tell me about you."

"For example?"

"Are you a threat?" she asked, opening

another can of beer.

"What?" just in case, I sat a bit farther from her. "Don't worry, Tissa. I'm not going to touch you."

"Not that!" she waved it off, scooted toward me and smiled. "It's okay to be a bit of a threat here," she said, waving with two fingers. "Knock yourself out, I will be fine. I'm talking about Dis! Were you given threat status because of Patrick's curse?"

I opened my mouth to give the honest answer that I didn't get threat status over the town drunk's curse, but she stopped me.

"Actually, stop! Stop, stop, stop! Shhhhhhhhh!" she leaned over to cover my mouth with a hand as she shushed me, but she lost balance and plopped down on my knee.

"Uh, sorry. I wasn't..." she put her hand back over my mouth.

I tried awkwardly to help Tissa up and my hand touched her breast. It was through her sweatshirt, but there was still no mistaking it. This was a secondary sex characteristic. And quite a hefty one at that. How did I just happen to grab right there?! I froze, afraid to move. Seemingly she had no bra on. At the very least, that was my impression.

"There. Shut up," Tissa said calmly, not trying to get away. "You can hold it if it helps you keep your mouth shut. And don't drool! Alex!"

I snorted something in approval and she continued:

"Sorry. Anyway, I was wrong to ask! If you're a threat, you cannot tell anyone about it! Ever!" She thought for a second. "Remember just a few days ago, that necromancer guy who turned into a class-Z that we eliminated."

"That day Ed came late?"

"Yep. Just one day later the devs stuck him with a huge social value penalty, and now he'll pretty much never make citizen. And as I'm sure you imagine, he didn't get a reward. His character was simply deleted from the sandbox, and he was biometrically blocked from accessing any world of the Gaming Consortium for the next three years. Do you understand me, Alex?"

"Not really." I tilted my head, imitating confusion and drunken sleepiness, but it was just an act. I understood perfectly. This game had very harsh rules, so it was always a good idea to obey.

"And that's good," Tissa muttered, embracing my knees. "If you don't understand what that means, you don't need to. And I was right..."

Not holding back, I kissed her on the neck. She gave a barely audible moan, and I kept going. Tissa smelled so good, like some elusive flower combined with an enticing aroma all her own. She started breathing quicker, and my lips started tingling.

I don't know how much time passed, one minute or one hour, but eventually she gingerly moved away and raised her head:

"Sorry, Alex. I've gotta go. Father will be worrying."

"Too bad."

"Yeah, it is..." she fell silent, then added: "Maybe some time you could... Take me to school."

We both stood from the couch in silence. She threw her hood down and took her backpack off the hook. We left just like that and, not letting slip a single word, walked to her flying car. We made it with no stupid kisses goodbye, either. Tissa just got in the car, nodded and flew away.

* * *

The sun was probably quite high when I woke up. I say probably because I couldn't actually see it. Rain was pouring down again and leaden clouds seemed to cover the whole city. I looked out the window and shuddered. The cold got under my skin and my teeth started chattering.

Much to my dismay, I left the window wide open. I was feeling sick and wanted some fresh air. My head was so heavy, and I really wanted to drink. Is this what my parents experienced after their wild nights? Is this a hangover?

I brushed my teeth and drank probably a quart of water. My bones and muscles ached so badly that I decided to get my blood pumping with some exercise. Either it helped or the contrasting shower after, but I felt better. Physically better, because mentally I was already doing quite well. The late night I spent with Tissa wouldn't leave my head and that kept a smile glued to my face.

AT, sensing my mood, turned into a dog. He jumped, ran, wagged his tail and barked, staring loyally into my eyes.

Stroking his ear, I called up my parents. In the course of the conversation, I was subjected to an impassioned interrogation from mom about the dark circles under my eyes. Meanwhile dad whinnied, spinning a few yarns about how I might have spent last night, starting with an everyday orgy, and ending with an all-night marathon of all nine *Back to the Future* movies. Dad had a very particular idea of a wild night. Old movies were like catnip to him. So of course he imagined I'd invite a bunch of geeks over to watch old crap.

By the end of the conversation, mom put on a guilty face and said they were gonna be stuck there another few days. Dad sent me a hundred phoenixes just in case, mom gave me a million instructions about everything she could think of. Finally, I had to swear ten separate oaths that I

---

would behave myself before they let up and finished the video call. Based on the view behind them, my folks were somewhere in the mountains designing something top secret on their client's property and had no way to access the global internet.

I didn't make any big plans for today. Me and the Dementors had planned our expedition into the instance under the Olton Quarries for tomorrow. Today, Saturday, they decided to spend giving Bomber and Infect fully fledged training so they could get some important dings and skills.

And that meant today was the best possible day to keep my promise to Trixie and go pay him a visit in Cali Bottom. The money my parents sent me would easily cover that.

It was hard to understand Tissa's behavior yesterday. So in the end what was that? Friends don't kiss each other, but can't a friend invite a friend to the movies? Or a cafe? We had flying cars at our disposal, we could even take a little getaway to the beach!

What was more, I had one hundred credits! Awesome! Dad understood perfectly that I could live just fine on what we had at home without any money, but he sent me money anyway, and lots of it! It was damn nice to be on the same page as my parents.

And if Tissa refused, I had stuff to do in Dis.

I planned the day out as I ate breakfast, then poked my head outside. Weather conditions were too extreme for manual control, so I set a route to Cali Bottom with a stop at a pastry shop, then sat back in the seat and opened the *Disgardium* forums.

> ***Disgardium > Forums > Sandboxes > Tristad***
>
> *Tristad / Search by topic / New topic / Display mode — new first*
>
> **Pinned** – *Author:* **Whiteacre** – *Welcome: please read!*
>
> *Author:* **Ancientgod** – *For those who know what they want out of Dis.*
>
> *Author:* **Strazigg** – *A guild for friends. Come join up :-)*
>
> *Author:* **Riman** – *[Axiom] Recruitment for second backup static! Priority to tanks and healers level 12 and up.*
>
> *Author:* **Teller** – *How to beat Pherax in the jail?*
>
> *Author:* **Yukawa** – *lvl 10 archer seeking clan with non-braindead leader!*
>
> *Author:* **Ozanax** – *Video. Lvl 6 noob shreds lvl 12 warrior in the arena!!! MUST WATCH!*

Well, well... Was this about me? I opened the thread but I didn't have time to watch the video.

The flying car had landed.

"First destination reached, Alex. Tia Raquel's Panaderia," the pleasant woman's voice announced.

"Wait here."

"Yes, Alex. Standby mode activated. Rate: one hundredth of a phoenix per minute."

I ran in for donuts and got two boxes of twelve each. That would be enough to treat Trixie, the old man and their friends. There was no line. In this weather most opted for drone delivery.

Back in the car, I told it to resume route, then got back to the forums. The video was shot from the eyes of a player in the Arena stands and from a distance. And it started after Crag had taken a few hits, and the commentator was surprised he was stumbling.

I took an intrigued look at my character. He looked like a poor person or bum compared to the big broad-shouldered warrior in plate armor. But that impression blew away as soon as I saw how I attacked. Abrupt lightning-fast strikes, swinging through the air, they went straight through the armor like Thor's hammer. Nether, that special was just level thirty-six! I was afraid to imagine what would come after one hundred!

I was planning to take a peek into the Gnoll Quarry today. The level of mobs there was higher than twelve, which would mean *Unarmed Combat* and *Resilience* would both be able level. I skimmed the comments under the video:

> **Strazigg**: *We know that "warrior!" Rat. Serves him right.*
> **Ereado**: *Wait, but wasn't this battle scaled? Every one of Scyth's attacks hits. That isn't possible at that level difference!*
> **Zoran** *[in reply to **Ereado**]: Yeah, they're definitely scaled. But that doesn't change the point. This unarmed whelp in* green *equip with zero chance of winning just breaks a guy tinned in plate. Doesn't that seem odd to you?*
> **Teller** *[in reply to **Zoran**]: Not really. Scyth is protected by the Dementors, if they haven't already let him in the clan. Crawler is a harsh judge of candidates. I don't think they'd even consider a true noob. I'm sure they gave him some sweet buffs too!*
> **Yukawa**: *So that's how a clan leader acts when they're not braindead!*
> **Plancka** *[in reply to **Yukawa**]: Up yours, Yukawa!*
> **Mamkinglad**: *Nothing out of the ordinary. First, that idiot Crag gave him a head start for some reason. It's easy to see, because he's not even blocking with his shield. Second, it's obvious that Scyth has leveled*

---

unarmed to the max. Based on how he's only using one special, he doesn't have any other ones up there. That kind of tactic can only work against gigantic headasses like the unrepentant ganker Crag.
Born *[in reply to **Yukawa**] Up yours, Yukawa!*

The video had less than one hundred views, and didn't spawn further discussion, especially after Ereado clarified that our characters were scaled to equal level.

For the rest of the flight, I leafed through another couple pages of forum topics until I hit the beginning of the year, but nothing caught my attention.

A topic about Crusher, who got taken down three days ago, was filled with feverish discussion, but it all led to guessing who might have gotten that First Kill. The main candidates were people from Axiom. The Dementors were also mentioned, as were another few strong characters from the sandbox.

But there was nothing yet about the zombie wolf Punisher. That led me to certain ideas, but I didn't think them over seriously. I'd go to Gloomwood and check.

But for now...

"Second destination reached, Alex. Cali

Bottom. Warning: this building has a low safety rating. Code yellow. We recommend you lock the doors and leave immediately!"

"Open doors. And wait until I come back."

Chapter Thirty

Paying it Forward

THE WHIPPING WINDS and drizzle were enough that no one was up here on the roof. I ran to the entrance and thought. How could I find Trixie? We didn't agree on a precise meeting time, I just promised to come on the weekend.

While I thought, the building door went up with a hiss. But no one came out to meet me and I took that as an invitation.

There was a metal stairway going down in front of me. The way was lit by an old dim luminescent bulb. It hummed and crackled, and the flickering light and playful shadows made it seem like someone was hiding somewhere. For a second, I almost chickened out and went back to my car. But I overcame the fear. I no longer had any illusions about the orbital crime identification system, though. Like hell they were gonna identify something out here, especially under the roof. The only remaining hope was my health status being sent to the Department of Health. If something happened to me, an ambulance would be here in ten minutes.

As for the lighting, I had never seen anything like this. In our building, it was all luminescent walls and ceilings. No one had used bulbs like this in a long time. Everyone knows, it's bad for the environment.

Holding tight to the railing, I went down and found myself in a long corridor. Large lettering on the wall bore witness to the fact that this was block thirty-nine, floor one hundred. How could I find Trixie in this giant building? He like the deceased Clayton, lived in thirty-six but I didn't know the floor or room number.

Should I turn down this hallway, or keep going? I went back to the stairs and stopped unconfidently.

"Hey!" I saw a head of disheveled gray hair from a lower flight. "Down here!"

"Trixie?" I couldn't tell who was shouting from the gloom.

"Wixie! He's in Dis. He asked me to meet you! Now step to before I catch cold and die!" the voice below mumbled. "Come on, we gotta get moving! This isn't some ceremonial reception for you! Or me for that matter..."

I heard creaking wheels. The voice gradually went silent, growing distant and I, jumping down a step, dashed off to catch it. By all accounts, this was Trixie's grandfather, the very same old man in the wheelchair I'd seen before.

I went a few stories down and caught the old man at a turn in another hallway.

"Sorry, Mister..." I paused for him to say his name, but the old man kept mockingly silent. His weathered eyes studied me drowsily. "Are you Trixie's grandfather?"

He nodded, waiting for more, but his gaze didn't express even a drop of interest.

"I promised I'd come over and bring him some donuts. If he's busy, could you give him these for me?" I pulled out my backpack and started unloading boxes of pastry, but the old man stopped me, grabbing my hand. "Excuse me?"

"Furtado," he said, introducing himself. "The name's Furtado. And nobody has ever called me Mister, so don't you start now, boy. Alex was it? Trixie's been buzzing in my ear about you. To be honest, I'm not sure why. But I remember you. You flew over to visit Clayton. You can call me Harold. Follow me."

Deftly working his arms, he rolled down the hallway, which was littered with all kinds of trash. The primitive illumination was also quite spotty, with some bulbs burnt out or just smashed. And the less light there was, the faster the man rolled. I though was constantly stumbling on boxes and buckets, eventually tripping on a brick. I fell and hit my hand on some small pieces of broken glass, and a couple feet later painfully slammed my thigh into the corner of a table that almost totally blocked the already quite narrow passage.

The old man laughed hearing my groans and cursing. He muttered something to himself.

"Keep up!" he grumbled again. "We're almost there."

We went around another few corners before reaching the cubby he shared with his grandson. Shadows ducked down the halls, cigarette cherries flickered up in the dark. I could hear feverish whispering on the other side of the thin walls. Here, life bubbled over. I could hear hysterical laughter, quarrels, screams and normal conversations.

A narrow door slid aside. Old Furtado turned his wheelchair with virtuosic grace and rolled inside, almost hitting the edge of the door. I came in next.

Inside I saw a cramped closet one third of which was occupied by a virtual reality pod. Not the same as the one I had, just a base model like they issued to all noncitizens. Under the closed lid, there was something happening. A little screen on the pod showed logs reflecting the player's status. Pulse, blood pressure, exhaustion level. All were yellow. I guess Trixie was very physically active in Dis. Maybe he was fighting?

"You'll have to wait," his grandfather Harold acknowledged. "Put a kettle on. We can have some tea."

"Will it take long?"

"Who knows," the old man shrugged. "When they kill him, he can leave. What's with your hands? Did you cut yourself? Get the sanitizer from the shelf, put some on. You could catch all kinds of diseases here. Not that long ago, some poor schmuck died of tetanus..."

I found a plastic bottle of alcohol gel among a heap of sticky tape, wires, screws, nails and coupons.

"This?"

"That's the one," Furtado confirmed, squinting. "Squirt some on your hand and rub it in."

I squeezed out a couple drops and did as the old man instructed, barely holding back a scream. It really stung the cuts on my hand. Harold snorted in approval.

Then I poured water from a huge canister into an electric tea kettle as the old man instructed, plugged it into the wall and spent a long time looking for the button to make it boil. It did not obey voice commands, and had no cleaning or disinfection functions. That bothered me. As if it wasn't enough thinking about where the water in that canister came from...

While I figured out the antediluvian device, the geezer called out to someone:

"Yes, he's here. Come over for a cup of tea, you can meet him."

I got on guard, but Furtado raised a hand in reassurance:

"Everything is fine. It's a friend."

"A friend?" That didn't calm me down one bit! "What friend?"

"You'll see," the geezer ambivalently rolled past and set up at a small folding table. "Get out your donuts."

"Here," I set the box on a disheveled and cut up tablecloth. "Do you have any way to heat them up? They've gone cold."

"They'll be fine like that," the old man waved a hand.

I didn't want to meet this "friend," especially because Trixie was liable to set something slip and that meant there was a chance my whole plan was about to go tits up.

"Sorry, I've gotta go, Mr. Furtado. My flying car is waiting. Say hi to Trixie for me."

"As you wish," he said, pouring something a small shabby porcelain kettle with a broken spout then filling it with boiling water. "Can you find your way back up?"

"Uh... Straight, left, straight, right?"

"That's what I'm saying. You'll never get out of the building like that. And it isn't so easy for me to shepherd you around. So wait for Trixie to climb out of the grave, or Hank will drop by. One of them can take you."

"What? Did you say 'Hank?'" that name meant nothing to me, and I got even more on guard.

"You know, the guy you met before. I mean, other than my boy. I don't understand what he wants with you, but as soon as Trixie said your name he just lit up," the geezer grumbled. I lifted the lid of the tea pot and took a sniff. "Oh, nice! Try as you might, you'll never find a nice tea for brewing. And the crap they sell costs so much you'd have to sell a kidney. And that powdered 'tea,'" he said as if spitting out the word, "you can keep it. Alright then, make yourself at home, take a seat. I'd bet my head that you've never tried something like this before!"

"I've drunk tea before!"

"He's drunk tea he says!" Furtado mumbled indignantly. "Tea isn't meant to be drunk, it is not water. Tea is to be enjoyed, savored, taken in tiny sips! Preferably with a lump of sugar. It's a shame there's no sugar, but these donuts will do just fine.

Oh, with sprinkles!" he extended me a mug with brown lines under the rim. "Take this and drink a few tiny sips."

A sharp piercing sound rang out from the door. I shuddered and spilled a few drops on the table. If this was that Hank, I had no cause to expect anything good.

"Well, don't you scare easy!" Furtado rolled back from the table in a fit of anger. "Drink the tea! What are you afraid of? That was the doorbell, someone's here. Go let them in!"

The old man was starting to get on my nerves. Who was he to be barking orders? Even my parents said "please" when they asked me for something. In the end, I flew across half a continent to see them, and came bearing gifts. What did he ever do for me?

I didn't say that out loud though and, getting up from the creaky stool, headed for the door. Thankfully it was just four steps. Well alright, seven. Respect for his age and disability made me hold back and do as he said. Although I could easily have told him off. Who was this guy? I didn't know much, but he was a noncitizen, which meant he was basically a nonperson.

"Turn the lock three times, then undo the latch, but don't take off the chain. See who it is first."

That was all complete gibberish to me. But

for some reason I didn't ask him to explain. I guess I didn't want to look like a bonehead. Acting on pure intuition, I turned everything there was to turn, clicked open the lock, moved the metal bolt aside and reached for the handle.

"Good day," I greeted the man standing at the door. "Alex-slash-Scyth I presume?"

"In the flesh. And you must be Hank."

"Yep. Hank friggin' Almeida. You gonna let me in?"

"Let him in, boy!" the geezer shouted. "He's a friend."

It was hard to tell how old this new guest was. He looked young, but there were spiderwebs of wrinkles around his eyes. Lean, veiny, with clear-cut shoulders. He had on track pants, running shoes and a black shirt. They didn't seem like the freshest clothes but everything in Cali Bottom looked past its prime.

Hank pulled up a nightstand and sat on it between me and old man Furtado. Then he reached for the tea pot like he owned it, splashed some in his mug and, without asking permission, pulled a donut from the box. Based on the old man's lack of reaction, Hank really was a friend.

"Nice to meet you, Alex," the guest said.

"What do you want from him, Hank? I've got some ideas," the old man said.

"I can't say it directly," Hank led his large

hooked nose over the donut and drew in the aroma, but didn't take a bite. Then he carefully put it back in the box. "What a smell! I wanted insanely bad to have an apple pie a few years ago. Not like they serve in Dis, a real one made of dough and apples. Like grandma used to make..."

"Oh, don't remind me," Furtado sighed.

"No promises Harold, but I'll try," said Hank. "I started dreaming about the flavor of apple pie! Basically, I couldn't stop myself. I friggin' lost it! I scrimped and saved everything I earned, then flew into town for flour and apples. I walked into a supermarket, got a cart and choked on my spit! Real food! Ham! Meat! Pasta! Real live vegetables fresh from the farm! And the smells! Nether, the memories are so vivid..." his stomach gave a distinct burble. "Sorry 'bout that. The store, by the way, was called Pherax... You ever heard of that, Alex?"

Pherax? So that was what this was all about... If Hank controlled the final boss in the Tristad Jail, he'd have seen everything! Nether!

I gave a short nod, letting him know he'd gotten his point across. He continued:

"Anyway, I just walked and walked... I was looking for cheaper flour and egg powder. First I thought I'd get real eggs, but the prices... were a bit beyond my budget. You feel me?"

"Yes," I swallowed, figuring he was going to

try and blackmail me. And honestly, better if he was. He could just be turning me over to some preventers.

"And I was overcome with such anger!" He sipped the tea, savoring it. "Why do they pay us so little? Why is there no work? I could do so much with these two hands!" Hank showed his palms. "So why do I, a healthy guy with a sound mind have to earn money in an imaginary world?"

"Who were you angry at?"

"Everyone!" he said, pounding on the table in a fit of rage. Trixie's grandpa cringed in disapproval. "Why does my family have to eat these synthetic blends? I've had it up to my neck with these damned UNBs! They make me want to barf! If you ask me, even rubber tastes better! And that shit is all we got to eat. My whole family! My parents, me, my wife and kid, my brother, his family. Every last one of us! And all of us except the kids spend days on end lying in these graves mining imaginary resources for a half phoenix a day!"

"So, did you make the pie?"

"Yeah, I did," Hank said, tired. "And I swear on my life it was worth it! You should have seen the look on Casey's face. My little girl Casey! It was hard on her stomach though; it wasn't used to solid food. And every blessed day since then, she remembers that pie and asks when we can make another one. And I always wonder what I should tell her. I mean, her mother and I would have to spend whole days locked in our capsules after that! And who would watch the girl?"

"Maybe you could take a couple of these donuts for little Casey?" I suggested. "I assume Trixie and Mr. Furtado won't be opposed."

"Harold?" the guest raised his head.

"Of course, Hank," the old man nodded. "Take a whole box, give half to your brother."

"Thanks!" he replied, sincerely grateful.

"Thanks to him for taking Trixie on," Furtado answered.

"Taking him on where?" I asked.

"As a miner in the quarries," the old man said with a shrug. "I don't know why my grandson did it. He lost out monetarily, but a lot depends performance. After he levels his mining skill, he might get lucky and find something more valuable than stone and copper."

"So that means he's there until evening? I know miners have a full work schedule."

"Yes, Alex," the old man said, calling me by the name for the first time. "Sorry I had to trick you to keep you here. Hank just really wanted to meet you. I've been looking out since this morning. Trix asked me not to miss you, but the weather... I had to sit at the window and watch for a flying car. To tell you the truth, he was hoping you'd show up later, after work."

"I saw everything," said Hank, aka draconid boss Pherax. "What made me tell the story about the supermarket... Well that was when I started hating all of you, the citizens. To be honest, I didn't especially care for you before but when I made sure with my own eyes that you live in the lap of luxury while we don't even dare hope for something better... I saw a boy like you there, Alex. He had his whole cart filled with ice cream! Why did he need that much ice cream? Is he eating whole containers of it at a time?"

"Uh... Sounds like it," I said, embarrassed at my memories of eating whole bags of chips. "For us it isn't that expensive."

"That's what I'm saying! Who gave those mooks at the top the authority to decide who's worthy of citizenship," he puckered up like he just ate a lemon, "and who isn't? What the hell is going on with this world, huh?"

"Hank, Hank..." the old man put a hand on his guest's shoulder, calming him. "What does this have to do with the boy?"

"I'm getting there," the man said, now calm. "Alex, I'm gonna tell it to you straight. I decided to sell you out. As soon as the battle ended, I left Dis. Thankfully my shift was over anyway. And I went straight to the forums. I was gonna write a quick message to a couple preventer clans and sell to the highest bidder. I could already see myself taking my wife and daughter to the supermarket for real groceries!"

"I don't know what you're talking about," I said, drenched in cold sweat and thinking that Hank was about to ruin all my life plans right now over one basket of groceries.

"What? You don't get it?" he laughed. "Nothin' gets past you, kid! But I'm no fool myself!"

"Clayton said such nice things about him," old Furtado noted, as if in passing. "My grandson also sees something in him..."

"And clearly there was good reason," Hank said. "But I'm going to end this story so you know what's what. Basically, I climbed out of my pod to wet my whistle, and my older brother was over. And wouldn't you know it, he told me the craziest story!"

"What was it?"

"Well it ain't news to you. He said the guys at the quarry were losing it after something that happened in the Bubbling Flagon! I think you know who I'm talkin' about, Alex."

"Who? Your brother?"

"Yep," Hank said with a broad smile. "His name's Manny. My asshole older brother is named Manuel Almeida, Manny for short. And you know what? I'd have to be a real douche bag to do anything that might hurt you now!"

Chapter Thirty-One

Conflict of Interest

O N MY WAY back from Cali Bottom, I thought about how lucky I'd gotten. Lucky that Manny Almeida was brothers with Hank, and lucky that he was in charge of the right wing of Tristad Jail. And I tried not to think about what I did that time in the Bubbling Flagon. It was really stupid to put my fate on the line like that.

We spent around an hour talking. And without delving into the details, I told them about me and my plans. Harold and Hank meanwhile just clicked their tongues when I mentioned space. For them it was something extremely distant.

"I see why Clay liked you so much," said old man Furtado. "You got kindred spirits."

"I don't think that's all," Hank disagreed. "Alex has a big heart. And he's no wuss. I mean, come on. This kid went against one of his people to protect one of us!"

By then I was well and truly embarrassed. After all, I felt I was simply repaying a debt to Clayton. But I didn't explain that and shifted the conversation to Hank's role as dungeon boss.

He wouldn't answer directly but, from his confusing and veiled explanations, I understood that no one controlled Pherax other than him. So when Hank was not in Dis, control over the draconid was transferred to an artificial intelligence, a neural network which adopted the behavioral patterns of the "prime HCMO[3]" as Snowstorm cleverly named Hank's position.

Of course, they had all failed their citizenship tests: all of Hank's family and Harold and Trixie Furtado, whose parents were alcoholics and had burned down their cubby in a drunken fit while their son was visiting his grandpa.

Hank had even tried again two times by saving up, but every time he was missing something. Society had no need for low-skilled labor, Hank had little aptitude for creative thought and the test showed that he didn't even come close to having enough intellect points to get a scholarship. And intellect points, by the way, were not the outdated IQ. They were the result of complex analysis and testing. And your score

---

[3] HCMO – Human-Controlled Mobile Object, i.e. a mob controlled by a human.

could be improved, but the self-taught very rarely achieved the kinds of results that university graduates could get. And they quite literally had intellect "acceleration" available to them, because expensive modern technologies could be used to enhance brainpower.

I flew the flying car back manually. That was either because of talking with the noncitizens, or I just missed the feeling of control. At any rate, I took a roundabout way home, avoiding the airways and enjoying the views of the turbulent but beautiful ocean. I landed near the California coast to get lunch from a taco stand on the beach and, squinting in the sun, ate my dinner. And that must have been my best half hour in recent memory, not counting last night with Tissa.

I came home late that evening and the flight lasted long enough that I was hungry again. So I had to eat a "Basic Dinner №9," which our culinary oven could make from liquid concentrate. I had a long night of *Disgardium* ahead of me, and it was better to go in with a full stomach.

It was very lonely without my parents. I missed them and couldn't imagine how I'd live alone, after I moved out. At least I had the purring AT to keep my company, curled up on my lap in cat form.

I had big plans for the evening and night: from levelling *Cooking* to completing all the quests

I'd picked up in the jail. If there were no witnesses, I could kill local bosses in one hit, then collect the reward from the jail warden. But that would take preparation. I'd have to spend time filling up my plague energy bar after tripping Curse of the Undead.

Loading...

I appeared next to the Bubbling Flagon, where I had discussed tactics for passing the bosses from Evil from the Depths with Ed and the crew the night before.

Going through the back door into the tavern, I entered my personal room and unloaded all my goodies. My rare *blue* ingredients were there waiting to be sold. I also had the *Skeleton Club* and *Lynx Paws* from my first battle in Gloomwood, a *Daredevil Blindfold* from a normal pack in the Jail and the loot I'd kept from the bosses – the *Two-Handed Mechanic's Wrench* and the *Silent Boots of the Assassin*. The shoes and weapons were not unique but, due to their bonuses, I kept them all. I still didn't know what class I might get at level ten. I would of course have a say in the matter, but the gods would limit me to three options based on my previous acts, gameplay and style of battle.

I also had the quest locket and *Whistle of Summoning* for the legendary spectral wolf. So I now had just one free slot in my chest. And that fact made me think long and hard. In the last few days I had been walking on the edge of a steep precipice, not considering what was around the bend. But for the first time in a while I had a minute to think.

I opened my profile and judged my progress in cold hard numbers:

Scyth, level-6 human
Real name: Alex Sheppard.
Real age: 15.
Class: not selected.

Main attributes:
Strength: 10.
Perception: 12.
Endurance: 5.
Charisma: 2.
Intelligence: 7.
Agility: 2.
Luck: 2.

Secondary attributes:
Health points: 280/280.
Mana points: 17/17.
Plague energy points: 10000/10000.
Recovery speed: 15 health points per minute.
Movement speed bonus: 2%.
Base damage: 4.
Carrying capacity: 325 lbs.

Disgardium Book One

Accuracy: 70%.
Spell power bonus: 8.4%.
Dodge chance: +4%.
Critical damage chance: +10%.
Vendor discount: +2%.
Chance of receiving a unique quest: +0.2%.
Chance of receiving improved loot: +0.2%.

Fame: 0.

Skills:
Unarmed Combat: 36.
Bashing Weapons: 1.
One-Handed Swords: 1.
Night Vision: 5.
Resilience: 36.
Stealth: 4.
Swimming: 1.

Abilities and special attacks:
Hammerfist: 36.
Battering Ram: 1.
Sneak Attack: 1.
Stoneskin: 36.

Trades and professions:
Cooking: Journeyman (100/250).

Special skills and abilities:

Mark of the Destroying Plague: 5.
Ghastly Howl: 2.

Achievements:
I'm on Fire!
I'm on Fire – 2!
I'm on Fire – 3!
The Lich is Dead! Long Live the New Lich...
First Kill: Crusher

Hidden status: Emissary of the Destroying Plague.
*Hidden status: Class-**W** threat with **L** potential.*

The last two lines had appeared only after my letter from the corporation and they were flashing a foreboding shade of red. I closed my profile, about to get to my missions, but something stopped me.

I opened the chest again and sat for a long time staring at it and not understanding what was bothering me. And the thought proved elusive. As I thought, I looked at each item in turn.

There was the *Skeleton Club*. It was for level-fifteen minimum and maybe I wouldn't need it, but I didn't see any reason to get rid of it yet. Logically, no matter how much I raised *Unarmed Combat* and *Hammerfist*, the base attack from the *Bashing*

Weapons arsenal, *Battering Ram,* would do much more damage.

That thought led me to another: I needed to go to a master of *Unarmed Combat* ASAP and learn some new attacks. From there a chain of associations led me to the idea of buying cheap weapons of various classes and leveling a few weapon skills in a dungeon.

But when I thought about dungeons, I got a vague suspicion I had missed something and those several minutes of thinking bore fruit. It dawned on me how big a risk I was taking by sitting alone in an ins for hours on end. After all, if anyone walked up to a portal while I was in the dungeon, they'd see:

> **The Tristad City Jail dungeon is being completed by another group of players.**
> *Current group progress: battle with* **Wimpy** – *100%. Alive: 1/1 group members.*

I spent a long time in battle with the mad gnome inventor that time. And they might have questions both about the number of group members and the length of the boss battle. Either of those could be explained – a high level player might go in to farm gold solo, while some especially beefy tank or high-level healer might take a long time on a boss. But the seconds between my death and respawn would eventually show them:

*Current group progress: battle with **Wimpy** – 100%. Alive: 0/1 group members.*

And a brief sliver of time later, it would show the same but now with that group member alive once again. And that would look quite strange indeed! What was more, who could say which of the bosses were controlled by a person?

Something in that system had me baffled. The devs thought the threats made their game unique. Dungeons controlled by people were clearly going to be their next big feature, and what was happening now was something of an alpha test. They would probably be using the results to decide whether to expand the function to the rest of Dis. And it was also worth remembering that common mobs could also be someone like Trixie.

So how did that all come together? I was lucky Hank was a good guy. What if he wasn't? I opened the tech support window to immediately write a message asking these questions, but after typing the first line, I erased it all.

Players weren't supposed to know any of the mobs were controlled by people. Hank hinted that vengeance could be fearsome for spreading that kind of information. I still didn't understand why he was revealing himself indirectly and with hints.

After all, the fact was that he already knew that I knew Pherax's true nature.

I again remembered Clayton's mysterious death right after he opened up to me. And I decided the risk to Hank would be too great if I asked Snowstorm the question I was planning to.

But still I had to get this settled. I had finally figured out what had me so bothered all that time. So, pulling at that thread, realized what a spaz I was. Nether!

I imagined myself as a noncitizen finding a huge pristine diamond on the street. But much to my dismay, I was already surrounded by a group of thugs and they were closing in. No, I'm not gonna play that game!

Responding to my mental outburst, I opened my messages to write one to Snowstorm. I carefully thought over what to write and how. I realized I could protect Hank by only mentioning Dargo/Clayton. Hopefully that couldn't hurt him now.

But beyond that, there was a more relevant question!

Where to start? Alright, I figured. I'd handle that as I went. I brought up the virtual keyboard and...

"Dear developers!" No, no. Not like that. "Hey..." my fingers flittered in the air, tapping at the ghostly keys:

Class-A Threat

Greetings, omnipotent gods of Disgardium!

My name is Alex Sheppard, game nick Scyth, Tristad sandbox. A few days ago I was named a threat with potential class L. The explanatory message said that, after the threat in my person was eliminated, my character would die once and for all.

Does that mean all my personal items, including those stored in the chest in my room in the tavern will be lost for good? I would like to know before any of the preventers identify and eliminate me. I have been fortunate enough to find some unique loot, a legendary spectral wolf. And at auction it might be worth in the millions of gold. I can't activate it and summon the wolf though, because I do not meet the level requirements. Beyond that, when I lose my character – and that will happen sooner or later for reasons I will go into below – I'm afraid the mount will also be lost.

I could sell it at auction, but I cannot withdraw money into the real world until I get into greater Disgardium, which means I stand to lose it all together with my character.

Now I feel forced to play passively, sitting in my personal room where no one can touch me and waiting until I come of age. And that is because, among other things, one of the bosses I encountered in the dungeon Crypt of the Temple of Nergal the

---

Radiant by the name Dargo was not a normal mob. He was pretty clearly controlled by a person. And the nature of my abilities as a threat are too obvious for someone not to notice.

That means that I have nowhere to really progress in level. In the open world players might notice me, but in closed locations there are real people lurking inside bosses. In both cases, I could be found out. My potential is higher than average, and the reward for elimination is attractive enough to bring in even high-level players. I have already seen some preventers discussing the search for my character. Thanks for the global notification, by the way! Good thing they don't know my name!

So, would you like to see me playing the game passively? As a teen, I am required to spend at least one hour in Dis every day. I will do that. But I will not stick my nose out of my room, and my apologies if that upsets any of your plans.

In hopes of a speedy reply,
Alex Sheppard, aka Scyth.

Let them play their own game of threat and preventer. My future was in that chest, and I was in no mind to lose it. Too bad I'd be abandoning the Dementors tomorrow. But here, as my Uncle Nick said, "you gotta look out for number one." If the whole wolf selling idea was going up in flames,

I guess I'd have something material to give my classmates. But I was absolutely not going to sell it before I had the ability to withdraw money.

Dad always taught me to be consistent in my decisions and actions. So, I sent out the letter and made sure I had finished my required hour of *Disgardium* then calmly left the game.

Chapter Thirty-Two

Might makes Right

BEFORE BED, I watched some dumb new comedy, then easily drifted off. I didn't feel the least bit worried, just a quiet joy that my main problem was solved.

Before that, I scrolled through an auction on my comm, setting a filter for "legendary," and "terrestrial" in the mounts category. The results disappointed me somewhat. I was not going to become a millionaire. Yes, my spectral wolf was unique and legendary, but it couldn't fly. And that meant it was completely impractical, because terrestrial animals were all three or more times slower than flying ones.

And that meant it could be of interest only to mount collectors, which was a totally different market. The spectral class was quite common and had a relatively low value. What was more, it was just some wolf, no dragon turtle or fighting lizard. A common gray wolf, even if it was a ghost.

Such land mounts were worth no more than three hundred thousand gold. Even if I got all that for it, withdrawing money into the real world through the Snowstorm bank takes so much in conversion and transfer fees that only two hundred thousand phoenixes would reach my account. Plus, I'd need to find some money for the commission first. With Snowstorm, nothing was free.

Nevertheless, if everything turned out, I could be sure my first few years of school were paid for. And two years would be enough time for me to think up a way to pay for the rest.

I slept like a bump on a log and didn't dream at all. In the morning a call to my comm woke me up.

"Hi!" Tissa was in a good mood, and her sonorous voice made me smile. "How did you sleep, Alex? Ready for adventures?"

"Hi," my voice was groggy and crackling. "What adventures now?"

"Big ones! Sorry for waking you up, but we're gonna meet you at the city gates in an hour. Alright, we're waiting! Don't be late!" she hung up, not giving me the chance to answer.

I sat mute for a minute, trying to figure out what she was talking about, then facepalmed. Evil from the Depths! Aw, nether! I called her right back to say I wasn't coming, but she didn't answer. Seemingly, she was already in her capsule.

I started getting undressed to enter Dis and write to her there, but then I noticed a blinking message on my comm. It was an answer from Snowstorm, and what followed was another message from an unknown number, some guy named Grant Acharria.

First I opened the developers' answer. Under the recognizable company-logo header, I saw a message that was read aloud by a pleasant feminine voice:

Dear Alex!

Thank you for your very important questions. We truly appreciate when our players work with us to solve problems like this. It is prudent and allows us to avoid unforeseen consequences and potential conflicts.

Fortunately, your question has a very easy answer. In the world of Disgardium, *private property is always retained as long as it does not violate the rules of the game for others (for example, a player that defeats you in battle has the right to take items and money that drop).*

In your situation, everything you own at the precise moment the threat is eliminated (including bank accounts, personal chests, and whatever

432

does not drop with your death both on your person or in a bag, and the bag itself if of a higher class than basic) is stored and transferred to your new character.

As you see, there is absolutely no cause for alarm in that regard.

As for gameplay style, of course we cannot make you do anything in Disgardium. After all, complete freedom of action is our guiding principle!

At the same time, we do not see any reason for your character to remain inactive. You have nothing to lose! what's more, by increasing your threat class, you increase the size of the reward you stand to receive after elimination.

In our turn, we would like to remind you that you are required to spend no less than eight hours in Disgardium *per twenty-four-hour period*. Yesterday, your game session consisted of less than two hours, so please try to make that up.

Thank you for getting in touch with us! May the skies of Disgardium *always be blue over your head!*

Most sincerely,
Marianna Da Silva, Customer service department,
Snowstorm Incorporated.

Was that all? I scanned down, reading my

quoted email, but there wasn't a word about Dargo or human-controlled mobs. It was all redacted so smoothly that I doubted if I even mentioned it at all. Was it all in my head?

In a flurry, I opened the second email. It had a built in "Burn after Reading" feature, evidenced by a fire icon next to the subject line "To Scyth from Grant." A mechanical voice read out the letter:

> **Alex, hey!**
>
> *First of all, let me inform you that all information provided in this email is of an informal nature and cannot be construed as an official statement by or position of Snowstorm Incorporated, or any related corporate entity, including but not limited to...*

What followed was a long list of registered trademarks and corporate entities I just skimmed. Following that was a list of restrictions on disclosure or dissemination, after which I noticed the address the email came from. It was registered to a domain that provided single-use email accounts.

I snorted and kept reading:

> *So then, now that the formalities are out of the way (just copypasta, haha) let me get to business.*

Class-A Threat

Marianna answered your other questions. As for the one about mobs and the human factor, that is out of her depth, so I will be answering. I will not give my name, and it does not matter.

Just between us, the theory of probability really screwed us. The chance that Tristad, which we chose to test our new function, would get a threat as obvious as yours (you know what I'm talking about) was close to zero.

But even one one-millionth of a percent, as our Skynet (the joking name for our super AI) calculated, in your case is greater than zero. And that means it was possible. Still, Skynet has run the tests and nothing in your situation could really go beyond the pale. All participants in the test, such as the person in the Crypt of the Temple of Nergal the Radiant have signed a non-disclosure agreement. In the scenarios Skynet ran, those people kept mum every time.

So none of us gave any significance to yet another threat arising in Tristad, even if the potential was higher than average. You're not the first or last player with threat status in that sandbox, let me tell you. In the last year and a half alone, you are the fourth (and honestly the last still standing, haha).

But you are right. After people discover a threat, they will try to use that information to their advantage. We cannot allow that. There is a conflict *of interest there. To us, our new project is equally important as threats progressing.*

And thus, we have made some minor adjustments. Now, if you enter a dungeon with mobs controlled by people, the system will kick them out of Disgardium, *replacing them with AI.*

Beyond that, you missed a minor issue, but we already fixed it, taking your gameplay style into account. Portals into dungeons show the status of the group inside, but in your case they will always show that the location is temporarily closed for maintenance. That is not unusual in Disgardium, *so no one will raise an eyebrow.*

Good luck increasing your threat class, Alex! And, to paraphrase a classic, put more destroying fire under your enemies' feet!

Grant (not actually).

I read to the end and the email disappeared, leaving me with an empty screen. I was brought right back to the incoming mail folder, and there was nothing there from Grant anymore.

I looked at the time. I was cutting it close, but there was enough time to quickly wash up and eat breakfast. I no longer saw any reason to break my promise to the Dementors and leave them in the dust.

Class-A Threat

* * *

Sunday morning in Tristad. Everything was almost like normal, just three times as many people. Wearing the gear Tissa gifted me, I almost felt like one of them as we walked through the concentration of people. And I had twenty-two gold clinking around in my virtual wallet, which I got for selling the Pherax loot at auction. Inspired by my first successful gear sale, I put the *green* knife from the Jail with plusses to *Thief* and *Break-in* up for auction as well.

And from there I ran to the tavern to leave my money in the chest. I didn't want to lose it, after all I didn't have any more. I finished that and got back to running, only this time to the place I was going to meet the Dementors.

In that time, I got a few messages from them, and their tone changed from cordial and happy to baffled. They didn't understand why I was late or where I even was until I realized I had activated the privacy setting to not show others whether I was playing Dis. I answered shortly: "omw."

The four Dementors were standing on grass next to the city gates. They saw me and stood up. When I got near, Crawler nodded with his arms crossed. I could read concentration not only on his face, but all of theirs. Mentally they were already in the dungeon. Even the normally jovial Infect was in no mind to kid around.

The boys squeezed my hand, Tissa smiled and gave a barely perceptible head-bob. And I understood why. Friday night didn't happen, act casual.

"Ready?" she asked.

"As far as I understand, I just need to raise whoever dies. That doesn't take any preparation…"

"He's ready," Crawler reported. "Let's move out. We'll give you the *Stone of Resurrection* when we get there."

I nodded. It was not a cheap artifact. Crawler was just playing it safe. I got added to the group, Tissa buffed us for speed and regeneration, and we jogged lightly off to the northwest toward the Olton Quarries. Hired workmen were transported there on special carts, but we had to hoof it.

It was not a short path. Thankfully it was well-trodden though, so mobs generally avoided it with the exception of one brazen level-ten black bear. Anyway, two *Hands of Nergal* from Tissa and a fireball from Crawler were too much for him. Bomber, as the strongest player with the highest carrying capacity, looted the body and we moved on.

The sun was sitting high and just frying my skin. We were all drenched in sweat and, even knowing this was just false realism, we were still constantly reaching for the canteens of water the

Dementors had thankfully brought along. They already knew what they were getting into. As it turned out, beyond the several stacks of health and mana potions, they had also brought lots of food with impressive bonuses.

"Spicy roast catfish in mango sauce, five gold a piece!" Bomber boasted, licking his lips. "And yeah it's tasty, but it's also gonna make the group better. It gives plus five to all basic attributes!"

"I should remember that and learn the recipe," I thought.

"I don't think it's tasty," Tissa didn't agree.

"Well it's better than what we eat out there!" Infect exclaimed, not clarifying what exactly this was tastier than, or what he meant by "out there."

Everyone already knew, and that tiny little thing finally made me realize just how drastically citizenship status can affect living standards. And that was a matter of just a few points on the test. They all had lower-status families than me. In mine, organic food was not considered a rarity.

In two hours and change, we were at our destination next to the crevasse. Crawler stopped at a tall stone pillar covered in carved letters. The top was adorned with a three-dimensional double-cross, the symbol of respawn points.

"Everyone set here if you haven't yet," said Ed. "Scyth?"

"I don't need to, did you forget?" I answered.

"The restless soul thing..."

"You know best. Alright, let's go. I'm gonna toss a *Feather* on everyone!" he got out a scroll.

There was a descending path carved into a steep stone wall and it was so narrow we couldn't get through two at a time. And it would have taken us half an hour at least, but with the air magic spell, it all went much faster. One after the next, the Dementors walked off the edge. I made sure the magic worked and jumped after them.

Flying, what a feeling! I couldn't control my speed at all, though it was relatively low. In fact, it was slow enough that I managed to take a look around.

Below me, there were miners scurrying around regardless of the fact it was technically a weekend. At the far end of the crevasse, there was a black tunnel entrance with a set of rails running into it. Miners hauled carts of ore out.

We landed and walked up to the cave. Now I understood why the guys came to town so rarely, and came back loaded like mules. They had no mounts, there were no portals into town, and the idea of wasting a half a day getting there and back for nothing made my fist tighten. And the hamster was about to hang itself.

Not paying any mind to the quarry workers, Ed led us past them into the mine shaft. I sensed someone staring at me, turned and saw Manny,

Hank's brother. He raised a hand and I waved back. He made a donut with his fingers and rolled his eyes back, smacking his lips. I smiled, nodded and ran off to catch my group.

In the gloom of the mine shaft, my night vision ability switched on and, when we turned down a side passage leading sharply downward, and the torch-light the miners worked by was left behind. Experience started pouring down like a river.

Night Vision skill improved: +1.
Vision radius in the dark increased by 60%.
Current level: 6.
Improve this skill by staring into the darkness, but take care. It might start staring back at you!

After that up, we went to the portal, which completely covered the passage down the tunnel.

Next to the portal, there was a short boy standing in the shadows. He took a step toward us and held a hand out in front.

Arador, level-15 human
Clan: Axiom.
Real name: Mikha Pavlyuk.
Real age: 15.
Class: Tracker.

"Dementors, stop!" he ordered sharply. "I can't let you in there."

"Arador, hi! Are your guys inside?" Ed asked in a business-like manner. "What's their progress?"

"The ins is empty, but you can't go inside, Crawler. As the strongest clan in this sandbox Axiom is claiming this dungeon until we complete it and get First Kill. In the future, after we're done, you may apply to enter, but it won't be free of course."

"What the heck?" Hung asked derisively. "You're alone, there are five of us. Try and stop us."

"Wait Bomber," Crawler frowned and turned to Arador: "Since when does you being the strongest clan mean you get to just claim dungeons? The arena is the arena. You're number one there, no arguments. But since when does that affect PvE?"

"Since yesterday. Big Po and Jay agreed. The Night Stalkers joined Axiom and now members of any sandbox clan that dares to defy us will be put on Axiom's KoS list. So Crawler, think well if it's worth being a stubborn ox like your boy Hung," Arador spat underfoot. "For what it's worth, our guys are already on the way."

"Son of a bitch!" I could hear Infect's voice distinctly. "We should have come yesterday..."

"You should have," the tracker smiled. "But

there would have been no point. We have a group: everyone is fifteen at least with max buffs and equip! And even still we keep going down on the last boss. We got him down to five percent on our last try, it was almost enough! But that was us! And who did you bring?" He nodded in my direction. "A level six in *green* gear! Crawler, I'm starting to think you might be a bit slow!"

"Don't you dare," Ed said gloomily. "We're leaving. Say hi to Big Po for me. Let's go, guys."

The Dementors turned, preparing to leave. I stood in place, feverishly thinking... Hm-hm-hm...

"Crawler, I still don't understand about the noob," Arador shouted, glancing at me. "Is this a little side hustle? I remember you told us off for doing that, got indignant... But now you're power leveling?"

Ed's eyes flickered indignantly, but he didn't manage to open his mouth before I answered for him:

"Something like that. What's in there anyway? Is that some kind of portal? Where does it go? I've only been playing for a week, I'm still learning..."

"Are you joking?" the tracker asked in astonishment. "Definitely a noob, although... Hey, you're that Scyth, I remember you!"

He guffawed. The Dementors stopped tensely and watched our dialogue. I weighed the consequences and came to a decision. With a mental command, I quickly sent a message to the group chat: "Don't kick me out of the group! I'll tell you more later."

"Haha!" Arador kept laughing. "You must be kidding! And what, in a whole year you've never been in an ins?"

"Yep, I admit, I haven't," I snorted stupidly. "Listen, Mikha, do you think I could just take a peek? Just to see what it's like and stuff..."

"Ha, no problem! I hope you haven't left your respawn point in Tristad! I guess it wouldn't be so bad though, it would get you right back to town. Please," he bowed mockingly, extending his hands toward the ins. "Be my guest."

"Guys!" I shouted foolishly to the Dementors. "Thanks for getting me to the mines, but I'll take it from here!"

And I dove into the portal.

Chapter Thirty-Three

Evil from the Depths

*T*HE CAVE I FOUND myself in was lit by flickering crystal formations on the walls. The evil magic emanated a dead light, but that was still better than absolute darkness. It allowed me to see fifty feet of the downward-sloping tunnel ahead of me, which got wider as it got deeper.

Water was dripping off the ceiling everywhere, and I could hear something rustling quickly in the darkness, but I made sure no one was coming to attack me. Then I sent a message in the group chat.

> *[11:27] [Group] [Scyth]: Tell Arador a timer turned on asking me to leave the instance. They're going to kick me out and I'm heading for the exit. I'll explain later.*

[11:27] [Group] [Crawler]: I see. We'll have to come back later...

[11:28] [Group] [Scyth]: Say I asked you to come back and meet me. There are nasty little millipedes in here...

[11:28] [Group] [Bomber]: They're blind. They only aggro if you attack. Don't piss yourself.

[11:29] [Group] [Crawler]: So are you really leaving? Should we wait at the portal?

[11:30] [Group] [Scyth]: Just do as I said.

[11:35] [Group] [Tissa]: Alex, we're here. Where are you? We can't see you.

[11:35] [Group] [Scyth]: What did Arador say?

[11:37] [Group] [Crawler]: He's in a great mood. He's yelling. The ins has been closed for maintenance. Where are you?

[11:38] [Group] [Scyth]: Great. Now tell him I got sent to the Tristad Cemetery. And also tell me what exactly it says for dungeon status.

[11:38] [Group] [Infect]: Uh... Just a sec, there's a lot.

[11:38] [Group] [Infect]: The location Evil from the Depths is temporarily closed for maintenance. We apologize for any inconvenience this may cause. Try again in: unknown.

[11:38] [Group] [Infect]: Ugh... So where are you exactly?

[11:38] [Group] [Crawler]: Yeah, Scyth. We lost you.

[11:39] [Group] [Scyth]: Everything's fine. I'm in the ins, but the devs gave me a little trick because of Patrick's curse. If I'm in a dungeon, it says it's out of order. That's so players don't aggro on me. Now we need to figure out how to get you guys in here.

[11:41] [Group] [Scyth]: Hey, answer me!

[11:41] [Group] [Tissa]: Alex, we're leaving the area. Crawler is talking with Axiom. Wait. We'll have to get rid of them before we can get to you.

[11:42] [Group] [Scyth]: Ok, I'll wait.

[11:58] [Group] [Crawler]: Sorry for taking so long, we were thinking. Axiom is gonna keep watch here until morning. After that, they're all gonna fly off to school. So we'd have to wait until tomorrow morning.

[11:59] [Group] [Scyth]: And?

[11:59] [Group] [Tissa]: Alex, we can't ask you to do that. But if you do...

[12:00] [Group] [Bomber]: I'll kiss you, Scythy boy!

[12:00] [Group] [Tissa]: Hilarious! Haha!

[12:00] [Group] [Scyth]: Alright, I'm gonna leave the darkness.

[12:01] [Group] [Infect]: Hung, are you cheating on me?!

[12:01] [Group] [Bomber]: XD XD!

[12:02] [Group] [Crawler]: Enough side-tracking! Well, Scyth. You don't have to. Hanging around an ins for almost a whole day is not the same as just running around Dis. It bites that we didn't have time to get you food or water. Anyway, we'll understand if you just leave.

[12:03] [Group] [Scyth]: Guys, do you only need the final boss for the achi?

[12:03] [Group] [Crawler]: Yes.

[12:03] [Group] [Tissa]: Yeah.

[12:03] [Group] [Infect]: Yep.

[12:04] [Group] [Bomber]: Uh... That's right.

[12:04] [Group] [Scyth]: Great! Then I'll see you at seven AM. I'm gonna kick a couple mobs around and level skills.

[12:05] [Group] [Tissa]: I told you!

[12:05] [Group] [Crawler]: ...

[12:06] [Group] [Crawler]: Scyth, it's a real mess out here. Bomber is doing some weird dance with Infect. I'm not celebrating with them and Tissa yet, because for now it's just words, but if you actually do this, I don't even know... Consider your rep with all of us up from neutral to respect.

[12:06] [Group] [Tissa]: Alex, you're the

---

best! I love you!
[12:07] [Group] [Bomber]: *Me too!*
[12:07] [Group] [Infect]: *Hung, you cheater!*

I smiled. Big old Hung and tan Malik were always playing a couple, but they were just acting. In fact, half the upper-class girls would kill to be with Malik, and Hung used to play on the school football team and now was carrying on with a few ladies.

[12:08] [Group] [Scyth]: *Alright. Well then, seven AM it is. Don't sleep through it! I'm off to beat down a millipede. Leroooooy!*
[12:09] [Group] [Crawler]: *Jenkins! Good luck, Scyth!*

I closed the chat window, kept the armor set I had on and bound it to a button. Now I could get dressed instantly. With all the damage from the mobs it would be a small miracle if it survived, but I hoped the gear would give me at least some protection. I was getting the impression that they turned the pain filters off for threats to the world, and the only thing keeping me sane was my *Resilience* cutting down on the pain.

By the way, while I chatted, my *Night Vision* improved. That led me to the idea of levelling *Stealth* and, what was more, the first mob I came across had exactly what I needed.

Spiny Flesh-Eating Millipede, level 18

Eighteen! That meant the bosses would be at least twenty! And that would mean I could level my skills to sixty. What a good move I made coming in here. Now I would spend almost a whole day in the gloom of a dungeon, teeming with monsters. But that didn't scare me. I had eaten a big breakfast, and my body could handle one day without food and water.

I lay down on my stomach, slowly crawled over to the millipede and lied down when it raised its head, looking toward me. I spent ten minutes lying like that, but the time was completely wasted. *Stealth* didn't grow by even one percent. Clearly neutral mobs were not counted as enemies.

And honestly, the millipede didn't try to attack. It ran past, tickling my leg with a clump of its long stiff hairs. I wasn't planning to go any further until Curse of the Undead tripped, so I attacked. It hissed and responded right away. We exchanged blows and bites, after which two of my skills dinged at once – *Unarmed Combat* and *Resilience*.

Then I died. The poison from this monster's bite gave a very strong DoT, reducing my health points right before my eyes. As I lay there, I looked at the logs: my accuracy against a mob that surpassed me by twelve levels was cut by one hundred twenty percent. If I hadn't levelled *Unarmed Combat* to thirty-seven, giving me plus one hundred ninety percent accuracy, I would have been better off just puffing bamboo until the Dementors showed up tomorrow morning. You can't fight too well with a negative hit chance.

With those thoughts in mind, I respawned, activated *Ghastly Howl* and *Stoneskin*, managed to smack the insect in its mandibles after the *Fear* ended and I died again.

Pain spread from the place the acidic bite landed. When I stood back up the beast snapped me in two again. But now I was used to that.

Twenty-nine deaths later, my *Resilience* was up to level forty, *Ghastly Howl* had levelled and the RNG worked its magic:

> **You carry the mark of the Destroying Plague and have evaded fatal damage!**
> *You have been given Curse of the Undead: all damage taken reduced by 100%!*
> *This curse will remain active until you completely restore your health.*
>
> **Mark of the Destroying Plague improved: +1.**

Chance to receive Curse of the Undead: 6%. Current level: 6.

First thing I noticed was that my plague energy reserves were still the same size, as was the percentage of damage I could convert into plague energy. The skill description said nothing about that, but if I considered it logically... I got plague energy at skill-level five. That meant at level ten I'd either get a new ability, or an improvement to my plague damage. And hopefully it would be both.

A thought flickered up that it was a good idea to try and level *Mark of the Destroying Plague* at least up to ten. But I set that very important thought aside until I was done with this ins. Six percent was less than ten. But if the Dementors saw me in this haggard, semi-decayed state, it might be too great a temptation. They'd either kill me themselves or sell my identity to well-heeled preventers. Imagine looking at this from an outside perspective...

> *[12:34] [Group] [Tissa]: 20+ deaths in seven minutes! Alex, are you already at the boss or something?*
> *[12:35] [Group] [Crawler]: I counted thirty. Who's doing that to you, Scyth?*
> *[12:35] [Group] [Scyth]: A millipede. I'm getting some damage in between deaths, so*

sooner or later it'll die!

[12:37] [Group] [Bomber]: Ahahahaha! A millipede!

While they had fun in the chat, I looked into my privacy settings and kicked myself. The group chat was showing all of my deaths. Oh no, can't let that happen. I put a restriction on everything including achievements and loot.

[12:42] [Group] [Scyth]: Sorry guys, but laughing at the less fortunate isn't nice! Show's over!

I just ignored their whining until they got it out of their system. Meanwhile, the millipede kept hissing fearsomely, biting and poisoning me, but its white bar was empty.

Thinking, I decided not to waste plague energy, and started levelling *Unarmed Combat*. From an outside perspective it probably looked pointless. My normal blows did no damage, and *Hammer* took just forty to fifty points. And that was only because it ignored thirty-six percent of armor.

You have damaged Spiny Flesh-Eating Millipede: 0.
Health points: 1982/2300.

You have damaged Spiny Flesh-Eating Millipede: 45.
Health points: 1937/2300.

At that point I regretted that I had no more *Roast Undead Rat Chitterlings* with their massive boost to skill progress. But it was no problem. I was not in a hurry. My Unarmed Combat bar was filling up right before my eyes, improving with every blow I landed on my three-fold stronger enemy.

By the time the millipede issued a hysterical chirr and flipped onto its back, fitfully twitching its legs, my *Unarmed Combat* was up to forty.

I spent a few minutes just sitting on a stone and savoring the calm. After the uninterrupted chirring and hissing, prolonged silence was music to my ears.

After a quick breather, I kept going, now back in *Stealth*. But this time it bore fruit. Before me loomed a pack of hostile mobs.

Foul Poisonwing, level 20

The three living breathing fruits of a sick designer's imagination hovered in the air, unhurriedly flapping their large wings, which were crowned with long claws tipped with glimmering poison. And they had huge faceted eyes on a bug-like face with mouth tentacles that glimmered a foreboding shade of red. Their long bodies gave way to a dangling sharp tail divided into scaly segments which flexed menacingly, sometimes down sometimes up.

The fact that the poisonwings didn't move around much played into my hand. I lay down in *Stealth* as close as possible, a distance I determined by walking up until one of the mobs sharply turned in my direction. Okay then, no closer than that.

If there were a patience skill in Dis, mine would have been very high already. I lay in the same pose then, afraid to move and thus break *Stealth* for almost four hours. Curse of the Undead was long gone, but I was at peace with that. I did have something else bothering me, though. Dis' realism. All my muscles were cramping, everything itched and the sweat trickling down my forehead stung my eyes. Four hours! I remembered a story from my great grandfather about some local war where he had to hunker down in a sniper's nest for hours on end and that helped me hold out. My great grandfather was risking his life. I was risking nothing, not even experience points if I died.

Seemingly, the system considered not only difference in levels, but the fact that there were several mobs and every one of them generated experience for my skill every second I spent unnoticed in their aggro radius.

Stealth skill improved!
Chance of remaining unnoticed by enemies increased by 60%.
Current level: 60.
Improve this skill by hiding near enemies of your level or higher!

After hitting the level cap, I stood up and was seen right away. All the poisonwings tore off in my direction. I activated *Ghastly Howl* and threw on *Stoneskin*. Let's see what you got!

✳ ✳ ✳

In the real world, it was approaching midnight. To me the twelve hours in the dungeon were filled with endless levelling of everything in my repertoire. The Dementors wouldn't show up for slightly over seven hours, and I had only gotten past the first boss.

And it took me a very long time to get there. I came across too many hostile packs. And they were varied and high in number.

The first three poisonwings were daisies in comparison with the ten spiders after them. Those hellspawn covered me with razor-sharp webs, entrapping me and holding me just out of reach. It took a very long time. So much in fact that I started to think I had gotten myself into a jam. Cool. I would be just stuck in this never-ending dead-end battle until the Dementors showed up, and they wouldn't even be able to enter the dungeon because I would be in battle. But all good things must come to an end. The glands that produced web secretions eventually ran out and the arachnids ran at me for melee. After that they didn't last long. Afraid that their web reserves might be recharging, I emptied all my plague energy on them right away.

After that came some slow-burn battles. First with scorpion-like creatures that attacked from underground; next with some pesky crustacean-like bugs who were all too happy to use their chainsaw claws; and finally some poison-spitting flies...

I used every opportunity I had to improve my skills. In the end I raised *Unarmed Combat*, *Resilience* and *Stealth* all to sixty-three. *Night Vision* hit fifteen too, which meant I could now see a one-hundred-fifty-foot radius in the dark. Sure it wasn't exactly bright as day, but I could see about like in the twilight.

Mark of the Destroying Plague levelled on the poisonwings, and Curse of the Undead now had a seven percent chance to trip. I also levelled *Ghastly Howl*, it hit level nine and its radius was up to sixty feet.

I was level eight by the time I got to the first boss. The abundance of high-level mobs rained down experience, more than ten thousand in fact. And that gave me two levels and change so level nine wasn't exactly beyond the horizon. I put the ten attribute points into luck on a hunch.

When I thought about it, with plague energy, additional strength would only give me crumbs of extra damage. And with Curse of the Undead, I didn't give a damn about the health I would get from extra endurance, or the dodge chance and movement speed from agility. Charisma was nice for leveling via quests and getting unique chains, but that was clearly not my path. Raising perception for accuracy no longer made any sense. *Unarmed Combat* was levelled as all hell, and that was pretty well enough.

But crit chance, which was now up to fifteen percent, was very important. And the hamster inside me greedily rubbed its little paws together at the extra one-percent chance of receiving improved loot. That topic was very easy to understand in Dis. No matter what might drop, there was always a chance for an item to go up by one quality level. *Green* might turn into rare *blue*, and in its turn a *blue* might become a fully-fledged *purple* epic.

The boss was a colossal overgrown praying

mantis named Faras, level twenty-one. A real freak, he was protected by a shield of fog, and you had to take it all the way down before you could even start on his health.

I had to take down that two-thousand-HP piece of crap five times because, every time Faras lost twenty percent health, he would go underground and come back up with a full shield. But it was only a breather for him. Up where I was, the battlefield flooded with waves of tiny praying mantises, which was nothing short of a nightmare. I had no AoE damage abilities, and I had to take down those little shits one by one. Crawler could have just put up a *Wall of Fire*, but he wasn't around. Anyhow, I didn't really care. It fit perfectly into my tactics. I took down the boss's shield with plague energy, then twenty percent of its health with my next attack. After that, I would refill my energy with the attacks of the tiny buggers.

The battle lasted over ten minutes, and that tripped *Enrage*[4]. Faras began vibrating and inflated either with blood or lymph fluid. At any rate, he turned red and sharply grew in size. And that was how he looked when he died. I didn't wait to see what the boss had in mind, dove under him and slammed his gut with all my power. The chitin

---

[4] *Enrage* is what happens when a dungeon boss gets mad. If you take longer on them than is allotted, they go psycho and start dealing massive damage.

dented, my whole face was covered with stinging hemo-lymph fluid, and his massive body collapsed to the cave floor.

You have critically damaged Faras: 290!
Faras is dead.

Experience points received: 1200.
Experience points at present level (8): 4600/5400.

The battle had me stressed out. My liveliness figure was down to zero, my legs were giving out. I laid down next to the boss. Taking a breather, I read recent chat messages and smiled.

The Dementors were supporting me as much as they could all day, constantly asking if I was doing alright, and how I was feeling. My parents' care was something that just seemed matter of course, but having my classmates worried for me was something new. Of course, Eve gave me something like that, but her personal problems always came first. Any interest in my problems was more a debt of politeness in her concept of friendship.

To put it briefly, it was... nice. I understood perfectly why they were supporting me. It was so I wouldn't give up before the end, but still it came in very handy. It helped me not lose my mind in the gloomy infested dungeon.

The last message was a PM from Tissa:

[23:48] [Private] [Tissa]: *It's stupid to wish you a good night, Alex. But still try and get some sleep. I know how spooky it is down there and I understand you probably won't be able to sleep. Pill bugs, cockroaches, fire ants, worms... We decided to get to bed early so we can be fresh in the morning. See you tomorrow. Kisses.*

My mouth drooped in an idiotic smile. I mechanically picked up the loot from Faras and smiled again, this time consciously.

The *purple* on the gear's name meant I had just got my very first epic.

Chapter Thirty-Four

Out of the Fire!

YESTERDAY on my way back from Cali Bottom, I set the car to autopilot for a while and, sponge-like, absorbed all kinds of basic information about Dis. It was rash on my part to dive headfirst into this game hoping to succeed without finding out as much as possible about it first. When I first climbed into my capsule, I was upset at my parents' divorce. Then Chief Councilman Whiteacre gave me an impossible but mandatory quest, and I got swept up in the vortex...

So I decided to use every free minute outside Dis to fill in the gaps in my knowledge. And here's what I managed to find out.

At the dawn of the first game world, when immersion pods existed only in fantasy books and characters had to be controlled by pressing buttons, *World of the Trade of Warfare* was one of the most popular games in the world. The founders of Snowstorm were reputed to be big fans of that primitive game. And for that reason, there were a ton of references in *Disgardium* to "WotToW."

One of them was a color graduation in item names, which they lifted directly. *Gray* was for low-quality items, trash basically. *White* was for normal stuff, without any bonuses. *Green* was for unusual items with minimal bonuses. *Blue* was for rare; *purple* was for epic, but still not unique; and *orange* was for legendary items of which only one existed in the whole game world.

Snowstorm also added another two colors: *gold* for scalable items that, as a rule, could not be of a class lower than epic, and *red* for godlike items.

Scalable was exactly what it sounded like. Their attributes and bonuses grew along with the wearer. They could not be stolen, lost or broken. What was more, they bound to the soul of the owner and no one else could ever use them. The main downside was that there was no such thing as sets of scalable items.

Red godlike items were as rare as they were valuable. It was the absolute top class of equipment and artifacts, combining all the upsides of legendary and scalable. There was only verifiable information about a couple such items, and nowhere near all of them belonged to the leaders of the most powerful clans. And that was all because they bound to the soul of the first person to pick them up.

No one who ever got a godlike artifact had said how they got it. Going off the name of the item class, some had brought their faith level with one of the gods of *Disgardium* to maximum. They completed magnificent quest chains from the gods, but it was all in vain. Yes, they got untold rewards, but there were no godlike items among them.

There were rumors, which the developers neither confirmed or denied, that godlike items were invented as a stimulus for players who kept to themselves. They said, in the *World of the Trade of Warfare*, the so-called founding fathers, the very best stuff could only be gotten as part of a strong clan or static (big raid groups with permanent member lists). And those who preferred to play alone were left out in the cold. The chance of succeeding with a randomly formed group was minimal.

It was as if Snowstorm decided that stubborn loners deserved a reward as well. So receiving godlike objects did not require combat prowess, just a flexible mind and adventurous gameplay.

Class-A Threat

I had never considered my style of gameplay, nor had I considered *red* or *gold* items. Sure a few days back I was elated by *blues* from Dargo and Crusher and had gone to great pains not to give them up to Crag or the Dementors. I'd earned them with the sweat of my brow after all. But ever since then, something was different in my perception of the world and surroundings.

> **Chance of receiving improved loot: success!**
> *Reward quality improved to epic.*

That message flittered past my attention in the heat after battle, but now I could see that epic stuff wasn't guaranteed to fall from the bosses of Evil from the Depths. A rare item was supposed to drop, but... I got lucky.

And here was the *purple* epic from the ghastly praying mantis Faras. I focused on the object and before me came a laundry list of text:

> **Gloves of Evil from the Depths**
> *Epic, part of the Evil from the Depths set*
> *Cloth armor.*
> *Armor: 24.*
> *+19 Intelligence.*
> *+17 Endurance.*
> *+9% critical damage chance.*

+7% spell power bonus.
Durability: 300/300.
Requires level: 20.
Sell price: 93 gold coins.
Chance of losing after death reduced by 90%.

Evil from the Depths set: belt, armbands, crown, gloves, neckpiece, robe, sandals and pants.
2/8 of the Evil from the Depths set: Reduces magic damage taken by 15%.
4/8 of the Evil from the Depths set: When taking damage in battle, the wearer has a chance to spawn a 350-HP shield.
6/8 of the Evil from the Depths set: +20 Intelligence.
8/8 of the Evil from the Depths set: +100 armor, +33% mana regeneration.

My first epic loot was definitely made for mages. And it was part of a set! I thought it would be just as good for Crawler as for Tissa. We had never agreed on how to split the loot, and they didn't know what I just got.

But I didn't want to lie. Still, I wanted to check something first. Even if this low-level epic could be sold for a couple thousand gold, I preferred to take a risk and show it to the Dementors first, then see what they said. I could decide what to do next from there.

There were another seven bosses in this dungeon but, if I killed all of them myself, even my friends would start to ask questions. Plus, I only signed onto this to sit quietly off to the side and resurrect them if they all died. So let the Dementors do some work tomorrow as well.

With these thoughts in mind, I set the interface alarm clock to six forty-five AM and fell asleep.

✳ ✳ ✳

"Wake up Alex, wake up," whispered a soft and charming female voice.

The tone started increasing in intensity and eventually I realized it was not a dream, but the interface alarm clock. I opened my eyes, and closed them right away. I wanted to sleep so bad, but I had to get up. I saw that the group chat window was blinking frantically. That meant very many fresh messages.

I opened my eyes again. Still lying there, I made sure my health was all the way back and Curse of the Undead was gone. Then I skimmed the chat:

[6:32] [Group] [Crawler]: Scyth, we're close. Infect went in stealth to check the entrance to

the ins. How's it going?
[6:33] [Group] [Tissa]: *Good morning, Alex! Hey, are you inside?*
[6:37] [Group] [Tissa]: *Alex?*
[6:41] [Group] [Bomber]: *Hey, Sheppard, I picked up a couple quarts of fresh-brewed halfling coffee in the Bubbling Flagon! I'm gonna personally make sure you drink all of it!*
[6:47] [Group] Infect *has entered Evil from the Depths.*
[6:48] [Group] [Crawler]: *Scyth, we're in the mine. There are no Axiom guys here, we're going in. The portal says the location is unavailable, but Infect already went in.*
[6:48] [Group] [Infect]: *I'm inside! It worked!*

Oh nether, they're already here! Unsticking my eyes, I got up and felt my bones and back aching. And those were sensations in my real body.

I jumped up, shook my head, but still felt like crap. My throat was totally dry, I wanted badly to eat and not here, there in the real world. My body was giving signals that I needed to quench my hunger and thirst as quickly as possible. Among the debuff icons, I noticed an interface warning that I was at risk of dehydration and, in five hours, I would be forced to exit *Disgardium*.

[6:48] [Group] [Scyth]: Everything is fine, I was asleep. Some coffee is just what I need, Hung! I'm waiting at the first boss. To be fair, he's a bit of a corpse now... He couldn't take the long hard fist massage and just died. And yeah, hi!

*[6:49] [Group] **Crawler** has entered Evil from the Depths.*

*[6:49] [Group] **Bomber** has entered Evil from the Depths.*

*[6:49] [Group] **Tissa** has entered Evil from the Depths.*

[6:50] [Group] [Bomber]: Ah-ha-ha! So what, you tickle him to death?

[6:50] [Group] [Scyth]: I spent half the night tickling. By the way, it dropped an epic!

[6:50] [Group] [Crawler]: Well I'll be! You beautiful boy! Link to loot, plz.

*[6:51] [Group] [Scyth]: **[Gloves of Evil from the Depths]** – something like that.*

All activity in the chat stopped. Clearly the set epic had so struck them and driven them into a frenzy that they were running to reach me as quickly as possible.

In ten minutes, I saw the Dementors entering Faras's cave. And Infect appearing behind me, covered my eyes and whispered tenderly:

"Guess who?"

"Don't even start," I groaned and broke free. "I'm already in enough of a fog here!"

Tissa, when she caught sight of me, for some reason cast *Holy Renewal*, which wasn't much help, then she ran up and embraced me, whispering in my ear:

"Thanks."

Ed patted me on the shoulder, then I found myself in the embrace of big old Hung. He gave me a strong squeeze, nearly breaking a rib then shouted, unable to hide his glee:

"It worked! We did it! I can only imagine how pissed those Axiom jerks are gonna be when we snatch the achi out from under their noses! Big Po is gonna blow a gasket!"

"Don't run in front of a flying semi, Bomber," Ed said. He looked me in the eyes with compassion, taking me by the shoulders. "Scyth, you can leave your pod now. We'll wait."

"Uh... But what about the progress? Won't it zero out?"

"Not as long as at least one group member is alive in the instance. Will a half hour be enough?"

"Hm... In theory yes, but I wouldn't mind a shower," I said, thinking it over.

"No problem," Rodriguez nodded. "The four of us have gotten to the final boss before, so take your time while we clear mobs. Don't worry, just get yourself together. It usually took us six or seven hours to get to the last boss. But you already took down the first, so we can get it down to five. Alright, go on."

"If you want, you could even get a bit of sleep out there," Tissa suggested.

"That's if he doesn't want the experience," Infect noted. "If he isn't here, he won't get any."

"I mean, we're different enough levels that he won't get much xp," Tissa didn't agree. "Alex, do you care about a couple experience per mob? You stand to gain three maybe five hundred points total including bosses, but it's up to you. I bet that's what you were getting from one pack of mobs before."

"Yeah, good point," Crawler said. "Don't worry about the loot. We have a fair system for sharing it. Needs take prevalence. If an item is no use to anyone, which is not likely, we sell it and put the dough in our clan coffers. But your share is twenty percent, and we of course will let you have it. If you don't get anything, we'll pay your share of the gear at market value."

They all looked at me, waiting for a decision. I considered whether I wanted to spend another five or six hours hanging around here, risking death from some boss's mass ability or aggro'd mob. After all, this place was full of traps, and you could easily just fall down a hole. I could not afford to die. I'd help them damage on the last boss by adding plague energy though. In theory, it would look plausible. They were not beginners and should understand that, with the ability to respawn in where you just died, you could level *Unarmed Combat* very fast.

"Good. I'm heading to sleep," I said. "If it's not too hard, give me a call on my comm if you need me."

"Sounds good," Ed said. "About... Okay, later. Go get some rest."

I activated emergency exit and this time I got no warnings about lost progress. The world around started draining of color then went black.

Emergency exit activated!
Exiting in: 3...

"You'll come back right here. We'll send Infect back to lead you to us. After this, it gets into these mazes..." Ed's voice went silent.

"Hey, what about the coffee?" came Hung, sounding offended. And that was the last thing I heard.

What did Crawler want to talk about?

"We got lucky too," Infect boasted. "Locust, the fourth boss, dropped another epic. This one is chainmail armor. The rest is good equip, but not *blue...*"

"We didn't come here for loot," Ed interrupted and handed me the artifact they had put such hope into. "Here you go, Scyth."

The little rock was the size of a chicken egg and made no impression. It wasn't a proper shape, it had flakes and chips. To touch it, it was just a normal rock. But pores in the mineral emanated a barely visible light.

> ### Stone of Resurrection
> *Artifact*
> *Use: resurrects a dead group member.*
> *Cooldown time: 1 hour.*
> *Value: 2000 gold.*

I estimated that at auction this stone might be worth as much as ten thousand. After all, two thousand was just the vendor purchase price.

"Yeah, it cost a pretty penny," Tissa said. "Please don't lose it. Best thing would be bringing it up on the panel and activating it from there."

"I hope we don't have to use it," Crawler said. "Well, are we ready? Scyth, do you need me to go over tactics again?"

"Give me a couple minutes to drink that coffee," I said, nodding at Hung. "I just woke up."

The tank eagerly dug in his bag and handed

me a large hot wineskin.

"It doesn't get cold in your inventory," he chuckled. "Sorry, there's only one. We kept it for you special. The other one already got drunk."

That break was exactly what I needed. When I climbed out of the capsule, I wanted to drink so badly I couldn't take my mouth off the kitchen tap for five whole minutes. Then I ordered three portions of breakfast of various kinds from our multicooker (all told, I got a tomato omelet, hot dogs, bacon, toast, beans, cheese croissants and a tuna sandwich), then went to take a shower. I ate, drank a whole carton of orange juice and, just as I entered the bedroom, collapsed into bed.

I woke up to a call from Tissa, answered that I'd be there soon and went to wash up and brush my teeth. While I did that, I thought over how I would handle the talk with the Dementors if Curse of the Undead kicked in or Ed started asking questions about my threat status. I was calmed by the fact that, if that happened and I had the curse, they would have no way to kill me. In fact, I would probably kill them. Then I'd go to the Mire, and hang out there until I was old enough to leave the sandbox. There were no preventers here, and I could handle high-level mobs with my curse, even if every one in the Mire came at once. Nothing was stopping me from levelling *Mark of the Destroying Plague* to cap either.

Class-A Threat

"Scyth, it's time to go!" Ed said nervously.

The team was very high-strung, after all there was just one more step to the target. Another issue was that they had been unable to beat this boss before, but this time they'd have a few chances.

"Yeah, let's go," I got up despite myself and returned the empty wineskin to Bomber.

On the way, Ed repeated the tactics we were going to use for the hundredth time. To me it seemed like a big waste of time considering that no one had ever killed this boss yet. I mean, that meant all known tactics had failed. Beyond that, we agreed that I was not taking part in the battle, just trying not to die and I would only join in the final phase, when Murkiss – the level twenty-three boss – was down to less than twenty percent health. Then the group would need all the damage it could muster, because Murkiss would *Enrage* and quickly mow down the whole party, starting with the tank if they couldn't kill the boss first.

We spent a long time walking the spiral ramp down, which was lit by Tissa's magic. We carefully crossed a narrow path carved into a cliffside over a lava pit and finally reached the entrance to a huge cave.

And there I saw the undefeated main dungeon boss. This was the very incarnation of Evil from the Depths – a gigantic scorpion. It's carapace was black and its many appendages were orange. Its searing pincers and segmented tail flexed menacingly. Plus it had thirty thousand health points.

The main problem came from the boss's magical abilities. Beyond very strong physical and poison attacks like *Stinger* or attacking with its powerful claws, Murkiss had a couple other ways to make problems for our group.

He was spontaneous and unpredictable. You see, at random intervals Murkiss teleported to a random point in the cave and attacked whoever was closest. And it might never happen in a whole battle, or it could happen once per minute.

The teleportation took less than a second, so it always threw a wrench in our battle plan. While the tank ran over to the boss, whichever of us ended up in hot water might go down. And usually they fought back, using all defensive abilities at once and frantically slamming health potions. There was no way to run because the boss cast a three-second AoE *Earthquake* wherever he appeared, which slowed everyone in a ten-foot radius by fifty percent.

The boss also often used *Ignition*, beating the ground with its fiery pincers, which caused lines of flame to run every direction. And another special, *Fire of the Depths,* could burn anyone to death in just three seconds.

"Out of the fire!" Crawler repeated for the tenth time. "Out of the fire!"

Sometimes Murkiss chaotically spit *Seed of the Nether* too, covering the cave with small puddles of black slime. If you stayed in one for too long, it came at a high cost. In a few seconds a player would be pulled down to the Depths. And down there, they couldn't do anything until the end of battle. But usually they would die before that. The Creatures of the Depths were small and blind, but they could smell living flesh, and were drawn to it. When they got what they were after, they would grind a person down in an instant. And so I heard "Out of the puddles!" at least twenty times from Crawler.

And although the boss's last two abilities didn't worry the Dementors much – just be smart and run out of fire and puddles and Tissa will heal you – the fourth and first had everyone very worried. It was basically a lottery.

Murkiss could also summon *Nether Worms*, which would swallow a random player and go underground. There was no way to avoid them either. After getting swallowed, if you couldn't get out in thirty seconds by killing the thing from inside, you would die. And we would be screwed if the worm swallowed our tank or healer. Bomber didn't have high enough DPS, i.e. damaging speed, to kill the worm that fast, and without a tank the group couldn't survive long. Meanwhile if it swallowed Tissa, the tank would fold. *Squeeze* and *Stinger* could take half of Bomber's life even with his defensive abilities, and without the healing power of the priestess of Nergal, he would be dead in just eight seconds.

Out of nine attempts by the Dementors, one every week, which was the maximum the system allowed for a raid dungeon like this, the worst happened five or six times. That meant the tank or healer got swallowed.

"The theory of probability is on our side," Crawler said. "Plus, we've got Scyth with us now."

"I really hope you're right," Tissa snorted. "Swimming in acid inside a worm is not exactly a great experience."

"Don't start, please! Think positive!" His harsh tone left no doubts about Crawler's own positivity. He scratched the back of his head, trying to decide whether he had considered everything or not, then he just barked: "Is everyone ready?"

"Yes!" we answered in unison.

"Then let's go!"

Chapter Thirty-Five

All Hail the Heroes

I FELT IT WAS TIME to step in. Up until now, I was busy avoiding the lines of fire and jumping out of the Depths puddles.

The panic started when Ed shouted: "Worm!" The earth yawned underfoot, and an instant later I could feel myself falling into its behemoth maw. The fear of dying and revealing my status as a threat was so high that I put half my plague energy into one *Hammer*. The worm exploded into smithereens, and I got splashed with a bunch of its innards.

"Hell yeah!" Crawler shouted.

I rolled away just in time, one second before the earth beneath me gave way.

The worm appeared when Murkiss was at fifty percent health. For the next thirty, the Dementors were inspired by the quick defeat of the worm attack. So successfully and methodically, knowing exactly what to do, they hectored the scorpion and even when it suddenly teleported for the only time in battle to Ed, nothing went wrong. The mage didn't flinch and activated a fire shield that absorbed and reflected damage. And that lasted long enough for Hung to get the boss back on him.

The whole battle, Bomber held the boss away from the group. Crawler and Tissa stood at maximum distance and had no problem seeing the trajectory of the fire lines and taking a few steps away when necessary.

On the other side of the boss, winding between the scorpion's appendages, Infect was running as a ghost, doing the highest DpS of all. His predatory daggers moved so fast they looked blurry when he used specials. And as if the huge damage wasn't enough on its own, there were also regular messages about DoTs renewing: *Bleeding*, *Slowed* and *Poisoned*. Beyond that, Murkiss had a constant bunch of debuffs on him from Tissa and Crawler.

The speed of the battle was impressive. It had started just a few minutes ago, but that was child's play. Murkiss entered *Enrage*, and everything turned on a dime. The boss grew larger and one and a half times faster...

"Heal!" Hung shouted.

"I am!" Tissa noted. "I can't get you to full!"

"Plus ten percent damage every five seconds!" Crawler shouted. "Bro, turn on *Tenacity*! Scyth, help us with all you got! Stay away from the stinger!"

I joined Infect from the same side and slammed full force with my ability, adding a dose of plague energy for two hundred points.

You have damaged Murkiss: 239.
Health points: 5426/30000.

The rhythm of battle was cyclical and I very quickly got the hang of it. Jump under a *Cleaver*, dodge the fire, *Hammer*, land a series of blows, out of the puddles, jump...

I added thirty or forty points of plague energy to normal blows and I think I was doing no less damage than Infect. I would use *Hammerfist* after cooldown and got so caught up in the fun that I nearly burned up in a line of fire. Thankfully the thief pushed me out, barking:

"Look out below!"

I didn't make any more errors like that. The scorpion's health bar was barreling down and that made it angry. That was having a very bad effect on Bomber. Tissa clearly wasn't doing enough.

"Pedal to the metal!" the barely living tank shouted, parrying the boss's attack with a screech and hitting back with *Shatter*. The scorpion stumbled and threw itself back on the attack. "Take this!"

That was the last thing Hung managed to do. With two snips of its pincers and one big bite, our tank was dead.

Infect was next on the aggro list. Spitting out Bomber's lifeless body, Murkiss turned to the thief.

"Inf, *Dodge* then smash *Disappear!*" Crawler yelled.

"Where would I be without you...?" Malik snarled.

But he didn't have time to go invisible. His *Dodge* gave a very high, but not one-hundred-percent chance of evading an attack.

This was not his lucky day. The scorpion one-shotted the thief and headed straight for Crawler.

"Alright guys, easy does it!" he admonished us, kiting the boss and throwing on a fire shield. "Almost there... Almost... Easy, let's not make any mistakes... Okay..."

"Scyth, now!" Tissa shouted.

"Tiss, regen on me and get to the other side," the leader of the Dementors had an infectious calm about him. "Just a bit more..."

You have critically damaged Murkiss:

289!
Health points: 1356/30000.

"He-hee-heee!" Tissa shrieked, reminding me of an enraged banshee. "Okay guys! Three percent!"

Understanding that if we fell now we'd have to start over, I put all my plague energy into this attack. That didn't kill the boss, but then someone's DoT ticked...

The scorpion let out a death chirr so ferocious it made my ears lay back. The stone arches of the cave shuddered and the floor shook when its monstrous body collapsed at our feet.

The mad cry of three throats filled the cave. I'm sure Hung and Malik, watching all this from their dead bodies, were shouting just like us, too:

"Yessss!"

We didn't jump for joy for long, though. While Tissa rezzed the dead, Ed and I studied the heap of notifications filling our field of vision. I immersed myself in reading mine:

Experience points received: 280.
Experience points at present level (8): 4880/5400.

You have passed the dungeon Evil from the Depths!

Achievement unlocked: First Kill: Murkiss!

Of all the players in your sandbox, you were the first to kill this local boss. Murkiss, the nightmarish level-23 scorpion is the spawn and incarnation of Evil from the Depths. The breath of a Sleeping God birthed this terrifying creature with the sole purpose of exterminating all intelligent life because it is said that the Sleeping Gods will only awaken when not a single thinking creature remains in Disgardium.

Murkiss is dead but, before it shuffled off this mortal coil, it inadvertently transferred you a modicum of its power.

Reward*: Depths Teleportation.*

Depths Teleportation

Active skill.

Current level: 1.

You will instantly be carried to a random known location in Disgardium.

Warning! Use this ability at your own risk. Always bear in mind that the ways of the Depths are inscrutable. Where you end up and why is not decided by chance. In fact, it's all up to the scheming minds of the fell spirits whose breath powers this ability.

Cooldown time: 24 hours.

All hail the hero!
Would you like to make your name public? Doing so will give +300 reputation with the city of Tristad and +25 fame.

"No All Hail the Hero! We can't give ourselves away!" Crawler shouted. "Everyone got that? And another thing... We had two epics drop as loot! A bow and a halberd!"

Based on the next message, everyone decided against the "Hail."

Attention all sandbox players!
Anonymous players *have completed the location Evil from the Depths in the Olton Quarries and got First Kill of the final boss* ***Murkiss****! Residents and visitors of Tristad, hats off to* ***the anonymous players****! All hail the heroes! All hail* ***the anonymous players****!*

Bomber and Infect, back from the dead, shouted out in tandem:

"All hail us! The glory is ours!"

"*Depths Teleportation*? What?" Infect asked in surprise.

"Now we can 'port right to ins's!" Hung shouted in glee. "Hooray!"

"Read it again, dumbass," Tissa said. "The

teleportation is totally random! If it spits you out in the Mire, let's see if you get out..."

"Oh yeah!" Hung frowned. "But the skill is called *Depths Teleportation*, not Random Teleportation! I bet if we level it up, we can have it bring us wherever we want!"

"He's right," Crawler confirmed and gave a broad smile. "But the skill is useful enough as is, especially to Scyth. If any gankers attack, this way he can just run. Isn't that right, buddy?"

"Yep," I answered mechanically, realizing what he was implying just after.

With a snort, I kept reading the system messages. I got another achievement the Dementors didn't get.

> **Achievement unlocked: I Came, I Saw, I Conquered – 1!**
> *You got a First Kill achievement on your first try! Verily, the gods of* Disgardium *have smiled on you!*
> **Reward:** *+100 main attribute points.*

I couldn't believe my eyes. One hundred attribute points? That was as many as you got by level twenty! Nether yeah! I opened my mouth enthusiastically, feverishly checking the chat and realized the Dementors couldn't see my achievement. I considered whether it was worth sharing my joy with the guys and decided it was too early.

> **All hail the hero!**
> *Would you like to make your name public? Doing so will give +500 reputation with the city of Tristad and +100 fame.*

I of course refused that fame. If I wasn't a threat, it would have been another thing. High fame could open the door to unique quests all the way up to royalty level, which was to say nothing of the crazy discounts you could get from NPC vendors. Reputation with the city meanwhile, would have given more social quests to complete. But I didn't want that. Most important was surviving until the greater world and...

Current threat class increased: T!

Chapter Thirty-Six

Class-A Threat Potential

*T*HE SUDDEN pop-up message about my threat level made me shudder. That meant the system considered me stronger not simply when my level increased, but when I got advantages that distinguished me from other players? The teleportation skill, even if it did bring me to a random location, and the one-hundred attribute points definitely made me stronger and... less predictable.

At the same time, a global notification flew throughout the sandbox about some unknown hero. I quickly turned to look at my groupmates, but they were discussing the twists and turns of battle and the epics that dropped. No biggie, they'd find out later. Nothing to worry about. We did it together, and the fact I was here for the first time was no secret to them.

"Scyth," Ed called. "There's a bow and a halberd here for level twenty-five. We don't really need them. What did you decide about your class? I know you can't see the future but, based on your style I'd say you're gonna be melee, so a halberd might come in handy. And by the way, that's what I wanted to talk to you about. We wanted to ask about the epic from the first boss. It is yours and yours alone, no question there. But, if you are looking to sell, we'd be willing to buy."

"If it isn't too important, let's talk about that later," I suggested. Shooting arrows imbued with plague energy could be used to work miracles, but my soul called out for steel. Like it just seemed more reliable or something. "I need to think about it."

"Okay, sure! If everything is sorted out, I suggest we get out of here before Axiom comes back from school."

Ed headed toward the passage to the surface that opened after the boss died, and we followed.

"Yep," I nodded. "Actually... Just a minute."

There was a stubborn notification icon drawing my attention.

*Miner **Manny (Manuel Almeida)** would like*

to add you to his friends list. Accept?

"Is something the matter?" Crawler noticed I had stopped. "Scyth?"

"Wait."

My group stopped, exchanging bewildered glances. I accepted Manny's request, and he immediately sent a message, then another right after.

[14:56] [Private] [Manny]: Hello, Alex. Sorry if I'm distracting you. First of all, thanks. Both for the warrior and the donuts. Hank told us a bit about you. He said you seemed like a nice kid.

[14:56] [Private] [Manny]: Second... I don't know if this is relevant to you, but the quarry just filled up with high-level players from Axiom. They keep asking our guys if anyone went into that dungeon. We've been on shift since eight this morning and we're saying no one has gone in since then. And that is true.

[14:57] [Private] [Scyth]: Hi, Manny! Thanks for telling me, but what do I have to do with this?

[14:57] [Private] [Manny]: Drop it, Scyth. There are no secrets between me and Hank. First came a First Kill message, then I heard your name being dropped by these players. I

---

put two and two together... Alright, it isn't my place. I won't keep yapping.

[14:58] [Private] [Manny]: And another thing. There's some big fat guy walking around with them, he's real mad. He says wants to find you and talk. Basically, just so you know, the whole quarry is packed with Axiom.

[14:58] [Private] [Scyth]: Gotcha. Thanks, I'll keep it in mind.

"Well, well, what have you got there, Alex?" Tissa asked quietly.

I shuddered because of how silently she walked up, nodded and said to the others:

"Alright, guys. There's been a slight change of plans. We might have problems."

Everyone walked up and Ed asked:

"What kind of problems?"

"Axiom. I have a workman friend in the quarry and he just wrote they're brimming with people. They're looking for whoever was in this instance."

"And what about the 'location is temporarily closed for maintenance?'" asked Bomber.

"Think with your head, Hung!" Ed said in a lather, calling the warrior by his real name and breaking his own rule. "A global notification went out! We didn't get out before they got back!"

"I am thinking!" Hung said, offended. "Now here's a question – can we just teleport out of the ins?"

For a few moments, we all stared at him, dumbfounded. Then we all started laughing at once.

"Exactly! That's it!" Crawler exclaimed. "Big Bomber, you're a good dude!"

"Hold up, don't celebrate just yet! Let me check first," said Tissa.

She focused her gaze on an icon only she could see and... disappeared. A few seconds later, we got a message:

> *[15:03] [Group] [Tissa]: Wow, awesome! It works!*
> *[15:04] [Group] [Tissa]: I am in the land of the Murlocks though. It'll take me at least until evening to get back to town.*

"Great!" Crawler laughed. "Meet you in Tristad, boys!"

We all exchanged glances and activated our new ability at the same time.

"Axiom, su..." Hung's voice disappeared mid-word.

The world blinked and I found myself up to my knee in muck. I was sinking deeper and deeper every second. Fitfully looking around, I saw only more of the same. The impassable swamp stretched to the very horizon in every direction. I started panicking, then floundered and sank up to my chest. I froze and the sinking slowed down.

I opened my map and saw that I was in the Mire. And to reach the nearest inhabited place would take me a week through the swamp. And that was if I walked a straight line.

I looked at the flickering log window and focused.

> **First use of Depths Teleportation!**
> *Known locations: 4 (Tristad, Gloomwood, Olton Quarries, the Mire).*
> *Origin point: Olton Quarries.*
> *Possible destinations: Tristad – 2%, Gloomwood – 39%, the Mire – 59%.*
> *Destination determined: the Mire!*

Of all the options, I was now in the only "known" location I had never been to. In fact I was in the very patch of swamp Patrick had sent me to!

Meanwhile, the more I struggled, the deeper I got sucked in. I couldn't find a single thing to grab onto. I started having a real panic attack, and the fact that I clearly realized it was not reality did not help, nor did the fact that I had already survived hundreds of deaths of all kinds. The fear of drowning in stinking grimy muck was stronger than my mind.

When only my head was still above the surface, I was just about to activate emergency exit, because I didn't want to die like that. But I held off. I'd have to come back here eventually.

So I closed my eyes, pursed my lips tight, gave a twitch and sunk beneath the fen. The system timer pounded in my ears like a heartbeat.

You are suffocating! Damage: 6.
Health points: 324/330.

You are suffocating! Damage: 12.
Health points: 312/330.

The damage was growing in a geometrical progression every thirty seconds. I got myself together and completely stopped moving in expectation of the inevitable. I had heard somewhere that a bog was like a predator. It reacted differently to different living and dead objects that fell into it: it wouldn't touch dead things, but it sucked living creatures. Dead stuff would just get stuck or stay on the surface. Those thoughts served to distract me from the inevitable: when my lungs ran out of oxygen, I would frantically open my mouth and inhale mud.

The pulsing in my ears was growing stronger and more frequent, then my chest exploded in blinding pain.

> **You are suffocating! Damage: 192.**
> *Health points: 0/330.*
> **You are dead.**

    The first tick killed me again, but the worst was behind me.

> **You are suffocating! Damage: 6.**
> *Health points: 0/330.*
> **You are dead.**

    The words "You are dead" came up another twenty-four times in the logs. Then I stopped dying. What was the quote from that classic book? That which is dead can never die? I would have laughed, but I didn't want to choke on swamp muck.

> **You carry the mark of the Destroying Plague and have evaded fatal damage!**
> *You have been given Curse of the Undead: all damage taken reduced by 100%!*
> *This curse will remain active until you completely restore your health.*
>
> **Mark of the Destroying Plague improved: +1.**

Chance to receive Curse of the Undead increased to 8%.
Current level: 8.

And then I had to open my eyes. In the clumpy muck, the interface elements shone bright as daylight. I reckoned the direction of the quest marker and, slowly overcoming resistance, after many long unsuccessful attempts, I finally got turned in the right direction and tried to lay my body out head first. While I floundered, I probably just went further under. I tried to move my legs cautiously...

Two hours experimenting with various kinds of movement taught me to move the way I wanted. I'm not sure this would work in real life, but the game conventions could do the impossible. At an unknown depth in thick muck and ooze, I was not crushed by its weight and could actually still move.

By then I had become an object of interest to all kinds of nightmare creatures from small forearm-length leeches, who stuck dead to every part of my body, to strange magic spheres with impressively large mouths, which glowed a dim blue and tried in vain to swallow me whole. The glow from the spheres helped me see in the cloudy muck and not only them, but all the other nasty fauna teeming around me.

If not for *Hammer*, I might have been eaten up. But the ability didn't care how thick the muck was, or how high the pressure. It bashed through the muck to the enemy and, reinforced by plague energy, did crazy damage.

Resilience skill improved: +1.
Resilience skill improved: +1.
Resilience skill improved: +1.
Resilience skill improved: +1.
Resilience skill improved: +1.
Resilience skill improved: +1.

My *Resilience* was going up with no end in sight. That was because I was being damaged by the swamp itself, which had no level.

This was levelling on steroids. After all, the DoT from lack of oxygen was ticking and growing exponentially. The ticks of *Suffocation* had reached the millions at this point and were only continuing to go up.

Resilience skill improved: +1.
Resistance to all types of damage increased by 90%.
Pain reduced by 90%.
Current level: 90.
You have reached the maximum level in this skill!

If added to *Stoneskin*, that gave me almost complete invulnerability without Curse of the Undead: ninety-five percent resistance to all damage for thirty seconds.

My *Unarmed Combat* was up to seventy-two, *Night Vision* to thirty and even *Swimming* was progressing quickly, now all the way up to forty. But the swamp had nothing more to offer me. I had lost track of time, fighting off the monsters and slowly moving toward the island the quest marker pointed to.

The monsters surrounding me ranged from level twenty to twenty-five, and experience flowed like a river. In fact, I made three new levels and hit eleven.

You are now level 11!
115 free attribute points available!

I had saved the attribute points for a more appropriate time to choose where to put them. I wasn't going to dig around in the interface while I was stuck in this dirty old swamp muck.

At level ten, a message flickered in that I could now choose a class, but for the same reasons I left that for later as well. Only one thing had my attention – getting to dry land as quickly as possible.

At a certain point, my hands hit something

hard. I felt a thick root and pulled myself toward it, then another one... Grabbing one after the next, I started up the sloped bottom. I had the complete sensation that I would lose my mind and the whole world was like this: impenetrable, slimy and full of dangerous invisible creatures. Only the periodic messages from the Dementors in the chat and the skill increase logs kept me remotely sane. Honestly, though, I wasn't answering them.

I don't know why I hadn't just gotten out of my pod. It was either because I could clearly see that I was moving but very slowly on the map, my target was relatively nearby, and I wanted to crawl out of the bog before leaving Dis... Or it was the strange cold whisper sounding out in my head, giving me words of encouragement. I started to feel that I was doing everything right and heading exactly where I needed to go. And that feeling kept me going.

At first the voice was like an indistinct rustling of someone else's thoughts in my head. Broken fragments of sentences, with a refrain running through them like:

"Co-ome... Helllp... Ha-as ar-r-ri-iv-ved..."

And with every foot I went the right direction, it grew stronger and spoke more often.

"Co-ome... Go-o-od... Ex-xce-el-ent... Co-ome..."

It was also approving of every swamp

monster I killed:

"Wo-on-nde-er-rfu-ul...   Mo-o-ore...   Ag-gain..."

The dead monsters disappeared, dissolving into wisps of inky blackness and heading in the same direction as me. And then I realized the voice was also growing stronger with every leech I killed.

And that very same voice greeted me when my head stuck up above the surface. Then I pulled myself out with difficulty:

"You m-ma-ade iit... Fi-in-na-al-ly a sui-uit-ta-ab-ble spe-ecimen... Finally..."

Everything around was slightly vibrating, and a monotone hum was coming up from under the earth. I raised my head and I saw a small island the size of my room and overgrown with sickly grass. The feeling that I was where I belonged grew stronger. And it wasn't merely the quest from town drunk Patrick, who told me to come here and help some spirit.

This spirit had a name.

Behemoth, Sleeping God
Level: ???

"You c-c-ca-ame, Scyth..." his voice rustled in my head. "Have you come to help?"

"Yes, Behemoth. I have come to help."

"Wo-on-n-nd-der-f-f-ful..." the spirit was

500

suddenly right next to me. "Let me in..."
So I did.

Current threat class increased: Q!

New potential threat class!
Potential class: A.

Build on your threat potential, Scyth and let the whole world shiver!

End of Book One

Want to be the first to know about our latest LitRPG, sci fi and fantasy titles from your favorite authors?

Subscribe to our **New Releases** newsletter:
http://eepurl.com/b7niIL

Thank you for reading *Class-A Threat!*
If you like what you've read, check out other LitRPG novels
published by Magic Dome Books:

Level Up LitRPG series by Dan Sugralinov:
Re-Start
Hero
The Final Trial
Level Up: The Knockout (with Max Lagno)

Adam Online LitRPG Leries by Max Lagno:
Absolute Zero

**The Way of the Shaman LitRPG series
by Vasily Mahanenko:**
Survival Quest
The Kartoss Gambit
The Secret of the Dark Forest
The Phantom Castle
The Karmadont Chess Set
Shaman's Revenge
Clans War

Dark Paladin LitRPG series by Vasily Mahanenko:
The Beginning
The Quest
Restart

Galactogon LitRPG series by Vasily Mahanenko:
Start the Game!
In Search of the Uldans

**The Bard from Barliona LitRPG series
by Eugenia Dmitrieva and Vasily Mahanenko:**
The Renegades
A Song of Shadow

**The *Dark Herbalist* LitRPG series
by Michael Atamanov:**
Video Game Plotline Tester
Stay on the Wing
A Trap for the Potentate
Finding a Body

Mirror World LitRPG series by Alexey Osadchuk:
Project Daily Grind
The Citadel
The Way of the Outcast
The Twilight Obelisk

**The Expansion (The History of the Galaxy) series
by A. Livadny:**
Blind Punch
The Shadow of Earth
Servobattalion

Point Apocalypse *(a near-future action thriller)*
by Alex Bobl

You're in Game!
(LitRPG Stories from Bestselling Authors)

You're in Game-2!
(More LitRPG stories set in your favorite worlds)

The Game Master series by A. Bobl and A. Levitsky:
The Lag

Moskau by G. Zotov
(a dystopian thriller)

El Diablo by G.Zotov
(a supernatural thriller)

More books and series are coming out soon!

In order to have new books of the series translated faster, we need your help and support! Please consider leaving a review or spread the word by recommending *Class-A Threat* to your friends and posting the link on social media. The more people buy the book, the sooner we'll be able to make new translations available.

Thank you!

Till next time!